FARM WINDOWS

ISBN 978-1-62806-475-9 (print | paperback)
ISBN 978-1-62806-476-6 (print | hardback)
ISBN 978-1-62806-477-3 (ebook)

Library of Congress Control Number 2026904415

Published by Salt Water Media
29 Broad Street, Suite 104
Berlin, MD 21811
www.saltwatermedia.com

Cover art by ValintinaG of 99designs.com
Title font, Grindy Brush, used with license from developer, Sronstudios

FARM WINDOWS

Joel Summers

Dedications
(in no particular order):

Thank you for everything, Dad. This book wouldn't exist without your support. Your encouragement fueled me every step of the way. I hope the cheeky hidden rock references make you smile. You are the reason this book is as polished as it is. To Keir and Talia, the original members of the Saga Writers' group, you both have been supportive since the beginning. For that, I can't thank you two enough. Keir, your thoughtfulness and capability to convey an impactful message through storytelling is something I admire. Talia, your ability to paint worlds with words has always impressed me, both in written form and as a game master. To Sabrina, you are my best friend in the world, and I love you immensely. Thank you for all the support and inspiration. To my late grandmother, who was loved. To Andrew, who really loves Sonic and is an amazing friend who puts up with this crap. To my late dogs, Nibbler and Rya, who would have much preferred one last walk than words on a page. Thank you to all my friends and family. If you were not mentioned here, I just want you to know you were thought of. You are all loved and appreciated.

DRAMATIS PERSONAE

The Cast

Mannhouse Perjurer: A servant to something terrible.

Carl Parson: A father trying to cope.

Bethany Parson: A mother amidst odd circumstances.

Leon Parson: A good kid in the middle of it all.

Edda Macson: A daydreamer who lives by the beach.

Francesca (Fran): Edda's best friend and a party animal.

Carter: A lonely beach retiree.

Ward: A caretaker to his grandmother.

Darcy: Ward's grandmother.

Greg: Friend to Peter.

Peter: Friend to Greg.

Master: A cruel, evil man.

Drull: A pitiful victim.

Ralberhetth: ~~A malevolent trickster entity.~~ Trustworthy.

Cactus and Spider: A Cactus and a Spider, obviously.

Any likenesses to real persons, places, events, or anything else in this book is completely coincidental.

CONTENTS

1.

WINDOWS

Windows into other spaces.

Unknown, long-forsaken places.

When peering into such lost mazes, the mind, it boggles.

Who made this? They are faceless.

Insatiable thirsts burden those who cannot quench the tightening in the back of their lustful throats. They gasp for oxygen, an inevitable drowning slowly flooding their lungs like vintage wine poured into a zip-lock bag. Horror is not designed; it is not a game or a fairytale. It is of the self, nurtured. Within us all skulks the great potential for hate, deeds indescribable by those who wish to ignore them. Circumstance is the ultimate foundry. It forges carnage into one's souls, many hands stained with madness, deathly indulgences. Architects of hell.

"What is this shit?" Peter asked.

"What are you on about?" Greg discarded his cigarette into a potted plant made permanent ashtray. It sparked, flashing like flint before flickering out.

"This shit!" Peter pointed at a poster on the wall. "This supposed to be porn or some shit?" He absently picked at a scab on his forehead.

"It's a movie poster, dumbass. Some old sexploitation flick Paw worked on... or something like that."

"BRAVE WARRIORS CLAIM THY REWARD! BECKON FORTH THE BABES OF BEDROCK!" Peter bellowed out the poster tagline, trying his best to sound like a narrator in a film trailer playing exclusively in his own head. "Who the hell writes this shit anyway?"

"How have you never noticed that?" Greg laughed, bemused.

The wind outside laughed along.

A storm was beginning.

The previously mentioned potted plant was, specifically, a cactus. The Cactus didn't particularly mind the accumulating ash from the cigarettes. In some ways, it was reminded of the black sands in its lost homeland. The heat from the dying butts and smoldering filters also brought some morbid comfort, as Greg kept their apartment relatively cool.

The Cactus *did* mind the swearing, however. Cactus counted multiple instances of the word 'Shit' uttered by Peter alone. Perhaps Cactus was old-fashioned, but they rather disliked cursing. Still, Cactus sat by the window and got to watch the world go by day after day and was watered every few months. Life was mostly pleasant, so Cactus never audibly complained.

3 ·

STORM WALKER

Outside, it was storming as if the world was ending. Dramatic storm clouds painted the sky in colorful, brooding brush strokes, shadowing the land below. Rain pierced from the heavens, dancing in the wind at odd angles, sluicing against windowpanes, and puddling in concaves on the ground. Thunder crackled and echoed for miles, heard by hundreds, most of whom were huddled in their homes. One person, however, was outside in the streets alone, browbeaten by nature's fury.

Mannhouse Perjurer grew up on the outskirts of downtown Letterfaux, Ohio, on an old Farmhouse (the town was a medium-sized, rural community with a dwindling population in the thousands), and he seldom left its borders anymore. In any other situation, Mannhouse would be sitting on his couch in his living room, watching television. Perhaps he'd be drinking whiskey or wine and smoking a bowl right about now. This night defied normal.

It contacted him out of the blue, Mannhouse's benefactor, after nearly a decade. The instructions were vague: cards, a home address, a basement, the entrance. Before rushing out into the streets, Mannhouse pulled on his boots, a trench coat, gloves, a winter hat, and wrapped himself in a scarf. The elements would not be his downfall, he'd make for damn sure.

Mannhouse grabbed his keys, a switchblade, and a deck of cards, sliding them all into his right coat pocket. Given no time to prepare, this was the best he could do. That morning, Mannhouse had dropped his car off at the dealership for repairs, someone had randomly smashed his rear window with a beer can the night before, though nothing valuable was kept in his car. He'd hitched a cab ride home. He planned to pick it up when ready in the next day or so. So, of course, of all nights, his contract had to come due. Perhaps the smashed window was not so random after all, but on the other hand, they did seem to have a strange sense of humor.

Mannhouse knew downtown Letterfaux rather well, its alleyways and back streets, and could picture in his head how they curved around themselves like snakes wrestling. It would be easy to get lost in this mundane brick scape under no duress. The wind howled like wolves, and a slushy rain pummeled him like blows from a towering boxer. Mannhouse could hardly see ten steps ahead and navigated by instinct and muscle memory alone, forsaking his eyes' guidance almost entirely. Years of nights in bars and blackout benders finally served him well.

Mannhouse weaved past storefronts, back doors, and alleys toward his destination. Passed Cheshire's, The Drunk Eagle, Mason Street Brewery, fond memories of these places were now clouded by the storm raging, especially the one inside his head. It was foolish to believe it was over. It had been so long, so he'd started to hope maybe, *maybe they* forgot? What better time to drop your car off for repairs than during a storm? Get it off the street. Not like he'd need it anyway. Blame, self-indulgent blame. It was a well-honed skill of Mannhouse's.

Mannhouse leaned against a familiar concrete wall, catching his breath, as a low laugh escaped him. The absurdity of the situation, really. Abruptly, his laugh turned to an uncontrollable, aching cough. Most days, he could forget about the cancer slowly eating away at his lungs. Mannhouse had forsaken medical treatment; he didn't want to die a wasting skeleton, immobile and strapped into an uncomfortable bed with tubes flowing in and out of him like an augmented monster. They told Mannhouse he had a few months to live. After that night… he was going on ten years.

Mannhouse fell to his side, his outstretched arm and shoulder breaking most of the impact on the ground. It hurt like hell, and he let out a pathetic whelp. Water splashed from a puddle into his face, muddying him even more.

Propping himself back up against the brick wall, Mannhouse

gasped, his breath still not returning to him. He clutched his chest, wiped his face, then covered his mouth with his right hand. Shimmering, twinkling light popped in and out of this vision like an endless horizon of stars. He coughed more and more violently, a spurt of blood and vomit bubbling up. He wiped the mess from his nose and mouth as best he could, yet the coughing would not cease. The wind howled mockingly, the air piercing his skin like invisible darts as he struggled and shivered.

To Mannhouse, it quickly became apparent that the cold was a ruthless and imposing enemy, unstoppable, ever-present, but just now truly appreciated. Mannhouse shook uncontrollably, his body flailing as he coughed, bringing up more phlegm and blood. Struggling, begging for composure, the grasp on Mannhouse's lungs and muscles finally loosened as he regained autonomy. The shivering would not stop though.

Stepping from the smoking area behind Mason Street Brewery's side alley, contumacious against the cold roaring night, Mannhouse let the rain overtake him and wash away what sick it could. Continuing his journey, his steps labored and unsteady, he eventually found his way beneath an awning on some side street, a temporary relief most welcome, though limited in coverage. Even if he did reach his destination, Mannhouse thought, he doubted he'd be in any shape to do anything worthwhile at all. The home, the Farm entrance was streets away, and the storm an omen.

The rain changed to sleet from black clouds above, their forceful impacts like meteors. Mannhouse held his arms and hands in front of his face, taking occasional hits to his limbs, hands, and body. He bruised easily, like tomatoes. Bled red like them, too.

One step turned into a million. As if his shoes were concrete, Mannhouse dragged himself across flooded streets, empty parking lots, and deserted sidewalks. Lamp poles, street signs, traffic lights. They swung wildly, their metal frames clanking against themselves, like giant wind chimes. Plastic bags, refuse, and dirt, all twirled and hurled themselves up and down streets and corridors, colliding haphazardly with anything in their way.

The hail, their average size around golf balls now, continued to batter Mannhouse, breaking and bruising his skin. A car windshield shattered nearby. The cold still stabbed at his bones. His teeth chattered like rattlesnakes. A gust of wind kicked up, and his scarf unraveled from his neck, flying away into the cold dark before Mannhouse was even able to think of reacting.

A large, splintered tree branch launched towards Mannhouse like a spear, unnoticed until it nearly impaled him. He dodged it at the very last second by ducking down, surviving via some combination of luck and instinctual reflex. He wanted to scream and did; his words absorbed by the wind.

"FUCKING BASTARD!" Mannhouse raged against existence for a moment. The universe seemed to take fervent pleasure in indulgences regarding his suffering. Sometimes, he wanted nothing more than to cry, huddle up in a ball, and die wastefully in a corner. Despite these temptations, failure wasn't an option Mannhouse could accept. He had sacrificed so much to live and learned death was a reward to be earned. He was an arbiter, dispensed by fate, wielding will and hate like laser beams. Tonight, tonight was just the beginning. He feared maybe death was too good for him. Maybe, Mannhouse thought, he was due something else.

. . .

Nearly an hour of slow, difficult travel passed. It was only a few blocks from here, his target. Mannhouse had walked about a mile, but the journey seemed continental. Death by exposure was becoming more and more of an inevitability each second, he remained outdoors. Going inside their however... the very thought shuddered Mannhouse to the core more than the elements ever could. Mannhouse was awaited for some hellish cause unknown.

Every instinct, every voice in Mannhouse's head screamed in opposition as he approached the residential road. Fear tried to sway him, sadness tried to overcome him, rage tried to burn out his will. But Mannhouse's stubbornness would prevail this night if nothing else. He would be king of the pig-headed bastards if such a title existed.

Mannhouse walked up the dirt road, muddied by the storm, which led to a few residences nestled behind a row of trees. Mannhouse had driven by these homes before, never giving them much mind. It was one of the nicer communities in the area, right on the edge of downtown, where it became slightly more rural.

Eventually, Mannhouse found the home he was looking for by spotting the address on a mailbox. He took a moment to double-check the address, partially hoping he wouldn't find the right place. He could turn around and pretend the evening was nothing more than a journey to hell and back again. It was the right place. Mannhouse crept up a brick driveway that led towards a large single-family home. A few spruce trees periodically lined the side of the path, dotted about in an attempt at symmetry from some landscaper. The trees swayed and danced in the wild winds.

It dawned on Mannhouse suddenly. He was so preoccupied with his destination he wasn't sure how he'd get inside. The entrance to that place was in the basement of 1459 Farmstead Drive. All he was given was an address and an entry point. Mannhouse had no idea who lived there, if anyone at all. Were they armed? Perhaps a couple? Did they have kids? Animals? If Mannhouse had been given some time, he would have done some research and preparation.

The end of the driveway led to a clearing of grass and a small parking area. It was next to a garage, which was connected to the front entrance. One car sat outside, covered in a tarp that had been carefully strapped down for the storm. Perhaps other cars were parked inside, or maybe not. Mannhouse was hoping to get a rough gauge on how many people lived here based on the number of vehicles, but this didn't indicate much of anything. A few lights shone through the upstairs windows, and a porch light illuminated the front doors and stoop. There was no way to know if anyone was home or how many. But probability dictated at least someone was around.

Mannhouse walked around the backyard. It had a nice outdoor

patio, a covered firepit, and some small gardens lined in a row, though the wind and rain had whipped the neat plants into frenzied knots of vines. There was a back door entrance connected to the patio. He tried the handle, but it was locked tight. Mannhouse hoped for a cellar door or something along those lines but had no luck.

Mannhouse liked to believe he was usually rather mild-mannered. He avoided conflict most of the time. He wasn't without the capability for anger and even aggression, but it took a lot for him to get really riled up. But finding himself in this circumstance, pseudo-willing, unprepared, and exhausted, he felt such a roil of emotion that it seemed as if the storm was his mirror. It was a beast, nothing but impotent rage, throwing things about and damaging whatever was in its path... A tantrum of sorts. Lightning flashed and thunder boomed and banged in succession over and over, warbling and distorting in the winds. It was a cry from a beast, a roar of vengeance from an angry ancient god, a proclamation of Gaia's might (but a fraction of her power). It was jazz, a chaotic orchestra, a cacophonous melody forcing an audience. Mannhouse screamed in frustration.

Mannhouse had never done a B and E before (breaking and entering). Now, here he was, creeping around some stranger's home looking for the best way to get inside. Maybe he could ring the doorbell? If someone was home, he could explain his situation. Maybe complete strangers would listen? He could monologue about why he was on their property, standing at their front door at 1:00 a.m. in the middle of a hurricane. *"Excuse me, sorry to bother you. I need to get inside your basement. Would you be a dear and brew some coffee?"* What could go wrong?

Mannhouse shook his head at the idea before abruptly convulsing and gagging from another fit of coughs and rigors. Thunder clapped, loud as a stampede. Thankfully, Mannhouse was able to regain his breath quickly this fit. Blood trickled from his nose, blending into his mud-splattered face. Looking around more, Mannhouse spied a window on the western side of the house with curtains drawn open. Peeking inside, it seemed the window sat above a kitchen sink. He could see stairs leading upwards adjacent to a connecting hallway. The first floor had no lights on, and what minimal illumination existed was mostly ambient sources filtering from the second floor. If someone was home, they were probably upstairs sleeping. This could work. He just needed a way in.

Mannhouse found a loose brick sitting in a garden plot out back. He was growing anxious. He was running out of time and energy. Mannhouse stared through the kitchen window, the one with the curtains drawn back, brick in hand. He shook himself, working up his nerves in anticipation of the act.

Mannhouse waited in the storm. Leaves bustled and swayed; branches creaked. Any minute now. A vortex gave form to leaves; they spiraled and danced, kicking up dirt. Any minute now. Heavy rain drops stabbed at him. Any minute now.

Lightning illuminated the skies, then...

BOOM! Thunder broke once more. Mannhouse launched the brick from his hand with the force of a cannon. It impacted with the window, the glass shattering like grapeshot, and the wood frame buckled inwards.

Mannhouse carefully climbed through the window, doing his best to avoid shards of glass, which had scattered everywhere. Besides minor scratches on his jeans, he was successful. Sliding over the sink and falling to the ground, glass cracked beneath Mannhouse's shoes. Water dripped and pattered from his wet clothes and skin onto the shards and tiled floor below.

Mannhouse's heart thundered as panic overwhelmed him. He swung his gaze around the room wildly, getting his bearings in the near black kitchen the best he could. Wind funneled inside from the broken window, howling, a natural banshee announcing its presence. A few seconds passed, but time seemed to move in slow motion for Mannhouse. He was seeing stars again.

Sounds of shuffling and movement came from upstairs, accompanied by lights being turned on. He had to hurry and find that basement. Moving as quickly and quietly as able, Mannhouse crept. Though no longer blinded by the storm, he moved without vision, praying to find a door leading downstairs somewhere. Living room, nothing. Some bathrooms, no. Front entrance, nada. Just a shelf for keys, a coat hanger, and some shoes. There was nothing in the kitchen either, save for a pantry. A small hallway adjacent to the front doors caught Mannhouse's eye. A rusted red metal door hung slightly ajar, allowing Mannhouse to see partially past its frame, which was lit dimly with a faint yellow light.

Someone began walking downstairs. The floorboards...

CREAK!

With nowhere else to go, Mannhouse stepped into the garage, closing the door behind him.

"Lock the door." A muffled voice came from upstairs, nearly inaudible, covered by swooshes of wind blowing in from the kitchen. Distant footsteps descended downstairs. Mannhouse ventured farther into the garage. The place was a mess. Boxes, crates, and plastic storage bins formed a makeshift maze of clutter. A nearby table saw was turned into an improvised storage shelf, with all kinds of detritus piled on top of it.

Mannhouse was riled, trying his best to find the basement entrance. There had to be a ladder, some old stairs, a hatch, anything. Desperately darting about, looking for an exit or the entrance, all Mannhouse found was a random accumulation of things obtained over a lifetime, and cobwebs. The red rusted garage door swung open. Mannhouse ducked behind the table saw, holding his breath. A cough crept into his throat.

"Whoever's in here... I have a gun!" The voice, now clear and deep, echoed menacingly through the garage. "No sudden movements or I will shoot!"

Mannhouse choked on his saliva, the back of his throat turning drier than cotton on a 100-degree day; he greatly struggled to hold in an attack. His throat collapsed in on itself like a dying sun. Then, a raspy screeching whelp muttered from his mouth before breaking into another session of coughs. Death felt certain for a moment.

It was instantaneous. A man in loose gray shorts leapt upon Mannhouse, the force of the impact throwing him backwards. In the dark garage, it was hard to make out many features, but one thing was plain to see, though. Gripped in the man's hands shone a silver revolver. It sparkled like fool's gold, luminescent, glowing marvelously.

"DON'T MOVE! Ah, I... I'll fucking blow your brains out, man!" The homeowner's hands shook. A shiver overtook Mannhouse, his wet clothes like icicles, his constitution dwindling. Mannhouse, still coughing, held his hands above his head slowly in surrender. He shook, both from fear and cold.

"Please, please, do... don't shoot. I..." Mannhouse coughed, leaning his head into his shoulder. The man with the gun flinched for a moment. Mannhouse was pathetic; indeed, he wore it deviously well.

"WHAT THE FUCK, what the hell are you doing in my house?" The gun was cocked. One sneeze, one itch, one moment of blind rage, all could be Mannhouse's doom. "Did you smash my FUCKING WINDOW OPEN?!" The man's face was twitching. Fingers too.

"I'm sorry I... I don't mean any trouble, please just..." Mannhouse pleaded. Without warning, the guy with the gun kicked Mannhouse in the chest, pummeling him with such force it caused his body to go limp, crumpling on the cold concrete floor. Negotiation suddenly seemed far less suitable to the situation. Mannhouse's coughs turned to screeching wheezes.

"So what? You a thief, murderer?" The man paced a little, his gun slightly lowered but still readied. Mannhouse gasped, his breath forsaking him, his muscles contracting around themselves. "Well?" the homeowner asked. "What is it?"

"I..." Mannhouse could hardly speak. After some time spent coughing with a gun placed against his head, his breath returned. Despite his regained capability to talk, Mannhouse was unsure of what to say. Sounds of Hurricane Nester's crazed rampage continued to pour in from outside. Mannhouse's teeth clattered as he asked: "Do you have a basement?"

"What?" The homeowner was dumbfounded. "You looking for a tour?"

"I mean..." Mannhouse shook his head like a dog shaking water from their coat. "I needed shelter, hoped nobody was home."

"Well, we are!" In the man's hand, the gun lowered slightly and uncocked. A click echoed in the garage. There was stillness, the two unsure what to do next.

"What's your name?" Mannhouse cautiously lifted himself from the ground into a sitting position. "I'm Ryan." Mannhouse believed in never giving his real name to strangers unless entirely necessary. Especially when held at gun point.

"No, we're not fucking doing this. We are not buddies!" The man stepped backwards; his dilated eyes looked like black pools in the dark. He scanned Mannhouse up and down, back and forth. "You the only one here?"

"Just me." Mannhouse stuttered. "Like I said, just... needed shelter." A large thunderclap echoed like a cannon in a recording studio, startling the two. The homeowner, unintentionally, pulled the trigger of the revolver in fearful reflex. Another large clap, man-made thunder, boomed. *BANG!* The gun lurched backwards in the homeowner's grip as he struggled to retain his hold on the weapon. A bullet whizzed past Mannhouse's head, barely missing. If Mannhouse was just a little bit to the right, his head would have been splattered, shredded like lettuce. The bullet slammed through a stack of cardboard boxes behind him before embedding itself into a cinderblock wall. Shredded cardboard, paper, and concrete particulates fluttered through the air in the aftermath.

"FUCK!" The man holding the gun screamed, visibly shaken. Mannhouse fell backwards, catching himself with his hands to lessen the impact. A loud ringing echoed in both of their ears, a funeral to frequencies never to be heard again.

"DON'T SHOOT! DON'T SHOOT!" Mannhouse cried, his entire body stiffened, his hands shaking to such a degree his muscles ached at the palms.

"It was an accident..." The man said, huffing. He loosened his grip on the gun, and the cock unwound. "Christ..."

A minute or three passed. Mannhouse slowly lifted himself

back up into a sitting position. The homeowner was looking down at the gun in his hand, the weight of the weapon heavy, demanding respect. Subtly, unnoticed, Mannhouse slipped his right hand into his jacket pocket, gripping his switchblade tight. Time passed, but everything felt motionless. Even the storm, with all its rage, had fallen quiet.

A slight sound of pacing footsteps came from upstairs. Looking away for but a moment, the stranger's attention was drawn to the red door. Grasping at any opportunity for survival, he could take, Mannhouse lept suddenly like a frog from a tree. The homeowner noticed, but his reflexes were not fast enough.

Mannhouse pulled his switchblade out from his jacket pocket. He clicked it open with a satisfying swoosh. The guy with the silver gun and the grey shorts began to ready his aim, but was too slow. Mannhouse pounced upon the man as if a wild fanged beast. The two toppled to the floor. Due to the momentum of the fall, Mannhouse nearly cut the bastard's throat open as he landed upon the man. Mannhouse held his blade against his enemy's throat, ensuring they could feel the sharp edge.

"DROP THE GUN! DROP THE GUN!" Mannhouse raged, pressing his blade tightly against the man. Blood trickled ever so slightly down onto the floor, absorbing into the concrete like a sponge sucking up dishwater. A metal clank hit the ground as the gun loosened from the man's grip. Mannhouse pushed the revolver away from the stranger with his free hand. It slid across the floor a few paces away before bumping into some storage boxes labeled 'Photographs'.

"Move and I'll cut your throat!" Mannhouse threatened, slowly rising up while he kept the blade as close to the man's neck as possible.

Mannhouse walked backwards to the gun, keeping the knife trained on the prostrate homeowner, readying his newly acquired weapon before putting the knife away. The weight of the gun felt familiar in his hands. Making sure he kept more than an arm's reach away from his enemy, Mannhouse spoke. "Now... what's your name?" Mannhouse pointed the gun at the man in gray shorts.

"Carl," the man said, attempting to stand up.

"STAY DOWN!" Mannhouse screeched. Carl flinched, falling back on his ass. Mannhouse took in his surroundings, and as his eyes adjusted to the darkness, he found a light switch. Flicking it on, with an electric buzz, the room was engulfed in a pale-yellow fluorescent glow. Mannhouse returned to Carl, still seated on the floor, and looked him up and down. Carl's face was long, his lips pale and chapped. His hair was brown, short, his eyes no longer black orbs, but blue oceans, still filled with life. Mannhouse could take that life so easily now; the thought sent a dread-filled fear tingling down his gullet. A sound from upstairs could be heard again, like furniture sliding.

"Tell me, Carl, who else is in the house?"

"Nah... no one."

"Lying doesn't help here. Try again." Mannhouse leaned forward, gently placing the gun against Carl's brow.

"OKAY OKAY! I... it... it's my wife, and... my son," Carl pleaded, his voice heavy and fearful. "She's probably already called the cops! Please! Just take what you want and leave!"

"I'm not here to rob you," Mannhouse explained. He was exhausted, in pain. His voice heavy like Carl's. "The faster you help me, the faster you never see me again."

"Anything, anything! Take my money, take...take my car... the keys are..."

"FUCK SAKE!" Mannhouse pushed the gun with greater force against Carl's forehead, tilting his neck backwards slightly. "Listen to me! I want to know one simple thing. Where is your BASEMENT!?" Mannhouse's voice didn't sound recognizable to himself anymore. It was as if someone was speaking through his lips, like he was a megaphone projecting for an invisible other.

"What?" Carl shook his head aghast, the barrel following along with the movement. "We don't have a fucking basement!" For a moment, Mannhouse was still, shocked. It wasn't possible, he was lying, he had to be. But he could tell there was truth in Carl's fearful glistening eyes.

Mannhouse kicked Carl suddenly in the chest. Now Carl was the one who collapsed to the floor, rag-dolling for a moment before his face hit the ground. Carl shouted in pain, weeping and moaning; he looked like a worm on the ground, wriggling. Blood trickled from a newly formed gash on Carl's forehead.

"Don't lie to me." Mannhouse put his foot on top of Carl's head, applying an uncomfortable amount of pressure. Momentarily, Mannhouse wanted nothing more than to grind Carl's brains beneath his boots, to indulge himself in a murder most vicious. He reminded himself he was not a killer (not entirely convinced). The way he felt in the moment, the bloodlust… it was disgusting. He hated himself and was incapable of recalling a time he didn't feel as such.

"I am not a violent man. Tonight's incident does not demonstrate who I really am…" It probably did. Mannhouse began to monologue, a sudden second wind swirling within him. Something inside was blooming. "I'm sure you feel the same way about yourself." Mannhouse wiggled his foot, digging into the side of Carl's head with worn, wet outsoles. "Hell, I don't want to be here either."

"Fuck… you…" Carl spat out in defiance, his mouth wedged between the floor and a boot.

"BASEMENT!" Mannhouse wailed, applying more pressure, like a clamp on a watermelon; flesh crunching between leather and rubber.

"WE DON'T HAVE A FUCKING BASEMENT!" Carl's voice was raspy, rough like sandpaper. His spittle puddled on the floor.

"Okay, okay…" Mannhouse stepped off of Carl's head, walking backwards. "Sit up." Carl began standing up.

"I SAID SIT! Not stand…" Mannhouse demanded. Carl sat, legs crossed, shaking, crying. "Do you love your family?" Mannhouse remembered a story a friend of his told him about training dogs.

"Yes!" Carl bellowed.

"I love mine too." Mannhouse frowned. "Would you do anything for them?"

"Yeush," Carl whimpered pitifully, nearly unintelligible. His sobs were louder than any hurricane. Mannhouse wanted to cry and laugh at the same time.

"How old's your son?"

"No, no." Carl shook his head.

"HOW OLD!?" Mannhouse's voice echoed in the garage.

"Sev...seven!" Carl's bewailing was like that of a newborn's, all raw emotion, unfiltered.

"Ahhhh, wonderful age." Mannhouse pointed the revolver at Carl's crotch. "Do you plan for more?"

"No, no... Just, just the one." Carl shuddered.

"Well, good. Here's what I'm thinking, you following me, Carl?"

Carl nodded rapidly.

"Good, good. Now, tell me... Where is your basement?"

Carl put his hands over his eyes like he was trying to stop a dam breach with a strip of clear tape; it was impossible, and the water flowed.

"We don't..."

"No! NO! NOO!" Mannhouse screamed, stomping his right foot against the floor. "If you don't tell me right now, I'll blow your tiny little raisins off!" Mannhouse was shaking, mostly from adrenaline. Everything he'd ever done, all his past mistakes, led him to this. It was too late for Mannhouse to disobey his commands, but he wished he had. He should be home in bed, not here, not cultivating this violence.

"Then... I'll go upstairs and drag your family down here and make you watch everything I do to them..." Mannhouse threatened. He knew he was irredeemable, and yet he continued to play the villain, undeterred, bound to another's will, or maybe his own.

"Sound fun?" Mannhouse asked. "Like I said. I'm not a violent man. My terms are rather reasonable."

"I swear! I swear! We bought this place ah' couple years 'go! Never had a basement." Carl spoke so quickly, his words jumbled together. He was helpless, a duck in a pond being fired upon by a distant hillside sniper. Snot ran down Carl's nose, past his lips, dripping down his chin.

Mannhouse, believed Carl. He'd believed him from the start.

Yet... how could his information be wrong? Was it some divine clerical error? Regardless, he had to act. Maybe this was some twisted test? Mannhouse cocked the gun back, ready to shoot. Carl continued to weep and beg. Mannhouse was going to fire; his fingers began to pull back the trigger...

Then, a buzz, sudden and surprisingly loud, vibrated nearby. If the storm hadn't begun to die down, Mannhouse would not have noticed it at all. The rumbles were coming from Carl's pocket, which was glowing. Someone was calling him.

"Who's calling?" Mannhouse intuited the call was important, somehow. "Go on, check." Mannhouse waved the gun at Carl, then rolled the cylinder dramatically. From a maintenance perspective, Mannhouse was aware that spinning the cylinder of a revolver was not recommended, but the delightful clicking sound it made was invigorating. And hell, maintenance of someone else's gun was the least of his concerns right now.

"Check?" Carl sucked some snot back into his throat, snorting, confused.

"Yes, yes, hurry up!"

"Okay..." Carl took out an old, beat-up cell phone from his pocket; its screen was cracked and dirty. Carl looked at the caller ID. *Unknown number, potential spam.*

"Answer it," Mannhouse demanded.

"Okay..." Carl hesitated, taking a moment to regain his composure.

"Hello?" Carl spoke into the phone. A few seconds passed as Carl silently listened to the mystery caller, not speaking a word. Then his eyes widened like two full moons, one hanging above the night sky, the other reflected in a clear pool of water below. Mannhouse noticed the change in his expression.

The caller hung up. Carl let the phone hang loose in his hand.

"Well?" Mannhouse asked

"He... it... they knew my name... They said to tell you..." Carl breathed in hard, sweat beads dripping down his face. "To say..." Carl grew silent, weary.

“What!?” Mannhouse felt an overwhelming impatience stirring within him. His finger tightened on the trigger. Perhaps his benefactors played some cruel trick on everyone involved.

“They said to make your own entrance....” Carl muttered.

Mannhouse reflected on Carl’s words for a moment. Outside, the storm grew a little louder. Mannhouse began to laugh, a pitiful chuckle.

“Hah... Hah... Of course...” Mannhouse shook his head. “Well then, if it wasn’t some bullshit, it was bound to be something else...”

Mannhouse extended his free hand outwards to Carl, gesturing towards the phone.

“Can’t have you calling the cops now.” Reluctantly, Carl handed it over. Mannhouse slipped it into his coat pocket.

“You have a sledgehammer or shovel or something?” Mannhouse asked.

“I think so,” Carl replied hesitantly.

“Well, then, grab it. We’ve got some digging to do.”

RALBERHETTH

Among the molten heaps of homes
housed past grieving mounds of bones,
beneath the dire darkest depths
dwelt the everlasting Ralberhetth.

Of songs of old did sirens sing
to lure great men to parts unseen.
Wicked mires filled with spite,
rouse visions of ghoulish fright.

There, Ral took soul in hand, the wills
and dreams of all of man.
Unburdened from their malicious form,
Ralberhetth began to mourn.

The dead Ral ate whose power stolen,
sculpt and shape began remolding.
No semblance found in past lover,
take a body, add another.

Ralberhetth, drunk with hate,
raked a roar through time and space.
When all did hear Ral's impossible wallow,
a gasp of dread mankind did swallow.

DRIPPING CRIMSON LIPS

Edda Macsen lived on the corner of 144th and Wight Street on the first floor of a small six-unit condominium named Ocean Heights. Her home, though small, is her sanctuary. It was lightly furnished, and Edda didn't own much. She preferred it that way.

Ocean Heights sat upon a slightly raised plot. Concrete steps with a metal railing led to Edda's porch and back door (which she used as her front). The paths were surrounded by small pockets of lush green grass. Opposite side of the building was a parking lot for residents, and stairs leading to the second floor.

Edda slid her screen door open, stepping out front, a cup of freshly brewed coffee in her hand. Waves crashed in the distance. A breeze drifted inland. Seagulls screeched. It was morning, the early days of April, an average Monday in Purple Beach. Though beginning to warm up, there was still a bit of a chill in the air.

The best part of Edda's home, in her opinion, was the porch. She spent a majority of her time sitting outside, be it working from home or enjoying the view. The space was small, barely enough room for an outdoor couch and chair. However, the view more than made up for any faults. The patio overlooked the public outlet beach entrance, which cut through two oceanfront homes. Besides watching the waves, Edda equally enjoyed watching the dune grasses flow in the wind.

Most of the beachfront houses on Wight Street were raised, cantilevered, sitting on large concrete pillars with cars tucked neatly below, forming strange hybrid spaces of simultaneous indoor and outdoor garages. Occasional family homes and McMansions dot parts of the street as well. The way that Wight and 144th intersected created a strange space. Beachfront homes formed artificial walls, partially blocking the view of the beach for the homes behind them. Between these places were roads and alleys and intersections and parking spots for locals. It created these concrete hallways, in which wind would funnel and blow, and the voices of distant people would echo and reverberate off the buildings. Sand collected in the corners of these spaces, and in those patches, weeds would grow.

There weren't a lot of full-time neighbors, and Edda was thankful for that. Many of the homes around here were strictly rentals, abandoned during the long winter before being spruced up and rented to tourists during spring break and the summer season. Many preferred the beach on warm, bright days, but Edda loved the stillness of cold beach nights, only the waves and the wind interrupting the silence. A sense of calming isolation overtook her soul in those moments, when she was barefoot in the sand, hugged by the dark; only the city lights behind her shattered the illusion of true isolation.

Edda worked as an accountant for William and Son's Mattress Company, a local business that helped provide homes, hotels, and motels with beds in a variety of frames and sizes. It wasn't the most thrilling employment Edda ever had, but she rarely needed to go into the office, it was stable, and the pay was decent. It allowed her to live comfortably and pay her mortgage simultaneously. The demand for mattresses in a town whose economy ninety percent relied on tourism was immense. Edda was thankful she didn't have to haul the heavy bastards around herself.

Edda sat down, facing the ocean view. She sipped her coffee slowly, savoring the flavor and its accompanying bitterness. Edda could hardly sleep last night, tossing, turning. She lay there for hours, thinking arbitrary thoughts and staring aimlessly at the ceiling. It was the kind of night where she was desperately tired, but her mind kept her up with endless anxieties, with no sign of slowing down.

At least, today would be an easy day. Work was a bit slow lately. Besides handling some billings and calling a few clients about due fees, her day would be spent looking at the ocean and wasting time scrolling the internet on her laptop.

Slipping inside quickly to grab her computer, Edda set up her workstation for the day, clocking in. The outdoor couch was positioned right against the railing. She liked wedging herself in the corner. It gave the best view of the beach and both streets. It also gave room for the power supply, which was plugged into an outdoor outlet snuggly hidden behind the opposite side of the couch. Best view in the office.

Emails were replied to and sent, a couple of phone calls were made, and before long, it was nearly noon. Edda was thirsty, hungry. Closing her laptop, she gathered her coffee, long, cold, and mostly empty, and returned inside. After rinsing out her mug, Edda dug into her pantry to retrieve the last two pieces of rye bread she had. She slopped the remnants of a jar of mayonnaise onto the bread, then put a few dry turkey slices on top to create the world's most pathetic-looking sandwich. It tasted alright.

After lunch, Edda returned to work with nothing to do but waste time. Soon, it was four. Edda clocked out, closing her laptop. She had spent the last slow and crawling hours browsing random forums. They discussed a wide variety of topics ranging from punk rock, coding, sculpting, and a hundred other passing interests Edda had accumulated throughout her life. It was a satisfying feeling, getting paid for downtime. These were halcyon days, lazy and fruitful.

"Hey!" A voice called out, startling Edda. It was her neighbor, Carter, one of the few full-time residents on her street. Carter was a retired guy in his sixties. He could get very talkative if you let him, and Edda wanted nothing to do with his conversations.

"Hey," Edda waved back.

"You see that fox running around?" Carter asked abruptly. "Called animal control... damned thing looked rabid. Didn't even seem scared when I was close n' nearby."

"Nope, haven't seen any foxes." Edda looked down at her phone, feigning distraction.

"Well, if you do, best keep your distance." Carter waved goodbye, his cane clanking against the concrete rhythmically. "Be seeing you."

"You too," Edda sighed. She was tired, despite such a lazy day. Edda liked to go for walks on the beach, trying to see how far she could go before needing to turn around. She tried to walk a little further each day. Each public beach outlet posted a sign that displayed the number of the connecting street. Yesterday, she'd made it to 122nd before turning around. The cardio was killer. Lately, the bottoms of her feet had begun to callus. Though somewhat painful, it also brought her a warm feeling of pride. Physical evidence of progress. Edda decided to go on her daily walk, despite her exhaustion. She grabbed her phone, locked the patio doors, and headed towards the beach. The sun kissed her skin, and the wind was perfect out.

Suddenly, a subtle flash of light and a stir of movement in the corner of Edda's eye caught her attention. Through a window, a flicker of brightness popped in and out of existence, barely noticeable in the daylight. It came from a home, one of the cantilevered estates on Wight Street to her left when facing the beach. The home was flamingo pink, and wedged between a blue and yellow home of the same design. There was no car parked beneath the pilings, but most homes were empty this time anyway. Again, a flicker drew Edda's attention. From where she stood, it was impossible to tell what she was seeing. *Simply a light turning on and off in some room,* Edda thought, *probably a bulb dying.* She'd never seen anyone in that house before. *New renters, perhaps.* Trying her best to pay it no mind, Edda continued to the beach. Still, something about that flashing light lingered in her subconscious.

The beach outlet path at 144th was small. Though it gained a minor amount of traffic during prime season, it wasn't a very popular entrance overall. The sandy path was surrounded by beach fencing with small posts in the ground connected by wires on the top and bottom. It was loosely held together, weathered over the years. Once white paint was now mostly stripped away, the few bits that remained yellowing. The fence's shape followed the gentle curves of the sand dunes, sprinkled with tall grasses, cactuses, bayberry, and holly.

Edda stepped down a slope onto Purple Beach, past the bench, past the designated smoking area. Almost no one was outside. Someone flew a kite in the distance past the Delaware line, another walked their dog. All in all, maybe four people were on the beach, including Edda. Treading past the line of dry and wet sand formed by the tide, Edda let the waves subsume her toes. The wind picked up, tangling her long brown hair. The taste and feel of the ocean spray was magnificent. She kicked up some sand, watching the wind whisp it away for a moment. Simple pleasures like this were what Edda craved. She felt like dancing. If nobody was around and she had more energy, she would.

Throughout her walk, time ebbed like waves to the shore. The beach ambience seemed to absorb Edda's worries, letting her daydream during her peaceful ventures.

Edda called Purple Beach home for two years now, though the move felt as if yesterday. When living in Ohio, Edda managed to save up just enough money up front to take out a mortgage for buying a place. Securing a job at William's before she even moved across borders definitely helped with the acceptance of her application as well.

Edda's move-in weekend was exhausting, and, despite how long ago it had been now, those days still felt fresh in her mind. She'd rented a small truck and asked an Ohio friend to help her. Her friend drove the rental truck while Edda drove her car up. It was about a ten-hour drive from Letterfaux to Purple Beach with stops. They unpacked everything Edda owned during the same day, which thankfully wasn't much.

Despite some shame in feeling this way, Edda seldom missed her old Ohio friends. She still kept in touch with a few, but distance and time were consistent wedges in their relationships. Making friends at Purple Beach was never her priority either. With such a small population during off-season (and an inclination to stay inside during on), Edda mostly kept to herself.

Francesca was the major exception to this fact. Fran lived on the bay side, down on 110th Street, near a barbeque spot Edda used to work as a server for. Edda was Fran's co-worker at that restaurant, named *Nicks*, though at the time the two women's personalities couldn't have clashed more. Edda was naturally withdrawn, content with silence, seldom rambunctious. Fran was a party animal, a socialite who fed off attention. Yet, despite this and a few minor work-related spats over shifts and tipping out, the two eventually stuck together like Velcro. They met up every few days or so, doing anything from watching horror movies to hopping buses between bars and putt-putt golf courses. Most nights, though, they just drank on Edda's porch. Perhaps their clashing personalities are what helped them get along so well. Francesca could get Edda to leave her bubble, and Edda could keep Fran in check when her inner party animal became a bit too rabid.

Edda noticed the sign for 118th Street was at the upcoming outlet. She'd broken her walking record considerably without consideration, lost in thought and daydreams. She was breathing hard, her calves and lungs burning, thirst tightening in the back of her throat. She turned around, headed toward home. It was almost time for dinner anyway. She thought about the old meals her mother used to make, how she'd sit there at the table talking about Dad.

. . .

As a child, Edda grew up in the middle of two Farms in rural Ohio. Her neighbors to her left used to raise dairy cows. To her right, they grew soybeans and corn. The Macsens used to live in Cleveland but moved to Letterfaux when Edda was six. Her parents had wanted less of the city life, less crowds, less noise. Though her family had never been rich, Edda never wanted for much either. The family was always teetering on the edge of lower and middle class. Some years growing up had been rough, especially during the recession, but Edda never went without a meal, shelter, and most importantly, love.

Edda's mother still lived in Ohio. She worked in downtown Fresno at Hanworth Regional Bank, where she'd worked since the family moved to Letterfaux. The bank was about a forty-minute commute from Edda's childhood home, where mom still resided to this day, all by her lonesome, which was a point Edda was often reminded of during their weekly phone calls (regardless of who called whom).

When Edda was very young, one year after moving to Letterfaux, her dad went missing. He disappeared one summer day like dandelion seeds into lush grassy fields. Police couldn't find anything; nobody could find him. Sometimes, Edda's mother swore her husband was still out there. She couldn't accept the possibility of his death. Instead, she insisted he abandoned them. Edda could not recall her father's face or voice.

As a teen, Edda wanted nothing more than to leave Letterfaux. It was boring; nothing happened there. She dreamt of moving to California to enjoy the city and beaches. Maryland proved to be a rather reasonable compromise in the end, though Edda still wondered what her life would have been like if she made the leap to the West Coast. Now, as Edda walked the calm, windy shores of Purple Beach, she found herself pining for days spent with friends in her youth. Nostalgia is a powerful thing; even when content, the soul wants for what it once had.

Edda's toes crunched across a patch of fragmented seashells; the sand and debris gave way beneath her skin, embedding the shells further into the wet sand. Looking down, Edda avoided stepping on the remnants of a dead crab, its rotting carapace picked clean by birds and other scavengers. A few flies buzzed around the remains.

Edda's stomach growled, and for a moment, the long walk home seemed daunting. Pleasantly, it occurred to Edda that the 'problem' of needing to walk home on the beach was a rather wonderful 'problem' indeed. She noted the streets as she made her way home. 119th: That's the street with the good Pizza place on the corner, Legalize Marinara. 122nd Street, there was the old Dollar Store and a surf shop. The putt-putt course at 121st Street was just okay, themed around Australia, of all things. There was another putt-putt course on 130th Street, which had nice gardens. She and Fran had gone once. Francesca climbed on some prop rocks to take a selfie, which prompted an intense shouting match between her and the cunt manager (Fran's words). *Get off my props!* The seashell store kept strange hours on 140th. On the second floor of the store was a museum full of washed ashore artifacts with mostly credible historical markers. There were shelves of pirates' gold and treasure chests, flintlocks covered in coral. Hell, the place even had a whale's penis bone. A dork. It was an awesome exhibit, even if most of the props were fakes. The last time Edda had visited the place, she went with Fran after they'd smoked a joint. They found themselves giggling at every little thing, especially the penis. Finally, Edda reached 144th Street and, veering off the beach, she could see her corner home.

Up the path past the dunes, crossing the street, onto the sidewalk, up the stairs, Edda unlocked her porch door and stepped inside. She checked her phone for the current time; it was almost five thirty.

Dinner was nothing special. Edda boiled some noodles, defrosted and pan-fried meatballs in garlic and butter, then added marinara sauce to the whole mix. She ate quickly. When she was finished with her spaghetti, Edda put the remnants of her meal on the mound of dirty dishes in the sink. She was running out of clean dishes. For a moment, she was about to walk away, to save the task for another day, but Edda sighed and gave in to the necessity of the chore. Unloading the previously run dishes from a week or so ago, Edda packed the dirty ones into the dishwasher like an unfulfilling game of Tetris. *Do Doo Do Doo...*

Procrastination was a general problem of Edda's. She was never tardy with due dates but rather put herself in positions of last-minute dealings in all manners of life. At work, she'd turn a week of labor into a few days of frantic catch-up sessions more often than not. It led to a lot of downtime, until it didn't. Nobody was the wiser, save Edda's semi-frequently ruined sleep schedule and accumulated work-based anxieties.

Edda stepped outside with a bottle of red wine and an empty glass. The wind had grown restless since her walk, but it was most welcome. She had worked up quite the sweat between walking, dinner, and dishes. Edda slid into her outdoor couch nook, setting the wine down, gazing at the waves. It was a little past seven. The sun was setting slowly, and shadows cast long angles across the streets and low buildings. Lamp post silhouettes appeared as creeping creatures, cars cast darkness like deep quarry pools. Pouring a generous glass of red wine for herself, Edda savored the smell for a moment. It was nothing special, but it was comforting, cheap, and got her drunk. Taking a sip, Edda's pocket vibrated. It was a text from Francesca.

Bitch I love you, the message read. Edda could hear Fran's voice in her head, a bit southern, slightly loud, and energetic. *Can I come over?*

Yes! Edda texted back. The answer was always yes. Edda took another sip, the bitterness of the red clinging to her crimson lips.

Out of the corner of Edda's eye, she spotted abstract movements. Edda saw another blinding bright flash and turned towards it reflexively. It came from the Flamingo pink home, from the second-story window on the left. Edda's view from the porch was not very elucidating; she could not make out what she was seeing through that window. It did make apparent the odd angle at which the phenomenon was witnessed. Standing to lean against the railing, Edda stared intently at the light source. It flickered rapidly, then slowed, with no consistent pattern. The strobing looked as if it came from a distant room. Squinting, Edda could just make out an angled doorframe, and from it a sliver of light projected. The line of sight oriented ever so exactly from where Edda was positioned that she could see slightly through the frame, just a crack, and only when the light flickered. The door appeared to be closed or ajar, and the light was pushing between the gaps between the door and its frame. The details were fuzzy; it looked strange. The periodic flashing light made it appear as if the room was moving, wriggling. Shivers shifted down Edda's spine. It felt like she was looking at something she wasn't supposed to, something wrong, grotesque.

Taking another sip of wine, Edda continued to look onward, fascinated, though unsure why. Illuminations flashed randomly. Sometimes the light would rave and riot, pulsating at quick speeds. Other moments it would dim for but a second, then linger at different lumens. On, off. Flicker, flash. Zip, zap. Bright, Dark. Perhaps a spinning ceiling fan was the source of the light's flickering. Edda was only speculating.

A car door slammed shut, instantly snapping Edda to attention. A familiar sedan with a rusted frame and faded blue paint had just pulled into a parking spot next to Edda's. Out stepped Francesca, her long blonde hair tied into a ponytail, which flailed in the sudden gusts of wind like string tethered to a weather pole.

"Heeey!" Fran waved, grinning ear to ear.

"It's good to see you." Edda smiled. Francesca walked up the stairs to the porch and then set her purse and keys down on the table.

"You've got no idea how good Edda." Fran teased, her eyes scanning the bottle of red up and down. "I'm grabbing a glass." Fran slid the screen door open and stepped inside, heading to the kitchen.

"Help yourself... You know where to go." Edda smirked. From the corner of her eye, once more, Edda spotted a flash from the window. It was jarring, like briefly spotting an aberration in one's periphery, never getting a full picture of what one saw. On and off, the light pulsated. On and off. In its jittery flashes, Edda imagined dark figures.

Francesca stepped back outside with a glass in hand, closing the screen door with a thump. She sat next to Edda, pressing against her so their shoulders touched. Fran poured herself a drink.

"So... guess what I've got..." Francesca smiled, sipping wine before setting her drink on the table. She reached for her purse and began digging through it.

"An STD?" Edda laughed, turning her full attention towards her best friend. Fran gently kicked Edda's leg in retaliation.

"No, you bitch! This..." Fran pulled a thin white plastic cylinder from her bag. Squeezing it gently with two fingers, a lid popped open on the top of the tube. Angling the container downward, a gorgeously rolled joint, filter and all, slid out of the tube into Fran's hands.

"High Speed Killer... awesome strain...smell it!" Fran held the joint to Edda's nose. Inhaling, Edda noted the pleasant musk. It smelled of a blend of fragrances: cherry, flowery aromas, maybe even a hint of tangerine.

"Wow. Smells like fruit!" Edda was excited; it'd been a few weeks since she'd last smoked. She'd loved to get high. "What's the occasion?"

"Just wanted to get my favorite dumbass stoned."

The two smiled, their gazes meeting for a moment. "Plus, interview went smooth as hell."

"Oh shit, that's right!" Fran had told Edda about the prospect a few days ago. "You get the job!?"

"I think so." Francesca smiled, flicking a lighter, holding it to the joint. She puffed and stoked the paper.

"Incredible news." Edda smiled back, eyeing the joint in gleeful anticipation. Francesca got the joint rolling, inhaling a few deep puffs before blowing clouds. She then handed the burning bud to Edda.

Edda took the slow-burning joint by the filter between two fingers. Placing the pre-roll to her lips, Edda sucked deep. The taste going down was sweet, subtle. Then, as the smoke hit Edda's lungs, she coughed rapturously, barking and heaving. Handing the joint back to Fran, Edda wheezed smaller and smaller coughs until her breath normalized. Taking another sip of wine to quench her burning throat, Edda felt a sudden sensation overtake her, a pleasant numbness of the body and excitement of the mind.

"That'll do it." Edda laughed.

"Lightweight." Fran teased. The two giggled in tune to the sound of the waves.

"So, what'll you be doing again? If you get the job, I mean..." Edda asked.

"Something to do with rental bookings. Figured I'd learn on the fly." Fran lazily puffed hits from the joint as it sagged from her lips.

Edda felt her spine tingle as she listened to her best friend. There was a pleasant humming in the back of her head, and she immediately forgot what the job was.

"Here... you need more of this." Fran passed the joint to Edda.

The next inhalations became much more pleasant for Edda. They were smooth and tasty; smoke pulled in and blew out with ease. It was a comfort. A sensation of calm washed over Edda like low tide. She could feel pressure on her eyelids, an elevating rumbling in the brain and soul. The two spent minutes passing the joint back in forth, mostly in silence, save for a coughing fit.

"Fuck yes." Edda grinned, passing back the joint to Fran. "Finish it, I'm good."

"Well, this shit's true to its namesake. You died quick."

"Oh, I'm alive." Edda leaned against the railing, looking out towards the ocean. Fran let the joint linger in her grasp and, with the same hand, picked up her wine glass, sipping at the rim between tokes.

The two lingered in the quiet spaces between conversations. Edda watched the world go by. A pleasant breeze picked up again, tussling Edda's hair and blowing away some ash and fire from the tip of the joint in Fran's hands.

"Fuck!" Fran exclaimed as a small ember of burning weed landed on her bare left thigh. Francesca quickly stood up, wiping the ash to the ground.

"You alright?" Edda asked, partially concerned, partially giggling at the sight.

"Yeah... yeah..." Fran sighed, setting her glass on the table. She handed the joint back to Edda. "I'm guna' go run some water over this." She pointed to a barely noticeable burn, a small dot of red on the skin of her thigh, then slid the porch door open and walked inside. As Francesca walked into the bathroom, keeping the door open, she shouted, her voice faint but legible. "You need an ashtray!"

"We got bushes!" Edda replied. Edda took small puffs of the dying joint, then flicked ash over the railing into the greenery below as if to prove her point.

Looking back toward the ocean view, Edda watched the grass

in the dunes sway. An elderly woman crossed the street, carrying a white garbage bag to the trash bin on the corner of Wight.

Then… a familiar movement caught Edda's glance once more. It was that damnable flicker. The inside of the flamingo pink house looked dark; everything seemed to have been turned off. When the light randomly shined, it briefly illuminated the interior with a bright white glow. The angle at which Edda sat made everything seem uncertain in scale and shape. The doors, the walls, they seemed to funnel the light like a focused laser beam aimed at Edda's exact position.

Edda wondered if anyone else had seen the flash? If she saw it from the street earlier, and now from her porch, surely there were other angles which someone could see this? Edda considered later walking down Wight to see if she could get a better view through the window. It felt very silly to Edda to even entertain such an idea, and she hated to be such an obvious voyeur. Yet the light was compelling for some strange reason.

Fran stepped back out onto the porch.

"Whatcha looking at?" Francesca inquired. Edda paused; she genuinely wished she knew the answer. It was… a lightbulb dying surely. She felt uneasy at the thought of mentioning it. She turned to face Fran, who sat down on the couch with a quaint thump. The breeze blessed the two with its presence once more, though it was growing slightly colder outside with the coming evening.

"Nothing. Just looking around… zoning out." Edda turned to Fran, noticing someone turning the corner sidewalk as she did so.

It was Carter once more, now in a teal windbreaker. He came to a halt as he got close to Edda's front stairs, slamming his cane down with a small *plock*. Carter stared directly up towards the porch where Edda and Fran sat.

"Hello again." Carter waved. "No sign of that fox, thank goodness." He spoke rapidly, making getting a word in difficult. "Thought I might see it again… I'm guna' head down to the bay get sum' more walkun' in. Maybe I'll see em' there…"

"Sounds good." Edda nodded.

"Well..." Carter smiled, looking directly at Fran now. "Think I might've found that fox after all." For a moment, an awkward silence boomed. The sentence lingered in the air, heavy, like iron raindrops from a steel cloud. Carter began scuttling onward once more, his cane clanking against the concrete with each other step.

"Have a nice night!" he called as he waved goodbye.

The two friends gave some time for Carter to get far enough down the street before reacting. He eventually turned towards the crosswalk, vanishing out of sight.

"That's a fucking buzz kill." Fran shuddered.

"Yeeeeah..." Edda grimaced. "That line came out of nowhere." The two poured themselves more wine.

"Maybe..." Fran's horrified expression shifted suddenly, a sly smile replacing it. "Maybe he's rich!"

"No. No!" Edda protested, waving her hands back and forth like how a referee would call a timeout. "You're not gold-digging my creepy neighbor."

"Just saying..." Fran shrugged, tension tightening in her back as she stretched her neck upwards for a moment before resetting to a sitting position. "Could be a millionaire! Maybe a widower?"

"I've only ever seen him alone." Edda shook her head, raising her eyebrows, egging on the conversation while pretending to protest it.

"See!" Fran quickly drank a large sip of wine in a single swallow before continuing. "We could both get in on the action, get all his inheritance! Then I wouldn't even need this job."

Edda squealed and snorted out an absurdly high-pitched chortle.

"Well... his dick probably doesn't work half the time anyway..." Edda raised her hands up and down like scales weighing out options. "Fuck that, though! That's gross in so many ways. I already have enough trouble sleeping as it is."

"Money makes anyone beautiful," Francesca spoke solemnly, in a way that could be taken both as a serious statement and that of parody.

"I hate that," Edda said, drinking more.

"Me too." Fran nodded, drinking more.

The two friends spent the rest of the evening continuing to drink, immersed in each other's conversation. They talked of hobbies, dreams. When the drink ran low, another bottle was opened, and the merriment continued. Francesca regretted only buying the one joint.

The streetlamps turned on. Hours passed. Soon the sun began to set, casting wonderful pink and orange hues across the sea. The dunes and beach turned a slight lilac color for but a moment, living up to the beach's namesake.

Nighttime at the beach was Edda's favorite. Edda took Fran by the hand.

"Let's go for a walk." She suggested, and Fran nodded in agreement. The two, barefoot, drunk, giggled as they crossed the street towards the dunes. Past the beach grasses and the wooden fence, the two made their way out onto the beach. When far enough away from the town and facing the endless horizon, a person could trick their senses into believing they were in a void. Only the stars above and the roils of the ocean anchored reality in place. That and the sand between one's toes. And Fran's hand gripping theirs... Without such measures, Edda felt as if she could float upwards and disappear into the atmosphere, becoming one with the clear night sky.

Fran and Edda sat down in the middle of the beach, letting the sand below conform to their shapes. Edda dug her feet into the sand while Fran lay backwards, nearly immediately. There was nobody else out on the beach that night, and it was a bit chilly, but tolerable.

"This makes everything worth it." Edda was sentimental when drunk.

"Yeah." Fran agreed, making sand angels with her arms for a moment. Edda fell back into the sand as well. The two gazed up at the night sky. The moon was new, only a slight sliver in the sky, and even that was mostly covered by a few clouds, moody and dark, splattered with hues of blue. Some constellations could be seen clearly, however, or at least parts of them. Each star seemed a beacon, a glowing dot aimlessly radiating from the heavens without intent or meaning, only existing for viewing pleasure. The two sat in silence, admiring the skies. Edda had no sense of time, especially when buzzed, and what was in reality nearly half an hour felt like fleeting seconds.

"I'm cold, and I probably need to go home." Francesca finally said.

"Nooo." Edda softly protested, half awake.

"I know, girl. Come on." Fran stood then reached for Edda's hand. Edda lingered, then reluctantly grasped it. Fran pulled her upwards, helping her come to a standing position, sand falling from the two of them.

"Unfortunately, I got the old job in the morning. Not much longer..."

"Me too," Edda groaned.

The two pattered slowly back home. On return, Francesca got a large cup of water, drinking it almost entirely in a single go. Then she hugged Edda, gathered her things, and walked to her car.

"I'll text you when I'm home," Francesca promised, opening the driver's side door.

"You good to drive?" Edda asked.

"Yeah," Fran reassured, waving back at Edda on her porch. "Been sober for an hour or so now. Night!"

"Night!" Edda smiled back. Edda resumed her seat on the outdoor couch. She watched Fran drive out of sight, turning towards the coastal highway. Checking her phone for the time, it was nearly ten. Edda was tired but wasn't quite ready to go to bed.

She peered at the flamingo pink house, staring into its windows, expecting to see a flash, but there was nothing. No lights, just pitch black inside the home.

"Finally." Edda quietly spoke out loud to herself, as if some important task had been accomplished.

Turning back to the beach, Edda stared towards the dunes and darkness, waiting to hear back from Fran. Her drive home was only about fifteen minutes, less at night. On evenings when the two partied excessively, Edda repeatedly pestered her friend to text when she got home.

Who are you? My Mom? Fran retaliated the first time Edda texted her if she'd gotten home safe.

Home? Edda inevitably texted Francesca. A few minutes passed before she received a reply, her phone vibrating in her lap. Looking down at her phone, swiping past the password screen, Edda read Fran's reply.

WINDOW

Edda lurched upward, grasping the porch railing as she focused on the flamingo pink house. Adrenaline pumped rapidly through her; a rapid, inexplicable terror overtaking her momentarily. The window, the one on the second story, was now fully illuminated, clashing against the darkness in the rest of the house. The light did not flicker, but remained on, constant, brighter than some stars in the sky. Edda looked back down at her phone, a sense of utter madness over taking her. Edda reread the message once more:

Home safe. It read. *Must have misread it.* Edda sat back down, upset and bewildered. She was exhausted, drunk. She was feeling a bit paranoid, obsessed. Edda looked back at the flamingo pink house once more. The single illuminated window light was unchanged, still glowing blindingly bright in the night.

MARROW BLUE

Carl longed to be free. He was eager to see his family to safety. Eager to dispatch the intruder. Yet he was helpless. A maelstrom of a million emotions, sick and ugly, clawed at him from the inside. It was the primordial instinct deep within each of us, the one that overtakes our perceived selves in times of danger. Such mental monsters taunted him; if only he was stronger, faster. Slowly standing up from the garage floor, wanting to shout and maim and kill, Carl shuffled to a nearby workbench. His hands were trembling; hell, his entire body was.

Mannhouse cautiously watched his hostage. Carl reached above his head to tug on a dangling pull chain. Scattered across the ceiling, three caged fluorescent lights lethargically blinked on, illuminating the garage and giving the homeowner and the intruder a good view of each other for the first time in the buzzing glow. They were no longer shadowy blobs, no more silhouettes veiled in gloom, obscured by confusion and the dark.

Carl was a healthy-looking man who Mannhouse estimated to be in his early forties. His face was handsome, clean-shaven. His chin sharp, his jawline well defined. His hair was short, light brown, slightly bloodied, matted from the recent scuffle. Carl's eyes were amber, his pupils dilated like inflated black balloons. While he had a bit of a tummy, Carl's muscles were noticeably toned, tense from the situation. Comparatively, Mannhouse felt like a shriveled raison. Carl was no Michelangelo's David, but compared to Mannhouse, he might as well been a male model.

"I think it's somewhere back here," Carl spoke meekly, his mind racing as he searched. The phone call Carl received left him confused; the situation he found himself in now seemed much larger than he initially realized. Someone knew his name, number and had great timing, or was watching them remotely somehow. Perhaps his captor was putting on a show, creating a distraction, though to what end he was unsure. For now, all Carl could do was speculate and cooperate.

"Find it." Mannhouse grew more impatient each second, his right foot tapping the floor rapidly. Coming from upstairs, the sound of hurried footsteps against old creaking floors echoed through the house. A child's wails pierced through the halls. Someone was fleeing the house, crashing footfalls echoed through distant rooms.

"DON'T HURT THEM PLEASE!" Carl shouted. He bargained and groveled, offering anything he could think of to Mannhouse, who only ignored Carl's continual pleas. He continued to hold the gun directly towards his hostage, his finger twitching. Mannhouse imagined some demonic aggressor, ready to burst into the garage with a force so powerful it'd detach the door from its hinges. He waited, listening, drowning out Carl the best he could, ready to react if anyone dared peek their head past the rusted red door. His hands shook like an old blues musician's.

The sounds of movement headed opposite the garage, however. Then, the sound of a distant door slamming echoed through the house. Someone made it outside.

"Thank god," Carl whispered to himself. Nothing was said for a long time. Mannhouse stared at the red door, his caution waning.

"Nothing about tonight makes sense," Carl spoke up, feeling emboldened. "People don't just break into a place without intent."

"I intend for you to find that sledgehammer." Mannhouse walked to the garage door, closing it all the way before turning back to Carl. "And I don't intend to explain myself." Mannhouse waved the gun commandingly, his voice cracking from exhaustion. "Hurry up!" Mannhouse needed to cough but managed to contain it.

"Fine..." Carl searched for a bit more. From behind a VCR stacked upon an old tube television, Carl picked up a hefty tool, worn and aged, the wood on the handle was splintered, the steel of the hammer rusted. "I knew it was back here." Carl didn't move, afraid he'd be shot for holding a weapon, or some other form of backwards logic such as that. Carl had no reason to believe his captor was sane.

"Good," Mannhouse said, but nothing felt good right now. The two stared at each other for a moment.

"So?" Carl asked, interrupting the stillness.

"So?"

"What now?"

The middle of the garage was mostly uncluttered by junk. A small section of clear floor sat unobstructed, nothing but a charcoal slab of concrete, speckles of blue and black scattered here and there. One of the fluorescent lights above cast a perfect square patch on the floor, like it was an art piece on display at a museum. World's most boring exhibit.

"Why not there?" Mannhouse pointed with the revolver. "Start digging." Mannhouse backed himself against a wall near the entrance, keeping his eye on Carl like a cat stalking a mouse. He'd never get used to being the predator. For so long, he felt like the prey.

"Seriously?" Carl drowned in disbelief.

"Do it or I shoot, simple as that," Mannhouse demanded.

"Whatever you say," Carl muttered, walking hesitantly towards the middle of the garage.

"Grovel all you want... we still gotta do this." Mannhouse struggled to get his words out; his throat was dry like desert sands. A glass of cold water would be heaven right now.

"Just... start swinging?" Carl asked, unsure of what any of this could accomplish.

"Just start swinging," Mannhouse echoed, holding in a cough that scratched like sandpaper against his flaking throat. Mannhouse knew better than to question the illogical at this point.

Carl arced the hammer high into the air. Mannhouse watched intently, ready to retaliate in case Carl decided to try and pull an impulsive Gallagher-style attack using his head as a melon. With all his might, Carl swung the hammer down upon the garage floor. On impact, the hammer head made a loud *thunk,* which reverberated through the room. The concrete was unscathed, not even a crack in the floor. The only thing the first swing accomplished was to kick up a large cloud of dust and dirt.

Again, Carl swung the hammer down upon the floor.

Thunk!

Clang!

Pow!

Slowly, swing after swing, minute after minute, the concrete began to give way, forming fissures and cracks in its foundation. Time crawled, and soon Carl heaved and panted, lungs burning, arms heavy.

"I..." Carl huffed, grabbing his shoulder, wincing in pain. He leaned the hammer against a stack of yellowed plastic folding tables. "I need a break."

"Okay." Mannhouse agreed. "We both could use a drink."

Carl nodded, surprised his captor didn't crack the whip. Carl headed to the kitchen with Mannhouse behind him every step, the revolver still looming, nearly pressed into the notches of Carl's spine. Mannhouse looked around, still cautious of an ambush, but the kitchen was only two rooms away. As they headed through the mostly dark house. Carl flipped on a few lights.

The kitchen was soaking wet, the floor still covered in shards of glass. Outside, hurricane Nester was also taking a breather. Carl grabbed two cups from a cupboard, walked to the fridge, and filled them with ice water. Carl guardedly handed over the glass of water to Mannhouse, still holding him at gunpoint. Mannhouse chugged the water, nearly drinking the entire glass in a single gulp.

"Ahhhh!" Mannhouse exclaimed. "I needed that..."

The two took some time to quench their thirst. Mannhouse never lowered his gun. When satiated, they headed back into the garage. Carl, though fearful, was abundantly curious.

"What's this accomplishing?" Carl asked. His back was screaming in pain, his shoulders like sandbags pressing down on him. Hesitantly, he lifted the sledgehammer back up.

"I said I'm not going to explain myself. Besides, you wouldn't believe me," Mannhouse said.

“I’m open-minded.” Carl raised his brow.

“You’re pretty chatty for a man held at gunpoint.” The weight of the gun felt natural now, like it was a part of Mannhouse, an extension of his hand.

“Look, I’m cooperating, just…” Carl leaned on the hammer for a moment like a walking stick. “I just want a little context.”

“Okay, fine…” Mannhouse scratched at his forehead, pondering what excuse to make. “Your house is built on an ancient Indian burial ground, and I need to find the Ark of the Covenant.”

“Is that right?” Carl almost laughed.

“No! Of course not!” Mannhouse almost snapped. “But nothing I say to you is going to sound any less insane!” He waved the gun nonchalantly once more. “Just keep at it!” Mannhouse was fearful authorities would arrive soon.

“Fine.” Carl didn’t bother to ask questions or argue anymore but continued to work at the threat to his life. The only comfort Carl currently had was knowing his family was out of the house, far from the maniac with the gun against his back. Hopefully, they’d found shelter and called the police by now.

Carl chipped away at the concrete until small fissures became large chunks. Endless painful minutes passed, the weather outside growing in fierceness once more as the epicenter of the storm shifted away from the county.

After each swing of the sledgehammer, Carl felt unable to raise the tool high once more. His lungs burned, and every time he gasped for air, dust and debris filled his mouth. Yet Carl persisted. He felt obligated to survive, not for himself, but for his family. He desperately hoped he could buy enough time until help arrived, or Mannhouse found whatever the hell he was looking for. Despite the water break not long ago, his mouth was drier than a wilted summer flower. The labor seemed never-ending. Sweat beads occasionally rolled into his eyes, blurring his vision and stinging. His muscles tore and veins popped. Still on he persisted.

The floor, repeatedly bludgeoned, looked more and more like a spider web with each blow. At first, it was one crack, then two.

Now, with a hundred strikes, thousands of fissures created the illusion of interconnected silks, forming a web of rubble.

Slam!

One last time, with a great heave from Carl, the hammer hit the floor with a tremendous quake. In unison, outside, thunder broke, rolling across the county. A powerful blue glow suddenly began to beam through the cracks in the floor, illuminating the entire garage in an intense light. The rubble on the floor seemed to fall, crumple in on itself, falling into a massive black pulsating pit below Carl's house.

Initially, Carl believed the source of blue light to be from the crackles of lightning outside. However, the garage's only window was covered, and the doors were shut. The lambent lingered, consistent, and unchanging, and when Carl noticed its persistence, it became clear this was no weather phenomena. The source was coming from below.

"Holy shit..." Carl's mouth was agape, his eyes wide. "What is that?"

"Wait..." Mannhouse recoiled, lowering the gun, his attention turning from the floor to Carl. "You can see it?"

"Of course! Asshole!" Carl huffed. "Who wouldn't notice THAT!"

"Everyone..." Mannhouse slumped backwards against the door in shock, rust scraping off onto his jacket as he slid to the floor. His legs sprawled outward as he scratched his head with the pistol barrel.

"I'm sorry..." Mannhouse sounded despondent, like a doctor trying to give news about a dead patient. "I didn't want... You shouldn't be able to..." Mannhouse sat the gun down next to him, no longer caring for its weight.

"Fucking hell," Carl panted, both from exhaustion and shock. He tossed the hammer to his side, the metal head clanking against the floor.

"You weren't lying about the Indians." Carl walked towards the light. Leaning downwards, he reached out to touch it. He was drawn to it.

"I wouldn't do that," Mannhouse warned. He stood quickly.

"It's ... beautiful." Carl's eyes shimmered. A fuzzy forgotten memory, long discarded, popped into his mind's eye. It was a lovely recollection. When Carl was a child, no more than five, his mother took him to a local carnival. The first time Carl witnessed those bright neon lights in the dark summer fields, he was filled with a sense of wonder never fully experienced again, at least not until now. The blue light, it's shine. He felt like a kid again, complete with the accompanying ignorance and awe. Carl extended his arm towards the glow; he needed that feeling forever. He could hear beautiful melodies.

Mannhouse grabbed Carl by the arm, pulling him backwards forcefully.

"I'm serious!" Mannhouse spoke from experience. "You'd rather put your balls in a blender! Trust me."

"I, uhmm, what happened?" Carl spoke in a daze.

An encore of thunder outside cannonaded like drums without rhythm, interrupting Carl's confusion. The blue mystery light seemed to flash in synchronicity with the thunderclaps; the brightness and dimness fluctuating with the intensity of the heaven's holler. As the rapturous weather calmed, Carl muttered an uncertain question.

"Am I dead?"

"No, we're very much alive... least I think we are." Mannhouse laughed. He got a sense of Déjà vu, like someone had just asked him that question. He was interrupted by a different kind of storm, cancer. Coughing up blood once more, Mannhouse wheezed a sickly gasp. Steadily, Mannhouse regained control, inhaling the particulate-filled garage oxygen. It smelt of dust and tangerines.

"So, if I'm not dead, what's happening?" Carl sounded intrigued, yet his voice was tinged with animosity, a burning hate towards Mannhouse for bringing some anomaly into his home like it was shelter for forces unknown. Part of him felt thankful. The ghastly blue glow terrified Carl as much as it did tantalize him.

Mannhouse felt a vibration in his jacket and pulled Carl's phone from his pocket. Looking at the home screen pop-up on the cellphone, it appeared to be a text from a person named Bethany.

"Here." Mannhouse handed Carl the phone. "I think it's your wife."

Carl snatched the phone from Mannhouse, looking at the screen to see one word: "Safe." They had ventured to a friend's house a street away and were able to find shelter.

"They're safe... somewhere else." Carl didn't wish to disclose where.

"Wonderful." Mannhouse smiled awkwardly. A mother and a child were not deaths he wished to claim responsibility for.

For a moment, the two didn't know what to say. Each of them was bathed in a solemn blue light. The light turned the garage atmosphere into something akin to a haunted house or laser tag center. The hazy dust floating in the air aided in the aesthetic as well. The crack in the floor almost looked like a window. Sparks vibrated inside it, like they were deep, electrified pools. Carl had never seen such a brilliant thing, and Mannhouse hadn't gazed upon the blue in a long time. He didn't need to look upon it again to know what it looked like, however. Its glow had long been burnt into his retinas.

"My name," the home intruder hesitated, "is Mannhouse. I was lying earlier."

"Okay." Carl listlessly acknowledged Mannhouse with a nod, transfixed once more upon the rays emerging from the floor. Walking over to the revolver, which still sat next to the red door, Mannhouse picked it up. Flicking the safety on, Mannhouse held the gun by the warm barrel.

"Here." Mannhouse offered the weapon to his once hostage. Carl looked up from the shimmering, almost just as shocked by Mannhouse's act.

"Why?" Now that Carl regained control of the situation, part of him longed desperately to beat Mannhouse within an inch of his life, though his better judgement prevailed. He was sore and exhausted, and even with a gun, it was proven earlier that any situation could turn on a dime. Plus, violence wouldn't explain a thing about the anomaly churning upon the ground. Carl hated himself for not killing Mannhouse where he stood.

"Violence is a part of being human." Mannhouse sighed, really wanting a drink, something alcoholic, bitter, and smooth. "But it doesn't have to be what we want."

"I could kill you." Carl looked at the gun dangling from his hand, the trigger guard hanging around a few of his fingers. Its metal shone in the blue, sleek and bright. "Part of me wants to."

"Either way seems reasonable." Mannhouse knew Carl wouldn't, but hoped he would.

"What is this, really?" Carl set the gun onto a plastic storage bin near himself. "You know something about this. Why else would you warn me?"

"It's... difficult to explain." Mannhouse deflected.

"Try," Carl insisted.

"Okay." Mannhouse sighed. "I'll try to make a long story short." Carl sat on the floor, looking up at Mannhouse like a toddler about to be told a story by their grandparent.

"When I was twenty... Oh... fuck." Mannhouse inhaled deeply, to his surprise he fought back tears. He hadn't told many this story, let alone a stranger. "I went upstairs into my attic, and I tried to kill myself. I put a hunting rifle to my chin and pulled the trigger. It was my grandfather's."

"Christ." Carl gulped.

"Yeah. Well, the crazy thing is the gun didn't fire. I pulled that trigger three or four times, but nothing."

"Why'd you try?" Carl asked.

"Look, don't ask a thousand questions, or I'll be here when the cops arrive." In truth, Mannhouse didn't want to tell anyone about his loss.

"Fine." Carl agreed.

"So, figuring maybe the safety was on or it was jammed, I pulled the gun away from my head. The moment I did, though, it fired directly into the ceiling. Insurance didn't cover that shit. It was the strangest thing. I'd put the gun against my chin once more and pulled the trigger. The weapon refused to fire. Then, the moment the barrel was pointed away from me, it discharged. I tested this, over and over, until my ceiling was riddled with bullet holes and I was out of ammo. I went unharmed."

"The hell..." Carl wouldn't normally believe such an abnormal tale, but he didn't know what normal was anymore.

"Yeah," Mannhouse agreed. "I tested it over the years, with other guns, I mean. Shotguns, pistols, whatever caliber, make, it didn't matter. Every time I'd put a gun to my head, the gun didn't fire until I pulled it away."

"Why were you afraid of my gun then?" Carl asked.

"Well," Mannhouse said, "Never did test it with other people shooting at me."

"Huh." Carl was fascinated but felt insane.

"Eventually, I accepted suicide wouldn't work," Mannhouse sighed.

"Did you try other methods?" It didn't occur to Carl how morbid a question it was until it slipped from his tongue.

"I..." Mannhouse's lips curled. "I'd considered it, but the means I could think of seemed too painful or risky. I don't want to be a brain-dead husk. Don't misunderstand me, I don't think I'm immortal, nothing like that. Just... something wouldn't let those bullets blow my brains out."

"Prove it." Carl wanted evidence. It excited him slightly.

"Really?" Mannhouse asked, shocked by the response.

"Yes." Carl stood up, reaching for the revolver. "If what you're saying is true, then you'd risk nothing, and I'm willing to believe anything now." He handed Mannhouse the gun, who hesitated. There was a long pause in which only the storm was heard. Mannhouse believed he'd be fine, though every new attempt did bring uncertainty. Could this be the time? It was a different circumstance than usual. Perhaps being in the presence of someone else who could see the blue window would change something?

"Okay, sure, why not?" Mannhouse sat up, looking around. "Uhhh, anywhere you want me to point?"

"Your head."

"I mean, where in the garage do you want me to fire?" Mannhouse asked.

Carl tilted his head slightly in thought. It was surreal, contemplating where best in his home for a stranger to discharge a gun in order to prove suicide by ballistics was impossible. "I guess the floor is already fucked, what's a little more damage?"

"Alright." Mannhouse agreed as Carl handed him the weapon.

Never yet in Carl's life had he experienced such a violent, absurd, and fantastical night. He was fearful he was about to watch a man blow his brains out. Yet, the glow from the floor seemed to assure him otherwise. Despite the irrational nature of Mannhouse's claims, it felt real. His dying seemed more impossible than naught.

Mannhouse removed the safety, showing it to Carl to confirm his actions like a magician setting up a performance. Then, placing the gun directly on his temple, he pulled the trigger. *Click.* He pulled again. *Click.* A third time. *Click.* Nothing.

"Now watch this." Mannhouse removed his finger from the trigger, resting it on the grip. Rapidly, Mannhouse pointed the gun towards the concrete floor. The revolver fired near instantaneously into the ground, kicking up dust. Carl jumped backwards. Thunder struck again a moment after, as if wishing to participate in the noise-making.

"Damn, that never stops being loud." Carl was amazed, his ears ringing, amplifying his headache. The proof seemed worthwhile for some reason.

"I can do it again if you'd like." Mannhouse offered, his ears also ringing.

"No, no... that's okay, I believe you!" Carl paced, dumbfounded, his vision blurry, his stomach churning. "What does this have to do with the light in my garage?"

"Well, I think I'm cursed." Mannhouse sighed.

"Cursed?" Carl asked. He laughed a little, an uncomfortable laugh.

"Yeah," Mannhouse continued. "See, I eventually got out of my 'slump', cleaned up, got work. I met this beautiful girl. We fell in love, had a kid, and..." Mannhouse paused, thinking. He stared into the blue.

"And?" Carl leaned in, both wanting to hear more and struggling to do so, watching the glow in the side of his vision.

"Well... I think I owed a debt. For my life... to something. Whatever had saved me... stopped me from killing myself. It came to collect..." Mannhouse coughed slightly. All this talking was agitating his throat. "Cancer, the big one. Doctors said I didn't have much time left." Mannhouse sighed. It hurt reminiscing.

"Jeez..." Carl kind of pitied Mannhouse in a way.

"But a debt can't be fixed with more debt..." Mannhouse asserted.

"And this has to do with that," Carl pointed at the light, "how?"

"I still can't believe you can see it." Mannhouse grinned, perversely glad to share the weight a little. "I tried to show it to people at first. All it did was make me seem crazy. I started to believe I was... for a while." Mannhouse returned the gun to Carl.

Carl set the weapon down, no longer feeling like a hostage nor a hostage taker. He wasn't sure how he was supposed to feel in this situation, which he could give no name.

"How many people did you try to show, I mean... the light and the gun? Who'd ya' tell?" Carl poked.

"I'd never dreamed of showing the family my neat little trick with the rifle... Not worth the risk of traumatizing them if it ended up killing me anyway; not to mention it was old history... I did, however, one day, tell my son about the light. Mannhouse looked like he was ready to cry. "He told me to get help..."

"He didn't believe you?" Carl was both surprised and not.

"How could he?" Mannhouse scoffed. "I never was a good father... I should've known it wasn't for me. I would've been the same way in his shoes. Sons no fool."

"Yeah, it's a hard sell." Carl's body was heavy. A lot had happened in a very short amount of time. "So...?" Carl urged the story onwards.

"Right." Mannhouse continued. "Rewind to before I saw the light. Anyway... I still hadn't told my family about the cancer yet. So, I decided to get piss drunk, went down to Cheshire's."

"Oh, that place gave me food poisoning once." Carl laughed.

"Yeah, I don't go there to eat." Pub food was hit or miss in Letterfaux, and Mannhouse preferred a liquid diet anyway. "Eventually, while drinking, as one does, I really needed to take a leak. So, there I am, pissing, when suddenly everything is blue like it is now. I didn't even notice it at first. Gradual. Then, to my right, I saw it. On the wall, past the urinals, that same light." Mannhouse pointed to the floor. "I'd thought maybe I'd drank too much. But I couldn't look away. I was just like you when I first saw it. The light called my name. I touched it, and when I did, something pulled me inside..."

"Inside to... where?" Carl stuttered.

"It's... hard to remember what's beyond the portal." Mannhouse was sweating. "But it's a terrifying place, and sometimes I'm obligated to visit."

Mannhouse paused. He wished he had some sort of time machine so he could stop himself from ever approaching the blue light all that time ago. His head hurt; recollections of the Farm pounded at his temple, haunting ill-defined images and flashes. He had visions of a field, a garden long unseen.

"So... like... you... go on scavenger hunts looking for this thing?" Carl felt like his entire worldview was a snowflake, melting away on a salted road.

"Yeah, something like that..." Mannhouse looked deep down past the depths of the blue sparkling glow.

"Do you hear that?" Carl asked suddenly, listening intently. He positioned his left ear towards the blue gap on the floor, focusing on some sound.

"What? The storm?" Mannhouse asked.

"No... music. Sounds like something grandma used to play." Carl's teeth trembled and clacked. Hastily, Mannhouse grabbed Carl by the shoulders, staring straight into his soul.

"Listen to me, Carl!" Mannhouse shouted, spitting unintentionally. "Nothing good comes from the blue! It ruined my life! STAY AWAY FROM IT! DON'T LISTEN TO IT! IGNORE IT!"

"Okay! OKAY! Jesus! You're spitting!" Carl pushed Mannhouse away.

"It took everything!" Mannhouse ranted. Even when threatening Carl at gunpoint, screaming demands, Mannhouse did not seem as intense as he did now.

"That place... that thing... It has done nothing but torment me!" Mannhouse's voice was deep, raspy, worn out. "I don't know why you can see that fucking light, but whatever you do, don't touch it! Don't interact!"

"Alright, alright!" Carl swore. "I believe you!"

"I'm sorry I put this on you." Mannhouse's guilt weighed heavy on him like elephants on a trampoline. Carl could still hear the music, though it seemed more distant than previously.

"I don't know if you can blame yourself for... that." Carl believed everything Mannhouse had said. Regardless, a great temptation tugged at him. He wanted nothing more than to reach out and touch the blue glow. Carl's will was strong.

"Well then." Mannhouse offered a handshake. "I guess I should get going then."

"That's it?" Carl almost didn't want this night to end but wished it had never started.

"That's it." Mannhouse nodded.

Reluctantly, Carl shook hands with Mannhouse. He felt a flurry of emotions as he did. Hate, rage, confusion, intrigue, concern. Some emotions churning within him didn't feel like they could be named.

"Goodbye," Mannhouse said, praying he'd imparted the severity of the burden blue. The beast which sucks marrow from bone, soul from body.

Mannhouse walked up to the ominous blue glow in the ground. Gazing deep down into the hole, which looked like it went straight toward the core of the Earth, Mannhouse felt a familiar sensation of horror and anticipation wash over him. He had wished never to return to the Farm. Mannhouse inhaled deeply, lingering, hesitant. In the blue, the unknown always waited. He hoped this was his final task.

Hopping forward into the pool of light, Mannhouse sank beneath the floor. Carl watched as Mannhouse's body seemed to vanish through the hole, falling through the ground. With Mannhouse's descent, so disappeared the light and the black pit. Now, where the glow had previously emanated, only broken chunks of concrete on a dusty floor remained.

"Goodbye," Carl muttered.

Carl was alone in the garage. Pulling out his phone, Carl dialed his wife, uncertain of what he would say. He just wanted to hear her soft, loving voice and his son's wonderful laughter. As the phone rang, Carl looked down at the floor, wondering if he'd regret not following Mannhouse into the light. It felt like he'd both avoided a disaster and discarded a miracle. In the distance Carl could hear approaching police sirens distorted by the storm.

LONE WINTER NIGHTS SPENT STONED IN A WEIRD WINDOWLESS ROOM

Ward was in his twenties, living with his grandmother Darcy, in a small two-bedroom apartment at Grassy Acre's. It was a large brown building that sat on Cattle Run Road. About five months ago, Ward's grandmother, Darcy, fell while changing into her pajamas. Hitting the floor hard, she shattered her hip, immobilizing herself in a most painful manner. Thankfully, she remained conscious, and after a painful crawl to the phone, she managed to call for help.

After being discharged from the hospital, Darcy moved into Citizens' Way Retirement home for a few months to rehabilitate. Eventually, Darcy regained some mobility while she used a walker, but could no longer operate independently. When she finally moved back into her home, she needed someone to take care of her. Darcy had COPD and struggled to breathe. In addition to helping his grandma with daily chores, Ward watched over her health and hygiene. Darcy had an oxygen machine, which sat plugged into the wall at the entrance of her bedroom, pumping air all day and night: a robot lung. Darcy wore a breathing apparatus in her nose, which connected to a large plastic tube from the machine. It essentially became Darcy's leash. They'd gotten her an extension to her tube that allowed her to reach most sections of the apartment. She had to drag it around with her everywhere, and it would often get tangled around her walker wheels and furniture. Ward was constantly untangling his grandmother's tube. For times when Darcy needed to leave the house, she had a portable oxygen tank which she could carry on her person. It was a cylindrical tank, one with a mask and nozzle. Darcy simply had to hold the mouthpiece to her face and press down on the nozzle for a burst of oxygen. They could fit a lot of oxygen in a tiny tube.

Taking care of Grandma when she left the retirement home was a difficult family decision. Ultimately, Ward was the perfect solution as he already worked from home. Thankfully, he could set his own hours and required very little interaction with coworkers. It was a data entry job, nothing special. Additionally, since he owned a one-bedroom flat, he began renting it for extra income after moving into his grandma's place. It wasn't the life he wanted, but it was a good deal overall. Darcy had been retired for some time and paid for all the utilities and groceries. The situation was financially advantageous for Ward and medically advantageous for Darcy, family helping family.

It did cause Ward's social life to go down the tube, however, as he needed to be there for Darcy at any given moment. Sometimes his mother, aunt, or uncle would visit, giving Ward a day or two off, but the occasions were infrequent. He lost contact with a lot of in-person friends. Now, most of his friendships were formed online. They were people he played Counter-Strike and other competitive multiplayer games with.

So, sequestered in a small flat with his grandma, Ward's life had grown rather plain. He cooked Darcy's meals every day, helped her change her clothes and diapers, and helped her sponge bathe. Anything and everything she needed. It was far from enjoyable, but someone needed to do it. The two didn't particularly get along with each other. There was already a pre-existing generational gap, which, combined with Darcy's declining mental state, made for tenuous interactions. Ward saw her as a miserable old woman who cried frequently about how sorry she was for being a burden and how she just wanted to die. The only pleasure she seemed to draw from life was drinking. Ward loved her very much but hated her in equal parts.

Darcy loved to drink screwdrivers. Ward tried to limit her consumption, but it felt futile. For a while, he stopped buying orange juice altogether on grocery runs. This led to grandma taking shots, and she ended up drinking even more this way. Eventually, through some form of familial attrition, Ward was browbeaten into compliance. He found himself looking away each night as she drank herself into a stupor. Hell, he mixed her drinks.

Darcy was a very schedule-oriented person. She wanted to get up at eight, eat breakfast at nine. She would watch *The Price is Right* midday, then eat lunch at noon. Dinner had to be exactly at five, which was also when she would start drinking. Finally, eight o'clock was bedtime. Each day, the process would repeat, all while Ward juggled his work during what downtime he had.

Because of Darcy's scheduled lifestyle, so did Ward's follow suit, like a planet rotating around a sun. After eight, when Darcy retired to bed, was when Ward felt most free. He would wind down his evenings by smoking weed. The high was a great evening relief. Darcy didn't much approve of marijuana but was in no position to protest.

On warm days, Ward would smoke outside on the front entrance patio, which was partially covered. The walls were pink stucco, and the ceiling overtop was made of the same material. Smoking in the apartment was a no-go. For one, it would agitate Darcy's COPD. Not to mention neighbors would surely complain of the smell, and it violated HOA smoking rules. The patio had a small, neglected garden. The view overlooked a plot of grass with a single tree in it, some roads, and adjacent apartments.

In the middle of winter, when temperatures sometimes dropped to single digits, if Ward wanted to get high, he would have to get creative. First, he headed down into the parking garage, smoking in his car. One night, a close call with a nosy resident nearly ended disastrously. Since then, he didn't dare try smoking in his car again. That was probably for the best, as Ward didn't want to make the pleather smell of pot anyway.

One evening, after putting Darcy to bed, Ward decided to explore the apartment complex for a new place to get high. He soon found a perfect spot after some aimless wandering. The apartment building was four stories tall. In the center of the building was an elevator that connected to each floor and the basement parking deck.

In the basement, to the left of the elevator, was a small, pitiful room. It was an oddly arranged spot, sort of shaped like the letter L. The space seemed like it was an afterthought of the architect. The room was only about ten meters in length, and eight meters wide, give or take some while accounting for the strange shape of the space.

The L-shaped room had been turned into a makeshift gym, though it's doubtful if anyone would be generous enough to give it such a title. In truth, the gym had a single treadmill, some small weights, and a mounted pull-up bar. All the equipment was donated by previous tenants, most of whom had since passed. There was a poster on the wall regarding gym rules, safety, and workout tips.

In the workout room, the walls were concrete, painted a bright lemon yellow. There were no windows, and the only entrance to the gym was a double door, which was painted a bright lime green. The floor was a dirty shag carpet, horribly inappropriate for a workout environment. On the wall outside the entrance was a plaque that warned residents to use the gym at their own discretion.

The place was dusty, neglected. Nobody in the building used it. Hell, the only reason Ward was aware of it was because of its adjacency to the basement elevator. To Ward, this was the perfect place to get high. All the residents of Grassy Acres were old, mostly retirees, and were seldom out and about during the evening, especially during dark cold winter nights.

So, the gym became Ward's new place to smoke. He would lean against the green gym double doors, right in the center, just in case one day someone did decide to wander in. They only opened one direction, inward, fortunate for him. Ward wasn't too worried about the smell but brought a small bottle of ozone spray with him every time he'd smoke, just in case.

Setting up camp, Ward opened a Crown Royal bag. He pulled from it a glass pipe, a grinder filled with a variety of strains, and a lighter. Ward would use a plastic sandwich bag to dump his ashes.

Phone reception was hit or miss in the basement, but Ward would try to watch videos on his phone while smoking. Tonight, however, he couldn't get anything to load. Ward sat in the quiet L-shaped room, smoking with his thoughts.

It was pretty creepy sitting alone in the tiny gym in the basement at night, especially with nothing to watch. Ward wasn't one to get scared easily, but the environment did evoke bizarre feelings. The overhead fluorescent light hummed loudly, bathing the entire room in a pale green. He was adjacent to the boiler-works, which would heave and gargle, as if the entire complex was wheezing. When the garage doors opened for a vehicle, wind funneled through the hallways, making it seem like the building was howling. This alerted Ward that someone would be coming from their car. The elevator *ding* was also a way to know someone was coming, but due to the elevator being a few footsteps away from the gym doors, the sound gave Ward far less time to react.

When Ward would hear someone heading towards or leaving the elevator, he would flick the gym lights off, remaining as quiet as possible. These were artificially tense moments. Nobody ever checked, but the apprehension still lingered while Ward would wait for the passerby to leave. Being unable to see who or what was on the other side of the doors did lend the imagination credence for running wild. Logically, Ward always knew it was a person on the other side of the doors, but he sometimes imagined terrible beasts, hideous monstrosities, improbable anomalies. In his head, they stalked the halls of the boiler-works and skulked in the shadows of the garage.

The most disturbing thing to Ward about the L-shaped room, however, was its lack of a window. It was as if he was in a space completely cut off from the rest of reality. There was no visual anchor, no beacon to connect this location with another. When in the gym, Ward felt like he was in a box floating in an empty void. Since Ward always sat leaning against the double doors, he did not see any light or movement through the cracks beneath the door. It was a strange box; one he could isolate himself in.

When Ward was in this weird windowless room, he was truly alone, his only companion, his roaming thoughts. Here, Ward's ideas were most clear and unbound, regardless of whether he wished to ponder them. Ward had one cruel and constant recurring thought: he wished his grandmother would finally die. He hated himself for this, but the thought persisted at all times of the day. Darcy sometimes begged for it. She wanted peace, no more pain. She missed her husband, her friends, all her beloved dead. For Ward, he just wanted his old life back. He wanted to be able to wander out of the house in total spontaneity. He wanted friends who weren't behind a computer screen.

Ward lifted a smoldering bowl to his lips, inhaling the smoke. His thoughts stretched out into the halls of Grassy Acres, deep into the boiler-works.

Dying Light Bulb Hypothesis

It was another comfortable Friday night at Purple Beach. Another week had passed, and soon the month of April would as well. The air was unusually warm for the season, making it almost feel like summer. Favorably, a complementary breeze lazily swept through the air, lovingly gifting anyone outdoors with its presence, angel kisses. The waves in the distance danced, and the sun had just set. Lamp lights illuminated the streets of 144th and Wight minutes ago.

Fran had stopped by to visit Edda a few hours ago. She and Edda were through a bottle and a half of some cheap red wine. The first bottle was named Wisdom Keepers, cheap and bitter stuff Francesca had gotten at Rishad's for twelve and some change. The second bottle (the brand the two friends were currently imbibing) was purchased by Edda a few days ago at the same liquor store. It cost around twenty or so dollars. It was named Encumbered Panther.

"There it is again!" Edda pointed excitedly.

"I don't see it, baby," Francesca laughed. "You're obsessed!"

"I am not!" Mac, dramatic and jovial, spat out her words. "I've noticed it all week!" Another flash of light, indistinct and blurred, pattered through the window in the flamingo pink house on Wight. On, off, slow, then fast.

"There it is again!" Edda pointed rapidly once more, waving her finger forward like a spear stabbing at an enemy.

"See? Obsessed." Fran was drinking heavily. She had no limits past a certain threshold, which she had long since passed this evening. "Still can't see shit..."

"Stan... stand up!" Edda ordered, jumping up from her seat as if she were spring-loaded. "Switch sides with me."

"Nooo," Fran moaned. She was wasted, tired from a long day at work. At the moment, all she wished to do was become one with the couch. "Edda, this is stupid. I don't care about some light in a window."

"C'mon!" Edda begged, gently shaking Francesca's left shoulder. "Maybe it's a line-of-sight kind of deal. I've only seen it sitting here, I think." Edda practically forced Francesca from her seat, narrowly avoiding knocking both of their glasses over. The two swapped positions, Francesca protesting the whole maneuver. As Edda sat where Francesca previously was, Edda confirmed her suspicions. She could no longer see the flash.

"It was a location thing, see! I'm... a genius," Edda self-congratulated.

"Ughh, this is why I drink." Fran sighed.

"Bitch you drink because you're an alcoholic," Edda said coyly, picking up her glass and taking another sip.

"So are you!" Fran also partook, as if on cue.

"Oh, I'm absolutely a drunk!" Edda laughed. The two loved to shit talk one another; it was endearing. "Anyway, look." Edda pointed towards the flamingo pink home. It was incredible to her that just a slight shift in her position angled the geometry of the home's window in such a way that one could not peer through the window, but only be able to see its frame.

"I... don't see anything." Fran hardly indulged her friend, hazily gazing through inebriated eyes in the general direction of the homes on Wight.

"There." Edda pointed once more. "Flamingo pink house, second story, the window on the left."

Francesca was never much of an observer. Perception was lacking, both due to apathy and constant daydreaming. In that manner, the two friends were most alike.

"This is silly," Fran quipped, scanning the home. She continued to see nothing. All the windows were dark. For a moment, Fran felt as if a trick was being played upon her, or some elaborate gag. Then, Francesca saw the flashing light, illuminating for a brief moment an otherwise mostly dark interior. The blinking continued at random intervals, the inside of the home was near impossible to make out, just formless dark shapes in ill-lit frames.

"Oh, yeah, I see it!"

"SEE!" Edda screamed way too loudly, triumphant in proving her trivial point.

"Yup." Fran held no interest. "It's a dying light bulb! Woooo…." She finished off her glass.

"Well? What'd you see?" Eagerly, Edda leaned in a bit, seeing if she could swivel or pivot her head in a manner that allowed her to see the flash again, to no luck.

"Jesus Edda…" Fran scorned, "It's just a light. We need to get you out of the house again…"

"I walk the beach!" Edda swallowed her spit. "Every day."

"You know what I mean!" Francesca reeled. "Anywhere that doesn't involve sand, errands, or office visits." Encumbered Panther had about a glass's worth in it, and Fran refilled her cup to the last drop, setting the empty bottle on the ground next to the other disposed one.

The night breeze continued to be pleasant. The light continued to flash, registering in Francesca's peripheral vision seldomly. Unlike Edda, it did not grasp her attention much. It was another mundane happenstance. To Edda, there was a limitless potential the light provided; within its very flickering concept lurked unanswerable mysteries, stories untold, thoughts to be conjured. It was romantic in a way. Behind that window could be anything. Edda just wished Francesca could see that.

CAGE AT THE CENTER OF THE UNIVERSE

In Ohio, in the city of Letterfaux, in the middle of an old Farm, in an unassuming field, stood a small green barn. The small green barn had two windows facing each other, one on the eastern wall and one on the western. Both were covered by tarps, which lazily draped over the frames, blocking most of the view inside or out.

There was a large barn door on the northern wall and a normal door on the southern wall. The northern door was barred and hadn't been opened in years, making the smaller door the only entrance and exit ever to be used. The rafters were dusty. Chains and rope hung from the beams. Bales of moldering long, long-forgotten bales of hay were tucked away in corners. A hose, hooked up to a water pump outside, twisted around itself on the floor, sprawled out across the barn like a stretching octopus's tentacle.

In the middle of the barn, sat evenly between the windows and doors, was a cage. It was a large steel monstrosity. It looked like a bird cage, though it was proportioned just large enough for a full-grown adult to occupy. The cage was welded onto a large copper plate. The plate had four large industrial hex screws on each end that bolted the rectangular plate into the concrete floor beneath.

The cage had a door with a hole for a lock. There was no lock, however. The door had not been opened in so long that its hinges and frame were rusted shut. Built into the door was a leather mask, one for the occupant of the cage to stick their face into. There were no eye holes in the mask, but there was a large, round gap where a nose and mouth could rest cupped between the stained leather form, which was splattered with many dried fluids.

Straw was layered over the copper plating and around the cage, like bedding for an animal. Feces coated the cage and much of the straw bedding, all of which was also soaked with urine.

Master did not put them in the cage for no reason. They had done something wrong long ago. They were always doing something wrong. At first, Master loved Drull. Master and Drull used to be friends. This was before Master took away their true self, assigning his current identity and eventual assumed name, Drull.

The cage was Drull's everything; all they knew was the excruciating familiarity of its metal bars and the surrounding barn interior. No longer could Drull recall their life beyond the cage. There were glimpses, flashes, distortions of a past now indecipherable, meaningless hallucinations that haunted Drull. Sometimes Drull was unsure if their memories were dreams, imagined worlds, or past lives. Flashes. They were images of a forgotten family, a lost life, a better self, but Drull could make no sense of the visions. They frightened them. Drull had no grasp on time. They weren't sure if they had been in the cage for days, months, years, or eternity. Drull wasn't even sure if they could die, but wanted it often.

Master would infrequently visit Drull. But when Master did, they used the only available door, and momentarily, Drull would be granted brief visions of the outside world. Not much would be visible beyond the door. It was mostly just some grass, trees. To Drull, someone who no longer knew the outdoors, it felt like a world unmapped. It was limitless, the things that could be beyond the foliage, beyond the door.

Drull stretched upwards as much as able. The cage never allowed them to fully stand. Drull could fit their legs and arms between the cage bars, making moving somewhat possible, though still restrained.

One of the bolts holding down the copper plate was slightly loose. Sometimes, Drull would rattle back and forth, causing it to create a fun clanking sound. Drull enjoyed this very much.

The sun was setting, causing orange light to cascade through a tiny sliver of ripped tarp on the righthand window. It was one of the only sources of light in the musky old barn, meagerly illuminating a pile of hay in a fuzzy, warm hue. Drull loved when natural light found its way inside the barn. A few cracks in the wood, tears in the tarp, holes in the roof allowed for minuscule reminders that there was more than the cage. Beyond the barn walls, there was a sun, a moon, life.

Drull stared through the bars of the cage, their vision focused on a sliver of light, orange and yellow, piercing past the tarp gap. It was but a trickle of sun, but the actuality that it even existed was a miracle. It was a thing of splendor, a void made bright by a star.

Drull's imagination could no longer be influenced by a normal person's experiences. Theirs was a mind's eye which was unrestrained, pure, free. The only influence upon their mind now was the barn, the cage, Master, and the endless days. Though such traumas were great, even in the tiniest cracks of light, Drull could often find brief states of wonder.

These moments, intensely experienced and spiritually immense, existed for milliseconds. Though not hallucinations, within the eye of the mind were sights so defined and exact it was almost like projecting visions of the soul unto reality. It was molding clay with the heart, making it take form of anything and everything, shapes impossible, subsuming their surroundings like weeds breaking through pavement. These were dreams impossible to be experienced by most, only given to those warped a certain way. They were glances into other planes, into the treasures of insanity.

Drull watched the light disappear through the rip in the tarp as night fell, growing melancholy as darkness overtook the barn. They could hear the clicks of crickets and a few remaining songs of the cicadas. Night was cold, dangerous when they were at their most vulnerable. Sometimes, the rats would come and nip at Drull's toes and rip at their flesh. Some unmeasurable time ago, Drull managed to kill the largest rat among a small group. Drull broke its spine and ripped apart its fur. The rats relented mostly since then, but recently they've grown emboldened again.

It was dark. Posts, bales of hay, tools, all figures familiar to the setting of a Barn, were now shrouded in an absence of sunlight. As Drull could envision things in light, so could they in the dark.

Drull piled up some of the dry hay beneath them, forming as comfortable of a bed for themselves as able. They flicked away the clusters of hay with a lot of excrement covering them. They covered the rest of their legs and huddled tight. Master would only allow them luxuries such as blankets and heaters during winter freezes, and this was moderate weather. The day had been rather warm in fact, though even warm nights could offer rigors and tremors if not mindful.

Truly all things physical were made painful by the cage. Sleep was no exception, but it was achievable. Drull would stretch their legs through the bars in the cage, resting their back against the door. Leaning their head backwards, they would place their skull in the leather mask indentation, using it as a pillow of sorts. Their arms, not as flexible as Drull once recalled, would grasp onto the bars in front of them or slouch by their side while they slept.

Drull closed their eyes. The nothingness behind their eyelids was much more tolerable than the ever-warping shapes among the witnessed dark. The immobile and mundane are more prone to take the form of monsters when Drull would look around the barn at night. Monsters of the head could not be defied; one could only wish for good dreams. As such fates would occasionally grant, no nightmares had assailed Drull in some time.

Drull was nearly asleep when suddenly they sprang to attention, hearing a loud rustle of movement disturb the stillness of the barn. Drull's eyes dashed about rapidly; they listened with intent. No more sounds were heard; all was silent except for the crickets. Drull grabbed his left hand with his right, squeezing tightly, barely breathing. It could not be the rats, for no patter of their feet was heard. Cats would sometimes also make their way through, skulking for prey, but even in them, Drull had no friend. Eventually, calm and assured by stillness, Drull attempted to sleep again.

When in sleep we may be dormant, the world around us still lingers. The first weeks Drull spent in the cage were completely restless. It was a painful process, learning how to sleep in such hostile conditions. When Drull would sleep, they would often awake in panic, banging their head or limbs against the cold metal of the cage. In time, their brain 'snapped'. Such reflexes were calmed, their panic replaced with complacency.

Drull awoke again to the sound of chirping birds. The sun was rising, and through the left window, a new ray of light pushed its way into the barn. It was a small god-ray, formed by creeping past a piece of tarp that wasn't completely drawn shut. It was a gift. The color of the rising sun was a bright mix of yellow hues.

Drull's sight pierced through the rafters above, in which the sun poked, as well as the slight light which passed through both covered windows and the cracks beneath the barn doors. Drull imagined small realities within the gaps of light. Though the holes were sizes not even comparable to that of quarters, within the light, the spaces felt immeasurable, endless. They were entire galaxies, whirling and chaotic, ones made of blossoming luminance, explosions of sunlight. It was like an intangible flower, its petals warming, impermanent. Dust particles floated past blotches of light. It looked like watching stars burn up in the atmospheres of a million Earths. Though Drull was lost in their imagination for a moment, such barren pleasures they held could not be cherished for long.

Drull heard strong stomping feet sloshing through muddy ground approaching the barn. Master was visiting. The barn door swung open violently, its hinges slightly bent. Light from the outside burst into the barn, blinding and brilliant.

Behind Master and the ajar door was a line of tall trees, forming a natural wall of roots and branches. A rusty metal thing could be spied to the left of the door before being cut off by line of sight. It was an abandoned car, some old construct heap that had spent decades lying in the field. From Drull's perspective, it was but an abstract monument, a thing to be glimpsed, but miniscule seconds at a time. The door creaked shut as Master entered.

Master's face was covered by a brown hood, as always. Master's lake blue eyes pierced through the hood eyeholes like sunrays through windows. His lips were grey and chapped; they poked out just beneath the bottom of the hood. Master wore jean overalls, which were tucked into his large brown steel-toed boots and strapped over his shoulders. Underneath he wore a tattered and yellowed white tank top. On his hands he wore gloves, brown leather, which were worn from extended use. A German cross could be seen tattooed on his wrist, partially covered by the gloves. Master was tall, and the perspective from the cage made Master seem as if a giant to Drull. Master's voice was rough, crackled and cruel.

"What good is a slave? Master spoke loudly, their muddy boots stomping as he walked past the cage. "Without a master?" Master grabbed the water hose, draping it across his back like pelts being hauled from a tannery. Running through the center of the green hose was a red line. At the end of the hose was a simple brass nozzle, which could be turned counterclockwise to control pressure. Master threw the hose to the ground in front of Drull's cage.

"What good is a pet?" Master approached the wall-mounted reel and faucet, where the hose was connected, turning a bronze valve; its metal squeaking as it rotated. Water rushed through the hose, inflating it, creases smoothed, turning to curves. "Without someone to care for it?" Master walked back towards the cage.

"What good is a child?" Master continued to monologue, pointing the hose at Drull. "Without a parent?" Adjusting the nozzle, water sprayed outward in a pathetic splash. With some finetuning, Master adjusted the nozzle until a narrow line of water sprayed forth with considerable pressure.

The water was cold, shocking Drull on contact. It was painful, like piercing arrows. Drull held their arms over their face instinctually. Master compensated for his aim, trying to hit Drull in the face for a while like it was a twisted water balloon game at some local carnival. Master laughed gleefully; his chortle sounded uncharacteristically jovial, like Santa Claus.

Shit and filth washed off Drull slowly, layer after layer. Hay was swept away by water pressure. It soaked up in puddles, which rolled out of the cage and off the copper plate, clumping at the sides. Drull flailed in their cage, huddling and trembling. Their teeth chattered from fear and pain and shivers of cold. Drull grasped their arms around their knees, tucking his face inwards. Their once grime-covered skin began revealing its natural color. Drull's skin was pale and bright, pink and spotted. It was like cheap deli ham on the brink of turning.

It had been a while since Drull had had a bath.

Drull didn't like baths. They were abrupt, often leaving Drull shivering. However, considering the feces and urine that would accumulate and cake upon Drull and the cage, it was the closest thing to hygiene to be had in the barn.

Master was filled with amusement watching Drull squirm, but eventually, he relented with the water. Setting the hose down, it sprayed wildly on the ground like a wriggling worm. Returning to the wall-mounted reel, Master turned the water pressure valve tight, which squeaked as he did so. Hay and hair floated on puddles of water, mimicking ships lingering in harbors or corpses floating down rivers.

"Maggots are worth more than you." Master spat on the floor; the drop of spit merged with a blot of liquid on the ground. He strode towards a wooden chair near the barn doors, grabbing it, before returning to Drull.

"Don't forget that child." Master sat down, a leg's length away from the cage.

Drull feared looking at Master. Master's eyes seemed to leap out from his skull through the holes in his hood. They were unblinking weapons, ones that pierced souls like torpedoes. A person's eyes can hint at their true character; it holds their emotions, their traumas. Master's eyes, they were different. They were windows into the worst aspects of mankind. Though he was a man, he carried himself like a beast.

Master leaned back in his chair against a wooden beam. Taking out a packet of cigarettes from a pocket, Master pulled out a lighter and three smokes. He placed each to his lip, lighting them all simultaneously, rapidly inhaling, puff after puff. The smell, ashen and foul, wafted through the barn, lingering like old ghosts. Master glared at Drull, who slunk and shivered, water dripping from their naked body.

Master was so enamored with his project, Drull, that he saw fit to take time every now and then to visit. He loved to bask in his accomplishments, to enjoy the fruits of the conquest which lay before him. In the cage was his victory taken form, an avatar. A person reduced to a token, discardable, forgotten, lost. This was the purest indulgence of man: power over another. Power over an enemy's fate. Master wore such wicked delusions over himself like impenetrable armor; he saw through a visor, limited, but bloody.

Drull's head was turned, staring out past the cage bars towards cracks in the ceiling. Out in the sun, beneath the sky, Drull imagined no such torments existed for any other creatures. It was a heaven for those bathed in light, so impossibly jubilant that each millisecond experienced could only be bliss and enlightenment. If such an imagined realm were made from soul alone, then only those who lived so impossibly low would know how to build towards the dreamed utopia.

Master smoked for a long time, but eventually finished his cigarettes, putting them out against the wood beam his chair leaned against. Often, Master would put out his smokes on Drull's skin, so Drull felt fortunate to be spared this occasion.

"Drull," Master spoke, standing from his chair. "I'll bring your meal soon."

With those words, Master left the barn. As Master departed, Drull looked out upon the scenery behind the door frame once more. Drull's eyes were wide and blinded, absorbing everything that could be seen. Within Drull, an intoxicating lust for the unreachable swelled up from their belly like whirlpools in water bottles. This overwhelming emotion drove Drull to grasp at their restraining bars, reaching outward towards freedom, an animal trying to push through impenetrable steel. Drull fought against the bars, as if their flesh would defy reality and phase through solid matter.

As the door swung shut, that brief recess, that momentary glimpse of the world beyond, was once again gone. Now only the cracks of light remained. Some god rays shot through slivers in the rafters above. Such pitiful views, still whimsical and wrought with potential daydreams, nevertheless felt lacking. Especially when compared to the landscape painting that was the open door. Drull often fantasized that Master would draw back the curtains, but such a dream would not be permitted.

It had been a while since Drull had eaten. The grumbles in their stomach acted as one of the few grounded reminders Drull had of time's existence at all. The sunlight's changing position was a prominent reminder as well.

Drull heard laughter in their head. This was a pain similar to when Drull tried to recall their life before the cage. Drull wept to the sound of a child's giggle, soft and familiar. Drull grabbed the cage, shaking it violently, the metal banging against the floor. Drull grew still. They were soaking wet, sobbing.

Soon the sun was readying to set, yet Drull had been brought no dinner. It was erratic and often infrequent when Drull was fed. Sometimes, Master was consistent, bringing meals regularly. On other occasions, Master simulated famine. Master had always managed to feed Drull just enough to allow them to survive, though there was not a day gone by that Drull did not know great hunger and all its accompanying pains. The promised meal could have been a taunt, some trick, or a mind game. Master's words were misleading and obscure. Drull's mind is just as much a plaything for Master as their body.

Dinner did eventually arrive, however. Initially, Drull was too absorbed in hazy hallucinations and didn't notice Master's entrance. Drull turned, hearing Master's approaching stomps, just momentarily glimpsing the outside beyond the door. Master held a tray in his hands. Drull's dinner had arrived.

Master placed a metal bowl and a large canteen of water in front of the cage. In the bowl was an offense to the very concept of the culinary arts. The food's consistency was that of gray, burnt mashed potatoes. Chunks of diced rubbery protein, a chewy mystery meat, were sprinkled on top of the meal. The pile was odorless, save for a faint background scent akin to old vinegar. Drull was given no utensils, as ordinary.

"Enjoy." Master's voice was dull, drained of prior enthusiasm. Feeding Drull was but another chore for him.

Drull wasted no time in consumption, frenzying to action. Master did not stay and watch; it sickened him. Drull paid no mind to the outside world beyond the door as Master exited. The bowl could not fit through the cage. So, Drull scooped up large globs in their palms, pulling the meal past the bars before stuffing down the gruel like a starved beast. Drull put his face up against the bars, sticking his tongue out to lick the bowl. The feasting was glorious. Drull ran their fingers across the bowl's inside and rim, ensuring every particulate of food was consumed. They licked up droplets on the cage bars, scooping up any bits of vittles that could be found scattered about the cage or their person. It was a great meal, though Drull held no standards.

After this, Drull was thirsty. Grabbing the canteen, Drull took large sips of water, greedily satiating their dry mouth. It was a joyful feeling, one of a few for Drull. After big thirstful chugs, Drull returned to the bowl, searching for the tiniest specs of food. When Drull was certain not an atom of sustenance remained in and on the bowl, they pushed it away from the cage. It rolled away on its side, eventually slowing to a halt, rattling back and forth in equilibrium until the bowl settled motionless on the floor. The movement and clanging sounds delighted Drull. Drull continued to sip at the water in their canteen. When not a drop remained inside, Drull tossed it as well. Master did not like it when Drull had objects. Master claimed they could be weapons, or toys. Neither were acceptable to him.

After dinner, Drull needed to urinate. They began to piss, holding their genitals out past the metal bar. Drull tried to direct the flow of piss away from the bar. It trickled down the barn floor, towards a drain. Drull's urine was sickly smelling. It was foul like roadkill and burnt like gasoline. Drull splashed themselves slightly. Afterwards, Drull cleaned themselves with some wet hay.

The day had been eventful and long. As the evening rolled forward and crept into night, Drull watched the last shimmers of sunlight and beams of light dwindle. Drull longed to be free from exhaustion, pain, solitude. A day as vivid and demanding as this one was rare and wore out an already broken body. With eyelids closed, sleep came swiftly for Drull.

. . .

The barn door swung open suddenly. Drull awoke in reflex, banging their neck against metal, jumping at the thought of ghosts. Master approached the cage, holding a bowl of food in one hand, and a grey blanket in the other, the hem of which dragged behind him. Master placed the breakfast, the usual grey tasteless slop, in front of Drull's cage, then tossed the sheet to his side. The helpings looked extra plentiful today. Walking about the barn, Master collected the discarded bowl and canteen. Filling the canteen with water, he slipped it in his pocket.

Drull consumed the meal through the bars as he had with his dinner the night before, fingers dirty and slop dripping from their lips and chin to be later licked up by their pale white tongue. Drull was quite full, their stomach bursting through their skeletal frame. Several meals within relatively close time were not unheard of, but it was less than commonplace. Master lit up several cigarettes, inhaling and exhaling great puffs like plumes from smokestacks. He needed the smokes to endure watching Drull eat. Once Drull had finished, he spoke.

Then he said, "Today is a special day." Master paced back and forth through the barn. "I need you to be extra quiet for a while." The musk of smoke filled the barn, rolling from Master's lips and from beneath their hood.

"Don't make a peep. None of that cage rattling you're so fond of..." Master had smoke rolling from their nostrils; ash fell from the burning cigarettes to the floor like cancerous snowflakes. "You understand me?"

Drull, looking down at the ground, fearfully nodded their head complicitly. Drull's subtle movements went unnoticed by Master.

"DO YOU UNDERSTAND!?" Master screeched, his coarse voice cutting like razors, spit flinging from his mouth. "SILENT AS A MOUSE!"

"Yee-yess!" Drull stuttered in fear. "Yush… Yush."

"SILENCE!" Master screamed even louder.

Drull nodded their head up and down while holding a hand over their mouth, desperately pantomiming understanding.

"Good. Good." Master handed the canteen through the cage bars to Drull. "Conserve this. I might not be back for a few days."

Drull, whose thirst clawed at the back of their throat, immediately opened the container and chugged large amounts of water from its contents. Drull did heed Master's words, though, and set aside the rest for later when satiated.

"Remember, quiet," Master said, lifting the grey blanket from the ground. He covered Drull's cage with it, allowing in almost no light.

"Hide those legs!" Master kicked at Drull's feet, who recoiled in pain, pulling their legs under the cover. "And if you remove your cover, you will be punished." Master's menacing and threatening voice was all too recognizable, and Master's words always held true.

Drull tucked his legs against his chest. They huddled and grasped themselves, listening to the sound of their breathing. Master's muddy stomps grew distant, and the sounds of the barn door opening and closing rang through the rafters. Under the blanket, in the cage, all felt still. Though it was still morning, it now felt as if early night.

This was a new experience for Drull. Never before had Master tried to hide them, nor did they demand silence of them. Master's screams were impactful. It was clear to Drull that this was no test, no game. Drull knew fear; it was cultivated well by Master. But more relevantly, Drull knew obedience. Master had total control over Drull, his greatest pet.

The day's temperature, which was already abnormally hot for the season, was amplified by the blanket, which quickly turned the cage into an oven. Drull sizzled in the hotbox, marinating in their own sweat. The blanket also muted the ambience around the barn. Sounds of nature from outside the barn could not be heard; only Drull's movement and breath seemed to be audible.

Drull drank from the canteen, large wasteful gulps. Such cool water was an immense treat, and Drull wanted to savor it before it turned room temperature. After quenching their thirst, Drull closed their eyes. In the heat, sleep crept upon their constitution. The darkness beneath the blanket made holding their eyes open especially difficult for Drull, who curled up in a ball. Skin baking against the searing metal of the cage, Drull fell deep into slumber.

Drull's dreams felt prophetic. They were vivid, as real as the feeling of running your hands across fresh-cut grass. They were brief, yet beautiful. In Drull's rest, they heard music and smelled fruits freshly picked. Fields of green stretched endlessly underneath the stars in the sky. They were so far away, the celestial lights, yet Drull could reach out and touch them, could run their fingers across the heavens. There was laughter, of a lover, of a child. Drull tried to follow the sounds, but they were lost in a crowd of people who emerged suddenly around them. All the people in the crowd were kind and familiar, yet their faces went unrecognized by Drull. Each one of them wore a hood, the same as Master's, but unlike his, their eyes were kind. Everyone in the crowd held clouds in their hands. Drull lifted a cloud into their right palm, grasping it gently. They could feel raindrops slip through their fingers. Drull joined the crowd, and they watered planets in the sky.

Awakening, mouth dry again, Drull immediately drank from their canteen, which was now about half full. They were absolutely drenched in sweat, and their skin felt seared. The air in the covered cage was thick and humid. Body odors circulated through the box, stagnant and sickly. Time passed unperceived, to Drull it seemed all was still. Only Drull, their pains, and the cage existed. All beyond the veil was motionless, culled from reality.

Drull passed time by memorizing the pattern on the blanket. It was simple, a grey box in a grey circle, repeated in a staggered array. Under the blanket, after gazing intently at the stitch work for minutes on end, its shapes seemed to warble and change. Drull watched as the symbols danced like geometric monsters. When Drull closed their eyes, they could see, burnt into their retinas, a box in a circle.

Drull held themselves tighter. They wished to see the light which pierced through the torn tarps and the beams of morning sun which penetrated through the rafters and cracks in the walls. At least, when Drull was looking through the cage bars, it allowed for some depth. The light beyond the barn illuminated some proof that more existed in this world than the cage.

Drull had a thought: Why must they be hidden at all? To the rational, this question would be absurd. Yet, so brainwashed was Drull, so stripped of humanity were they, that they could no longer see themselves as anything other than a caged beast. Drull was as if a goldfish attempting arithmetic. They believed wholeheartedly that they deserved the cage. That the cage was normal for them. Others would see it as such, too, Drull reasoned. Drull was the cage, and the cage was Drull. It was no more abnormal than the sun. The only strangeness felt by Drull was their need to remain hidden.

Beyond the blanket, outside the barn, Drull heard something from afar. It sounded like two people walking and talking past the barn. Their voices were muddled, their words illegible, but they were loud. They were shouting at each other; in an argument it seemed. One of the voices sounded like Master's, though Drull knew no others to guess who the other person could be.

The voices continued to rise in intensity, and the walking came to a stop. Whatever the disagreement was, it sounded violent. The two continued shouting and screeching at one another, their words heavy with rage. Eventually, the quarrel grew to such volumes that the voices drowned out even the sounds of Drull's heartbeat. A few words here and there, now could be distinguished, mostly curses. Fucking lying nazi asshole! The argument seemed to reach an eruptive climax. Then...

BOOM!

A loud explosion echoed across the landscape and through the barn. It was intense, louder than lightning. It sounded as if a car backfired, but at a much larger scale. In the aftermath of the quake, sounds of feet running through the mud could be heard momentarily. Then, nothing but Drull's own breath made a sound once more.

Drull knew that sound somehow. It was a gunshot... It ripped through someone, for some reason. But Drull knew not what those variables were. Drull wanted to remove the blanket, see if they could get a better look, but dared not to. He grew thirsty, and Drull sipped water in the heat, wondering about the gunshot. Liquid sloshed within the canteen, diminishing slowly. Drull tried to resist drinking as long as possible between each pitiful sip. Drull would let their mouth, throat, and tongue wrinkle and wither like raisins, and even as their body begged for hydration, Drull would wait a little longer.

A day passed, then another. Drull had hardly had a single drop of water in the last twelve or so hours. Now, each sip Drull took was more hesitant than the last, and each droplet was savored. Then... only the canteen remained. Drull, despite their best efforts, had not a drop of water left. Drull hoped Master would return soon. He had entertained the idea that it was Master who was shot, but it felt impossible. Someone like Master couldn't be dead. Or perhaps it was foolish optimism, like a pet waiting for its dead owner.

Sweltering, their head burning like a grill, Drull blacked out from the heat. Their body violently spasmed and shook momentarily before collapsing into a comatose slumber. Drull, with no control over their body, sprawled their legs out beyond the cage, poking through the blanket. They drooped downwards along one side of the cage, their head resting on a bar in a way that twisted their neck. No dreams or nightmares came to Drull now. Only nothingness. They were unconscious for a very long time.

Violently awaking, Drull felt a terrible gnawing and ripping on their left leg. They launched forward with haste, grabbing at their leg. Drull screamed in pain, then, remembering Master's warning, clamped a hand over their mouth in an attempt at silence. Drull flailed their body and kicked their legs, which caused the cage to rattle and the blanket to slide off the top of the cage, dropping down upon the metal plate. From Drull's left leg flung an exceptionally large rodent, a mangey thing. A small amount of blood leaked from Drull's wound. The rat had just begun, or at least attempted, to eat them.

The foul creature crashed to the ground, landing violently. Its back legs twisted slightly on impact. This thing let out a pathetic squeak. Drull got a momentary look at the varmint. It was like no rat they had seen before. Its flesh was free of all hair and pocked with blisters, red and green. It was famished, and its ribs were visible underneath its stretched, leathery skin. Its tail was nearly all gone, save for a bloodied stump. Its face was scarred and battered. Its eyes were black and beady, wild and hungry. For a moment, Drull and the rat made eye contact. It was as if looking in a mirror.

The diseased rat snarled. It limped away out of sight beyond some crates. Even rodents roamed freer than Drull ever could. Even pests felt at liberty to take from Drull. It was as if Drull owed a great deal of endless debts to all things that saw fit to take.

Drull grabbed at their wound, inspecting it. The rat had managed only a single bite, and fortunately, it did not break skin. Though it was minor, the pain stung greatly. This was all accompanied by the absolute exhaustion from heat stroke and a thirst that could not be quenched.

Taking some time to calm themselves, Drull looked at the blanket that fell from the cage during the scuffle. Drull's first instinct was to cover their cage and hide themselves, but the comparatively cool air brought relief to their roasted skin. It was nearing night, and the temperature was so pleasant. The sensation felt as if Drull had traded burning coals for a hand-waved fan.

Drull needed to urinate. Sliding their legs through the cage and piling up some hay underneath their crotch, they pointed their trickle of piss away from the cage as best they could. Drull could do little more than pant with exhaustion. It was a strenuous process, amplified by thirst and sore limbs.

Miserable and tired, Drull had a sudden idea. The hose Master had used to bathe them was left unfurled, and part of it lay on the floor a little over an arm's length away from the cage. With a supreme lack of elegance and a form befitting of the weary, Drull stretched their arm through the cage. Drull's hands grasped at the very edge of the hose, its textured plastic smooth upon their fingertips. It was just out of reach, but with persistence and pulled muscles, Drull managed to grab the hose in time.

Drull wedged the empty canteen between their slender legs, holding the hose nozzle over its open top. Turning the nozzle on, a small and short-lived stream of water flowed into the canteen, some of it splashing on Drull's legs. Unfortunately, Master had turned the hose off after use. Drull sucked at the nozzle, absorbing its moisture, desperate for a few more drops of water. Then, Drull drank what pitiful amount had fallen into the canteen and was dry once more.

Though their thirst could not be quenched, Drull took appreciation in being able to see the light pierce the cracks of the barn once more. Drull sat still in their cage, watching the remaining light until nightfall.

Though it grew late and dark, Drull didn't want to fall back asleep, paranoid about another rat attack. Drull speculated it was only a matter of time before they were fending off a swarm. Drull had dealt with aggressive rats before. They usually came in groups, and none looked as sickly as the lone rat that had assaulted them earlier. Drull tried to stay vigilant; however, the tolls that burdened their body forced Drull into a restless sleep. Another miserable night passed. No pests attacked.

Upon the morning's break, Drull felt especially weak. Their vision was blurry, their skin tight. Though not as severe as their thirst, Drull's stomach growled relentlessly, accompanied by great pains in the gut. Drull kept hoping that Master would miraculously return soon with food and water. In the cracks of light, Drull imagined great feasts and cups of crystal-clear water.

In the distance could be heard humming, a delightful off-key melody. At first, Drull assumed this was Master's return, but quickly realized they were incorrect. Master did not hum pleasant tunes, and this voice sounded like that of a young girl.

Drull, with no heed to Master's commands, desperately tried to call out for help, for water, but from their voice muttered only heaves, low pitch, and inaudible. So it was by some chance variable that the barn door opened.

Through the door stepped a little girl. She was humming to herself, as if in a wandering daydream. She wore a white dress that had a pattern of oranges scattered across it. The girl must have been around eight years old. Her eyes were wide and her face curious. The girl and Drull made eye contact. Drull, delusional, and hallucinating, briefly thought they were looking at an angel.

The girl stepped into the barn, keeping a distance between herself and the cage. Drull did not see fear in the girl's eyes, but an innocent curiosity and confusion that could only be possessed by a child.

The girl wasn't sure what she saw before her. Most adults would be terrified by such a discovery. From a little girl's perspective, however, this encounter seemed like a chance for fun, like making friends with a goblin in some fantasy game.

"I'm exploring," the girl proudly proclaimed, as if a great adventurer.

Drull possessed no energy to speak, but with great effort lifted their right hand, waving slowly. *What could a kid even think in witnessing such a thing?* Drull wondered.

"What are you doing?" The girl asked.

Drull pantomimed thirst the best they could. They raised the nozzle to their tongue, panting.

"Wuh..." Drull wheezed, "ter..."

Luckily for Drull, the proud adventurer was a smart kid. The child followed the hose to the wall mount and turned the bronze dial. Water hissed through the expanding hose; it was the most wonderous sound. Drull immediately began to guzzle straight from the hose, adjusting the nozzle as they did so.

Drull let water run into and over his mouth, cooling his body. Steam wafted from Drull as water made contact with their molten skin. Drull held the hose over their head, letting water cascade down upon themself. It was the greatest relief ever felt, and Drull made such a jubilant and silly face that the girl, witness to this strange scene, began to giggle in an adorable, joyous laughter. It was a lovely accompaniment to Drull's satiation.

"I sometimes jump over sprinklers at my house." The girl proudly claimed as she giggled. "Mommy sets it up for me..."

Drull continued to guzzle water, the kid patiently watching.

"I never drank out of the hose, though."

Drull continued to satiate himself; nothing else on his mind.

"What's your name?" The kid inquired.

Lowering the water, greatly panting, Drull contemplated the question. So rare a concept to consider themselves at all.

"Nuh... no namm." Drull worked up the courage for a reply.

"Everyone has a name." The kid giggled.

"I bet you have a silly name." The kid skipped around the barn, dancing around the cage. "Something fun."

"Like what?" Drull managed a coherent-sounding reply.

"Something like a funny guy would have. Pillow. Or Vanilla."

Drull laughed. It wasn't something he was used to. It hurt his chest, which was constantly compressed due to the angles in which he rested. Still, it was a wonderful feeling. He smiled for a moment, watching the kid skip.

"Whut's ur namm?" Drull asked.

"My name's Edda!" She replied like an explosion.

"Ehhh-dda." Drull grasped the hose in shock, the flow of water reduced to a trickle. "Edda..." With a million neurons firing in their brain, memories of Drull's life before the cage flooded in. They were remembrances, ones Drull had tried to suppress. She was so young, only five, when Drull last saw her. Somehow, here she was. Their daughter... She couldn't be here... not her. Drull so desperately wanted their old life, their old identity, their old family. Drull wanted Edda to stay, to hear her voice forever. But Drull wanted the cage for no one, especially Edda...

Drull twisted the hose nozzle shut, ceasing the flow of water. Drull pushed their face through the cage bars as far as possible, which only allowed for their mouth and nose to poke through. This looked silly to Edda, who laughed whimsically once more. Such an innocent sound pained Drull immensely, each a dagger. Drull fought an internal conflict, trying to find any reason to let Edda stay a little longer. If Edda didn't see Master's body, it was a good chance he wasn't the one shot, and Drull couldn't take that chance. Drull knew what they must do, though the realization was heart-shattering. Drull howled a sorrowful command:

"Youhh!" Drull heaved, each word an anchor that weighed endless tons. "Need!" Drull clutched the bars so hard their palms began to bleed. "Tuh!" Drull panted. "LEAVE!" Drull's face, no longer amused Edda. It was mangled and warped, further distorted with each word. Drull's face was clay, sculpted like a gargoyle.

Edda began to quiver, but she did not scream. Tears welled up as innocent exploration turned to vivid horror. It was the first real fear Edda felt. She realized something was wrong, but did not know what.

"RUUUNNNNNNN!" Drull vehemently screamed a high-pitched wail, a shriek so visceral and haunting that it clawed past the eardrums into the basement of the soul, never to be forgotten. It was a sound Drull never knew they could make, and a holler they could never reproduce even if they tried. It took all the energy out of Drull, who collapsed backwards, slamming into the bars behind them. The roar boomed and echoed; it tore asunder the heavens so that the stars in the sky took notice. It sent ripples through the oceans, which formed into great waves and whirlpools. It was the last command as a father they would ever make.

Edda tumbled backwards. Picking herself up from the mud, she sprinted from the barn, leaving the same way she came. Drull watched as the girl stumbled out of sight. When Edda exited through the barn door, for a moment, she was bathed in a wreath of light and truly did look like an angel.

The days were long and empty voids. Drull withered until nothing remained. He passed, looking at the sunlight which made its way into the barn through little cracks. He was thinking of the beautiful angel who came to visit him. The rats eventually returned. The swarm first consumed Master. Then they came for Drull.

DYING, RICH, AND SOBER

"I'm telling you, man! Through that window is a gold mine!" Peter pointed at some privacy glass windows as they walked by.

"You're insane." Greg rebuked. Simultaneously, he grabbed Peter's hand, who squeezed back.

Greg was joining Peter on a visit to Citizens' Way Retirement Community, which was a short drive from home. Peter's grandmother resided there. The two approached the front doors, which slid open as they walked inside.

The building had an interesting smell, mostly of bleach and other cleaning supplies, but another dank and foul odor lingered in the background. After checking in briefly with the front desk, the two walked through corridor after corridor, all of which looked about the same. Peter's grandmother was at the far end of the western hall.

"Listen," Peter continued his sales pitch, "what do all these people have in common?"

"They're old and dying?" Greg laughed.

"Well, yes," Peter agreed. "But beyond that, they're rich!"

"So?" Greg asked.

"So!" Peter shouted a little too loudly, getting strange judgmental looks from an old woman who was passing by in her motorized scooter. "So..." Peter lowered his voice. "This place doesn't allow any drugs or alcohol. Which means there's a lot of old folks here desperate for a buzz."

"Again, you're insane." Greg shook his head disapprovingly, though a smirk poked through his façade.

"Think of the upcharge. These geriatrics are basically prisoners here. They'll pay anything." The two were a few doors away from his grandmother's room. Peter stopped, looking Greg right in the eye. "It's a hell of a lot easier to pull off with two people. We could cover more ground."

"Christ." Greg was actually considering it despite his better judgement. "I'll think about it."

"YES!" Peter jumped up, shouting a little too loud again. "I've already scouted the place, made a few sales. I know this old man named Will, always desperate for some gin."

"You're unbelievable." Greg could use the money, though.

"You won't believe how much I can charge for one of those pocket-sized bottles." Peter smiled like a true opportunist. Opening the door to his grandmother's room, the two friends walked in.

"Hey Gram-Gram!" Peter enthusiastically greeted her. "You remember my friend Greg?"

BRIGHT FUTURES

A few years had passed since that night. Carl Parson had never told anyone the full truth about the home intrusion during Hurricane Nester. Bethany knew Carl was hiding something, and Carl knew Bethany suspected he was withholding the truth from her. Not once, however, did Bethany insist that he tell her everything. Carl was unsure why.

Regarding the authorities, Carl had told the police most of the truth about the break-in. He left out the parts that would make him sound insane and fabricated a story about the events in the garage. Carl told the cops that the intruder attacked him with his own sledgehammer, and after a few missed shots were fired, the man fled. Investigators were skeptical that one person could shatter a concrete floor in a few blows. Carl had described the intruder as especially large and burly, hoping it would lend some credence to the story. The case was eventually closed, with a suspect never identified.

That night haunted Carl Parson every day of his life, despite years having passed. He still felt Mannhouse's switchblade against his throat every time he gulped. He remembered his gun turned against him. Vividly, Carl still felt, with horrid recollection, the overwhelming fear for his family's life. What Carl remembered most, however, was not his assailant, the threat to his family, nor the gun to his head. It was not the intense labor as he slammed the sledgehammer against the ground. It was not the relief felt when reunited with his wife Bethany, and son Leon. It was not the grueling interviews with police, nor the sleepless paranoid nights following.

It was the glow.

That blue, unnatural hue, yet so real, so true. That window. How it enveloped the garage with its aura. It was the muted sounds of music, coming deep from that unnatural light.

On rare occasions, every few months or so, the blue light would conjure to haunt Carl. This first time it returned, it felt as if a waking dream, but it was as real as the wind. It was always manifesting somewhere nearby like an inconspicuous prop. It could appear anytime, anywhere. In his home. At work. In random locations, indoors and out. One rule seemed consistent. It always appeared when Carl was alone. During each appearance, Carl fought ferociously against his curiosity, against his debilitating urge to reach out and touch the blue. All this time, Carl's willpower won out against the anomaly. He found ignoring it and keeping it out of sight to be his best tools to do so.

"I'll see you tonight. Don't forget to pick up Leo." Bethany waved goodbye. Some days, she felt vacant. Bethany suffered just as much from the night of the break-in. Though she had no supernatural encounters, it was an equally horrific experience. Beth would often replay parts of that night repeatedly in her head. Later, she confided in Carl how she'd holstered their son Leon against her shoulder, shushing him as he sleepily protested.

"I won't. Have a good day." Carl smiled, feeling immensely lucky. "Be safe." Carl waved goodbye to his wife as he headed to the kitchen to grab a cup of coffee. Carl watched Bethany through the kitchen window as she headed towards her car. He watched her drive away, sun gleaming off the hood of her car.

Leon had been away from home all week. He was attending his first summer camp at Bright Futures. It was a seasonal camp for youth at Salt Fork State Park. Carl had recommended it. Turns out they both went when they were kids. Bethany was hesitant, but Carl eventually convinced her they should enroll their son. While it could be argued that the costs were minimal for the experience provided, housing, food, and activity fees did add up to hundreds of dollars. Still, it was worth it for Leo. Carl had taken the day off, giving himself a nice three-day weekend. It was rare to have the house to himself and was a most welcome rest from the normal chaos of work.

Carl was a manager at Green King, a company that installed and maintained potted plants for corporate, government, and business sectors. They did a lot of work with malls, hospitals, offices, and other similar facilities. Green King offered a variety of trees, grasses, and plants for installation and long-term care. At work, Carl often felt like he was a glorified calendar. He scheduled meetings and helped oversee location assignments. Sometimes he'd have to work with new hires, even occasionally filling in on watering duty when short-staffed. Most of his job was spent at a desk in front of a computer.

Carl spent the morning doing some chores. He did some light grocery shopping and picked up some wine for the evening as well. After a simple turkey sandwich, Carl decided to enjoy the beautiful day. It was August, the temperature in the mid-eighties. A fantastic breeze billowed outside.

When weather and time permitted, Carl liked to bike. He was never into racing or charity rides. Carl simply rode for his own enjoyment. Aurora Creek was a local park on the opposite side of downtown Letterfaux. It was one of Carl's favorite haunts. It had an assortment of walking and biking trails, some of which were wooded. The whole area was considered a wildlife reserve, protected land. Biking there took about five or six minutes.

Carl pulled a tiny remote control from a bag that hung from the handlebars of his bicycle. Clicking the button, the garage door shuttered open loudly as Carl walked his bike outside. Closing the garage door behind him was an equally squeaky process as the door shuttered and rattled. With a helmet on, he climbed atop his bike. Carl drifted down his driveway and out of his small neighborhood.

Making his way downtown, he peddled slowly at first before ramping up in intensity. On the main road, Carl gained speed as his legs pumped until they burned. Carl pushed himself until finally his legs slowed. He idled, the gears churning as he held the pedals still, the chain still spinning as the bike rolled forward, its speed entirely relying on momentum. The wind racing past Carl's face was most invigorating.

A few cars passed Carl by now and then. Some Letterfaux residents were rather hostile towards bikers, so Carl always felt a bit apprehensive around drivers, staying as vigilant as he could. Main Street was rather small, just a two-lane road, with cars usually parked on the curb. Biking on the sidewalk was a no-go. The walkways were in terrible disrepair and could get crowded. Concrete slabs were misaligned, often having an inch or more in height difference between sections of the sidewalk.

Zooming through Aurora Creek's parking lot, Carl peddled towards the trails. There were two primary paths that forked off in different directions, which eventually intersected before looping back to the start. The entire loop was a little less than two miles. When riding on the trails, all of Carl's focus concentrated on the moment. He would find himself in a state of peace, distracted from all the anxieties of life.

The path on the left was primarily wooded, while the one on the right was mostly dirt hills and grass. Carl took the path on the right, saving the best for last. While mostly flat, the path did have some hills and slopes to maneuver. It wasn't terribly tricky, but the occasional roots popping out from the ground were obstacles to be aware of. Carl had flung himself from his bike once and did not wish to repeat the process. When that happened he nearly passed out, landing on his chin, but managed to avoid any serious injuries luckily.

The trail was adjacent to an old, abandoned Farm, separated by large wood fences. Generations ago, cows chewed their cud in the fields, but now the land was overgrown with weeds and bramble. Even still, the old place was beautiful in the warm day's light. There was a medium-sized homestead, distant, whose roof had collapsed in on itself. Carl had biked this trail for years now and noted the collapse happened after hurricane Nester that night. The home was backed up against a line of trees. A small green barn, to the right of the destroyed home, sat humbly discarded.

The trail began to veer to the left, away from the overgrown fields. Carl peddled through a patch of dirt spattered with tall bushes and thin trees. The path was its most ambiguous in this part of the trail, as the land transitioned from open spaces to wooded terrain. The sun's presence lessened under a ceiling of leaves. Carl loved biking under the canopy, in its shade, and through its sloped mounds.

Two boys, brothers perhaps, were walking their dog on the trail. It was a little white yappy thing, a poodle, it seemed. They stepped to the side of the path, courteously allowing Carl to pass, as one of the boys meekly waved hello. The fluffy ferocious beast, nicely groomed, its eyes beady, barked insistently, tugging against its collar towards the bike as Carl rode by.

Several minutes into the wooded trail was where the path darkened most. Though not nearly thick enough to block out the sun, it did leave blotches of shade, allowing only small beams of sunlight through. The breeze picked up, rustling all the leaves in the woods and shaking several branches. When the sun did briefly touch Carl's skin, it was a marvelous warm contrast to the cover.

Further into the woods was a small creek, whose waters were calm and lazy. A small wooden bridge crossed the gap. On it read a sign: No Vehicles. Carl was sure bicycles were an exception. Even if they were not, there was no troll to enforce regulations, nor an officer on duty.

The bike's thick rubber tires pattered rhythmically against the wooden bridge. The gentle babble of the stream was lovely, though its sounds hastily vanished behind Carl, who continued to pedal forward faster. It felt like he could break the sound barrier. The swooshing air rustled what few strands of hair poked out of his helmet.

Emerging from the woods, Carl, with great headway, reached the end of the trail in no time. Looping back to the start of the fork, Parson peddled past the parking lot to make his way home. He was exhausted, sweaty, and ready for a tall glass of water after an exercise well enjoyed.

Then Carl saw it.

He was so distracted by its presence that he nearly ran into a stationary car, one of the few in the parking lot. Slamming the brakes, Carl's bike jutted forward to an abrupt halt, shaking the frame as he stabilized. Carl, feet freshly planted, turned to face what he glimpsed. He glared at it with anger, that familiar menacing glow. A powerful panic prodded at Carl. He tried to swallow it the best he could, to push down that sinking dizzying feeling.

It rested on the ground, as casual as a pebble among rocks. The blue light. That window, that thing. Carl gazed at it. He could almost see movement, see beyond the frame, but it was opaque. It was a surreal sight, like a handyperson had installed a window into the parking lot asphalt to help let in some light to the underground.

It'd been several months since Carl last encountered the anomaly. Though not surprised that it once again appeared, he wished it hadn't. It was like an ethereal stalker, ever present and able to show up at any time. Music churned, from the depths of the glow, tantalizing. Carl could hear it in his head.

Carl fought against a great overwhelming urge to ride his bike straight into the glowing hole. He was uncertain if he'd phase through it, enter it, or smack his bike against it. He wanted to see Bethany tonight and had to pick up Leon from camp. There were bills to be paid, a life to be lived. Tempting fates was not on his agenda. Carl shook his head, coming to his senses, ignoring the blue with great effort.

Carl peddled his way home at a slow pace. He had no energy to ride fast, both from the intense ride and the horrible presence of the anomaly. His stomach felt sick. As he peddled home, Carl kept looking behind him. Though nothing was there, it felt as if he was being stalked. Carl made it home, opening the garage. Peddling inside, he let his bicycle slam to the floor as he tore his helmet off, rushing towards the first-floor bathroom.

Leaning over the toilet, grasping the porcelain with his hands, Carl let loose a waterfall of vomit. Chunks of today's lunch, stomach acid, and bile poured from his throat in waves of hurls. He struggled to regain his breath between great heaves, gasping and panting; he was *chunderstruck.* A great sense of awe overtook him, like he was witnessing something profound in the toilet bowl. When his stomach finally settled, Carl had painted the toilet with a variety of unpleasant splatters. He sat there for a long time, uncertain what to do, thinking nothing.

Standing up, Carl wiped his mouth with the back of his hand. Chunks of vomit were stuck in clumps of his well-trimmed beard. Cleaning up the mess in the downstairs bathroom, Carl walked upstairs. His bedroom, shared with his wife, connected to a personal bathroom. Stripping off his clothes and setting his phone on the sink, Carl climbed in the shower.

Carl was shaking, even as the hot water coursed over him, his hands tremoring from an intense apprehension. He felt like a coward, a pitiless fool. He wanted to traverse whatever realms lingered beyond that blue window light, but feared what could lie inside, and what it would do to his family. Such a thought was maddening. He felt crazy.

It was foggy in the bathroom by the time Carl stepped out of the shower. The mirror was clouded, the walls moist with condensation. He had forgotten to turn on the ceiling fan and did so on emergence. Getting dressed, Carl felt incredibly unmotivated to do much of anything. It was almost two in the afternoon. Carl had spent more time in the shower than he realized.

Carl headed downstairs, toweling off his hair as he went. He poured himself a glass of wine before walking to the living room and plopping down on the couch.

"Five o'clock somewhere," Carl sighed, taking a sip. The acidity was a bit rough on his sore throat, but the buzz was appreciated. There wasn't much to watch on television. Carl scrolled through show after show for some time, eventually just settling on some action movie that was halfway over, one he'd heard of but never seen. Taking a sip of wine, Carl leaned back on the couch. Carl was exhausted, and the midday drink amplified it. His eyelids were heavy, and soon, he drifted into a dream.

In his dream, Carl found himself, naked, standing in a dark pool of warm, shallow waters. A blue light, far in the distance, suddenly became visible to him. An overwhelming need to get close to its glow compelled him, the sensation growing stronger with each step. Soon, Carl was jogging, then running.

Carl sprinted feverously towards the blue light, huffing with each stride. His breath echoed amongst a vast chamber. Water splashed under his feet. The droplets suspended themselves midair, eventually motionless and glimmering. As Carl grew closer, it grew brighter and more striking, reflecting marvelously in the ripples which cascaded beneath each stomp of Carl's feet. Music, muddled and barely audible, echoed on the horizon. It was some old-timey song. A melancholy trumpet wailed, accompanied by an orchestra. A beautiful woman's voice was singing some woeful tale. She sung about sitting in her lonely room, filled with gloom.

Carl recognized the song, though he did not know the name. It was the same song he'd heard from the garage during that night. That night was like an apogee in which Carl's mind constantly circled. That music, lyrics distinct, only made his memories much more visceral. On the singer sang, woeful and wailing, claiming she didn't want to walk without her baby.

Once a blue speck in the distance, it now grew into a giant bloom. It looked like a blue sun rising over black mesas, coating the flatlands in malicious vibrancy. Now, the void took on a deep haunting hue, ever burgeoning as Carl bound closer to the source of the music. She sang about being left behind, her love abandoning her, and going for a walk to get them off her mind.

The music grew louder; it began to shake Carl's insides, his heart beating in tune with the macabre. As he continued to sprint across the abyssal dark, his pants ever louder, his skin began to peel off like a potato being prepared for a boiling pot. Then, his muscles unraveled into strands of red ribbons, leaping from Carl's bones. He was stripped down to nothing but a skeleton. Still, the music grew in volume, and still Carl sprinted onward in disregard of everything else. Carl's bones turned to dust, flowing like dandelion seeds on a spring breeze. Yet he was still running, just a glowing outline of his former physical self.

Growing in size, tall and imposing, the blue took the form of a window. It was massive, of such incomprehensible size that it consumed all spaces. Carl leaped into the glow, diving into its surface like it was a body of water. It gave way, but its consistency was like slightly soupy gelatin. The music grew muffled in the blue but could still be understood. The music turned to something else, slow, incomprehensible, warbling and wavering, the lyrics no longer recognizable, the instruments like hot screeching metal in boiling soup.

Carl swam through the depths. As he submerged further, Carl could see Bethany, distant in the murky blue. She was veiled in shadow but looked battered, injured. Carl swam frantically until he was upon her. She was standing over an unknown corpse. Bethany turned to Carl, her face whiter than snow and her eyes devoid of color. She smiled, baring monstrous rows of teeth like a shark with walrus fangs.

"Maybe it's genetic?" Bethany asked, as she ran her fingers down Carl's chest, moaning. Her toothy mouth split open like a lotus pod. Within her jaw was Leon, wrapped in a blue light. "Maybe... you're infectious..."

Carl awoke violently, panting. He stood from the couch, frantically looking around, awakening in a state between the dreamworld and consciousness. Carl realized where he was after a few moments and took a steadying breath. Grabbing his half-empty glass of wine, he took a substantial chug. It was bitter, and only dried out his mouth more, but it was relieving, nonetheless. Carl looked at his phone. It was three thirty, on the dot. Panic shot through Carl as he suddenly remembered an important obligation. He had to pick up Leon from camp at four.

Brushing his teeth and chugging a glass of water, Carl hopped into his car. He felt a little buzzed but knew he could drive. Salt Fork was about forty minutes away, but the ride was easy enough. Carl tried to distract himself by listening to the news and public radio, but if quizzed, he wouldn't be able to recall a single word spoken.

Pulling into the parking lot, much later than he should be, Carl turned off the car and headed inside the main entrance. The facility was an impressive place: a series of well-kept buildings and lodges wrapped around a central hub, creating a U shape.

Carl checked in at reception and was let into the campgrounds. Bright Futures accommodations were on the east side of the main building. There were nineteen rooms in total, divided into two wings. Most of the rooms had two beds, two desks, and two dressers. There were four communal restrooms in total, each on a separate side of the wings. There was a single window in the middle of each room opposite the door. Counselors got their own private quarters, which were similar to the kids' dorms, except they had their own personal restrooms. Carl looked around, reminiscent of a foggy halcyon childhood as he headed towards his son, who was waiting with some other kids in the rec room, which sat in the center of the two wings. It seemed most of the kids had already been picked up. The remaining children were huddled around a TV, watching some fighting game unfold in dramatic fashion.

"Hey, buddy." Carl placed his right hand on Leon's shoulder, who was just as enthralled as the other kids.

"Can we go after this game?" Leon was in the middle of playing, didn't turn from the spectacle, his voice sounding desperate. His fingers hit the buttons on the controller with the accuracy of a surgeon.

"Sure." Carl smiled, watching the game unfold. It was flashy.

The drive home was silent at first. Leon seemed reserved. Not necessarily hesitant to speak, but rather lost in thought. Carl wasn't in much of a talking mood either. Then he had an idea:

"How about pizza tonight?" Carl asked. It would pair well with the rest of the wine anyway.

"YES!" Leon fist-pumped excitedly.

"Any toppings you want?" Carl merged onto the highway. There was a pizza place in Newtext he'd been wanting to try.

"Pepperoni." Leon smiled widely. "And cheese!"

"You're really pushing the envelope..." Carl grinned. Being around his son seemed to melt a lot of his anxieties away. As chaotic and loud as Leon could be, he'd missed him this week. "So... tell me about camp."

"It was pretty cool sometimes... They had a rock wall!" Leon smiled, eyes wide. "Can we get a rock wall?"

"If the pizza place sells them... sure." Carl chuckled.

NECTARS

From living rocks did rivers flow, and so did sweet nectars grow.

Dripping down lost cavern halls, honey-coated sugary walls.

In this den, the first spiders dwelled, living under the flavor's spell.

So gave form a great arachnid queen, whose citizens lived in syrup dreams.

All was peace and prosperity, all feasted quite charitably.

Then the rocks of Earth did die, and so to their gifts all said goodbye.

Since no more nourishment came, a cannibal feast instead did reign.

All but one remained alive; it was the queen who did survive.

A message sent to generations did pass, that no such reliance shall ever last.

In honor of that sticky place, great webs were weaved and interlaced.

No longer sugar-deranged, the meals of spiders slowly changed.

It is forbidden among eight-legged lore to seek sweet nectars anymore.

AWAKENINGS

It was another evening of drinking just like any other, then Edda told Fran a troubling story.

"You... just left them there!?" Francesca's voice was unsure, a blend of doubt and fear.

Edda wasn't even sure why she mentioned it. She'd never told anyone about the cage. Now she was telling her best friend. It was a relief to talk about at first, but upon seeing the look of shock on Fran's face, regret jolted up Edda's frame like electricity through a live wire. *Why tonight?* Edda wondered. Of all the moments previously available to her, why now? Was she that drunk? That high? It was nothing but a memory until now. Edda trusted Francesca a lot, but up until this night, the magnitude of that trust was not comprehended.

"I was a kid... I didn't know what to do." Edda felt like she had to defend herself, her future, present, and past.

"Why didn't you tell someone?!" Francesa asked.

"Well... I thought I would get in trouble," Edda sighed, topping off her beverage. They were almost through the whole box of wine. "It was a really long time ago. I'm not sure what I was thinking."

"Jesus Mac... Fuck."

"Yeah," Edda agreed.

The two sat on Edda's porch, listening to the waves. It was almost two in the morning. After such a conversational bomb, any following words seemed weightless now. A familiar light, flashing from the flamingo pink house window, popped back into Edda's peripheral vision.

"I'm guna' use the bathroom," Edda said, breaking the silence.

After scooting past Fran on the couch, Edda headed inside. Walking made Edda realize just how inebriated she'd become. It didn't feel as if she was moving but rather gliding over the ground as her surroundings stumbled by.

Edda could still see that mysterious person, shriveled and dying in the cage. She could still hear its screams as it pressed its face through the bars, commanding her to flee. Edda remembered sprinting away in fear, through the woods, through an unpatched hole in the neighbor's fence. She was weeping the entire way home. On the toilet, in Purple Beach, drunk on a weekend night, Edda began to cry that exact way. She felt as vulnerable right now as she had that night.

Leaving the restroom, reluctantly sliding open the porch screen door, Edda tried to hide her tears from Fran as she shimmied back onto the porch. It wasn't the first time Edda had cried around Fran, but she still felt greatly embarrassed about it. Francesca was many things, but she was not a fool and noticed Edda hiding her face instantly.

"Hey, hey, it's okay," Fran said gently. Francesca transitioned from fun mode to emotional support mode naturally. She seemed to always know what to say. Her words were enunciated perfectly and spoken with great intent and emotional precision, even though she was very drunk. Standing up from her seat, Fran wrapped her arms around Edda, who at first recoiled but eventually allowed herself to be hugged.

Edda cried for a short time, her head resting on Fran's shoulder. They were painful tears, the kind where a person chokes between each heave. Francesca hugged Edda, her arms around her head. Slowly, a shudder turned to a chuckle as Edda regained herself. Edda hugged back, as tightly as she could, and Francesca squeezed back harder.

Pulling back from her friend's embrace, Edda looked Fran in the eyes. They were beautiful. Leaning in slowly, Edda spontaneously kissed Fran. Their two crimson lips collided. Fran's lips were sweet, like raspberries. Francesca was shocked at first, but then leaned forward, kissing her back. It was comforting.

"I..." Edda laughed, "I don't even like girls..." Francesca snorted loudly, caught off guard just as much by Edda's comment as her kiss.

"Sometimes a kiss is just a kiss." Fran smiled, leaning against her friend. They both sat down, and eventually, the two fell asleep lying next to each other, embraced by the sounds of the ocean and each other's warmth. Hours later, the two made their way inside. Neither had any weekend obligations, so they could sleep in. Edda made her way to bed. Fran decided to crash on the indoor couch.

. . .

Edda awoke the next day, a little past noon, the smell of coffee filling her nostrils. She was hungover, and her head especially stung. Francesca seemed to have some drinking-related superpower. It wasn't that she was incapable of having hangovers, but rather her hangovers seemed to only last for a few minutes. Usually, a cup of coffee was all it took to reset feeling like her normal self.

Edda shuffled out of her bedroom and toward the kitchen. Fran reclined on the couch, sipping at a freshly brewed cup. Like Edda, she was still in her previous day's clothes.

"Morning." Fran waved.

"I feel like shit," Edda complained, nodding towards Fran as she grabbed herself a mug from the cupboard.

"You always do after drinking," Fran replied, sipping at her mug. "Crêpes? Been craving them lately..."

There was a great reactionary growl in Edda's stomach. It was a perfect proposal, the best way to start her Saturday, and a great way to fight her hangover.

"Yes." Edda needed some food. "As long as you drive." Edda poured herself a cup, adding some cream.

"Deal, little Mac."

"Awesome." Edda smiled, ignoring the spike of pain in her head. "Just let me finish this."

Edda changed clothes (Fran borrowed some of Edda's), then the two departed with messy hair and shared hunger. It was a gorgeous day. Edda's neighbor, Carter, happened to be out. He noticed the two step outside. He power-walked across the street directly towards them, nearly dragging his cane behind him like an escaped dog would drag their leash. His sun hat and tan shirt made him look like he was on safari.

"Oh shit," Edda mumbled as Fran patted her on the back, while simultaneously stepping behind her slightly, desperate to avoid any interaction.

"Morning!" Carter enthusiastically waved at the two as he crossed the road. "Amazing weather today!"

"Sure is." Edda smiled, her eyes straining against the sun's glare. Carter and a hangover were definitely not a preferred cocktail. Carter had now fully stopped on the sidewalk, looking up towards the two friends past the bushes and the porch railing. He stood directly in front of the stairs leading to Edda's apartment, like a barricade.

"You hear? Bout over at 133rd?" Carter asked, ready to tell them all about it.

"No..." All Edda wanted was food.

"They caged 'em!" Carter's words stunned Edda. Coincidence and bad timing are often close associates.

"What..." Edda stuttered, nearly falling backwards. Fran clasped at Edda's shoulders, practically holding her upwards. Edda felt especially sick and dizzy, and with all her might, restrained herself from puking.

"They got a mama fox! I saw them cage it and haul the thing back to their truck," Carter explained.

"Oh..." Edda sighed, praying for an end to this conversation.

"Tax dollars at work." Carter rubbed his chin as he was struck by a wandering thought. "I wonder if they'll relocate it. I should've asked one of them animal control boys."

"Possibly." Francesca stepped in front of Edda, a tone of annoyance in her voice. "We're running late. Got to get going."

"Oh." Carter's voice rose in pitch, just slightly indignant. "Well, don't let me stop you. Have a nice day, ladies." He fluttered his hands as if he was some showman, then waved goodbye. Turning away, Carter's cane tapped against the sidewalk as he waddled down the avenue.

Climbing into Fran's messy car, Edda took a deep breath, letting residual panic drain away.

"You... okay?" Fran asked as she turned the ignition, and the car hummed to life.

"Yeah." Edda bit her lip. "Just hungry."

"Well, let's go eat then bitch!" Fran shouted, which caused Edda to wince. "Sorry, volume..." Fran laughed.

Crêpe King was on the boardwalk, about a twenty-five-minute drive from Edda's normally. The coastal highway was surprisingly empty for a Saturday morning, regardless of the season. Every light was green and seemed to synchronize with their passing perfectly. The only time Fran had to brake was at a few stop signs, which even then she mostly rolled through. Parking in a small lot, the two slammed their doors shut and walked onto the boardwalk. The wood planks beneath their feet creaked with each step. The smell of the sea and high cholesterol foods filled the air.

Francesca ordered herself the Crepey Rachel. It had roast turkey, Swiss cheese, thousand island dressing, and of course, sauerkraut. Edda ordered a Banana Pudding Crêpe, which was drizzled in a delicious caramel syrup. The meals were sticky, honest, and delicious. With a full stomach, even though she nursed a small headache, the day started to seem much more manageable to Edda. Francesca paid for the entire meal, insisting on it. Edda didn't know what she did to deserve such a fantastic friend, but was grateful for her. After breakfast, the two headed back to Edda's place. Traffic had picked up slightly, but it was still an easy drive.

"I'll text you later," Francesca smiled, pulling in front of Edda's place.

"Get home safe," Edda said, climbing out of Fran's sedan.

The condo was quiet without Fran, so Edda turned the radio on in the kitchen to help combat the blaring silence. Some chefs, a man and a woman, were talking about pasta and wine pairings. Edda had heard their segments on public radio before. Edda decided to take a shower, and the hosts' voices followed her down the hallway.

"Pinks often get bottlenecked into this negative perception," one of the radio hosts said. "People often think about Rosés simply as cheap boxed wines. But there are actually quite a few high-quality pinks in a wide variety of price ranges and containers."

The male host interjected with a soft laugh. "I'd be lying if I said I disliked a cheap boxed wine, however." For a moment, there was some brief static interrupting the radio, distorting the speaker's voice.

After her shower, Edda stepped out onto the porch. Her day held no obligations. Sitting in her favorite spot on the outdoor couch, Edda watched the waves. The distant radio could still be heard, the program shifting from the culinary arts to sports news. It didn't matter to Edda particularly much what the topics discussed were about. It was the noise the radio provided that was most welcome. Hell, she didn't even particularly mind pledge drive season.

Momentarily, Edda peeked toward the flamingo pink house, curious to see if any lights were flickering. All was still and dark within. Feeling some strange assurance from this, Edda closed her eyes. She was more tired than she realized and fell asleep relatively quickly; the sounds of the radio and ocean ambience made for terrific white noise.

The ocean breeze picked up for a moment, followed by the screeches of a seagull's repeated call, a high-pitched laughing sound. Awakening to the sounds of sea birds, Edda was feeling quite pleasant. It was a much-needed rest, and her post-drinking sickness was reduced to a minor discomfort in the back of her neck.

Edda checked her phone. She'd slept for about an hour; it was a little after one in the afternoon. Stretching her arms and legs outward like a starfish, Edda felt tension dissipate throughout her muscles. In her post-sleep haziness, Edda was tempted to drift back to sleep, but her grumbling stomach forced her awake.

A small blue car drove passed Edda's place. It rolled through the corner stop sign and turned left onto Wight Street. The car backed into the flamingo pink home's parking space, pulling in underneath the concrete supports that formed its pseudo-outdoor garage. Edda hadn't noticed at all until the sound of a car door slamming shut caused her to look up briefly. She nearly looked back down at her phone until she realized someone was arriving at the flamingo pink house. This excited Edda more than it reasonably should have. She watched with intent, feeling like an old gossip-prone retiree. A small, thin man, somewhere in his early thirties, stepped out of the car. The man approached the front door and pulled a set of keys out, opening it slowly. Heading back to the car, he raised his trunk open, pulling out several bags and some tools. They were cleaning supplies. After locking his car, the presumed cleaner headed inside, closing the door behind him. All these years living on the corner of Wight and 144th, Edda could not recall seeing a single person enter that home. Edda had little faith in her perception, however, and came to the conclusion she'd never paid attention until recently.

Pulling back the screen door, Edda stepped inside. It was lunch time, and though she knew she could not produce a meal nearly as satisfying as this morning's breakfast, she still wanted to concoct something delicious to the best of her capabilities. Thankfully, delicious is often easy, and she made herself a PB&J with some chips. Simple and invigorating.

Edda was still a little hungover but figured a walk might clear her head a little bit. She had no intentions of breaking her walking record today, but it could still be pleasant. Grabbing her keys, Edda locked the porch door and trotted down her patio steps. Just as she was about to cross the street to the beach, Edda found herself motionless on the corner of the sidewalk, staring at a sudden spectacle.

The man who parked at the flamingo pink house, the presumed cleaner, suddenly burst from the front door, frantic and driven by something primal. The door slammed shut behind him, which echoed a bit through the quiet streets. The man's movements were erratic, and his disposition panicked. Leaping into his car, the vehicle practically launched out into the streets, swerving past Edda's apartment onto the coastal highway as rubber burned. Smoke kicked up into Edda's stunned face. The entire sequence happened all within a couple seconds, and Edda hardly had time to process what she was seeing. It didn't appear as if the man had locked the door, nor did he have his supplies on him as he left. If he was a cleaner, he sure didn't spend any time on the job. Startled, unsure what to do, Edda stood flabbergasted and amused.

Hesitantly, Edda walked to the Flamingo pink home to check things out. The door was closed shut. Momentarily, Edda reached out to try the doorknob, but something in her gut restrained her curiosity. She considered knocking, but also could not muster the gumption. Edda looked around the front property. Everything looked normal enough. One thing Edda noted was a lack of props. No outdoor wall sheds, stools, hoses, beach chairs, umbrellas, boogie boards, no evidence anyone had ever been there at all. Nothing. Just concrete and weeds. No sound was coming from inside, but Edda dared not put her ear against the door. Eventually, Edda turned away, returning to her walk, uncertain.

The beach was not as comforting as usual. It was still a pleasant experience, and the exercise quite invigorating. The entire journey, however, was tainted with intrigue. What did Edda witness? She invented a myriad of possibilities and scenarios in her head. A murder? A robbery? Maybe the man owned the place and was getting it clean for the season when he received bad news? Perhaps he was rushing to the hospital to see a loved one? Maybe his wife went into labor? Maybe he had an existential crisis? Maybe the cleaner saw a ghost? Maybe it had to do with that flickering light? Edda continued to explore all possibilities in her head. In thought, she had wandered out onto the beach farther than her legs could take her.

Edda returned home early, the walk feeling like more of a chore than meditation. She knew she had witnessed something wrong. It was the same feeling Edda had felt all those years ago as a child, as she fled from the screaming person in a cage.

An intrusive thought lurched to the forefront of Edda's stream of thought. She should go back to the Flamingo pink house and try the doorknob this time. The man must have left it unlocked, she thought. Just go peek inside. No. Edda told herself. She wasn't about to commit home invasion to indulge a curiosity. Still, the urge to try and open the door continually itched at her brain.

Sitting in her living room with the screen door open, Edda fell into a nice book she'd been reading: *Power, Wealth, and Social Status.* It was smut disguised as a raunchy romance novel that took place during the Elizabethan era. It had a murder mystery plot and some political intrigue, but the author knew their audience and exactly why they were reading it. It was an easy read, but compelling. Simple to pick up but hard to put down.

Time sunk into the words on the pages. A growl, like a starving beast, roared from Edda's belly. Looking up from her book and at her phone, it was twenty minutes past five. She'd been reading for much longer than she realized. Edda had missed a call from her good friend potential spam. Francesca had also sent a text. Edda opened it. It was a picture of Francesca's fluffy black cat, Yang, lying in Fran's belly. The cat looked disdainfully into the camera, but that's just how Yang looked. *CUTE!* Edda texted back.

Edda contemplated dinner. She had some Alfredo sauce and ravioli she'd been meaning to make for some time. Her stomach growled approvingly in response to the idea. As she pulled the Alfredo from her pantry, Edda realized something. She'd finished off the wine last night with Fran. A nice pasta dish was, of course, incomplete without wine, Edda justified to herself. She grabbed her wallet, keys, and phone before heading outside. There was a liquor store two streets up from her house on 146th. It had decent prices and a neon sign with dancing cans of beer.

Compelled by curiosity, Edda walked down Wight Street, past the flamingo pink home. As she strode by, she looked the house up and down as if she were examining a crime scene for clues. Everything seemed normal. The door was closed, though there was no way of telling if it was locked with just the naked eye. There were no lights on inside, and all the curtains were drawn. All was still. The house made Edda feel lonely, isolated. It made her miss something she'd never had. The home looked like every other house on the street, but still, it didn't seem to belong. Though it was a narrow home, it seemed impossibly wide. Though it was a tall home, it seemed rather compact. The house itself looked as if it was staring back at Edda, examining her, its brow furled with intrigue, contempt, hunger, and scorn. It frightened her.

Edda resumed walking, taking a fast pace until she reached the liquor store. It was rather empty, business slow, more so than one would expect a liquor store to be on a Saturday evening. The lady working the register looked checked out. A few customers shuffled down the aisles. Overhead from the store speakers, a generic Top 100 radio station belted out unremarkable overplayed pop hits.

From the discount section, Edda found a cheap red *Coriander.* She bought it and, on her way back home, began to savor the notion of a nice meal alone and a quiet night. As Edda approached 144th, she considered avoiding Wight Street and heading home via the coastal highway roadside. Yet that compulsion, that curiosity, lingered relentlessly in her. *There was no reason to be apprehensive of a house,* Edda told herself.

A breeze bellowed down the back road. It was wrong. To Edda, it was the strangest sensation. She'd lived in Purple Beach for years now. She knew the breeze, the wind in all its forms, be it an inland gust or gale straight off the ocean. This was not that. This was stagnant air. The kind of air you'd find in a dusty, untouched basement. It smelled as if toxic chemicals lingered in the atmosphere.

Edda was nearly home. Ignoring the strange taste in the air, Edda passed the flamingo pink house. As if trying to avoid eye contact with a stranger, Edda leaned her head downwards slightly. As she drew parallel with the pink home's front door, Edda halted, noticing something strange in the side of her vision.

The front door (a white wooden door with peeling paint) was open, just a crack. From that gap in the doorway shone a haunting blue light, so fierce it seemed to distort and warble the edges of the passageway. It was of such intense brightness that underneath the concrete canopy, much of the area was bathed in a wicked hue.

Even the light seemed to creep across Edda's skin like a swarm of flies.

Edda Macsen's hands were shaking, violently so. The bag of wine she cradled rocked in her tenuous grip. A great, overwhelming series of emotions overtook her. Joy, relief, power... All things Edda rarely felt. She began to walk towards the door, compelled to see the inside. For but a moment, it felt as if she was lingering in a living dream.

Edda's grasp on the wine loosened, the bag slipping from her fingers and the bottle plummeting. Shattering on impact, the bottle sent shards of glass and splashes of wine all along the road. The breaking bottle, abrupt and loud, snapped Edda to attention, pulling her from a daze.

"Ahhh!" Edda yelped in reflex. The blue light, without notice, faded. It took a moment for Edda to realize her purchase was ruined, and when she did, she berated herself.

"Idiot!" Edda scolded herself as she stomped her foot in frustration. Picking up as much glass as she was able, Edda walked the refuse over to a trash can, leaving a dripping trail of wasted wine in her wake. The air smelled natural again.

HOMES BY THE SEA

In the past, Purple Beach was considered dead real estate. The area around the boardwalk, just about the only place to visit, was a bundle of hotels and bars. There were a few locals, mostly the kind of people who wanted to be alone. Nothing but sand and salt water, people would claim, not understanding the value of the sea. Over time, the general attitude shifted. People sought out the ocean. They wanted to visit it, to live near it. Over time, it would become a prime vacation location.

September 12, 1969, Purple Beach—Wight Street. Inside a small portable trailer gathered three men. There was no air conditioning in the trailer, so a few fans were set up and the windows were left open to help circulate air. Each of these men worked for Larry Masons, a home development firm.

The first gentleman, sitting in the corner of the trailer on a metal chair, was Williard Chapmen. He was the foreman who oversaw the construction on Wight. The trailer was, in fact, his primary office over the last half of the year. Will was a bit of a hard ass. He had no sense of humor and had no patience for small talk. He was a stocky gentleman, strong and short. He was nearly bald and had a short-trimmed beard.

The second gentleman, across from Will's desk, sat upon a wooden stool, was Barney Kellson. He was the head accountant for LM. He was a tall man, skinny, with short-cut hair and a clean-shaven jaw. Barney was especially drenched in sweat (hereditary thyroid issues amplified this), his white shirt and black tie drenched in human bog water.

The third gentleman in the room was Dean Cecil. He stood in the corner, smoking a cigarette. Dean was one of the company's in-house lawyers. He worked around zoning law compliance and cleared any legal minefields that needed to be crossed when working within the city limits. Dean was average height. Like Barney, he was also clean-shaven. Dean's hair was slicked back, stylized to impress. He wore a nice suit and a fancy watch and was a bit of a braggart when given the opportunity.

The three middle-aged men were waiting for a fourth person, Michael Richardson. The meeting was supposed to begin at one o'clock, and now it was more than ten minutes past. Michael was the regional director of Larry Masons. A head honcho.

"Can we begin?" Dean broke the silence. He inhaled another puff from his cigarette. The smoke and some ashes were whisked away by an oscillating fan and out through the ajar door.

"Yeah, Will," Barney chimed in, tugging at his collar. "It's a damned sweat box in here."

"We wait," Will groaned in annoyance. "Meetings between the four of us." Will picked up his mug of piping hot coffee, gulping it like it was ice water.

"How can you drink that in this heat?" Barney shuddered at the idea, continuing to drip.

"Keeps me awake." Will rolled his eyes.

"Quit your groaning, Barney." Dean hadn't seemed to even break a sweat.

"And don't get me started on you." Barney pointed at Dean like a stern teacher. "No idea how you're staying so dry in that suit." Barney wiped his brow with his hands.

"Louisiana born. This is nothing." Some ash fell from Dean's cigarette.

"Well, this is a waste of time, clearly," Barney whined, kicking his feet and tugging at his shirt with discomfort.

"I assure you. THIS!" Will emphasized his words, the impatience in his voice now turning into anger, "IS important!"

"Clearly it is if you'd have me drive three hours out to this damned glorified desert," Dean snarked. "Frankly, I'm still amazed people want to live out in these boonies."

"More of a swamp kind of person ay' Dean?" Barney quipped.

"Jesus, can you two just shut the hell up!?" Will slammed his fist on his desk. "Y'all giving me a damned headache! I got enough bitching between them *Cholos* and *union boys.* I don't need you adding on it."

Dean laughed at the whole situation, continuing to smoke. Barney melted into his chair at first, following the slow-moving fan with his face the best he could. Eventually, he waited outside the trailer to cool off. Dean had finished two cigarettes as they waited and was soon on to his third. The wall clock ticked on and on until finally, even Williard's patience broke. Will called Barney back inside.

"Fine," Will sighed. "Clearly, boss ain't coming. Guess we got to start someday." Will stood up. Next to his desk, from a filing cabinet, he pulled out a yellow envelope. From it, he slid out a thick stack of papers, all neatly stapled together. "Let me ask you two a simple question." Will stared at his two colleagues without blinking for a few seconds.

"Okay..." Barney spoke uneasily, breaking eye contact with Will.

Will looked away. He turned through the papers to a specific page, setting it down in front of Barney. It was an old, wrinkled page, part of the original project proposal document. On it, a number was highlighted in bright yellow, the number twenty-two.

"Tell me, gentlemen. What does that number say?" Will slammed his pointer finger down on the page like it was a finger from God smiting a wicked demon. Barney leaned in, and Dean walked behind him, peering over his shoulder.

"Twenty... twenty-two," Barney stuttered.

"That's the number of homes we built." Dean wore a look of confusion on his face. "What the hell are you getting on about?"

"So, I can fucking count," Will laughed, pacing. "Good to know I'm not insane."

"You called us here for math lessons?" Dean's expression grew more quizzical.

"No dammit!" Now Will was sweating. "There aren't twenty-two homes." He felt insane even saying this. "There are twenty-three."

"What?" Barney laughed. "No, that's not possible. We were already over budget, that woulda' put us way over the line on materials alone."

"Go count then." Will loomed over the desk despite his size. "I'm telling you, there's twenty-three."

"Okay, slow your horses." Dean flicked his cigarette out of the trailer. "I know for a fact the city registered exactly twenty-two new residences, addresses, and all. They've all passed inspection even."

"You're correct." Will nodded.

"Yet you're telling me we have..."

"Twenty-three houses, yes," Will cut in. "Listen, gentlemen, I know how this sounds. I wouldn't be calling this meeting in if I wasn't certain." Will looked visibly shaken, like everything that mattered was on the line.

"I can't believe it," Barney mocked, "They hired a foreman who can't even count."

"You want to count!?" Will shouted, lunging forward like a maniac, wielding a knife. Will slammed his palms on his desk. A pencil rolled off, plopping onto the floor. "Go count, asshole!"

"Jesus, Will, calm down," Dean said. "I'm sure there's an explanation for this."

"Oh really!?" Will lifted himself from the desk, huffing. "Well, if there is, I'd like one."

Barney stood, indignant, drenched, exhausted with the absurdity of the conversation. He headed for the door, walking out of the trailer as if nothing had happened.

"Where the hell you going?" Dean asked. Barney turned around in the middle of the trailer doorframe. The sun beat down on his back, forming what looked like an aura around his person for a brief time.

"I'm not spending another minute sweating my ass off in a metal box listening to that nonsense. I need a drink." Barney stepped down outside.

"Hey, wait a minute!" Dean stepped through the doorway, grabbing Barney by the shoulder.

"What now!?" Barney shook his head.

Releasing his hand from Barney's shoulder, Dean pinched the top ridge of his nose in frustration:

"Least we can do is count."

"Fine," Barney hesitantly agreed.

The three grumpy middle-aged white men toured Wight Street. Williard counted out loud, pointing towards each home as he did so with the force of a maestro's swing.

"One..." Will began.

"Oh god," Barney frowned. "He's counting out loud."

"Two..." Will continued, ignoring the comment completely. And on he counted down the street as Barney and Dean followed along.

"Eighteen." Will was almost smiling. He did love proving a point. Even if it was a bad thing to prove. "Nineteen."

The three were reaching the end of the road.

"Twenty." The foreman's voice was authoritative and loud. On-site, it seemed to amplify his roar. "Twenty-one."

Any moment now. "Twenty-two."

Sure enough, as promised. "... and twenty-three."

Will bowed, reaching his arm outright like he was a speaker introducing royalty.

Barney's utterly baffled face was priceless. He'd quite literally oversaw the books. Dean was equally baffled. Clearly, something was amiss.

"Okay..." Barney didn't like admitting he was wrong, but would in the face of evidence. "You're right. Twenty-three..." Barney bit his lip. The trio stood in a circle in the middle of the road on Wight, silent for a few seconds. Only the waves and their thoughts filled the atmosphere. The sea breeze was pleasant and cooling.

"I think this is all clear now," Dean spoke up suddenly. The other two turned to look at him perplexedly.

"That so?" Williard scrunched his face. Barney stood gazing awkwardly.

"Obviously, there was a mix-up with proportions," Dean explained. "I once saw a house built to four times its original scale."

"How does that account for the extra house?" Barney asked.

"If someone's idiot enough to misread some blueprints, they're liable to make other mistakes." Dean lit himself up another cigarette as if rewarding himself for an argument well made.

"You calling me an idiot, friend? Will huffed, leaning in towards Dean. "I've been working this job for almost two years now. We did everything to the letter. We did not build a twenty-third house." Will held back a loogie, swallowing his spit.

"Well, clearly you did." Dean shook his head in disbelief. "Hell, you counted it yourself."

"Listen, listen." Will shook his head. "It gets stranger." Will walked under a cantilevered roof, one of the recently finished homes, standing in the shade. The others followed. "I did some math. Numbers aren't adding up."

"In what way? Budget?" Barney inquired while enjoying some relief from the sun.

"No, no, no." Will rubbed his temples. "Square feet." The foreman felt insane just thinking about it. He felt insane in general. Two days ago, when he came upon the realization of the twenty-third home's existence, he ignored it. He told himself he was miscounting, hallucinating. But one cannot avoid truth, only hide from it. "Let me show you," he said.

The three walked back down the road towards the trailer. The site was quiet. Construction was wrapping up as the end of the week approached. Most of the work to be done was clean up and some final touches, anyway. As Dean walked, he lit another cigarette. Will walked quickly ahead as if marching onward to war. As Barney walked, he observed each home. They seemed to repeat batches of colors in groups of three. Tan, Blue, Yellow, all soft beachy pastels. Tan, Blue, Yellow. The pattern repeated, over and over. Then, towards the intersection of 144th and Wight, one house stood out. It was pink, flamingo pink.

Barney gulped. The home, besides its different color, looked completely normal. Yet, he felt a great fear when looking upon it. Fear for himself, for his loved ones. Despite this, Will started to walk towards the home instinctively. He wanted to walk inside, to be inside it. Frightful, he turned his gaze away from the front door, staring down at his feet as he trailed behind Dean and Will, fighting his urge to leave the group.

Stepping back inside the trailer, Will pulled out schematics of the house design exteriors and interiors, spreading the blueprints out on his desk. He put a stapler on one end of the paper and an empty coffee mug on the parallel corner to keep it from folding closed. Barney and Dean stood around the desk, looking at the presented drawings.

"Look." Will pointed at the written dimensions. "Each home is one thousand, three hundred and twenty square feet." Will sighed nervously, hesitating to speak momentarily. "The total area of both combined lots comes out to a little over three thousand."

"And?" Dean waved his dominant hand in a spiral, inhaling more puffs of smoke from his cigarette as it hung from his skeptical lips.

"And!?" Will shouted. "That means the lot can only hold twenty-two houses!" Will breathed rapidly, frustrated and flustered.

"You're proving my point," Dean replied. "Clearly, the homes weren't built to size."

"NOOO!" Will shouted. Dean and Barney stepped backwards, startled by the outburst. It was louder than usual, and Will was a loud man.

"I measured each and every one of them homes! *TWICE!*" Will emphasized his words with a guttural groan. "Exterior and interior! Every last one of them is correct! Took all damned day." Will shook his head back and forth as if denying a crime. "I'm telling you! It don't make no sense."

There was silence in the trailer for a moment. A few cars could be heard passing down the highway. The waves in the distance crashed as usual, and seagulls laughed their obnoxious call.

"Well..." Dean spoke with a momentary crackle in his voice. "I just don't see any logic..."

"What about the pink house?" Barney loudly interrupted. A nervous twinge roared within him, causing his eyelids to stutter for a few blinks.

"What?" Will asked in a startled tone.

"There's... uh', well, a single pink one." Barney said.

Will felt a familiar fear in his gut. Panic overtook him. He ran past his desk and pushed Dean aside. Stumbling out onto Wight Street, he scanned each house rapidly. Dean, taken aback, collected himself and followed. Barney stood in the doorframe of the trailer, watching Will with interest.

Will spotted the home immediately; there in plain sight. It was pink like a flamingo, pastel like the other colors. It was so obvious now upon recognition, yet it had been subtle enough that it seemed to blend in with the other homes. Upon a glance, the building felt as if it belonged, but as Will stared at it, something about its proportions seemed wrong. He wasn't able to pinpoint why, but an instinctual feeling gained from years in the industry tugged at his senses.

"I... never noticed..." Will cradled his face in his right hand, desperate to understand. "We never had siding in that color..."

The three befuddled men stood in the street, looking at the home. Dean felt a long-forgotten nostalgia, a childhood feeling just now remembered. He remembered summer fields, carnival lights, and chain link fencing. Ward was driven to understand, to solve the mystery. Barney looked down at the ground, avoiding looking at the home. The house was staring at each of them, smiling.

From the trailer, a phone rang. Will headed back inside his office. Picking up the phone, he quietly listened to the voice on the other end, urgent and panicked. Barney, still drenched in sweat, hung his head in front of a fan, following its slow oscillating movements. Dean stepped inside, watching the two. Will listened to the caller on the phone. Dean could tell something was off immediately by the look on Will's face.

"Oh..." Will set the phone back on the receiver and fell back into his seat, shocked.

"Good news?" Barney asked while speaking into the fan, causing his voice to distort and warble. He sounded like how one would imagine a robot to speak.

"That was his secretary." Will took a long pause. "Michael's... dead."

Barney turned from the fan immediately, and Dean's expression shifted from curiosity to panic. Nobody knew what to say. Nobody knew what to do. They stood desperately awaiting something, anything.

"How'd he die?" Dean asked. He and Barney looked at Will with macabre eagerness.

"He was driving. Got hit." Will wasn't a very sentimental guy. He was the kind of man who thought crying was for sissies. The kind of person who would bottle his emotions until they exploded violently. He had been working with Michael for over a decade now. The news was heartbreaking, a profound reminder of mortality. Moreover, Michael was a friend. He'd watched Michael's newborn boy grow into a wonderful kid over the course of a decade, and now that boy was fatherless. He'd gone to parties and dinners with Michael and his wife. She was now a widow. Will held back all indications of his sadness he felt in the moment.

"What a disaster," Dean sighed. He was dreading the upcoming business repercussions in the days ahead. Death always left behind a lot of work for the living.

"Yeah," Barney agreed.

"Fuck," Will moaned. "Meetings canceled. We'll figure this out another day."

"Give my condolences to the family," Dean extended his hand, "I know you knew him well."

"Of course." Will shook Dean's hand. They both had firm handshakes, though the ritual held an inescapable, ensorcelled sadness.

Releasing each other's hands, Dean left the trailer. Barney followed, scuttling behind, desperate to escape the awkward tension.

"Goodbye," Barney said as he left the trailer. He practically sprinted to his car, moving surprisingly fast.

Will closed the trailer windows and locked the doors, unsure what to do. He listened to the muffled sound of crashing waves. He smelled the ocean air mixed with cigarette ashes. Turning to his left, through the trailer window, he looked at the home, the pink one, house twenty-three. As if an animal driven by instinct, Will left the trailer and started walking towards it. Within a minute, he was standing in front of the pink home's doorway.

Stepping inside, the home smelled of fresh-cut wood and paint.

The downstairs was slightly smaller than upstairs due to the stairway immediately to the front doors left. There was a hallway adjacent to the stairs that led to the first-floor den, which was connected to a tiny guest bedroom with a small bathroom that had a walk-in shower. It was all the same exact layout as every other model on this street. Nothing unusual. Heading upstairs, Will recalled the schematics in his mind. There are eleven steps on each set of stairs. Will counted as he climbed.

"One."

"Two." Two steps taken.

"Three. Four. Five." Will looked upwards. The path ahead seemed extraordinarily long.

"Nine. Ten. Eleven." When Will reached the eleventh step, he realized the stairs extended much further upwards. "Eleven." He counted out loud, taking another step. "Eleven." He said again, continuing to climb upwards. It all seemed correct somehow.

On the stair walls were photographs of mutilated people, bizarre and terrible imagery. A black and white Polaroid of a boy whose face seemed inside out. A digital print of a smiling family hugging each other on the beach. Their heads seemed to be filled with several tiny pulsating holes. There was a painting of a woman holding an egg, her face charred and burnt as if she survived a horrendous fire. The pictures were distressing, and yet, all seemed normal to Will. To him, it was as if these were simply stock photos used by some realty agency. It was decoration for prospective buyers touring the home, he perceived.

After minutes of walking, Will reached the second story. The stairs opened up to a large kitchen with a center island. It had a lovely white granite top. The kitchen was the heart of the home. It connected to the living room, another bathroom, and the outdoor balcony. The view outside seemed normal enough. It overlooked the ocean, past the dunes and the sand. The waves seemed to crash backwards into themselves, and the beach was longer than it should be. The living room was barren of furniture, just a stretch of shag carpet that connected to the final set of stairs. As Will walked across the carpet, his feet seemed to sink deep into them, like it was mud and clay.

Will approached the final set of stairs, drawn to it. They were going down, deep into some hole with which no light was found, only immeasurable depths. What he was seeing was impossible. The stairs should be colliding with the floor below, yet they seemed to descend unobstructed. Even with this knowledge, armed with all his logic, Will felt strangely soothed. A great relief hugged him like loving arms, and absorbed in a trance, Will dragged himself downward into the abyss. As he descended, Will did not bother counting. Yet on occasional steps taken, he would find himself muttering:

"Eleven."

Past a hundred or more steps, Will swore he could hear music coming from below. Slowly, it grew louder the deeper he went. He was swallowed in true darkness, with only melancholy music his company. Will allowed himself to cry for the first time in years. He smiled as he sobbed, his skin stretched over his face like plastic wrap, his eyes bulging and pink. Each step downwards seemed to contract his skin, and his body grew ever thinner, stretched across a spiraling staircase.

. . .

Two days later.

Barney sat in his office at his desk, reading *Life* magazine. His office wasn't small, but it wasn't large either. The walls were covered in decorative wallpaper, yellow with a floral pattern. It wouldn't have been his first or last choice in regard to decor, but he didn't have a say in the building's design. The ceiling was concrete. A ceiling fan and light dangled in the center, the fan lazily swirling round and round. The floor was a light pink carpet (again, not how

Barney would have designed it), and the carpet pile was fuzzy. In the middle of this small rectangular room was Barney's desk, and behind it his reclining seat. On his desk was a typewriter, stacks of paper, and a variety of literature, both professional and recreational. Across from his desk was his door, which was firmly shut. The door had green privacy glass. It allowed one to see if someone was approaching the door, but anyone who did had their form reduced to a hazy green shadow. The room was basically windowless, save for a small slit of glass which sat near the top of the roof, barely allowing for any natural light in at all.

It was a Thursday, currently around three. About an hour before noon, an office memorial was held in remembrance of Michael. A few coworkers gave some kind words, and drinks and food were served. Barney ate a few too many cookies and drank too much scotch. One man's death is another man's cookie (and scotch), apparently. Work had been reduced to a slow malaise these last two days. The death of Michael caused quite a panic among management, and roles had to be filled.

Barney knew he should be working, but after the party today, he didn't feel right. He had no motivation to proceed with anything productive and knew he could procrastinate for some time. He had timesheets to approve, checks to write.

Being a department head at Larry Masons wasn't what Barney imagined he'd be doing with his life, but he stumbled into the job. He never really was sure what he wanted to do anyway, so it kind of worked out. The pay and benefits were way too exceptional to pass up. He enjoyed working with numbers and money. Something about mathematics and business theory always felt natural to him. It had rules, it was definable, solvable, yet an art form. However, being a manager was much more about keeping people in check. He was a taskmaster, the one with the whip. The work he had once enjoyed was now transformed into overseeing his old job's tasks and more.

His phone rang, startling him. Picking up the phone, Barney sighed. He nearly ignored the phone call but decided against it.

"Hi," Barney greeted.

"Hello," A monotone voice replied. "Am I speaking to a Mr. Barney Kellson?" The voice held an air of authority and power.

"This is he," Barney gulped. He felt unsure, hesitant. His buzz had mostly faded.

"Wonderful. My name is Detective Taft. I work down at Purple Beach precinct." Barney wanted to speak, but Taft spoke faster, and Barney held his tongue. "I understand you met with a Williard Chapmen a few days ago."

"That's right..." Barney was nervous. "What's this all about, sir?"

"Have you been in contact with Williard since you last saw him?" The detective pressed, his voice deceptively calm.

"No..." Barney began to sweat just like he did in the heat or humidity. "Officer, would you please tell me what this is about?"

Taft coughed momentarily, which crackled through the phone line and produced a miserable sound. Barney withdrew the phone from his ear slightly in response, the sound grating. The detective spoke again after reclaiming his voice.

"I'm afraid Williard's gone missing," Taft spoke bluntly.

"Excuse me?" Surprised, Barney spoke in reflex.

"Unfortunately, so. He hasn't been seen since Monday." Taft coughed once more, then continued to speak. "Some workers on site claim to have seen you and another gentleman conversing with Williard a few days ago."

"That's correct," Barney affirmed.

"May I ask who the other gentleman was?"

"Oh." Barney had assumed Taft knew Dean's name, considering he knew his. "That was Dean, Dean Harold. He works at Larry Masons, same as me." The muffled sound of papers shuffling, and a pen scrawling came through the phone speaker, another horrid sound of a different variety.

"Perfect," Taft said. "Can you tell me what the three of you were doing?"

Barney's throat was dry; he was nervous, trying his best to speak audibly and to enunciate. Taking a sip of cold coffee from this morning's brew, Barney spoke with a newly lubricated voice.

"We were having a meeting, discussing business."

"Anything important?" The detective was masterful at controlling the pace of a conversation. "Did Williard mention anything about going somewhere, plans perhaps?"

"No." Barney had nothing to hide, did nothing wrong, but as the conversation continued, he felt his nerves weaken exponentially. Barney had no reason to fear the police; in fact, he respected them. But this Taft fellow made him feel uneasy. "No, no, we just talked business." Barney needed something to drink other than old coffee; anything else would suffice. Water or a pop perhaps.

"What sort of business were you discussing?"

Momentarily, Barney contemplated telling Taft the truth but declined to do so. If Dean mentioned it, so be it.

"Just..." Barney took a moment to think of a plausible excuse. "... discussing plans for the coming days as we wrap up development."

"That so?" Taft responded in a voice fitting of command, deep and intimidating.

"Indeed," Barney spoke softly. If Barney and Taft were in the same room together, the detective would see the sweat dripping down Barney's face and have weaponized it against him. Barney had no doubt in his mind: he was a primary suspect. It was the only logical conclusion. He was one of the last people to have seen Will.

"Well then..." Taft thought on his words. "I appreciate your time. I'll be in touch."

Without giving Barney any time to reply, Taft hung up. Barney lay back in his chair, letting the anxiety drain from him slowly. His heart beat rapidly, and he had soaked his collar in sweat despite the pleasant AC blasting in his office. On reflection, the entire conversation was strange. It felt like all of Taft's words were veiled accusations. It didn't sit right with Barney.

Will's disappearance was another layer of shock. Larry Masons was losing good people practically in succession, so it appeared. Barney hoped Will was okay. He rationalized that it was probably not too much of a concern. People go quiet for a bit; it happens. Despite minimal interactions, in Barney's mind, Will seemed to be the kind of guy who liked to go camping. It was probably something like that, just miscommunication. Nobody in headquarters had mentioned Will, but often, people in the office and employees on site didn't interact.

The timing was strange, however, Barney thought. What were the chances of Michael dying and then Will disappearing within the span of forty-eight hours? Barney felt the kind of irrational unease children have when unable to confront the monster in the closet, the beast under the bed. Who else, he wondered, has Taft spoken to within the Larry Masons workplace? Taft couldn't have conjured his intel from thin air. Someone at the company spoke to Taft, and Barney wished they knew who that was. Moment by moment, things felt more conspiratorial.

Barney couldn't stop thinking of Michael, of Will, of the twenty-third house. Barney frequently found great comfort in numbers and mathematics. The logic and rules of math were absolute; only humans muddled the formula. Now, a simple number was burned into his head. Its very existence opened a world of implications that stabbed at the imagination. It was a symbol of defiance to reason. It was no longer just a number; it was a threat. And that color, that bloody flamingo pink, it felt sinister.

Barney picked up his magazine and began to read once more. Minutes passed. He was reading an article about the advent of space travel and the implications of the moon landing. Just as he was beginning to get engrossed, his phone rang once more. Barney jumped from his seat, startled. Dog-earing the current page, Barney set his reading down. Reluctantly, Barney picked up the phone.

"Hello." Barney gave the standard greeting, exhausted with the day.

"Hello," A familiar voice spoke. "Am I speaking to a Mr. Barney Kellson?"

"Ye...Yes." Barney replied, his sweat glands hard at work once more.

"Brilliant!" The voice spoke. "My name is Tim; I work as a detective down at the local precinct."

Every instinct Barney felt at that moment was to drop the phone and run, to flee so quickly and with absolute determination that he would abandon his old life and become someone new. No part of him felt safe. This fear, this maddening irrational emotion, overcame Barney so suddenly that he yelped before regaining himself. The shudder deep within him was so visceral it reminded him of all the bad occasions in his life. Of deaths of loved ones, of hunger.

"Ya' alright?" Tim faked concern, his voice uncannily similar to Taft's.

Barney didn't speak for a moment, calming his anxieties as best he could before his response:

"What can I do for you?" Barney cut to the chase.

"Well, I was wondering if you've recently been in contact with..."

"Will," Kellson cut in.

"Yes..." Tim, the voice on the line, sounded genuinely surprised. "Suppose you've heard then?"

"Officer," Barney explained, "I just finished speaking with Detective Taft. I'm sure any questions you have for me, he's already asked."

"Taft?" Tim sounded perplexed. "What precinct does he work for?"

Now, all of Barney's fears felt grounded, sensible. Something was gravely wrong. This was no longer a conversation. It was a test, or perhaps a cruel joke.

"Purple Beach, I reckon..." Barney cautiously informed. The man on the other line laughed curiously.

"I'm afraid that's not possible," Tim replied. "I'm the only detective on employ here, if you can even call me that. Maybe you're thinking of Ocean Pines?"

In a flash in his mind, Barney recalled some short story he'd read as a young adult over a decade ago. It was in some random edition of *Collier's.* It was this short about these creatures who took over people's bodies, mimicking humans' voices and behaviors. Barney didn't remember the name of that story, but the concept stuck with him, and he was reminded of it now.

"Maybe, maybe..." Barney shivered.

"I'll check in with them later." The detective coughed before continuing. "Well, I'll still need to ask ya' some questions, if you have the time."

"Of course," Barney nervously agreed.

Almost all of the questions the detective asked were identical to the previous caller. Barney answered the detective's questions nearly identically to the way he had with the last. Barney felt nauseous as he repeated himself.

All Barney wanted to do was continue to read about the moon landing until shift end. After he hung up the phone for the second time, he did. Barney's hands were trembling as he grabbed the earmarked page. He tried to read but found he struggled to focus much on the words, finding himself rereading paragraphs over and over. Thirty or so minutes had passed. Quite a large amount of residual stress lingered within him, but Barney's ability to manage his jitters was a well-developed skill. Years of running the accounting department honed him well.

Once more, the phone rang. Once more, Barney answered.

"Hello?" Barney's meek nature and learnt confidence were fighting with one another, a war in his crackling voice.

"Hi." A voice, once again near identical to Taft's or Tim's, spoke. "Are you perhaps Barney..."

"Kellson," Barney cut in. "Yes." His heartbeat sounded like a drum solo. It was all wrong. He needed to escape, to flee home, to another state, anywhere. The day felt cursed. His lips began to shiver, his teeth chittering.

"Great." The voice spoke. "I'm a detective. Names Tyler, I work for the city down at the precinct."

"Sir," Barney, despite his nerves, asserted himself. "This is the third time within the last hour or so I've gotten a call from someone claiming to be a boy in blue. Furthermore, they've all sounded exactly like you. You pulling some kind of sick joke on me? A man died... have some respect!"

"Really? Two others called?" Tyler asked, sounding quite naturally perplexed.

"Yes," Barney asserted, "So, this is some kind of game, some sort of grift?"

"I assure you I'm not playing games," the detective said.

"Uh-huh, sure," Barney scoffed, "Have a nice day." Slamming the phone on the receiver, the bell dinged on impact. Barney was breathing hard, panting. Both thrill and terror surged through him, adrenaline pumping through his core.

"Christ!" Barney shouted, wishing he'd stuck around at the open bar longer.

Barney stood up, no longer interested in reading. Pacing in his tiny office, Barney touched the east wall, then the west, back and forth. He was unsure if Will was even missing now. Nobody had mentioned it before, and clearly the 'detectives' on the phone were the same person. It wasn't Will, unless he was really good at changing his voice. Furthermore, Will was not the joking sort. Barney pondered relentlessly like he was a student cramming in one last study session before a big test. Maybe someone else in the company was pulling this stunt?

"Fuck it," Barney said to himself. He picked up his keys from the desk. He was checking out early. As came upon his office door, the phone rang once more.

"Come the fuck on!" Barney shouted, turning around. Picking the phone up, he sighed, ready to curse out the recurring jackass prank caller.

"Yes?" Barney answered, coiled like a snake ready to strike.

"Hey, Barney," A friendly voice spoke. "It's Dean."

"Oh..." Relief washed over Barney, who let his guard drop. "Hello."

"Do you have a minute to talk?" Dean asked. "I wanted to have a word with you at the party, but couldn't find a moment with all the tears and speeches."

"Of course," Barney agreed. "What's on your mind?"

"Did you by any chance get a phone call from a detective today?" Dean's smokey voice crackled.

"Three of them, in fact," Barney replied, frustration resting on his tongue.

"Three?" Dean seemed taken aback. "Are you sure?"

"Yup." Barney didn't know what to think now. Dean's confirmation added a lot of variables to the formula. Barney had told 'Taft' and 'Tim' about Dean, so it is possible they had called him after the first or second prank call. That still didn't explain how the callers got their information, nor why the persons pretended to be three different detectives, poorly at that.

"They claimed Will was missing," Barney sighed.

"Yeah, told me the same thing." Dean confirmed.

"Started to think it was some sort of prank until you called."

"Prank?" Dean's voice shifted. "Sir, I assure you I take my job very seriously."

"What?" Barney gasped.

"Have you been in contact with Williard recently?" Dean was no longer speaking. His voice had shifted to the previous callers' voice. This was no prank. This was something else, something terrible.

"What were the three of you discussing? What are you hiding?" The voice asked.

Barney fell backwards, landing on his tailbone. The phone dangled from the receiver over the desk, the spiraled cord springing up and down like a thrill-seeking bungee jumper as the phone twirled.

"Sir?" The voice over the phone continued to speak, quiet but not inaudible. "Are you okay, sir? Are you still there? Sir? Mr. Kellson?"

Barney sat on the floor facing away from his door, huffing and wheezing as a terrible anxiety caused his world to spiral. The room, once square, was now cylindrical as it pivoted around him like planets circling the sun. Crawling underneath his desk, Barney grasped at his trash can beneath it. Holding his face above the hollow square box, Kellson choked. It felt as if he was going to vomit, but nothing came out. He convulsed, but still, nothing would release. Barney continued to dry heave.

"Sir?" The voice on the phone continued to speak. "I know you're their Barney. I can hear everything. Twenty-Three."

Swatting the trash can away onto the floor and wiping spit from his lips, Barney emerged from underneath his desk. Letting the phone continue to dangle, Barney pressed the switch-hook down with his spit-covered finger, ending the call. Out of habit, he hung the phone back up.

Barney was done. He was calling it a day. Hell, he might quit and never come back. Gathering his things, Barney was ready to depart. He reached for his doorknob and realized things were not so simple now.

Where his door once was located, now instead was a metal plate. It was welded atop the door and fused to the walls like a tick to flesh. It was rusted and looked like it had been there for some time. Around the metal plate, stains in the wallpaper and spatters of mold seemed to pour out from behind the barricade. Panicked, Barney looked around. Where his small meager window was once located were now nothing but bricks. Everything else in his office looked the same.

"No," Barney shook his head. "No..." Closing his eyes shut with immense pressure, he could feel his brain shaking within his skull. "No, this isn't real." Barney counted to ten, hoping he was just stressed, seeing things. Opening his eyes, the metal plate remained.

"Noo!" He shouted again. Barney was already a sweaty gentleman on a good day. In a state of pure panic, he started to roast and drip like a rotisserie chicken.

Rushing the plate, Barney grabbed its sides and tugged at it, hoping he could peel it open like a can of tuna. No luck. Barney backed up, building up as much momentum as possible before slamming his shoulder into the metal. Besides nearly dislocating his arm and sending a great pain through his nerves, he accomplished nothing.

"Son of a bitch!" Barney screamed in pain. Barney leaned against the sealed off door, pounding on the metal plate with his clenched fists, screaming for help. "Hello!?" Barney shouted, his voice reverberating through his office space. "Can anyone hear me?" For minutes, all he did was beg and scream and bang on the door, but nothing changed. Barney was trapped. After a long fit, greater than any child's, Barney ceased his struggling, his throat sore, and his head pounding.

Leaning against the plate, Barney held his head down. He didn't know what to do, what was happening. What could he do? What could anyone do in his situation?

On his desk, the phone rang once more.

“Aaaarghh!” Barney bellowed. He stood in a flash, rushing his desk. “Asshole!” Barney grabbed the phone, ripping the cord from the wall and throwing it to the floor with an unsatisfying putter and ding. Still, the phone continued to ring. Barney kicked and stomped at the device. Metal bits shattered from the phone, yet still it kept ringing. Debris and destruction flew every which way as Barney reduced the thing to near rubble. Still, the call persisted. Hardware was made to last, but this was beyond reasonable.

The phone rang one last time. The tone, once a pleasant pitch, was now deep and prolonged, the death rattle of a living machine. Barney huffed. He was dripping sweat. One last time, he stomped down on the phone with all his rage and fear. The object no longer resembled a phone, only trash. Some metal chunks had wedged their way into the soles of his shoes.

Walking back to his desk, Barney sat down in his chair. Directly in front of him, the metal bulwark taunted him. Nothing was getting in, and nothing was getting out. Though his heart was beating through his chest so intensely he felt his rib cage pulsate, Barney tried to calm himself. No reason or rationale for his current dilemma could he conjure, so Barney instead focused on remaining composed. He told himself panicking would fix nothing, that he needed to conserve energy.

From the floor, from the rubble, the phone ‘rang’ once more. This time, however, it was not a bell nor a mechanism. It was a voice, the same voice that had mimicked Dean, the voice that played the role of detective(s).

“Ding... Ding... Ding... Ding... Ding!” The voice, which originated from the rubble, mimicked the sounds of a phone like a parrot. “Click Chuck!” The ‘phone’ answered itself. “Hello, this is Detective ████ Twenty-Three. I’ve been watching you since you were very young.”

Barney lifted himself from the seat, backing himself into the corner of the west wall like a cornered animal. Huddling himself, he covered his ears. He felt sick, dizzy. He begged to a God he long stopped believing in for reprieve, but on the voice berated.

"I've laughed at your every mistake." ███ mocked. "I reveled as your mother was raped and beaten by your father and brother." The voice was a chorus of chortling horrors.

"Shut up!" Barney screeched.

On and on, the voice cackled, "Twenty-three. I laughed when she died, the pig."

The voice grew bestial with each utterance. "You were a mistake, a loveless consequence."

"Stop it!" Barney's tears mixed with his sweat. He sat in a pool of his own fluids, trembling, undeserving of such a fate, as no man is. Sadly, such cruelty was Barney's only gift in life now.

"I've seen your weakness. Your cowardice. You've done nothing with your life. You're just like she was."

Barney made only animalistic sounds now. Grunting and screaming, fearful, angry, one with sorrow. Though he tried to speak, to retaliate, only tears and wretched sounds emerged.

"What will you do now?" ███ words continued to drub Barney. It mocked, spitting foul words like heavy raindrops from a storm. "Twenty-three. You'll never see another friend again. Twenty-three. You're always going to be alone. Twenty-three. You're useless, weak, unlovable. Twenty-three. Your dreams were nothing more than pitiful delusions. Twenty-three." The voice stopped, leaving a wake in its absence which echoed in the small space.

Curled up in the corner, dripping snot, sweat, and tears, Barney cradled himself, helpless. Minutes passed, all silent save for his heavy, churning sobs.

The room, the office, started to shake, as if it were a localized earthquake. Barney looked up, clearing snot and tears from his face as he used his shirt like a rag. The shaking intensified, then, from cracks in the wall, small plumes of dust filled the space. Sounds of distant machinery whirring to life and metal scraping boomed from beyond the office walls. A constant pounding sound, almost in four-four rhythm, rang in the distance.

The shaking halted, and the room stuttered briefly. Then, the floor began to sink downward at a slow crawl, down deep into some pit.

"SHIT!" Barney screamed, fear, confusion, and sorrow, his only companion. He crawled into the middle of his office, pressing his back against the right side of his desk.

The room fell downward as if it were an extremely unconventional elevator. The metal barricade blocking the door rose upward, and with it the ceiling and the bricked window. Now, only walls on all sides of the room surrounded Barney as the room churned downwards, the sounds of distant abstract machinery hard at work. The walls at first shared the same wallpaper pattern as the one in Barney's office, but as he fell, the walls changed. Soon, there were a series of metal beams that formed a cross shape against reinforced concrete. Pylons, gears, and wires littered the walls as if decoration, their function unapparent if at all.

Barney made all manner of joyless wails as he descended into darkness. Then, for a brief moment, a bright yellow luminescence filled the room as the office passed an industrial light mounted at an indent in the concrete wall. Beneath the light, in bright orange text, was a large hand-painted number: **1.**

The pounding grew louder, and the machine's whirring became more violent. Pistons slammed against metal plates, and electricity buzzed and crackled.

Sinking beneath the numbered wall, the room continued to fall, picking up speed. The sounds of clanking machinery intensified. Sparks flew from the walls as metal grinded against metal. They were like large, painful sparklers, which on occasion landed on Barney's skin, burning him slightly. They illuminated the office briefly with great flashes of white in the absence of light. Then, the room passed another fixed light source and a hand-painted number in bright orange text: **2.**

Barney looked straight upwards. He could barely see the office ceiling fan, which was now nearly just a spot of light that shimmered slightly with movement as it rotated. The ceiling was so far away it could be mistaken for a black night sky.

3.

Another number flew by, and sparks grew higher, bouncing about the room. The distant rhythmic pounding grew louder, and a funnel of wind formed around the falling office, howling like damned spirits languishing.

4 ... 5 ... 6... 7... Barney nervously started counting out loud.

"Eight." Barney gulped. Perhaps the number represented how many stories down he'd descended, but no real logic could be derived from the circumstance. Barney knew the number would end with twenty-three, and that something would happen then. What that was, however, was unknown to him, and it frightened him more than anything, the potential.

"Nine." Now the room began shaking once more. Another number flew by, and again, Barney counted meekly. "Ten." The sparks continued to fly, and the things on his desk began to vibrate, falling off the sides of the table. His typewriter fell from the desk, landing right next to Barney, who jumped to his feet in reflex. Standing in the middle of his office, wreathed in sparks, drenched in sweat, counting passing numbers on the wall, Barney began to smell something. It was a sweet smell, like oranges. The distant banging noise grew louder, and the sparks grew higher and brighter.

"Eleven. Twelve. Thirteen! Fourteen!" With each letter chanted, Barney grew louder. Though not emboldened, an intense anticipation, none ever greater felt in his life than this, boiled his belly like stew in a pot, and he felt compelled to chant along in dread.

"Fifteen! Sixteen!" Barney was crying, each word a shout of defiance.

"Seventeen! Eighteen! Nineteen!"

The room stuttered, a large screeching sound like rusty car brakes pierced his ears. The room began to slow, though barely. The office scraped violently against the rusted metal girders surrounding it, physics pushing the room down while machinery wrestled against nature's forces. "Twenty! Twenty-one! Twenty-two!"

Then, as if a violent craterous impact, the room slammed to a halt with a force so tremendous that Barney quaked, pressing himself against the desk to maintain his footing. *BAM!* One last time, the machine boomed. In front of him, in orange text, was the number **23**. There was no light above this number. He was in a dark pit far beneath the earth. Above him, Barney could see a row of lights extending upwards past the capability of his sight. The shaft above seemed endless. The sounds of machinery, the pounding sound, halted entirely, like an engine puttering off.

"Twenty-three," Barney whispered to himself. Beneath the bright orange number, nearly invisible, was a pathway, utterly wreathed in darkness. It was a doorway with no door, featureless. Reluctant but curious and with nowhere else to go, Barney stepped into the pitch-black hallway, pressing his left hand against a wall to guide himself. The wall was bumpy. He dragged his fingertips against the wall as he slowly stepped forward, hesitant. Wherever he was, it was quiet, cold. Barney could make out no sounds, save for his labored breathing and footsteps. Sweat poured from his brow, down his eyes, nose, and chin. Each step felt more difficult to take than the last, but he progressed, driven by instinct and fear.

He stepped into a chamber, of which Barney knew this because his fingers slipped free from the wall. The surroundings were just as dark, and he could make out nothing else. Standing still, Barney listened. Everything was silent; no ambience was heard save for his breathing. He could see nothing but black. Then, a ghastly realization overcame Barney. He was not just hearing the sound of his own breath. The source was near, across from him. Looking around in the inky dark, there he saw, just barely visible, the outline of a face. It was impossible to make out any characteristics, though its pupils were beady and glowed a dim blue. The entity, realizing it was spotted, spoke. Its eyes widened, forming blue orbs in the dark.

"It's me!" the voice shouted out to Barney from the dark. It sounded like a young girl, excited, as if reuniting with a friend. "It's me!" the shadowy figure repeated. "It's me!" The voice spoke in the same tone and speed each time, like a recording being played back over and over. "It's me!" The voice sounded absent of humanity. It reminded Barney of a pet bird a friend of his used to have. It would often repeat words and sounds heard around the house. *Pretty Bird!*

"It's me!" The thing continued to repeat itself, over and over. "It's me! It's me!"

Barney was frozen. There was nowhere for him to go. Behind him was a dead end, and his surroundings were so shrouded in blackness that he could hardly maneuver without stumbling. Even if there was an exit ahead, he dared not venture forward and risk contact with... Barney was unsure what it was, but his gut told him it was dangerous.

The voice grew silent momentarily. A strange shifting sound of twisting meat and bone gurgled and fractured, then a new voice, which sounded like an elderly man, masculine but taxed by age, spoke.

"Hungry!" the voice said, as if casually suggesting breakfast or lunch. "Hungry!" Just like earlier, it repeated itself over and over with the same cadence. "Hungry!"

Barney didn't want to know what this thing ate.

"Hungry!" it repeated.

Barney felt like a rat cornered by a house cat, some plaything to be disposed of.

"Hungry!"

Barney decided to slowly retreat. Trying his best to walk backwards undetected, the thing continued to speak. "Hungry!" Two steps back, Barney still faced towards the thing, whose glowing blue eyes faded into the void as he retreated. "Hungry!" Barney desperately wanted to run, but fought the urge, not wanting to trigger or alert the entity in the shadows.

Again, momentarily, the creature grew silent; a horrific sound of crunching bone and gooey flesh echoed in the room. Then again, it spoke in a new voice. It sounded like a young male adult, begging for mercy.

"HELP ME!" The voice was much louder and distressed than before. "HELP ME!" Barney tried his best to move faster. The thing started moving, the blue orbs growing closer. Barney could hear wet footsteps echoing in the empty chamber behind him.

"HELP ME!" The thing shrieked.

"HELP ME!" Each wail was identical.

Barney felt his chest tighten, pain igniting all throughout his body.

"HELP ME!" The thing begged. "HELP ME!"

Panic overtook Barney, who turned around, sprinting swiftly away from the screaming creature. He ran through the dark hall, once again dragging his hand against the concrete wall. Behind him, the beast broke into a sprint. Thuds and sounds of wet meat slapping against the ground splattered behind him. The thing was gaining on him, all the while continuing to scream the same thing over and over.

"HELP ME!" it shouted as it launched through the darkness. "HELP ME!"

Barney raced to his office (if it even was that from the start) in a panicked sprint. Rushing towards his desk, seeking the only place he could think of to hide, Barney slipped suddenly, falling backwards onto the ground. A rubbery chord and phone debris launched under the weight of his soles. Barney's hefty impact with the floor took the wind out of him, and for a moment, he could not breathe. Now practically on top of him, the formless thing continued to wail.

"HELP ME!" the monster screeched. Barney regained his breath and picked himself up, crawling underneath his desk and huddling into a ball. He was shivering, panting, and whimpering uncontrollably. He covered his mouth with his hand, pressing down on his lips as if to hold in all the sounds he could produce. With several great sloppy clonks, the thing stood over the top of the desk.

The thing huffed but was otherwise silent for a long moment. Then horrid visceral sounds of twisting flesh popped above Barney. Sounds of tendons snapping, bones locking into place, teeth gnashing, all spurted and churned. A wiggling noise like maggots writhing in rot was accompanied by a loud buzzing flutter akin to a wasp or beetle in flight. The horror spoke once more, now in a chorus of voices, all in great agony, all reveling in the moment.

"LOVE ME!" The creature's claws wrapped around the desk, digging through the wood, before ripping it from the ground and smashing it against the wall. Splinters of wood and chunks of metal, brackets and screws burst every which way, clanking against the floor and pelting Barney.

"LOVE ME!" the thing screeched directly at Barney, spewing globs of spittle and goo onto his face, chest, and arms. Barney wept, shaking, daring not to look at the thing in front of him. Barney felt a great pain piercing through his chest like knives through tendons. He grasped at his neck and head, his body stiffening and convulsing. His sight left him, as well as his thoughts and breath.

Barney looked at the creature in front of him. It was a faceless being, its form muddled and wicked. It smiled, despite having no lips. Barney died huddled on the floor, grasping at his face. Death came slowly.

. . .

Jon was having a good day. Though the 'party' was mournful, he took any opportunity to enjoy a drink. Jon worked in billing under Barney's management. They'd recently outsourced some contract work to a third party who'd been giving them strife about improper compensation, despite evidence to the contrary. Jon had prepared a paper trail of contract proposals and bank statements to prove otherwise, as requested. Knocking on Barney's door, he came to deliver his work and head home early for the day. He'd had plans for the night with his wife. After a few knocks and no reply, Jon cracked the door open. There on the floor in front of his desk, a motionless Barney lay wrapped around himself, dead, pale, his face warped and twisted. His skin was shiny like clay.

Jon, as well as many other employees at Larry Masons, spent much of the night talking with the police. Eventually, a coroner deemed Barney's death the result of a massive heart attack. It most likely killed him near instantly, the report claimed. Out of Michael, Will, Barney, and Dean, only Dean lived past the month and year of September 1969. Though no authorities or individuals would ever link the deaths of the three Larry Masons employees together (they were considered a string of coincidental, unrelated tragedies), Dean always held a grain of suspicion within him that something more had happened to his colleagues, though he was unsure of what.

Dean would occasionally think of the strange mystery surrounding house twenty-three, about the death of his coworkers. Upon Dean's death in 1988, no one thought of the flamingo pink home, home twenty-three, for a very long time. There it sat on Wight Street, inconspicuous, biding time, never rented, never owned, unnoticed.

FRIENDSHIPS AND LOVERS

Peter wrapped his arms around Greg. Underneath a blanket Greg pulled over them, the warmth of their bodies radiated against each other. After just a small amount of time in the cold and rain, Peter was shivering. Peter leaned against Greg's shoulders, which were soft and comfortable like pillows. Greg felt his heartbeat like a drum. All this time, and he'd still not gotten used to this feeling.

On the windowsill, Cactus sat, as they had for years now. It was a calm, rainy night in Letterfaux. Water pattered against the glass like smooth jazz; it ran down the sides of the roads and burbled into the drainage. Cactus enjoyed watching the weather. On rainy nights like this, Cactus got lost in old memories. They remembered the first rains after years of drought in Cactus's old homeland. Cactus longed to feel the storm breeze and rain every day of their life and held out hope that they one day would.

Cactus had made a friend recently: Spider. She climbed up a web and onto one of Cactus's spikes. Spider and Cactus seldom communicated, simply content with each other's company. Spider ate any harmful pests, and Cactus provided anchor points for her webs to be spun. Still, on special nights, they would occasionally engage in minor banter.

"Beautiful, isn't it?" Cactus said to Spider.

"The view or them?" Spider's meek, squeaky voice replied, their eyes focused on Peter and Greg, who still embraced each other under the comfort of their blanket.

"Both, I suppose." Cactus would smile if they could make expressions.

"I wonder," Spider spoke as she crawled across her web toward the window, "who will eat who after they make love?" The spider webs tickled Cactus's green, smooth skin.

"Humans don't sexually cannibalize," Cactus laughed, "that's a Spider thing."

"Oh." Spider sounded disappointed. "Shame." Spider crawled onto the windowpane, enjoying the soft vibrations through the glass from the gentle falling droplets. "They don't know what they're missing."

"Perhaps." Cactus was thankful to have such an interesting friend.

Greg ran his hand up Peter's right thigh. Pressed tight against his pants, he could feel Peter's passion throbbing. Peter's face was flushed, both from the cold and Greg's presence. Looking into each other's eyes, the two kissed. Their tongues wrapped around each other's. Greg gently bit Peter's lip, causing him to blush even more. Greg's beard was well-trimmed, while Peter was clean-shaven. Peter could feel Greg's soft beard hairs brush against his face as they kissed.

Peter ran his hand down Greg's chest. Greg shivered. He felt a great anticipation well up inside him. He wanted Peter more than anything in the world. He wanted to give him everything, physically and mentally. He wasn't sure when everything changed, when their friendship turned into something more. They'd never even given this 'thing' a title. Greg feared that if they did, this sudden love they felt would falter and die. So, they just let it exist, enjoying each spontaneous moment.

"I'm feeling much warmer." Peter smiled.

"Good." Greg grinned back, climbing on top of his lover. Chest to chest, the two pressed their hips against each other as they slowly removed each other's clothing. Peter's chest was smooth, his skin soft. Greg's body was covered in hair, which both tickled and excited Peter. Underneath the blanket, the two began to sweat, so soon the blanket was tossed to the floor.

With each other's clothing removed, the two stroked each other as they ran their hands across every crevice and curve of each other's bodies.

"I love you..." Peter said almost in reflex, shocked by his own words. He was terrified that Greg would recoil, run away in fear.

Instead, Greg replied, "I love you, too."

It felt right, and they kissed.

"Are you sure that big, hairy one isn't going to eat the tiny one?" Spider asked Cactus. "The tiny one's pinned down. This would be a good time to strike."

"Positive," Cactus laughed.

"Interesting." Spider shook her head, confused by the strangeness of humans.

"If you say so," Cactus replied. "Us plants don't reproduce that way."

"Now that's a real shame," Spider laughed.

"Can't miss what you don't know," Cactus rebutted.

"But you can imagine," Spider retorted.

"I suppose you're right," Cactus agreed, "Perhaps my imagination is limited."

All was peaceful in the apartment; all was perfect. Eventually, everyone inside capable of sleep did so to the sound of pattering rain against windowpanes. No better night could be constructed, and everyone inside that home felt loved that night. Eventually, around four in the morning, the rain ceased, and save for some howling winds, it was a silent night.

ALL WAS IN ITS PLACE

It was a cold winter night. It was also macaroni and cheese night. Bethany would be home from work soon, and Leon was in the living room playing games on the family computer. Carl sprinkled a layer of breadcrumbs on top of the cheesy noodles in the casserole dish. Sliding the meal into the oven, all Carl had to do now was wait for the top layer to brown to perfection. Leon loved macaroni and cheese but was otherwise a pretty picky eater. About a year ago, the Parson family went out to eat lunch one Sunday afternoon. They had ordered fried calamari as an appetizer and told Leon it was curly fries. He ate them right up without question, loved them in fact. Since then, Carl had been trying to sneak other foods into Leon's diet. Tonight, he'd finely minced mushrooms, mixing them into the macaroni. Carl hoped Leon wouldn't notice.

Bethany stepped through the front door; behind her, a blast of winter air sent a momentary chill throughout the house. Closing the door with a hefty slam and wiping wet from her feet on the welcome mat, she removed her boots and hung up her jacket.

"Hey, smells good," Bethany said.

"Should be." Carl beamed, walking to meet her at the front door. "How was work?"

"Not great. Not as bad as the roads," Bethany sighed, setting her wallet and keys on the entryway table. The two headed into the kitchen.

"Traffic?" Carl asked.

"Oh yeah." Beth headed into the living room to see her son. "Hey, my little man." Her voice always held much more joy when Leon was involved.

Carl set an alarm on his phone for the macaroni and joined his wife on the sofa. Carl and Beth snuggled close to each other, enjoying each other's warmth. Leon was focused intently on his game, some tower-defense game involving zombies and plants. To Carl, the moment felt like it should be perfect; however, he was on edge. He felt happy, normal, or rather told himself he should feel that way. Simple moments like these were all he wanted anymore. All was in its place, but everything felt shifted...

Bethany leaned her head against Carl's shoulder, who seemed tense. She felt the subtle beat of his heart. It was rapid.

"You alright?" Bethany looked at Carl. He seemed displaced from the moment, though she knew that feeling equally.

"Yeah." He smiled. "Just zoning ..." The three sat in silence for some time. Carl's phone rang eventually: the oven timer.

"Christ!" Carl leaped from the couch. Beth leaned back, and even Leon turned from the computer for a moment to glance at the ruckus.

"Startled me," Carl exhaled.

"You startled *me*," Beth laughed. "You sure you're fine?"

"Yeah ... just tense, I guess ..." Carl shrugged.

"Well, dinner will help." Beth stood up. "Let's go eat." Bethany walked over to Leon, who was back to being affixed to his glowing screen. She poked him on the shoulder, though Leon gave no reaction.

"That means you, too, buddy!" She spoke in her stern motherly voice.

"Let me finish this level!" Leon pleaded. He was starting to become rebellious as young teens do, but he was still a kind kid by all accounts.

"You can pause it," Beth negotiated. "We're having mac and cheese!"

"Okay." Leon tried to act annoyed, but Beth could see through his guise. Leon paused the game and rushed past his mother to the dining room. He plopped himself down at his seat with anticipation. Beth, exhausted from the cold day, could not help but smile.

The Parsons sat down to eat. Leon immediately began gobbling up his meal. He had a tendency to eat rather fast. Carl quietly celebrated to himself while watching his son. He'd never have gotten Leon to eat mushrooms willingly. Slowly, Carl thought to himself, he'd get his son enjoying a diverse palette. Despite this small, claimed victory, Carl couldn't shake an odd, rapturous sensation tightening around him.

"Don't choke on it now." Beth had not even had a single bite yet. Meanwhile, Leon was nearly a quarter of the way through his meal.

"You have any homework tonight?" she asked.

"Already did it! Just math," Leon said with his mouth full.

"Good." Bethany ate her first bite. "Oh! That turned out really well," Beth complimented. She looked at Carl, who once again seemed vacant.

Carl felt an urgent need to escape, like he didn't belong in his home. He didn't belong in his skin. Yet, everything was how it should be.

Nothing was wrong. His eyes dashed around the room.

The dining room table was the same old hunk of wood. His chair still creaked beneath his ass. The plates and silverware were the same as ever. Bethany was her usual self; she seemed tired, but that was by no means abnormal. Leon was also behaving normally.

Nothing was wrong. His eyes dashed around the room.

Time felt faster than usual. The walls looked normal, same old coat of paint. The floor, original hardwood, still had that beautiful oak stain. Carl could recognize each scratch on the wood, some of which had memories associated with them, move-in day, new furniture. The ceiling fan looked the same; it needed dusting. The rug beneath the dining table was the same old pattern.

Nothing was wrong. His eyes dashed around the room.

All was in its place.

"Maybe your best yet," Beth said, peering at Carl with concern as she ate.

"It's really good," Leon agreed, sipping at a glass of water.

Carl nodded in acknowledgement, unsure of what to say, his

focus misplaced. The table was quiet for a bit, save for clinking forks and the sounds of chewing. Carl didn't touch another bite. Beth was about halfway through her meal. Leon ran the edge of his fork around the rim of his bowl, scooping cheese up and consuming it until his bowl was near spotless.

"Can I have some more?" Leon asked.

"Sure," Carl replied, snapping out of his daze, trying his best to tell himself everything was normal. "It's sitting on the oven."

Leon left for the kitchen.

"I've got a doctor's appointment Thursday," Bethany informed Carl. "I'll probably take the rest of the day off, pick up Leon from school for a change."

"Sounds good." Carl stared into his bowl of food.

"No appetite tonight?" Beth asked. "Normally, Leon's the picky one."

"I heard that!" Leon shouted from the kitchen.

"No," Carl chuckled, "just thinking." He forced himself to take a few more bites.

"About anything in particular?" Bethany asked.

Leon walked into the dining room with an absolute mountain of mac and cheese in his bowl and sat back down in his seat.

"Well, the car needs its oil changed." Carl was a master of deflecting. "Been missing biking with all this cold. Ya' know, just thoughts." Carl took a few more bites. The meal did actually turn out really good, despite his melancholy.

"You'd think he'd been starving," Carl quipped, pointing his thumb outward at his son.

"Yeah," Bethany sighed. "I was ..."

"What's *that!?*" Leon stopped eating, interrupting his mother. He pointed to a wall in the dining room. His voice was a mix of both curiosity and timid uncertainty.

As soon as his son spoke, Carl noticed a nearby blue glow glimmering in his peripheral vision. Tucked in the corner was something most dreaded. It was an entity malicious, an unescapable cosmic stalker, intent veiled behind its glow. There was that blue window, the horrid thing, upon his dining room wall, like a painting on display, one which could not be taken down.

"You can see it!?" Carl trembled as he slid back in his seat and stood up. He loomed over the dining room table, bathed in blue. Startled, Bethany dropped her fork. It clattered on impact with her bowl.

"See what?" Bethany spoke, tepid and curious. She looked around the room, but all was in its place.

"What is it?" Leon inquired. He stared into the light, his eyes wide with childish elation and instinctual caution. Leon pushed his plate aside and slid his chair back from the table.

"I ... uhm ..." Carl had never thought of describing the blue light before. "Do you see the same thing I do?" Carl wasn't sure what to say. He was shaking. He had to be sure his son was seeing the same thing he was. "Can you describe it for me?"

"It's ..." Leon blushed. "Blue, square, bright."

Carl felt as if he was shrinking or the world around him was growing larger. Uncontrollable tears began to fall from Carl's eyes. He sobbed and heaved, a cry so visceral and frightful that Beth had only seen such reactions from her husband in the most dismal of occurrences.

"You ..." Carl shook. "You're not supposed to..." Carl was panicked, shouting and incoherent. His hands, which were pressed against the table, shook so violently that the furniture quaked with him. "You... you've..."

"What the hell is going on!?" Bethany stood up, alarm bells in her mind ringing at maximum volume. She felt a great urgency to defend herself, but from whom, she was not certain. Momentarily, she remembered ... something else, something from her past, but the memory left as quickly as it came, leaving her only with more dread.

"You're not supposed to *see* it!" Carl raged with a piercing urgency, his screams so loud they echoed from wall to wall.

"What the fuck!?" Bethany shouted fearfully. She sprang from her seat.

"Not YOU! Not YOU!" Carl continued wailing. He grasped the side of his neck and the top notch of his spine, squeezing with tremendous force. His knuckles popped outward from his fist like molehills.

"What's happening!?" Bethany tried to calm her husband, to get a grasp on the situation. "Talk to me, hun..." Carl continued to weep, his words illegible. Beth had never seen him like this. Carl was the type of man who was willing to cry, but he tried to keep it private, out of view. It had taken Carl years to feel comfortable opening up around Beth. Carl had never cried in front of Leon. Now here, on macaroni night, seemingly unprovoked and without cause, Carl opened the floodgates, and a dam of emotions poured forth.

Leon seemed unfazed by the entire situation. His focus grew ever more intently on the glowing light. To Bethany, it was as if Leon was staring at nothing. Leon's pupils were wide and filled with intent, elation. They looked bluer than normal. He stood from his seat and slowly began walking towards the blue, affixed upon it like an insect to a lamp.

"He, he ..." Carl panted, lost deep in his sorrows and panic.

"Talk to me! What's going on!?" She put her arm around Carl, rubbing his back. "It's okay." She assured him, her heart racing, her exterior calm. Bethany provided no comfort to Carl, despite her best efforts. All of her focus was on him.

Leon stepped more surely towards the light. He reached both of his hands out to the side, like he was balancing on a tight rope. His eyes were completely affixed upon the anomaly. Suddenly, Carl realized that his son was moving towards the glow, and Carl reacted. Instinctively sprinting, Carl shoved Bethany to the side, who fell to the floor, aghast and swearing.

"What the fuck!?" Bethany shouted as she picked herself up from the floor. The fall hadn't hurt, not physically at least. Carl had never been violent. He was always caring and gentle, but this side of him was something entirely different.

Carl rushed towards his son, almost toppling him to the ground. Wrapping his arms around his boy, he lifted his son from the ground.

"NOOO!" Leon screamed at maximum volume, his voice cracking, a raw screech of defiance. "NOOO!" He shouted again, kicking at his father as he was dragged away from the blue glow.

"IT'S NOT FAIR!" Leon declared. "I FOUND IT FIRST!"

Leon scratched at his father's arms, drawing blood with several furious swipes.

"Stay away from it!" Carl shouted, his voice overtaking his son's, echoing in the dining room. It was a command, both to his son and the anomaly. Neither listened.

"STOP IT!" Bethany screamed.

Carl lifted his son over his shoulder like luggage. Still resisting furiously, Leon continued to pummel and bruise his father.

"I found it first!" Leon's voice began to crack, his throat raw from shrieking. "It's mine! It's mine!"

"Stay away!" Carl commanded once more.

"STOP IT!" Beth continued to shout.

"I found it first! I FOUND IT FIRST!" Leon reached toward the glow like he was trying to steal a toy from a store shelf. He punched violently at his father.

"WE NEED TO LEAVE!" Carl screamed, grabbing his wife by her hand with his free arm. He felt the bruises of his son's assaults accumulating, and the weight of his growing boy hurt his bad shoulder and back.

Carl dragged the three upstairs into their bedroom, slamming the door shut. The three sat on the bed. Blood trickled from Carl's minor wounds onto the white sheets, like flower petals on snow. Leon eventually ceased his kicking, and Carl released his hold. A few seconds of silence descended as the Parsons sat motionless on the mattress. It was short-lived.

Abruptly, Leon attempted to launch himself from the bed. With impressive precision and reflex, Carl grabbed him by the scruff of his shirt. Pulling him back, Carl pushed Leon down against the springy mattress.

"Don't hurt him!" Bethany recoiled in horror, jumping from the bed.

Leon pushed against Carl. He raised his head slightly, just enough for his mouth to make contact with his father's palm. With a powerful underbite, Leon bit down hard on Carl's hand.

"ARRGHH!" Carl shouted in pain. Blood dripped from his son's mouth; the boy was like a predator ripping apart a fresh meal.

"ENOUGH!" Bethany slammed her foot on the ground, her voice so brilliantly resolute and imposing, it felt as though it shook the heavens. Despite forces unknown, the ominous anger in his mother's voice shook Leon to reason, who returned to his normal demeanor, at least momentarily.

Leon's face was a mask of confusion. He spat blood from his mouth, and immediately, Leon began to cry. He threw a tantrum, this time non-violent, reminiscent of his toddler years. Bethany ran to her son, holding him. She cradled him back and forth, weeping herself. She whispered soft, gentle words and melodic shushes into her son's ears.

Carl headed into the bedroom's en-suite bathroom, cleaning his wounds with some soap and water before applying a band-aid. Returning to his wife's side, Leon, calm for the moment, the three held each other. As the whimpers and trembling softened in the aftermath, Bethany asked:

"Will you please tell me what's happening?"

"Okay," Carl whispered.

Carl never wanted this for Bethany, for Leon. Carl thought it was his alone to carry... Now, it felt as if he'd passed on a terrible curse to his family. It amazed Carl that despite how blatant the portal's presence was, Bethany was unable to perceive it. It was like... Carl thought of the words to describe it... 'selective camouflage'.

"I need to tell you both a story..."

Carl struggled, but he disclosed every detail he could recall about the night of Hurricane Nester, the night Mannhouse broke into their home looking for their non-existent basement. He spoke without interruption, and the two listened intently. When the story was done, Bethany didn't say a word. Leon kicked his feet against the side of the bed, looking down at the carpeted floor like it was just a boring night time story. Carl waited anxiously for Beth to say anything, but she remained silent for minutes. Eventually, Carl spoke up.

"You don't believe me?"

"It's..." Bethany paused, "Just... it's a lot to take in. I want to take your word for it, I do... But magic lights? It's... I don't even know what I can say." More silence, painful silence...

"You didn't see it, Mom?" Leon looked up towards his mother, his eyes red from crying.

"No, honey," she said solemnly. Leon's question unnerved Beth, his words a quandary unsolvable. His intonation was innocent in a way only a child could sound. Carl looked down at the floor, and Leon as well. Leon kicked his feet a few times more, his shoes bouncing off the mattress. Bethany held her breath, only inhaling when at the brink of deprivation.

"How long does it last?" she asked.

"Excuse me?" Carl asked.

"This thing. How long does it stick around?" With her expression and tone alone, Bethany impressed upon her husband a willingness to cooperate despite her hefty skepticism.

"I've never stuck around to count." Carl hadn't ever considered this. He was always too focused on avoiding the thing's presence rather than observing it.

"Well." Beth stood up, her hand on Leon's shoulder the entire time. "If there is an... alien or whatever in our house, shouldn't we check to see if it's still here?"

"I guess..." Carl hesitated.

"Considering I can't see it..." Bethany continued.

"Okay." Carl stood, looking at his son and wife. "I'll check." He was terrified, ready to restrain his son once more. "I love you both." Carl descended down the stairs slowly, making his way back to the dining room.

After a short delay, Bethany stood up from the bed. She lifted Leon up from his sitting position, clutching his hand in her own.

"Mom?" Leon hesitated.

"Be as quiet as you can, okay?" Bethany whispered to her son. "It's a game."

"Okay," Leon agreed.

"Do exactly as I do."

"Okay." He agreed once more.

Down the stairs, mother and son crept. Making it to the front door undetected, Beth grabbed her car keys and wallet as she slipped on her shoes. Leon followed suit. Beth slipped on her jacket, and Leon put on a hoodie.

"It's still here!" Carl shouted from the dining room, not noticing the two were downstairs. Leon leaned towards his dad's voice, still drawn to the blue. Bethany swung the front door open, dragging Leon behind her in a single-minded sprint. There was a light drizzle outside, and the sun was setting.

"Mom!?" Leon clamored.

Carl heard the front door lurch open and the pattering footsteps of his wife and child. He turned from the blue glow, racing to pursue them. He couldn't let Leon enter the window, should it follow.

"NO!" Carl shouted. "STOP!" He sprinted outside in pursuit.

Bethany practically shoved Leon in the passenger seat of her truck, scrambling in after him before slamming the door shut, igniting the engine with a rumble. Carl sprinted, nearly reaching the driver's door. Beth's truck sputtered for a moment on the slick wet ground before racing down the driveway. Water kicked up from the back tires. It splashed against Carl's face, who raised his arms in reflex.

"Don't leave!" Carl pleaded, his voice the same as he begged for his family's life at gunpoint years ago. "Don't go!" He spat mud from his mouth.

Bethany and Leon headed down the road, out of sight.

"What did I do wrong?" Carl reached toward nothing. His family gone. Momentarily, Carl contemplated rushing inside to grab keys for the sedan, but decided against it. A high-speed pursuit of his son and wife seemed unwise to him, especially in his current distraught state.

Stepping back inside and closing the front door, Carl walked back to the dining room. The disruptive blue lingered, still washing the room in a single color. Music played, emanating from the glow, though so faintly that Carl barely heard it over his own ragged breathing. Carl knew he'd heard this song in his dreams many times before.

The only person left in the house was him, but Carl didn't feel alone. He stared into the swirling blue miasma that arranged itself upon the wall. Carl found himself watching sparks dance from its maelstrom. Flashes of lasers beamed in and out of the portal, forming impossible shapes and symbols. It was like the thing was putting on a show for him. Carl picked up a fork from the dining room table and threw it at the blue window. He expected it to absorb the item, but instead it bounced off the wall as normal, tumbling to the floor with a metallic clink. Overcoming the urge to embrace the blue, Carl turned from the anomaly, sick and exhausted.

IN ITS PLACE WAS ALL

"Where are we going?" Leon was worried. Bethany slammed the passenger door shut as Leon settled into the car seat. Bethany rushed to the driver's side, ferociously swinging the door open. Hopping up into the driver's seat, Bethany turned on the ignition. Her truck rumbled to life, the engine roaring like a panther. Beth slammed her foot hard against the pedal before she had even closed her door. The car launched forward like a runner at the start of a race. Bethany watched Carl get splattered in a little bit of mud via her side view mirror.

"Seat belt!" Bethany demanded, Leon complied. She pulled out of their driveway, leaving the neighborhood. Beth didn't bother buckling herself.

"Mom?" Leon's voice stuttered. He waited for a reply.

Bethany was unfocused, her mind somewhere else.

"MOM!" Leon shouted. Startled, Bethany gasped, lurching to the left momentarily, causing the car to swerve into the other lane. She was shaken but had her wits mostly about her.

"Where are we going?"

"I don't know, sweetheart." She really didn't know where to go, just that they had to leave home for a while. "I don't know." The car slowed to a halt at a stop sign. With her right blinker on, she turned onto local backroads she knew well. Beth was headed for the closest town, Newtext. She felt like a mother wolf protecting her pup. From what, however, she wasn't certain.

"Is this because of the glow?" Leon inquired.

"No," Bethany twitched.

"Are you sure?" Leon continued to investigate. One thing Leon did struggle with was reading people's emotions. An individual could have a raging scowl or a wide, gleeful smile on their face, and Leon could not tell the difference. It was an immense struggle for him at times.

"Yes." Bethany tried her best to remain calm, to quell her tears, but she was still shaking.

A family of deer poked out from a wooded area on the side of the road. Bethany slammed hard on the brakes, nearly avoiding thumping the bumper headfirst into some fawn. The foolish creatures gawked witlessly toward the general direction of the car. They looked sickly, pocked by boils and missing clumps of hair. They were skinny, too, from the looks of it. After a brief moment's pause, Bethany slammed her palm into the center of the steering wheel, blaring her horn several times. The deer scattered across the road into some high grass. Beth continued driving onwards, cursing at the animals.

"Do you think it's weird only Dad and I could see the light?" Leon kept asking questions. He didn't even seem to notice the deer, or care.

"There is no light!" Bethany screamed in a state of rage, fear, and frustration. Leon hopped in his seat, startled. "I don't know what happened ..." Bethany tried to keep her voice down, but had an issue with volume control when upset.

"But I saw it! And Dad said!" Leon spoke as persuasively as possible.

"I don't care what you saw or what your dad says!" Bethany cried.

"Okay." Leon looked down at the car mat, disheartened. Leon did not possess the skill set to express himself properly at this moment, nor did he possess the skills necessary to debate his mom. Leon knew his mom was upset to a level that he'd seldom seen before, but he just didn't understand why. All he knew was something was terribly wrong.

The two spent minutes driving in silence. Leon kicked his feet against his car seat. His head was turned into the seat belt as he looked through the window at passing blurs. Eventually, Bethany had a destination in mind. There was an old highway motel off one of the exits between Letterfaux and Newtext. Paradise Suites, Bethany believed it was called. It would be safe enough for the night. Beth only wished she kept a black light on her. Leon's stomach rolled. He'd not eaten most of his lunch, and dinner was cut short, even if he had gone for seconds.

Timidly, he spoke up, "I'm hungry."

"Me too," Beth agreed.

There were a few fast-food places to pick from on the road toward Newtext. Beth chose a place called Jack's and pulled into the drive-through. The joint was colorfully painted in red and white stripes. A neon "Open" sign glowed a bright yellow in the night. Around the frame of the drive-through window were several bulbs. The colors of the lights danced back and forth, from red to white, flickering on and off. Leon sat in the car, looking through the front passenger window. The colors refracted through the transparent barrier; they looked like large tidal waves to Leon. He could see himself, warped and distorted in the glass, his image flashing between surreal, incandescent blooms as the bulbs zapped rhythmically. Though they were marvelous and pretty, the man-made lights felt hollow compared to the marvelous marrow blue which hugged Leon just recently. Leon could find no such similar sensation in any other incandescence. No fireworks, no torchlight, nor concert shows could ever compare to that magical compulsion, that ecstasy in which the blue did.

"Have a nice day," The lady working the window said in a monotone voice as she closed the panel shut.

"Hold this," Beth said, handing her son a greasy bag of food as she cranked up the truck window. Placing their drinks in the cup holders, the wayward two left Jacks to find refuge.

. . .

The motel receptionist looked bored and smelled of weed. Bethany was handed the keys to their room. They were on the second floor, room twenty-three, on the corner next to the stairs. Carrying their food into the room, Bethany locked and chained the door behind them and closed the blinds. She'd made sure to park in a spot behind the motel, hidden away from the road.

The room was small. It had two beds, separated by a small table with a lamp. On it were some fresh towels and a note about amenities and hours. Opposite the beds was a dresser with a medium-sized, cheap flat-screen television. Next to the dresser was a mini-fridge, and to the right of that was the bathroom, which was cramped and had mint green walls.

Bethany claimed the bed closest to the door, deliberately. They each ate on their beds. Jack's was pretty terrible, at least in Bethany's opinion. Her burger was dry, her fries floppy. Leon seemed to enjoy his meal. As they ate, Bethany replayed the last hour's events in her mind, over and over, trying to understand what exactly had happened. She was unsure why she fled with Leon, but it felt like the safest option.

Wrapping her unfinished burger in its foil, Bethany tossed it towards the plastic trash can near the door. The detritus rattled against the rim of the bin, nearly knocking it over before settling. Bethany washed the grease off her hands in the bathroom before returning to her bed and checking her phone. She had several new text messages and a few missed calls. Beth huffed, remaining as stoic as she could.

Carl had called multiple times and sent several text messages. They were all along the same sentiment: asking where she went. Messages emphasizing the need to keep Leon safe, away from the blue light. Messages begging for forgiveness. Messages about how she needed to believe him. She read each text but didn't know how or if she wanted to reply. Beth ruminated on it. There was another text received, one marked as potential spam. Usually, Beth would just delete such a message, but she read it for some reason.

"Nearly 40% of energy use during the winter season is due to poorly insulated windows. With Westen Hurley's new sales program, it's easier than ever to book your free consulta..."

Bethany stopped reading. She marked the text as spam and deleted it. Her phone was sitting at around sixty percent of a charge. Since she didn't have a charger, she set it to low power mode and ignored the phone.

"Mom," Leon said after finishing his meal. "When are we going home?"

Bethany hesitated, but she fabricated an answer. "Tomorrow, honey." Bethany was sorrowful, her volume low.

"Why couldn't Dad come?" Leon continued to question.

"Well…" Bethany grew sick. Bad fast food and anxiety weren't a great combination. "Dad and I needed a little break." Her phone buzzed again, vibrating on her thigh. Carl was calling once more. Bethany decided she needed to talk to Carl eventually and figured now was as good a time as any.

"Why don't you find something to watch?" Bethany suggested tossing the remote to her son, who caught it with reflective ease.

"Okay," Leon huffed.

Bethany stepped out onto the second-story motel walkway. She didn't want to have this talk in front of Leon. It was dark and brisk outside, the cold winter air worsened by a consistent frigid breeze. The only illumination provided was by the stars, balcony lights, and a few vending machines scattered across the parking lot. The sounds of distant cars zooming down the highway added to the dreary ambience. Their headlights flashed between a row of trees along a curved section of the main road, creating speckles of dancing light between the leaves.

Bethany picked up the phone, holding it to her ear. She could see the heat of her breath linger in the air. Carl's panicked voice came through the phone speaker. He was distraught, in tears, his voice choked. It didn't seem Carl realized she had answered.

"Hello?" Bethany hesitantly spoke after some time.

"Oh Jesus!" Carl shouted, startled, relieved. "I didn't think you'd ever answer…" Though the reception was not great, the anguish in his words still carried through the static on the line.

"Sorry," Bethany said, her voice thick with emotion.

"Are you okay!? Is Leon safe!?" Carl's voice was rushed, anxious.

"We're fine." Bethany peered through the crack in the door. Leon was half-heartedly surfing channels, clicking through each one by one in reflex.

"Where did you go!? Why!?" Carl sounded just as angry as he did fearful.

"We're in a safe place," Bethany assured Carl while on the brink of tears. About five doors down, some stranger emerged from their room. It looked like an older woman; she was wearing a blue hoodie. The woman lit a cigarette. Beth turned away from the stranger, lowering her voice and swallowing the lump in her throat.

"You're both safer with me!" Carl shouted in frustration, his digitally compressed voice distorting somewhere along the process of input and output.

"Well, it sure as hell didn't feel like it!" Bethany retaliated, lowering her voice mid-sentence as she avoided looks.

"Baby," Carl tried to lower his temper, tried to soothe his wife. "I'm sorry ... I'm sorry for all of this."

Bethany was reminded of the gentle, wonderful man she'd fallen in love with, yet in this moment, his voice seemed corrupted somehow.

"Please just come home."

"I think it's best if we... we just need to keep our distance. For now." Bethany wanted nothing more than to forget everything and cuddle underneath a blanket with her two favorite boys. But her instinct continued to drive her away from this desire. Something was still wrong. The idea of returning home felt dangerous. Everything felt dangerous.

"It's just..." Carl began to rant. "You can't see the light like Leon and I can..."

"Not this," Bethany sighed, exhausted with the preposterous premise. She was shivering; it was miserably cold out, and saying she was underdressed was an understatement.

"Just listen... There's no way of knowing when and where it can show up. You can't protect him from what you can't see!"

"I can protect my son just fine, *damn it!*" Bethany screeched and shook. Her shivering combined with the harshness of her voice caused her shout to wobble. The smoker a few doors down leaned against the railing, casually watching Bethany through their peripheral vision.

"That's not what I'm saying. It's just..." Carl tried to defuse an already active bomb.

"And I'm saying I'll come home when it feels safe!" It took years after the storm for their house to feel secure again, to feel like a home again. Bethany was unsure if it ever truly went back to the way things had been, or if she'd just been lying to herself.

Carl grunted in frustration. "Okay, okay... Fine." Carl was hesitant but had no power over the situation, regardless. "Stay away as long as you need. Please, just keep my boy safe."

"Our boy... and always." Bethany wanted to scream at Carl and comfort him all at the same time. The nosy motel neighbor slipped back inside her room. Entertainment or not, the cold was quite a deterrent.

"I hope we can fix this when you come home," Carl said softly. Beth struggled to hear him, the distant highway and winds muffling his whispers.

"I'll call you soon." Beth hung up the phone, giving him no time to respond. She hurried back inside to the warmth.

Leon was sitting on his bed. He'd wrapped himself in blankets as he stared listlessly ahead. There was some action movie playing in the background. Carl would probably know the name of the film, Beth thought. Beth wasn't a big movie person and could rarely remember the names of films, even if she enjoyed them thoroughly. Carl, however, could name release dates, actors, and a hundred other random bits of trivia for a shockingly large pool of films. Bethany climbed into bed next to her son, trying to hug him, but Leon pushed her away. Taking the message, Beth retreated back to her own bed, sullen. She wished she had an explanation. One to tell herself, to tell Leon.

"Mom?" Leon turned to his mother. "What about school tomorrow?" Winter break was coming up, but it was still a few weeks away. Bethany hadn't considered tomorrow. The mundane obligations of life seemed a distant priority at the moment.

"Maybe we'll take the day off." Bethany produced a fake smile and tried to sound enthusiastic. "Could go do something fun..."

"Okay." Leon sank his head down onto his knees.

"Come on!" Bethany brusquely proclaimed. "You're the only kid in the world to be bummed about a day off from school!"

"I guess." Leon wanted this day to come to an end. "I don't even have my phone."

"We can go get it tomorrow," Beth sighed. The movie Leon was watching cut to commercials. There was an advertisement for a new menu item at Burger Bank playing. Leon sat motionless on his bed, staring down at the sheets.

"Do you want to talk about tonight?" Bethany asked.

"No!" Leon exclaimed. "I just want to go home!"

Bethany couldn't muster another reply.

A few hours passed with no conversation. Leon faded to sleep with the motel television volume set low. Bethany watched her son fall asleep. His breathing was fast at first, but eventually calmed. He looked peaceful, even in such bizarre circumstances. When she was sure he was out, Beth clicked the television off. The room flooded with darkness, save for small rays of light shooting through the window blinds. Looking at her phone, she'd received two more messages. One was from Carl.

I love you, it read.

The other message was marked spam. Again, Beth read it.

Smart windows can save your energy bill up to—

Bethany marked the message as spam and deleted it. The scam messages felt especially enraging given the context of the day. Any annoyance now seemed much more potent than usual. Silencing her phone and setting an alarm for nine, Bethany tried to sleep. She lay in bed for hours, twisting and turning, lost in thought. The motel bed wasn't particularly comfortable, but it was her mind that would not let her rest. Sleep did eventually come, and Bethany fell into strange dreams.

. . .

Bethany gasped, twisting upright in a panic. She was momentarily confused about her location. Letting her heart slow and her eyes adjust to the dark, Beth looked towards her son, who was deep asleep. He was a lump underneath some bed sheets, a blob in the dark. Regardless, to a mother, his form was instantly recognizable.

Bethany desperately needed to use the bathroom and to drink some water. Grabbing a disposable cup from atop the fridge, Beth stepped into the bathroom, illuminating the mint green room with a sickly yellow light. Beth filled her cup from the sink and wetted her dry mouth. The water here tasted strange, but it was quenching all the same. She drank her plenty before sitting down to urinate. Bethany's head was pounding. She held her forehead, desperate for a way to make sense of her life. Everything of late felt like a bad dream. She wished she was in her own home, her own bathroom.

Washing her hands, Bethany headed back to bed. In the aisle formed between both beds, Bethany stood over Leon for a moment, watching him sleep. Crawling back into bed, the mattress creaking, Beth checked her phone. She'd received another text, just more spam

Outdoors, too much of an eyesore? Window removal is fast and easy with our patented beleaguerment paneling systems—

Bethany marked the message as spam and deleted it. Putting her phone away, the room faded into dark. Now that she was awake, there was no falling back asleep. She lay in bed, staring up at the ceiling. Her head was aflame, whirling with thoughts. Bethany wondered how Carl was coping, if he was sleeping. Bethany kept thinking about Leon's violent fit. How he kicked and clawed at his father. His screams sounded so desperate. She could still hear the exact sound he made in her head. The fervor in Leon's voice, the desperation. Leon had never made those kinds of sounds before, never vocalized such intense enthrallment and urgency.

I found it first! Leon's screams had imprinted themselves into her mind. It was another vivid trauma for her to carry. Bethany closed her eyes, wishing she could toggle sleep on and off like it was a light switch.

A bright blue light flashed past the Parson's motel window, perforating the blinds before vanishing into the dark. Briefly, it illuminated the room in a sickly color, casting large blocky shadows from the shape of the blinds. The bumpy popcorn ceiling was illuminated and briefly looked like a rough stormy sea. Its ridges were tidal waves crashing through shadowy oceans. Through the fleshy veils of her eyelids, Bethany saw brief bright flashes of movement. Opening them, she was greeted by a dark room. Looking around, she felt paranoid, foolish. Bethany observed all corners of the room for minutes. Everything looked usual. Just as Beth was about to close her eyes, once more a bright blue illumination settled directly behind the motel room's window. It remained completely motionless, casting an ominous glow into the room.

Initially, she believed the light to be a car driving past the highway, angled just right to illuminate their room, only for a terrifying realization to paralyze her. She was on the second floor. No car in the parking lot could point its headlights directly through the window. The source was coming from directly outside their room.

Leaping from her bed, Bethany sprinted towards the door, double-checking it was secured. It was locked and bolted. Someone or something was outside their room. Carefully looking through the blinds, Bethany was unable to see out past the balcony. All her vision was consumed by a sickly blue, like it'd replaced the very atmosphere. The light, the glow, held no source. It simply sat in place, illuminating itself and its surroundings. Bethany reasoned to herself. This had to be Carl's doing. This all had to be some sick joke, some horrid mind game. This couldn't be real.

"Mom?" A sleepy voice called out. Leon raised himself out of bed, tossing his sheets to the side.

Bethany turned away from the window towards her son, staring at him in disbelief. Leon was lit in stripes of blue, where the lights poked through and bathed him in a glow. She was shaking, a great nausea and urge to collapse overwhelming her. She stood steadfast against the sickening barrage, determined to protect Leon and herself.

"Do you see it now?" Leon asked bluntly, standing from his bed in yesterday's wrinkled garbs.

"Yes..." Bethany shook. "Yes."

As if upon Bethany's acknowledgement of the anomaly's existence, it vanished, the room once more nearly pitch black. Bethany and Leon looked at each other as their eyes adjusted. The only accompanying ambience in the room was their breathing and the steady whirring of the furnace.

"Is it gone?" Bethany breathed uneasily. Her eyes now just making out her son's form.

A great impact slammed hard against the door, shaking the walls of their motel room. The door lock remained true, but the frame splintered upon impact.

"Jesus Christ!" Bethany screamed in terror! Leon gazed forward listlessly, expectantly.

Rapidly, the door handle shook back and forth, the metal creaking and rattling as the handle flung up and down. Another powerful force pounded against the barricade, and once more wood splintered. Several successive knocks bashed at the door. The bolted chain shook and rattled. The walls creaked and the floor shook, trembling just as Beth was.

"STAY AWAY!" Bethany screamed at the top of her lungs, peddling backwards slowly, maintaining eye contact with the door and window.

The blue light returned. It flashed and strobed as if at a rave. Each pulse was accompanied by a piercing metallic sound. Bethany covered her ears, her headache amplified. Leon did not flinch but rather continued to look onward placidly at the spectacle. The blue flashed, strobing quicker and faster through the motel blinds. Bethany looked around, hysterical, wrapped in a whirling devilish light; it was as if the entire room had turned into a zoetrope.

"It belongs to me," Leon whispered to himself, unheard by his mother. He jumped off his bed and began walking towards the door.

"Please!" Beth cried. "Stop!"

The door continued to be battered and assaulted, but still it held. The light outside shone, perpetually deceiving the eyes. Bethany looked down at her hands. As the lights gleamed, time slowed down, and she could see her skin vibrating. Leon passed his mother; his slow trod focused on a single goal. In the glow, it looked as if Leon was jittering forward rather than walking, like a stop-motion puppet. He reached toward the doorknob.

"NOOO!" Bethany screamed. She mimicked the same desperation in her wails as Carl had yesterday. Leon unlocked the door, pulling it open. As it swung ajar, the flailing chain on top prevented it from fully opening. Bethany rushed towards her son, dragging him away from the door and throwing him to the floor. She slammed the door shut, locking it tight once more. Just as she did, another force pounded on the door. Bethany tumbled backwards in shock, falling to the floor next to her son. The scratchy carpet floor did little to lessen her impact.

"Oh baby..." Bethany turned to Leon. She reached out to hug him, but Leon pushed his mother back, using her as leverage to stand. Bethany began to pick herself up from the floor as well, but as she did, Leon raged.

"ITS MINE!" Leon screeched. Raising his right leg behind him, Leon kicked his mother in her throat with as much strength as he could muster. Bethany reeled on her back, her vision blurry and filled with stars. She bucked reflexively as she held her hands to her neck, gasping and spitting. On impact, Beth bit down upon her tongue, leaving the taste of copper in her mouth as she choked. Unable to breathe, she kicked and gasped.

It was all black for a moment.

"It's mine," Leon repeated in a calmer tone. A merciless look glimmered in his eyes as he peered at his mother. Leon smiled. It was finally his.

Leon released the lock and chain, letting the door swing open fully. Behind its frame was nothing but a blinding glow, such a deep blue hue that seemed darker than the bottom of the ocean and brighter than the sun. Leon held his arms out to his sides and stood as high as he could, on the tips of his toes. A final piercing screech emanated from the light before fading into a pulsating hum.

Bethany slowly started to regain her breath. Wheezing, she looked up at her son, who was directly facing the light. He was wrapped in a dazzling aura that shone so brightly that it turned the corners of his silhouette into a pure white outline. It looked as if he was being kissed by the sun; he was the golden child, the blue boy.

"No..." Bethany tried to call out, but her throat collapsed. She spat up blood and snot.

A phantasmagoric arm reached out from the glow. Sickly pink tendons wrapped around the unhallowed limb, held together by tension only. Its muscles had long since rotted. It was horrible smelling, like moldy fruit and decaying roadkill. Another rotting arm emerged from the blue light, then another, and another. Hundreds of claws reached outwards, grabbing Leon, who began to chuckle like he was being tickled. It was a child's laugh, innocent and pure, unbefitting of the moment.

It was the first time in Bethany's life that her son's laugh made her so utterly discomposed. She looked at her son, horrified, as she lifted herself from the ground. As more and more claws emerged from the glow, Bethany could no longer see her Leon. Every part of his body was ensnared. Hands ran up and down Leon, who giggled with each sensation. With a force that could ignite the atmosphere, Leon was dragged through the portal. As he disappeared into the light, so did the blue.

Seconds later, a mighty shockwave, the kind experienced in localized atom bomb detonations, exploded where the portal had just been. The motel door was ripped from its doorframe, sent tumbling against the balcony railing. Every window in the motel shattered inward simultaneously, spraying Bethany and other unlucky guests with tiny shards of glass. Beth covered her head, screaming, huddled low to the ground, as glass showered above her. In the parking lot, each car's alarm began to blare. Bethany blacked out for a second or two, then awoke screaming.

Though occupancy was low this evening, there were still a little under a dozen occupants. Each emerged from the rooms in a panic, shouting, crying, screaming for answers. Most of the car alarms were silenced by people with their remote keys, but the rabble outside grew in volume. There was a crying child and a concerned mother.

"What the fuck happened!?" a deep man's voice exclaimed.

"Holy shit was that a bomb!?" another person cried, face covered in cuts.

Beth pulled herself up from the floor, using the television cabinet to lift herself. She struggled to orient herself, the panic of watching Leon disappear doing little to clear her thoughts. The world outside was a stir, and inside her brains felt scrambled. A tight pain in her neck flared through her back as she clutched her side, coughing and panting in agony.

Taking a moment to come to terms with what had happened, Beth concluded she had no time to waste. The blue light was gone, but it could still be home with Carl. No explanation was wanted now, no logic or reason for the moment's events was desired. Now Bethany only wanted one thing. Her son.

Bethany dusted glass from her clothes. There was glass in her shoes, so she went barefoot. She grabbed her phone and keys and emerged onto the balcony, glass crunching under her feet. The smoking woman from earlier that evening wore a look of confusion and terror on her face as she watched Bethany emerge from her room. An athletic man wearing nothing but his underwear and some socks stood behind her, his hands on her shoulders.

"Hey, are you okay!?" the woman asked, her voice coarse and unsure. "Heard screaming..."

"Do you know what happened?" the man asked, faking a look of calmness. He seemed like the kind of guy who would wear shorts in Antarctica.

Bethany paid the strangers no mind, moving opposite their direction as quickly as possible as she practically leaped down the motel stairs. She left small trickles of blood behind from her cut-up feet.

"Hey, wait!" A woman called out from the balcony.

Bethany sprinted to her car, trying to call Carl, but was unable to connect. She hung up and tried again, and again, but to no avail. It seemed she had no service, but after what she'd just witnessed, Bethany lost faith in the idea of coincidences. Reaching the parking lot, Bethany climbed into her truck. Several people, all standing outside of their rooms, were watching her. Bethany felt she must look as if she was fleeing the crime scene, but she peeled out of the motel parking lot, speeding towards the highway with reckless abandon.

Shaking, Bethany called Carl once more. The call didn't go through, and Bethany hung up, starting the process over again.

"Connect, asshole!" Bethany screamed at her phone. Her throat was raw, and while shouting hurt, Bethany could not restrain her panic. She had one hand on the wheel and her eyes half-focused on the road. She swerved past a pickup, which puttered along at a snail's pace. Bethany was driving on adrenaline, instinct, and muscle memory alone, all while spamming Carl's phone. Call after call, Beth still couldn't manage to connect. Her phone could act as a wireless hotspot, yet still, no call was able to be placed.

"Please!" Bethany begged her phone, her neck burning. Still, no call would go through. Beep, the phone would ring once, fail to make a connection, and automatically hang up. Still, Bethany persisted, hoping to regain reception at any moment.

The car practically drifted as Beth took a sharp right turn, going sixty in a thirty-mile area. She was almost near the exit which headed towards Letterfaux. Beyond the windshield, the headlights illuminated the dark country road ahead. Less than half a mile and she'd be on the highway.

"COME ON! Come *on!*" Bethany chanted as the phone dialed uselessly. She raged and shouted and pleaded. Tears and hysteria enveloped her. "PICK UP!" Bethany wailed as she stared at the phone. No bars. Her head was buzzing, a powerful migraine eating at her core.

From the side of the road, beyond some trees, a sickly-looking beast emerged. Momentarily, the two locked eyes. It was a deer.

Smashing her pristine truck into the horned creature, the deer died instantaneously, turning to mush, giblets, and bone, as the front fender wrapped around its corpse. Upon impact, Bethany was flung forward, crashing through her windshield. Shredded and mangled, she was launched onto the side of the road. Her truck tumbled and spiraled until it settled in a ditch with a catastrophic halt. The twisted pile of metal was mere inches away from crushing Bethany as it ceased its rolling. Settling still in the wreckage, the truck's horn blared out in the silent winter night for a moment before dying with a whimper, a small plume of exhaust smoke and vapor raised from the wreckage.

CATCHPHRASES

Darcy's apartment was a bit of a cave with no natural illumination. To Ward, it was a maddening place that felt more like a dungeon than a home. The place was located on the first floor facing the main road. The layout of the home was mostly one large open space. The main entrance was a combination living room, dining room, and kitchen, which connected to the rest of the rooms. Darcy's bedroom was the largest, being the master bedroom. It had its own connected bathroom, which stretched the entire length of the apartment and led to a back den, where Ward did most of his work. Ward's room was originally the guest bedroom, so it was remarkably smaller than Darcy's.

Ward plucked a baby wipe from the top of the container. Running it down Darcy's left thigh, Ward cleaned feces from her old, wrinkled leg. Picking up her diaper, he carried it to the trash can. Darcy began to sponge bathe herself. She hadn't had a real bath or shower since she broke her hip, and despite the attempts at cleanliness, had a generally disgusting smell which lingered about her. She'd regained enough mobility that a bath would be feasible, but the idea was daunting, and Darcy refused such suggestions.

Running the trash out to the garbage shoot, which was a door down at the end of the hallway next to the stairwell, Ward returned to the sound of her grandmother calling out to him.

"Ward!?" Darcy called out from the toilet. Darcy always sounded desperate, like she was dying or being assailed, even for the most mundane of requests or questions.

"What's up?" Ward asked, stepping through the den and into the bath. The toilet in Darcy's bathroom was tucked in a corner between the shower and the den doorframe. Darcy had dropped her sponge; it had fallen out of her reach.

"That." She pointed. Ward sighed, picking up the sponge and handing it to her.

"I'm sorry," she cried, her face dry. "I don't mean to be a burden." It had become her catchphrase, or at least one of them she'd been repeating of late.

"You're not a burden," Ward huffed, tired of replying to the same statement with the same response, day in and day out. Ward despised his grandmother's constant wallowing. It didn't take much anymore for her to upset him. He tried to disengage from such toxic conversations, but Darcy's words had a way of stabbing beneath his skin. He had a way of escalating things as well and was trying to be better.

"Yes, I am..." Darcy sounded sorrowful as she scrubbed her ass.

After bathing, Ward got Darcy into bed. The transition from standing to climbing into bed was always a slow and difficult process. Darcy would have to back into her mattress like a truck, then lean backwards as she lifted herself up. Ward would hold her, making sure she didn't fall. The whole process was exhausting for both of them.

Ward grabbed a jacket and his stash, which was kept in an old lunchbox of his. He could use a nice buzz. It was cold in the basement exercise room, especially on these winter nights, but it beat sitting on the outdoor patio. The entire previous week had teetered on lows reaching nearly zero, and this week was looking like a repeat of last. Readying to leave, Darcy called out for him. Ward set his stuff down momentarily.

"Ward? It's not working!" Darcy shouted out another phrase of hers as she pointed towards the TV with the remote. Ward had become Darcy's personal *IT* guy. Somehow, Darcy had managed to change the HDMI input on the television. After some finagling with the remote, Ward had the TV back to normal and handed the clicker (as she called it) back to his grandmother.

With Darcy successfully channel surfing, Ward headed

downstairs to smoke. He decided to mix up his normal routine tonight by taking the main lobby stairs to his left rather than descending the stairwell toward his right. Ward generally didn't like riding any of the elevators, be it the small ones on the end of each wing or the center lobby elevator.

There were ten other apartments between Darcy's and the main lobby. There were forty-four apartments in the building, mostly occupied by the elderly. Grassy Acres was like an unofficial retirement home for mostly able-bodied geriatrics. Reaching the lobby, Ward headed downstairs. He smoked a bowl or four in the odd L-shaped room, watching videos on his phone.

Smoking was always a nice end-of-day activity. It was a vice that partially helped keep Ward in a healthy headspace. With a nice high and thirty minutes gone by, Ward headed back up to check in on Darcy. She should be in the process of fading to sleep at this point. That or shouting for Ward for help with something.

Ward returned through the same way he came, but as he strode through the building, something odd caught his eye. An apartment door was swung ajar, idly lingering. It was the home just two doors down from Darcy's. Ward believed it was Mrs. Paula who lived there, but was uncertain. He'd spoken to the neighbors before but tended to avoid contact when possible. Momentarily, Ward considered calling out to see if everything was alright, but decided against it. Either someone had forgotten to close their door or was just slipping out momentarily, Ward reasoned. He thought no more of it and headed back home.

"Hello?!" Darcy shouted out. Ward made his way into her room. All he wanted to do now was hop on his computer and distract himself. When moving back home after her accident, Darcy got herself a bed that could raise and recline. She had herself propped up and was illuminated by the glow of the television in her dimly lit room.

"Just me," Ward responded with all the energy of a corpse.

"There's something wrong with the TV again," Darcy said.

"I'm sure we can fix it," Ward sighed; head turned away from the television as he snatched the remote from Darcy's hands.

"What's the problem?" He asked, turning towards the tube, barely present in the moment.

"He's gone," Darcy said, a hint of concern and bewilderment in her voice.

"What?" Ward laughed. Darcy was watching what looked like the local news, but it was just footage of a desk with digital infographics flashing in the background. There was the time in the corner, as well as some scrolling text about the stock market at the bottom.

"The news froze," Darcy said. "It's nothing but this..."

"Weird..." Ward scratched his chest. "Must be a broadcasting error or something. Try changing channels."

"Well," Darcy sighed, "It's not worth it. I'll just go to bed."

"Good idea," Ward encouraged her. "Good night."

"Before you go," Darcy spoke in a soft demeanor as if some pathetic beggar. "Can you get me some more water?"

"Of course." Ward smiled genuinely, a rare occasion.

Handing Darcy her cup, she took it from Ward's hands slowly. Her fingers were shaking. She sipped meagerly before setting it next to her. With a sigh of relief, Darcy whispered words Ward had heard a thousand times before. They were words he hated. Words that made him furious.

"I wish I could just die," Darcy mumbled under her breath. It blended into the sound of her oxygen machine's pumping. This too was a catchphrase, the most horrid of all her repetitions. Darcy was aware of how Ward reacted to such words. It was the cause of many of their arguments. But she couldn't stop herself from saying it, so instead she just reduced the volume to a whisper. She meant every word, and despite Ward not wishing to admit it, he wished she was dead as well. Momentarily, Ward wanted to scream and stomp and spit, but he was tired. Maybe his spirit was broken, but he didn't have the energy to retaliate of late.

"Do you like silence?" Ward asked in a shallow, low tone.

"Sure." Darcy was surprised by this response.

"I don't." Ward frowned. "I need to sleep with a fan on, or something like that."

Darcy turned away from Ward. Focusing on her grandson seemingly exhausted her. Her face was wrinkled, the shadows cast deep on her skin.

"Anyway," Ward sighed, turning away from his grandma. "That's what I imagine death is like. Silence."

. . .

It was too early for Ward's taste, who awoke to a droning electric beep. Grabbing his phone, he lazily swiped the alarm. It was 6:50 a.m. Even though he'd been waking up early for years now, it never felt right. Ward was a night person or wished he was. He wanted to sink back into bed, let the sheets embrace him a little longer, but his muscles were sore, and more pressingly, Darcy was calling his name.

"WARD!?" Darcy called from her bed. Darcy usually started shouting Ward's name the minute she heard his phone blare. It had become habitual at this point.

"Hello?" Darcy called out, knowing Ward was there, but feigning as if she was alone, ever the martyr.

Ward practically fell out of bed. Wearing only sweatpants, he shuffled across the laminated floor toward Darcy's room. Ward turned on the living room lights and opened the curtains to the porch as he passed, which let in a flood of morning sun.

"Hello?" Grandma called out once more.

"Hey." Ward sighed, sliding into Darcy's bedroom. The doors of Darcy's room had been removed since she couldn't fit her walker through the frame with them installed. Thankfully, she could just manage to squeeze through the bathroom doors, so she had privacy if there were guests.

"Morning." Darcy smiled. "I need to change."

"Yeah." Ward could smell the piss.

Ward helped lift Darcy out of bed. She grasped her walker and slowly made her way to the bathroom toilet. Ward helped Darcy get undressed. The entire process was a trial, and she panted and wheezed, taking in great huffs of oxygen. The bottom of her pajamas were soaked in urine, and the bottom hem of her shirt was drenched as well. Ward helped remove her clothes and threw them into the laundry hamper adjacent to the sink. Darcy always wore a diaper, and over top of those she wore a loose plastic nappy that tightened around her waist using a simple elastic strap and button. It was an extra layer of protection, sort of. The material was see-through and flimsy, but it cleaned easily and helped reduce leaking. Darcy struggled and kicked as Ward helped remove her undergarments. She got most of it off herself, but couldn't manage on her own when the disposable reached her knees. As Ward slid the diaper down Darcy's old, wrinkled thighs, shit smeared down the sides of her legs. With a soapy rag, Ward cleaned the shit from his grandmother's legs. Darcy had been soiling herself a lot recently, so much so that it started to degrade and peel away at the skin around her groin and inner thighs. Because of this, her doctor prescribed her an ointment, one that was applied every morning.

As Darcy sat on the toilet rubbing in her prescription, Ward got to work. He disposed of the diaper and cleaned the plastic nappy with soap and water thoroughly. He then stripped Darcy's wet bedsheets, putting them in the washing machine to start a load. There was a plastic cover over the top of Grandma's mattress, which helped protect against frequent leaks. Though the sheath looked dry, Ward quickly ran a baby wipe across it for good measure. Afterwards, he washed his hands and began to brew a pot of coffee.

"Doing alright?" Ward poked his head in through the bathroom entrance, which connected to the den (the side in which the toilet sat).

"Fine." Darcy sounded exhausted. In the background, her oxygen machine pumped. She breathed in deep. "Just need to catch my breath."

"Okay." Ward smiled, waiting for Darcy to regain her strength.

Tottering to her walk-in closet, Darcy picked out her outfit for the day. It was one of the few bits of autonomy she had left in her life.

"That." Darcy pointed towards an old, green sundress.

Ward helped Darcy get changed. With groans, agony, and dismal panting, eventually, Darcy was in her daytime attire.

"What are we having for breakfast?" Darcy asked as she sat down at the dining table. The coffee filled the apartment with a warm, comforting smell.

"Want anything specific?" Ward asked.

"No." Darcy shook her head. "Orange juice."

"Okay," Ward said, his voice tired and unenthused. He felt like each day was a perpetual loop. He was a Mobius strip, entangled by his obligations and sense of self. Ward looked at the calendar hanging via colorful magnets on the fridge, spying the day's tasks. He prepared two bowls of cereal and two cups of orange juice, carefully carrying them to the table in one go (a skill developed by years of serving and bussing tables). Darcy slowly lifted a spoonful to her mouth, crunching down oats and slurping milk. Ward headed back to the kitchen to grab Darcy's morning pills.

"You've got an appointment at Dr. Kane's at three," Ward reminded Darcy as he set her pills on a napkin next to her cereal.

"Oh, that's right. Good." Darcy nodded. She drank down her cup of orange juice in a single gulp before gently setting the tiny glass down. Darcy pushed her cereal away from herself towards Ward. She'd hardly eaten anything. "I'm done."

After a brief breakfast, Ward helped Darcy get in her recliner in the living room. Getting the television turned on, she gazed listlessly forward. Her memories, cherished phantoms, wandered far beyond the boundaries of Grassy Acres. Floating thoughts dispelled into the ether.

"I'm going to shower," Ward informed her. Darcy waved her hand at him, a careless acknowledgement.

Ward had a portable waterproof Bluetooth speaker, which he hung from the shower wall. Connecting his phone to it, he put on the playlist 'Shower Music' that he made and shuffled it. There were over four hundred songs on Ward's playlist, each hand-picked personal favorites. There was a wide representation of genres and artists in his mix. Funk, jazz, rap, metal, hard rock, blues, bluegrass, swing, electronic, prog, screamo, punk—hell, it even had specific songs from video game and film soundtracks mixed in. Ward added to the playlist constantly; it was ever growing as his tastes expanded. Regardless of what music Ward played, Darcy made sure she commented on it. Darcy disliked songs with lyrics in them, only having an ear for classical music. Words diluted the art form, Darcy had once claimed.

The portable speaker had a surprising amount of oomph behind it. An enthusiastic sounding rapper spat brutal lyrics about a man's face being blown off before having a new one sewn over his old burnt flesh.

The portable speaker had a surprising amount of oomph behind it.

Fresh and clean, hair combed, and clean clothes adorned, Ward emerged from his bedroom.

"Interesting music," Darcy sneered.

"Certainly is." Ward smiled, wearing a shit-eating grin. Lately, though he would never admit it, Ward had been listening to music he knew would provoke his grandmother. She hated rap especially.

Setting up his laptop on the dining room table, Ward clocked into work. He had to fill out a self-assessment by the end of the week, and figured he'd get it done today. He could reasonably claim he'd spent most of his half-day working on his assessment. In actuality, most of his time working was spent playing video games or scrolling through forums. Ward was never one to leave free money on the table. Darcy continued to flip through channels, mindlessly passing by one program after the next.

Darcy loved to watch her game shows before lunch. At 11:00 a.m., *Steal or Deal* came on. At 11:30 a.m., T*he Price is Right* aired. Darcy had been watching *The Price is Right* for more than four decades now. Ward passively enjoyed it. It held with it a certain air of nostalgia. Ward would watch it with Darcy when she babysat him as a kid. The host was lovable as well, though not a fan favorite like Bob was.

"What channel again?" Darcy asked, like she did each day.

"Nine," Ward informed her.

Darcy stared down at the remote, looking it up and down like she was diffusing a bomb. Eventually, she switched to channel nine. A commercial was playing, blaringly loud. Because of her poor hearing, Darcy kept the television volume up extremely high. Commercial volumes tended to be much louder than the actual shows, so during commercial breaks, it wasn't uncommon for the advertisements to be practically screaming.

"...alk to your doctor about Phemretroval and see if it's right for you!" the television boomed. Six years ago, when Darcy's husband, Ward's grandfather, was still alive and life seemed more normal, Ward had gotten his grandparents a soundbar for Christmas. He installed it the same day he gave it to them, made it so that it turned on and off with the TV, so they couldn't mess it up. At least the sound quality was nice when he watched a film or show with Darcy, but it made some ads unbearable.

The game shows came and went. They were the same thing every day, just with slight variations in the games and the products they advertised. When noon arrived, just like breakfast, Darcy asked, "So, what's for lunch?"

"We have plenty of leftovers, or I could make you a sandwich." Ward closed his laptop. He dragged his feet towards the kitchen, his socks sweeping the floor. He'd barely managed any work.

"Mmmmhhhmm," Darcy mumbled to herself, "What leftovers?"

Ward opened the fridge; the bulb inside hummed loudly. He needed to go grocery shopping soon, probably a chore for Saturday. There was enough food to last till then.

"Let's see..." There were three containers of leftovers that they needed to eat. "A little bit of pulled pork... Uhh... some raviolis and..." Ward forgot what was in the other container. Opening it up, he recoiled at the smell. "... and that's it." Ward tossed the entire container out with the trash. It was old and falling apart anyway.

When Ward first moved into Darcy's a year ago, he learned a few things about his grandmother's meal preferences as well as her lack of food preparation safety knowledge. She had strange and dangerous beliefs and behaviors regarding food. Stuff like the dangers of letting raw chicken touch other foods, for example, salmonella, no joke. Darcy frequently ate moldy bread, saying simply to "Pick around the bad bits."

One night, Ward made burgers and fries. After getting herself some ketchup, Darcy ran her finger across the top of the bottle, licking it with delight. Ward didn't use ketchup that night, and that bottle became Darcy's personal condiment. Darcy rarely washed her hands after using the bathroom, and Ward would constantly have to remind her to do so. Ward wondered how many meals she had prepared for him when he was a kid where she had used the restroom prior. When Ward raised complaints to his grandma, her go-to response was somewhere in the ballpark of calling him a *paranoid germaphobe.*

"I'll have my favorite," Darcy said. "And iced tea." Darcy's favorite was a sandwich that Ward found absolutely foul. It was a remnant of World War II, when rationing in America was at full peak. The sandwich was peanut butter and mayonnaise on white bread.

"Sure." Ward nodded. As he did, his cellphone dinged loudly. Checking it, the message was a reminder from Dr. Kane's office about today's appointment.

"Anyone important?" Darcy asked.

"No just a friend," Ward lied, scratching his ear.

Delivering Darcy her sandwich and tea, Ward headed back to the kitchen and microwaved the remaining leftover pork for himself.

"We have any chips?" Darcy asked as she chewed. Ward opened the pantry to check as the microwave spun.

"Pretzels, okay?" he asked.

"Sure." Darcy sounded disappointed.

Ward retrieved the bag of pretzels, which crinkled loudly in his hands. Removing the clip, Ward poured them onto Darcy's plate until she said when. She raised her hand up like an officer telling a citizen to halt.

The microwave beeped. Ward retrieved his piping hot pork from the microwave. When he lifted the paper towel from atop the glass bowl, steam simmered upwards, which sat in a pool of its own, bubbling fat. Ward had overcooked the pork a little bit, but it would still taste good, especially when doused in barbeque sauce.

Lunch was fine enough. Ward could always hear Darcy's chewing, and it bothered him slightly. Her teeth were like firecrackers popping. Ward sometimes felt he was finding reasons to hate his grandmother more and more frequently and wondered what it said about himself. Noon passed, and the day continued.

A few hours later, the power went out in the apartment. In the black cave of a home, the few windows, all covered, made apparent the tomb-like design of their home.

"Oh my ..." Darcy gasped, startled. Nearly immediately, only ten seconds or so after the outage, the power returned. Darcy's oxygen machine whirred back on, pumps buzzing back to life. The smoke alarms beeped, and electricity buzzed through the building. The television turned back on.

"... lucky you were around to keep ..." some show played in the background, given no heed.

"Brown outs..." Ward said out loud before turning his attention back to work. Fortunately for him, he used a laptop, so nothing was lost, nor any inconvenience due to the outage other than waiting for the internet to restart. The brownout was about the most eventful thing that had happened this week, hell, maybe this month.

A few more hours passed, and it was time to take Darcy to her doctor's appointment. The process of getting Darcy out of the house was arduous at best and horrendous at worst. Ward would first head to the parking deck in the basement. Passing his little smoking spot, he'd retrieve the car and park in front of the apartment patio, making sure Darcy's seat was closest to the curb. Then Ward would head inside, slowly escorting his grandmother out, making sure to hold the front gate for her.

Getting Darcy to climb in or out of the car was by far the most difficult process of traveling. If something could be described as the opposite of acrobatics, this would probably qualify. Not only did Ward have to carry the majority of Darcy's weight, but the whole time she trembled and shook, making it even more difficult. The cold amplified this tenfold.

Despite the obstacles, Ward got Grandma in the passenger seat and the two set forth to Dr. Kane's, which was about fifteen minutes away. He used to need the GPS to get there, but he'd driven Darcy so many times now that it became muscle memory. Looking down the road ahead, Ward realized he needed to wash his car window. A layer of film and grime had built up on it. It was still easy enough to see through the windshield, but it was pretty damn dirty.

Taking a puff from her portable oxygen tank, Darcy slowly regained her breath. About five minutes into the drive, Darcy said something new, something Ward hadn't heard his grandmother say before. Her words were hefty, like bricks in a fishnet tied to a kitten in a lake.

"Your face looks like his." She inhaled more oxygen.

"Excuse me?" Ward said, quickly glancing at his grandma before putting his eyes back on the empty rural road.

"You know I love you, and you mean the world to me," Darcy said. She took a puff of her portable oxygen.

There was a time, long ago, when Ward not only loved Darcy but adored her. When Ward was a kid, young and in the fog of youth, his grandmother seemed almost like a magical being to him. She would concoct wondrous games for him to play when babysitting. She would spoil him every chance she had. Ward still loved his grandma, but he didn't like her. It was now an obligatory love, one formed by circumstance, familial ties, empathy, and respect for one's past. Ward wondered if love for relatives was akin to a contract. He regretted the contract he was in tremendously, even if he was proud of his actions.

"Yeah..." Ward was confused. "Who do I look like?" Pulling up to a stop sign on an empty road, Ward idled momentarily to look his grandma in the eyes.

"My first son," she said bluntly.

"Like Dad?" Ward asked, concerned. "I mean yeah..."

"No..." Darcy spoke low, slow, and somber. Ward flicked the right turn single on, it ticked and ticked as he rounded an intersection.

"Well... Dan was actually my second..." Darcy shivered as she dropped the bombshell of information on Ward.

"What?" Ward was shocked. "What are you saying?" This was new information.

"He died so early... Just three months." Darcy's breath was labored, heavy, but she carried on. "He passed away in his sleep. Doctors couldn't tell me why... His name was Henry."

"Jesus," Ward said softly. Darcy puffed away at her oxygen. They were close to the doctor's office, only a few minutes away. "Why are you telling me this?"

"Even though he was just a baby, I can see his face in yours." Darcy cried gentle tears. "Sometimes I wonder, when I finally die, will I get to meet him in heaven? Will he be all grown up?"

Darcy paused for a long time.

"I... Uhmmm," Ward stuttered. He didn't know what to say, how to handle the conversation. He continued to drive in silence, wanting to say something but unable to find the words.

"I don't know if I believe in heaven." Darcy looked directly at Ward, like she was witnessing a miracle in him. "But I want to die and find out. I want to see my baby again."

Darcy coughed, struggling after her long monologues. This was the first real conversation Ward felt he had ever had with his grandma. For a moment, he saw a person once more. In that brief realization, he shuddered, holding back years of suppressed tears.

"What..." Ward was almost shaking, but remained calm. "What about your current son?"

"No one visits me anymore. You know that," Darcy said. Ward wanted to dispute her but knew she was right. Ward hadn't seen Dad or anyone else around in months. All they did was send token text messages or make short, awkward phone calls.

"Yeah," Ward huffed, his breathing matching Darcy's for a moment. "I... I..." Ward watched the road fly by as he spoke. For a moment, it felt like he wasn't driving, just gliding. "What... Oh man... What was his name again?"

"Henry." Darcy smiled.

"Henry," Ward repeated. The two stopped speaking for the remainder of the short drive. Only public radio and the sounds of the road were diegetic.

Ward pulled into a handicap spot when they got to the doctor's office. There were an unusually small number of cars in the parking spaces; only four other spots out of about twenty were occupied. Darcy pulled down the passenger sun visor, and from it fell a blue and white handicap parking permit, which she placed on the dashboard of the car. She took an extra second to make sure she had no streaks or smeared makeup. Even in the worst physical state of her life, Darcy found it necessary to look her best when in public.

Dr. Kane's office was in a small lot with a single commercial building. To the right of the doctor's office was a veterinarian. To the left was a Mexican restaurant, and to the left of that restaurant was a hair salon. The doctor's office looked dark inside, as if it was closed. Suspicious, before helping Darcy out of her seat, Ward checked the doors, and sure enough, the place was locked up tight. The sign on the door even read closed. Feeling insane, Ward checked his phone, and sure enough, the reminder text he'd received earlier this day confirmed he was at the right place at the right time. Maybe there was an error, he told himself. He did a quick loop of the parking lot; the restaurant appeared open, and there were a few workers and customers that could be seen beyond the windows. The salon appeared to be closed, as well as the veterinarians. Ward climbed back into the car, shaking his head in frustration and confusion.

"What's going on?" Darcy asked.

"Buildings closed, nobody's there," Ward answered.

"Huh," Darcy mused, "maybe you got the wrong day?"

"No." Ward shook his head. "I got a message from them this morning confirming the appointment."

"Strange," Darcy huffed.

"I'm going to call." Ward looked up Dr. Kane's office number online. After several rings, nobody picked up, and eventually the phone went to voicemail.

"We're sorry we couldn't answer you at this time. If you're

having a medical emerg..." The automated message played. Ward hung up, flabbergasted.

"No reply," he sighed.

"Try knocking," Darcy suggested. She inhaled several puffs in rapid succession.

"Careful with that, or you'll start seeing stars." Ward climbed from the car, leaving the door open. After several obligatory knocks on the office door to no result, Ward headed back to the driver's seat.

"Guess we'll reschedule." Ward hid his anger. He hated having Darcy exert herself for no reason. The drive back home was mostly mundane. Ward had to halt for a while as a group of deer crossed the road. They were sickly looking, as if wasting away. Otherwise, it was an easy trip. Ward kept thinking about what Darcy told him in the quiet, wondering if anyone else in the family knew about it. Seeing the tears in his grandma's eyes was the closest to connecting with her Ward had come in a very long time. With fortunately minimal struggle, Ward got Darcy back inside the apartment and parked the car.

The rest of Ward and Darcy's day was slow, save for the normal obligations of life. Ward scheduled a new appointment for Darcy online for tomorrow, same time. He then spent the rest of the afternoon playing video games, trying not to think, until dinner soon arrived.

"I'll take a screwdriver," Darcy ordered. It was almost five.

At her request, Ward obliged.

"Bless you, dear." Darcy momentarily grabbed Ward's wrist as she thanked him. He could feel her brittle fingers wrap around him with her wrinkly skin. It amazed him how much of a roil of emotion Darcy dug up within him. Halcyon memories, disdain, sympathy, disgust. Ward feared one day he'd become just like Darcy: wheezing for air, begging for death. Nothing but a mockery of his former self, imprisoned by his body's failing constitution, pining for better days while revealing long hidden secrets on a lark.

The phone rang. It was Aunt Clara wanting to speak to Darcy.

Ward handed over the phone to Darcy, and the two friends chatted for a bit. Between Darcy's slow labored speech and Clara's witlessness, the conversation moved at a snail's pace. When Ward first started taking care of his grandma, Aunt Clara had accused him of attempting to steal millions of her dollars in inheritance money. Of course, though she did have a substantial amount saved, it was not nearly that much. Ward was also never motivated by the money. Sure, Ward thought some inheritance would be nice, but he took on the role of caretaker to help his grandma and family first and foremost. That intent didn't stop familial drama from occurring.

Ever since then, Ward felt paranoid when Darcy spoke on the phone with family, especially Clara. Darcy tended to exaggerate the truth and play the victim. It, though albeit unintentionally, sometimes put Ward in a bad light, especially to people in his family who already saw him as a bit of a black sheep. Hell, he'd felt like a bit of an outcast from the rest of the family for as long as he could remember. In truth, Ward had made himself one. Ward was more like Darcy than he realized and had a bit of a martyr complex at times as well. He was still young and healthy enough that these traits hadn't been exaggerated by pain, time, and trauma.

Ward prepared dinner, eavesdropping on his grandma's conversation as she chatted away. He was making a simple meal. He had some baked beans warming on the stove top and was cooking up some frozen burger patties. He caramelized some onions, washed some lettuce, and sliced some thin pieces of tomato. Once everything was prepared, he set the table.

"I've got to go. Dinner's ready," Darcy said into the phone. "Alright, talk to you later."

The oxygen machine, a constant drone, buzzed in synchronicity with Darcy's panting. Dinner, like lunch, was passable. Ward overcooked the burgers a bit, but they tasted fine enough. Smothered in baked beans and ketchup certainly made it more palatable. Darcy had no words for Ward, having used most of them up, it seemed. Ward was pleased with this. The rest of the evening after dinner was spent doing chores and or nothing at all.

"I'm your host, Alex Treb..." The TV boomed. It was seven thirty; time for another one of Darcy's favorite game shows. Ward would sometimes watch TV passively with Darcy. Mostly, however, Ward would scroll through his phone to kill time, occasionally glancing up at the screen.

8:00 p.m. came.

"Well..." Darcy slowly lifted herself up from the couch, leaning against her rollator. "Time for bed."

Darcy had soiled herself again. There once was a time, not too long ago, when Darcy would let Ward know when she soiled herself, piss or otherwise. Now, Darcy didn't care. She'd rather stew in her waste than exert the effort required to go use the bathroom. Initially, if Ward would smell Darcy, he'd make a fuss, forcing her to clean up and get changed. Now, however, Ward had no energy to do so. If grandma wanted to sit in shit, it was her own priority. He'd gotten mostly used to the smell.

This essentially meant Darcy usually only headed to the bathroom a few times a day, sometimes only once in the morning and once at night. Burning skin and rolling liquids paid grandma no heed. No stink too foul could deter her amotivation for simple hygiene necessities, which many take for granted as a normal routine. Hygienic practices never were much of a priority in her life to begin with. Her age and pains only amplified such tendencies. Ward hated himself for not forcing Darcy to change more often, but he as well lost motivation via attrition.

Helping Darcy slip into her pink pajamas, Ward escorted her back to bed. He would have to go ahead of her, grabbing the oxygen tube to ensure it didn't get tangled underneath Darcy's walker's wheels.

"Thank you," Darcy panted as Ward threw a sheet on top of her. "Can you get me some more water?" Darcy handed her cup over. Ward was always happy to reply with that request. Grandma still probably didn't consume enough liquids, but she had improved drastically. Still, often Darcy would say stuff like: *X has water in it.* X being whatever alcoholic drink she was having at the time.

Ward couldn't help but think about the conversation the two had on the drive to the doctors. The revelation didn't bother him. Rather, it fascinated him that Darcy chose to confide in him. He wondered if it was because she trusted him, or if he was the only person she had left. There was seemingly no prompt. As if she was reading Ward's mind, Darcy spoke up.

"I miss him. Miss my friends, my family."

"Yeah." Ward didn't know what to say. He never knew what to say to those kinds of catchphrases. They were a barrage of miseries Ward was immensely underqualified to handle. Lingering in awkward silence, Darcy flicked the bedroom TV on.

"I'm going for my walk," Ward said.

"Okay," Darcy didn't turn from the flashing light of the television.

Ward had talked to Darcy about marijuana before. She was aware that he smoked it, but she believed dope to be a dangerous thing, a drug used by killers and gang members that could cause a sudden, deadly overdose or a sudden violent turn to a life of crime. Darcy would, of course, immensely disapprove of Ward using the gym as his own personal hotbox. He wasn't about to give her gossip ammunition that could cause him legitimate personal and legal problems.

Heading to the basement, Ward decided to go the same way he had last night to check if that one apartment door was still ajar. The hallways of Grassy Acres always felt strange to Ward. It was not that they were disturbing in any traditional sense, but they had an eerie atmosphere. The ground was green carpet, with golden lines adjacent to the walls, which were covered in a striped wallpaper pattern that repeated from yellow to white over and over again. The lights, which hung up between each apartment door, gave off an almost yellow-greenish hue, filling the interior with a sickly miasma of colors.

Dismayingly, Ward found that Mrs. Paula's door remained open, still slightly ajar, same as yesterday. Inside, the lights were dark, and almost nothing could be seen save for dim shapes and outlines of furniture. For a moment, Ward wanted to call out to ask if everything was alright. His neck tightened, and he gulped. It didn't feel safe to do so. Furthermore, he didn't want to be the person to discover the corpse of some elderly spinster. Ward hated interacting with the cops and didn't need more trauma in his life. Besides, if everything was okay, he didn't want to be accused of trespassing. Ward transitioned from the carpeted halls to the tiled floors of the main lobby, putting the ajar door in the back of his mind. *Not my problem.*

Ward decided to take the lobby elevator, contrary to his normal preferences. As he waited for its arrival, he felt suddenly tense. It seemed like he was being watched, despite the emptiness of the lobby. Looking down, he could see his reflection in the freshly polished floor. Everything felt normal, but a panic attack stabbed at his chest, and Ward felt a slight wooziness spinning in his head.

DING! The elevator door slid open, startling Ward. It was empty.

Stepping inside, Ward pressed the basement key. Slowly, like the old and durdeling contraptions they were, the elevator descended downwards. Its lights flickered briefly as the suspended box shook downwards. With another DING, the elevator doors slid open. The basement hallway connecting the gym, parking lot, and pipe works was particularly dark tonight. The light bulb that hung in front of the elevator was out, cloaking the area in a shroud that was only pierced by distant lights coming from the garage.

Ward stepped inside the gym, closing the green double doors and sliding to the floor with his back against them as usual. Retrieving from his Royal Scepter whiskey bag a bowl, a grinder, and a lighter, Ward spent a lot of time smoking. The strange L-shaped room always felt bizarre to him. He never felt a sense of danger here, but it also didn't feel safe. Nearly forty minutes passed as Ward filled the room with smoke; he tried to swallow as much of it as he could, but that wasn't always possible. Ward had watched a podcast on his phone, mostly zoning out and enjoying his accumulating high. Sufficiently obliterated, Ward packed up his buds and accessories.

Swinging open the gym doors with unnecessary muster, wind

bellowed like a screaming banshee from the garage past the gym into the pipework maze beyond the elevator. It ruffled Ward's short hair.

Ward waited as the elevator descended from an upper floor. *Ding.* Ward stepped into the elevator and pressed the button for his floor. As he did so, Ward heard a startling sound.

SHHRRRIIIEKAALL!

It was coming from deep within the basement pipe works, but the echo made its origin impossible to place. It was a high-pitched shriek, like a guttural death wail. It sounded nothing like the howls the wind made through the basement corridors. This sounded like it originated from a person. Shivers quite literally accelerated up Ward's spine, who clicked repeatedly on the door close button; a sudden flight reflex kicking in, pumping adrenaline through his veins. The howl continued, turning into a deep gargle that on the wind sounded like blisters popping. As the elevator doors slowly closed, Ward huffed a great sigh of relief.

"What the fuck," Ward muttered to himself, shaken and uncertain.

Creeping through the halls back home, Ward practically sprinted by Paula's door, not even bothering to look inside. Everything felt cursed. It seemed as if the very building could swallow him whole. Once at his door, Ward quickly unlocked it with his key. When inside, he slammed the door shut and latched it, sighing audibly.

"Shits making me paranoid." Ward wanted to blame the weed, but he knew that wasn't it. Something was wrong. Today felt off.

"Hello!?" Darcy called out from her room. "Hello?"

"Hey, Grandma," Ward called out, stepping into her dark bedroom, which was momentarily illuminated in deep blues and purples from the television. Ward could already feel his buzz dying. He wished he could stay high forever.

"It's not working." Darcy pointed towards the television. The local news was playing. "There's no sound." Darcy had the television on mute.

Ward's phone vibrated, but he ignored it for now. He had

explained to Darcy where the mute button was a million times. She was always accidentally pressing it. Regardless, Ward repeated his shtick and showed her the mute button. He even made Darcy press it herself. Audio returned, as always obnoxiously loud.

"...tring of disappearances. Police say to remain vigilant, be cautious, and report any suspicious activity to the authorities. In oth..." The newscasters blabbered in the background.

"Okay, thank you." Darcy turned her attention back to the news. "You're a good kid." The oxygen machine pumped especially hard as Darcy said it, as if it was laughing at the statement.

"Uhh-huh." Ward left Darcy's bedroom.

"...ergence of a new wasting disease that has been affecting local wild..." The TV audio faded into the background. Ward hated the news. It depressed him more than things usually did. Even if the story was just local dribble or heartwarming fluff, he couldn't stand it.

Ward checked his phone. He'd received a message from a friend asking if he wanted to play some video games. Normally, Ward would say yes, but tonight he didn't have much energy for it. This evening felt heavy, imposing. Ward was still experiencing the aftereffects of adrenaline; he felt uneasy. His hands tremored like his grandmother's. Ignoring his friend's outreach, Ward sat in front of his computer, staring at the desktop screensaver. His mind wandered for some time. In the background, the sound of central heat whirring on vibrated the walls. Darcy's television and oxygen machine were present, but difficult to hear, blending in with the noises of the complex. Eventually, Ward's buzz faded completely, and his mind returned to the moment. He realized he was doing nothing, just staring into nothing, just thinking of nothing, just being nothing, feeling like nothing, indulging in nothing, nothing.

Ward decided to go to bed early tonight. Checking in one more time with Darcy to confirm she was okay (she'd fallen asleep with the television on, which Ward turned off for her), Ward headed to bed. It wasn't even nine yet. Most nights, he found himself going to bed sometime between eleven and midnight. On rare occasions, usually against his better judgement, he stayed up to one or two in the morning.

Lying in bed, Ward didn't feel physically exhausted. It was mental exhaustion; his brain felt rattled. Ward decided to masturbate, hoping the post-ejaculation sleepiness could help him pass out swiftly. He just wanted to turn his brain off. Though he could become stiff and erect, the pleasure of his repeated stroking was almost nonexistent. He felt like he was going through the motions, up and down. Ward's orgasm was of no pleasure to him. It felt, in fact, like an inconvenience to even toss the tissue into the tiny trash can near his bed.

Ward's plan failed. When in bed, stirring and sore, certain sleep is an impossibility; it feels like each second is an hour. He had no power over his body, just like his grandmother. Underneath his blanket, Ward accumulated sweat and felt itchy. As soon as he threw the blanket off though, his body began to shiver. He was either too warm or too cold this night. Hours of kicking and torment and apathy eventually yielded Ward results. He began to drift asleep.

Ward's cell phone crackled, startling him to attention. He'd forgotten to put his phone on sleep mode. It was a loud, upsetting noise, a repeating, distorted electronic buzz which sounded like saw blades screaming into a synthesizer. Grabbing his phone from his side table, he saw it was an emergency alert message. A yellow flashing bar lit up his cell phone as he silenced the alert wail and set his phone to sleep. Wide awake again, out of curiosity, Ward clicked on the alert, expecting it to be a code Amber or something of the like. It was not.

The alert read: *Ohio State Emergency Alert System: Imminent Threat.*

That's all.

"What the fuck." Ward double, then triple-read the message, his eyes adjusting to the screen light in the dark of his room. "What threat?" Ward had seen plenty of emergency alert messages before, tests or otherwise, but none that read like this. Someone was probably going to get fired over a typo for causing undue panic. Ward lay back down in bed, trying to temper his anxiety and confusion while balancing an attempt at comfort on his painful mattress. His body was too sore, though, and his mind too curious.

Ward grabbed a hoodie, covering his otherwise bare chest. He was wearing tennis shorts and was barefoot. Zipping up, he opened the porch doors, bracing himself for a cold winter night. Wind bellowed inside as the doors swung open. Outside, the air was stabbing; it nipped and ripped at his bare legs. There was an incredibly deep fog that coated the land like a base of white acrylic upon an untreated canvas. Nothing but dark and rolling air could be seen beyond half a mile. Across from Darcy's patio, on the sidewalk, was a streetlamp. Normally, this late at night, it would be blazing bright. In this fog, however, even the brightest lights were swallowed up, reduced to specks the sizes of fireflies. Looking up, Ward could not even see the clouds. All his vision yielded was murky, dark, and thick mists.

Ward enjoyed the cool air for some time, despite the intensity of the breeze. He had been sweating a lot in bed, and the wind massaged his sore muscles. The shivers held off for a moment. It was extraordinary outside; Ward's senses felt heightened. It was silent save for the wild huffs of air, spirits free in the frigid lone. Visually, the outside was transformed into a surreal landscape that turned an everyday known location into an alien place shrouded in mystery. Ward could barely see past the fence boundaries of the patio, and all things beyond the fog turned to distorted shapes. It felt like there was movement in the beyond, or like the fog itself was moving in ways it shouldn't.

It was strange, though Ward had seen the view from this patio a million times, it never once was so beautiful to him as it was now. During clear summer days with boring blue skies and bright white puffy clouds, this area was but a mundane field with a few trees and a small road intersecting a parking lot. Now, though it felt like this place was a blank canvas, anything could be out there.

Ward began to shiver but wanted to stay outside a little longer. It was peaceful. For the first time in a long time, right now, he felt free. There was nothing that felt impossible anymore. Ward stepped forward, past the small, neglected garden, to the edge of the patio gate. He could see some cars, their shapes like blobs, edges round and soft. The sister apartment to the east was a large, imposing black rectangle obscured by weather. As the wind bellowed, the building seemed to shift some.

Ward headed back inside, freezing, but the image of the cold foggy night stayed prominent in his head. Climbing back into bed and snuggling into his bed sheets, he thought of the fog. He thought of the screams from the basement. He thought of his grandma, of her first son.

THE DREAMS THAT DIE WITH ME

The dreams that die with me await me in my slumber. Of fields white and gray, the clouds above rolling thunder. In past youth, we wielded unchecked ambition, no foresight, no friction. Only intention, imagination, a canvas, fission. These visions of the mind seen so clear as if sunlight. God rays and golden light, experience the limit, the hands that cannot mimic. For it seems dreams and schemes only are deemed possible in the beginning. When taken to task, deep-rooted beliefs batter the meek. There is seldom hope for winning in dungeons of the mind. The potential drives forward, a greater dangling carrot so close yet undefined, unreached, illusory, like the dreams that die with me; water yet breached in a black, empty sea. Floating upside down, we seek the surface. Yet deeper we swim with greater purpose. Until the depths convert us, invert us, assert mirthless our happenstance, birthless. No more pressure can hurt us. We are one with the water, and the water owns us; it collects on our debts. The dreams that die with me, I see them in my final breath. To drown could be a welcome rest.

THE SIXTEEN-FINGERED MAN

"Yeah, well... I really prefer not to know," Adrian replied.

"So, you don't finish movies!?" Shantel was shocked.

"No, of course not!" Adrian scoffed. "What's the point?"

"To..." Shantel was at a loss. "...see how they end, to finish 'em?"

"But if I know how it ends, it's boring!" Adrian laughed, taking a sip from his liter of Coke. He emptied about a quarter of it and filled the rest with rum. It was perfectly discreet so long as they weren't obvious about it. The campers had long since gone to bed anyway; it was a little past midnight.

"How is it boring!?" Shantel laughed. "Lemme get some of that!" She gestured to the bottle, snatching it from Adrian's hands.

"I don't know," Adrian said as Shan took a swig, "Half the time I can't even sit through a movie anyway, and when I do, the endings usually suck. I'd rather just stop when I get bored and imagine the rest."

"Wow... I can't believe you!" Shantel was agape in disbelief, despite her brimming smile.

I can't believe I met you at this shitty job." Adrian scooted closer to Shantel. The two were sitting in Adrian's rooms, using his bed as a couch. Accommodations were rather bare bones.

"Shut up, you weirdo!" Shantel laughed awkwardly, taking another drink as she shoved Adrian's shoulder to push him away.

"No, I'm serious!" Adrian smiled, his heart beating and pants tight as he imagined the fun he could have with Shan. Adrian was deviously handsome and diabolically charismatic. "Last year, I worked with this social worker. He was overseeing my training, but he hardly spoke to me or the kids. *That* was a real weirdo."

"Well, I'm glad I'm better company." Shan handed Adrian back the bottle. "It's late, I'm drunk, exhausted, I'll see you in the morning." Shan stood from Adrian's bed, the springs creaking from the movement.

"You sure you don't want to stay a little longer? Help me finish off this bottle?" Adrian shook the liter, the contents swooshing inside. As he did, he ran his free hand down Shantel's arm. Her skin was soft and warm.

"I'm good. It's almost midnight," Shan said, shaking off his advances. They were both pretty drunk, though sobriety most likely would not have prevented Adrian from hitting on Shantel at some point during the week. "I always stop right before I make a mistake." Shan winked at Adrian, heading out of his room.

"Okay." He was disappointed, like a sad puppy. "See you tomorrow."

Adrian and Shantel were working as counselors for Bright Future's summer camp program at Salt Fork Park. It provided minimal pay but went towards college credits. It was Thursday night, almost Friday, and tomorrow the kids headed home in the evening. They had rock climbing in the morning, lunch, then free hours until check out around four. Shantel was twenty and Adrian twenty-two. Each of them oversaw separate groups. Adrian was a camp counselor for a group of twelve boys, while Shantel watched over a group of ten girls.

Despite it being past curfew, four kids had snuck their way into a single room. The kids, in no particular order, were Harold, age fourteen. Bethany, fourteen as well. Edda, eleven. And finally, James, ten. James had brought his Game Kid, and the four were taking turns playing. Last night, Herald had 'acquired' some candy, chips, and soda from the kitchen. Despite the group's minor mischief, they'd managed to remain under the radar. This was the second night in a row they hung out after hours, and the counselors were none the wiser. The boys and girls weren't allowed to be in the same room together unsupervised, as one of the rules of law at camp.

"No, that's wrong! Ultra-Max doesn't transform into..." James was arguing with Bethany about a cartoon when footsteps rang through the hallway. Each kid gasped, holding their breath. The only light in the room was from the glow of the GameKid, which dimly illuminated the bottom of each of the breathless children's faces in an electronic green. The footsteps vanished into the night.

"That was scary." Edda was flushed from holding her breath, though nobody could tell in the dark.

"Yeah," James agreed, his voice timid.

"It's my turn!" Bethany snatched the toy from Harold, her volume control non-existent.

"Hey, I didn't die yet!" Harold retaliated, scrambling to regain control of the toy as Beth pushed him away with her left shoulder.

"Ssshhh!" Edda shushed at the two, holding her left index finger over her lips with her brow furled. "Keep screaming 'n' you'll get us grounded!" Edda loudly whispered.

"Sorry." James apologized despite his innocence in the rabble.

The three huddled around Bethany as she played. The level involved bridges and pitfalls, in which fish jumped from the water below, attacking the main character. She'd gotten the firepower up and was about to finish the level when the console flickered off, leaving the already dark room in pitch blackness.

"Oh, what the...!" Bethany shouted way too loudly. James, Harold, and Edda all shushed Beth, certain they'd be caught. It was fortunate for the four that Shantel had gone to bed, and Adrian was too drunk to care.

"Sorry. It turned off," Beth said. She flicked the power on. Briefly, the game lit up before immediately powering off again. She repeated this process until no flash could be produced. Now the four sat in darkness, save a sliver of moonlight which trickled in from the window.

"Batteries must've died," James grumbled, disappointed.

"Did you bring extras?" Harold asked, an urgency in his voice. "I wasn't finished..."

"No..." James almost cried. The room was silent, all but their breaths heard, and their silhouettes seen.

"Now what?" Bethany asked after a sip of her soda.

"It's scary in the dark." James jittered as he grabbed his GameKid from Beth, holding it tight like a stuffed animal.

"Do you like scary stories?" Bethany noticed James' nervousness and laughed deviously, like a supervillain.

"Not really." James grimaced at the thought.

"I do," Harold said while chewing on chips, raising his hand as if he was in class.

"Well, I know a scary story," Bethany proudly proclaimed. "My brother told it to me!" She didn't remember much of it at all, and in fact, the first time her brother told her a scary story she cried through the night.

"Cool." Harold continued to snack.

"Cool..." Edda faked enthusiasm.

"Cool..." James repeated after the other two like a mockingbird.

"Okay! I'll tell it then!" Bethany changed her voice to mimic something akin to the crypt keeper.

"Once there was a surgeon who went insane." Bethany began to unfold her spooky tale, "and one day he moved his lab into the sewers."

"Why?" Edda asked.

"Why what?" Bethany huffed, indignant that she was interrupted. Harold looked enthralled already, as he continued to snack. James looked like he was readying himself for a crash landing.

"Why did he go insane? And why did he move to the sewers?" Edda sought elaboration.

"It doesn't matter!" Bethany did a whisper shout.

"It seems like it matters..." Edda persisted. "What's his name?"

"Oh my god! Just let me tell the story!" Bethany shouted.

"Volume!" James reminded.

"Anyway," Bethany continued, "the surgeon found a human to experiment on..."

Through the small dorm window, past its frame, was a cloudy night sky. Scattered pockets of light fluttered through celestial cloudscapes, and a few rays of moonlight made their way into the dorm room. As Bethany told her story, she was bathed in moonbeams.

"Dragging his victim back to his lair ... the doctor put him on the operating table. The guy was screaming and stuff ..." Bethany tried her best to voice act, but with her mid-pubescent vocal cracks, it hardly was spooky. However, to James, it was intimidating.

"That's so unsanitary!" Edda continued to poke holes. So far, she was unimpressed by the story, having expected something a whole lot scarier.

"Let her finish!" Harold butted in, showing sudden interest in something other than snacking. "Gotta' let it get to the good stuff." Harold liked Beth, but his awkward affections went unnoticed.

"Fine." Edda sipped at her drink, looking out of the window at the night. She found it comforting.

"The surgeon cut off the man's thumbs and ate them!" Bethany felt proud that she remembered most of her brother's story, though she felt he told it better. "Then ... the doctor took a knife to each of the man's fingers and cut them in half! Blood splattered everywhere!" Beth tried her best to make blood sound effects. "Splurt! Splurt! Goosh!"

"Cool..." Harold sounded like he was hearing the most prophetic story ever told. James nervously sipped at his drink, uncomfortable with the situation. Edda rolled her eyes. She wanted to ask why the surgeon was a cannibal now, but was tired of being berated for pointing out bad storytelling.

"Between each finger, the doctor put knives and swords, then sewed them up!" Bethany made a few knife sounds. *"Sling! Slarsh! Swingg!"*

"Badass." Harold nodded his head in enjoyment.

"The mad doctor was proud of his work and gave a name to his new creation. The Sixteen-Fingered Man!" Bethany chuckled her evil villain laugh once more.

"Whoa..." Harold's eyes widened.

"Yeah..." James was looking away from the entire group.

"The surgeon tortured and drove Sixteen insane, until one night, it escaped ... and killed the doctor by chopping him into little bits. Sixteen went on a rampage and killed a bunch of people, eating all their thumbs ..."

Edda seriously wanted to ask what the thumb-eating thing was all about, but held her tongue.

"You know the thing is... he was never caught." Bethany scooted close to James as he hunched downward, looking away from her. She whispered into Jame's ear.

"Do you know where he escaped?"

"No..."

"Ohio... At this very camp... in this very room..."

Silence lingered, save for the sound of Harold crunching on some snacks.

"ARRRGHH!" Bethany screamed into James' ear. James flinched backwards, shouting as he dropped his GameKid on the floor.

"Seriously, stop screaming!" Edda hissed. Bethany ignored Edda, though she did lower her voice.

"Man... you're no fun to scare," Bethany complained, glaring at James disappointedly. "This sucks."

"It was a cool story," Harold chimed in, staring at Beth like a lost puppy.

"It was stupid," Edda sighed, monotone.

"Whatever!" Beth huffed. "This is boring..." She stood up, pointing at James. "You're no fun without your game! And you're boring to scare!" Bethany stood up and stormed out of the room, unconcerned about her volume.

"Wait, I liked the story!" Harold waved his crumb-covered hand, getting no response from Bethany as she stomped loudly towards her room. Edda was bunking with Bethany, which made the hangout session possible in the first place. They'd put their pillows under their bed sheets in case someone looked inside, as if anyone would.

"That was weird," James commented, unfurling and releasing the tension in his back.

"Yeah, she was angry," Edda commented. She wanted to wait a minute and give Bethany some space. After a week of sharing a room with her, Edda learned her temperament to be frightfully volatile at times.

"You think she likes me?" Harold interjected.

"No," Edda sighed. Despite her age, she often felt like she was surrounded by children.

"I like you," James offered his praise.

"Thanks." Harold frowned disappointedly before turning to Edda. "Do you know any scary stories?"

"No," Edda sighed again.

"I don't really like scary stories that much." James re-emphasized.

. . .

Bethany stomped out of the boy's room, flustered, though unsure why. She began to head back to her dorm, planning on using the restroom beforehand. Reaching the hallway that connected to the girls' wing to the boys, a familiar figure emerged from a doorway. It was Adrian, wearing nothing but his boxers and a white tank top. His form was obscured by shadows, making him look like a malicious ghost.

"What are you doing up so late?" he snapped, leaning against the door frame.

Bethany gasped, startled by his appearance. Adrian was tall and muscular. He loomed over her, a frightening and unwelcome shade in the dark.

"I..." Beth struggled to find words. "Was just going to the bathroom."

"Coming from the boys wing?" Adrian pressed. From his boxers, a bulge formed. He looked down at Bethany. She was skinny, her face cute, chest small. Her skin looked soft. He felt powerful, drunk, in control.

"I ..." Bethany stuttered, scared and unsure what to say or do.

"Lights out is at ten... sweety." Adrian looked down at the frightened girl. "What's your name?" Shantel interacted with the girls' group mostly, so Adrian didn't know most of them.

"Bethany," she replied hesitantly, looking away from Adrian. Her heart was pounding, and she desperately wanted to run and hide. This place had previously felt safe. Now, in this moment, it felt like a maze, a deathtrap, inescapable.

"Bethany." Adrian smiled, his teeth like fangs in the dark, his gaze burning with hellfire. "Cute."

With a sudden force, Adrian grabbed Bethany by the wrist, pulling her in close to him as she slammed into his chest. Beth began to scream, but Adrian covered her mouth with his free hand, allowing only a brief welp to escape her. Adrian dragged Bethany into his room. Using his feet, he kicked his door closed. He lifted Bethany onto his bed with ease and crawled on top of her, pushing his waist against Bethany's. She began to weep, desperately screaming muffled shouts through Adrian's palm, which was now drenched in spit. Bethany was confused, terrified, desperate, wanting nothing more than to go home. She kicked, flailed, and scratched, but the counselor was too strong to resist. Adrian leaned in closer to Bethany and whispered into her ear.

"Any more noise and I'll make it worse," Adrian threatened. "Understand?"

He pressed his hand hard against Bethany's jaw, so much so that it felt like it would break. Bethany shook her head in compliance, tearful, her neck straining under Adrian's strength. Bethany went limp, trying her best to be quiet, to hold in her tears, to ignore the pain.

"Good." He smiled, sliding his fingers between Bethany's thighs.

INTERGRADE COMMUNION DISPATCHMENT

Edda slid open her porch door, holding a cup of freshly brewed coffee in her hand. She had struggled to sleep last night, getting up earlier than usual this morning. Ever since yesterday evening, she'd been feeling strange, but tried her best to ignore the sensation. Glancing down Wight Street, Edda could see remnants of her spilled wine soaking into the asphalt. Edda had few obligations today (save for laundry), so she hoped to reset her mental state before the coming work week. Relaxation was the aim of the game today.

The morning sun rose slowly, casting an orange glow upon the Earth. Even past the dunes, Sunday morning mists sprayed Edda's skin and caressed her hair. It coated the atmosphere with a fishy smell, a homely smell. Sitting in her favorite spot, Edda sipped and watched the ocean waves crash and dune grasses dance. Lingering in her was a sense of curiosity, a portion of her thoughts solely devoted to the flamingo pink home. Edda glanced at the innocuous building from time to time. It had a similar draw to it, the same call the ocean held upon her.

As Edda sipped, her view unconsciously turned from the ocean towards the flamingo pink house. There was a faint flicker in the same window as usual. Edda was mesmerized, looking at all the features of the home: the pylons, the windows, the side paneling, and the roof. Something was off. She couldn't place it, but the house looked different. At a passing glance, it appeared normal. Yet it felt as if a trick of the eye was warping her perception. The home was larger, or perhaps smaller? Either way, Edda was certain its proportions had shifted. The change was subtle, so subtle that it was unrecognizable to the naked eye. It could only be intuited. Edda didn't know what was different about the flamingo pink house, just that it was.

It occurred to Edda how strange windows were in an abstract sense. Here were these see-through walls, these conduits, passageways that connected or obscured the outdoors from the indoors. Occasionally, windows allow brief glimpses into the lives of strangers. In their very nature, intentional or not, they are voyeuristic. You could see a flash of someone's television or a passing figure. Windows are like picture frames, and the paintings are ever-moving, formed by happenstance and the perspective they are viewed through. Even when nothing can be seen through a window frame, it tells a story.

Edda dawdled in her thoughts, exploring the very strangeness of being at all.

Edda spotted Carter, walking down from the coastal highway sidewalk toward Wight. Wishing to avoid interaction, she headed inside for a while. Closing the porch door behind her, she looked back at the flamingo pink home briefly. Edda made herself something to eat and did her laundry. The mundane provided no sanctuary for her; the flamingo pink house dominated her every thought. Changing into sweatpants and a hoodie, Edda decided it was best to go for a walk and try to clear her head. The beach provided less and less comfort these days; her mind always rushing, but the exercise was welcome.

Edda walked for a long time. She broke her record for most streets passed without even realizing it. Yet even thousands of steps in the wet sand could not bring Edda's mind farther from the flamingo pink house, its window, its open door. She kept thinking about last night over and over. In her head, Edda could hear the wine bottle breaking as it smashed against the hard ground. It terrified her, without rationale, both the idea of entering that home and never taking the opportunity to do so.

It was growing cold outside, much more frigid than it had been all week. The ocean mists turned to fog, and from the coast a slow and creeping haze overtook the beach. Edda hadn't noticed the heavy dew upon the air at first; she was simply too lost in her thoughts. It was only when she returned to her house, a few blocks to her inlet entrance, that she looked up from her feet and at the sand to see the thickness of the air around her. One could taste the salt stronger than ever in the atmosphere.

Years ago, a few months after Edda had moved to Purple Beach, there were severe wildfires in Spain. The fires brought smoke across the ocean, making the air quality in Purple Beach and the surrounding areas miserable for a little over a week. This rolling fog appeared similar to that smoke, without the unpleasant side effects of burning eyes and gasping lungs.

Bare feet transitioned from sand to pavement, and as Edda crossed the street back towards her home, an intrusive thought popped into her head. She stood motionless in the road, invisible in the fog's veil, pondering an idea momentarily.

"There's no harm in looking..." Edda whispered to herself. She lived in this neighborhood; there was no crime in walking down the street. What was the harm of looking at a home?

None, Edda told herself.

Slowly, through the mists, Edda walked down Wight Street. Through the curtain haze, Edda could see a familiar pink side paneling.

SCRACK!

In the center of Edda's right foot, a small shard of glass pierced straight through. It sliced into her skin, drawing blood from deep within her veins. It was an especially painful cut. Her wound felt as if it was burning, and her skin felt like it was peeling apart layer after layer.

"Ouch! *Shit!*" Edda cursed, hobbling backwards and trying in vain to avoid putting pressure on her injury. She was standing exactly where she had dropped her bottle last night. Lifting her foot from the ground, Edda could still see part of the shard wedged in her bleeding skin. Edda hobbled to the sidewalk, sat down, then grabbed the bloodied sliver of glass the best she could. With no hesitation and a great heave, she ripped it from her foot. It hurt even more coming out than it did going in, and a spurt of blood shot out of her foot with impressive force like a water display from a fountainhead.

"God damn it!" Edda roared, her shout echoed down Wight Street. She felt a little dizzy, and a slight wooziness overtook her. She'd always had that reaction when seeing blood, especially her own. Edda removed her shirt, her black sports bra her only cover, and wrapped it around he wound. It soaked up a lot of blood, turning from green to mostly red.

Looking at the front door of the pink home (which was shut), Edda sighed, frustrated with herself, frustrated with her aimless obsession. She felt like a fool. Hobbling home through the ocean fog, blood trickled down Edda's foot in small droplets, leaving behind a couple red droplets on the road. For a moment, she considered calling Fran for help, perhaps an ambulance, but Edda decided against it. In a way, she felt as though she was proving to herself she could survive on her own. She was living up to ridiculous standards she set for herself, a Macsen family trait.

Wishing not to track blood inside, Edda tried her best to hobble to the bathroom. It was a minimal success, but she did leave behind a few spots of blood on the living room carpet. Some blood, which had soaked into her shirt, dripped onto the floor bathroom tile when she removed it from her wound.

Underneath the sink was a box of medical supplies. Checking her cut, Edda saw there was a small piece of glass still embedded in her foot. Grabbing the tweezers, Edda clawed at the shard. Tugging, the remaining glass came out with relative ease. Nonetheless, the pain was tremendous, more so than it had any right to be.

"You bitch," Edda cursed at no one.

Running her foot under the bathtub faucet, the water ran the red away. Edda watched blood trickle down the drain. The water felt both spectacular and miserable on her wound. Once the cut had mostly stopped bleeding, Edda sat on her toilet to treat it. Splashing some isopropyl alcohol on a cloth, she applied it to her cut. It stung tremendously, and Edda clenched her teeth as she endured the misery. Once properly disinfected, Edda put an antibacterial gel on the wound and wrapped the injury in gauze. She used up the rest of it but had just enough to wrap her laceration once. The medical kit she was using was given to her nearly a decade ago by her mom when she went to college. It seemed ludicrous to Edda that the tiny red plastic box had stayed with her all these years.

"Least I cut myself after the walk," Edda grumbled. Yesterday's ghosts felt like they were still haunting her. Edda took an aspirin, then limped to the living room and peered outside through the patio doors. The fog was less dense, though still present. Sitting on the couch, Edda propped her leg up. She sat facing away from the outside, not wanting to look towards the flamingo pink home.

Wishing for someone to commiserate with, Edda texted Fran. After a few minutes of scrolling on her phone, Fran hadn't replied. Her foot throbbed occasionally, but she'd done a good job wrapping it, and the pressure helped alleviate pain. Edda turned the television on, surfing through show after show, with nothing catching her interest. She wasn't much of a film person, but watched some movies now and then. Eventually, Edda picked some shitty rom-com. It was something easy to zone out to.

. . .

Thunder clapped outside; it was a magnificent boom. Purple Beach trembled in its might. Edda shook awake, startled by the cannonade noise. Sitting up from the couch, Edda checked her phone for the time. It was just after three in the afternoon. She took a nap after lunch and slept much longer than she intended. She still felt sleepy; her head was heavy. Fran had yet to reply to her earlier text message. In the living room, the television continued to play. Edda looked up from her phone and watched it for a moment.

"Damn barbarians," a dirty caveman said on the television. He was hunched over, wearing colorful pelts. The actor was ripped and handsome, his pecs well-oiled and gleaming under studio lights. It looked like some old film from the sixties or seventies.

"Those bedrock bastards will never claim my babes!" The actor proudly posed under the limelight. "FOR ROGDOR!" the actor shouted, raising his hand triumphantly.

The movie was surreal, making Edda feel as if she was in a living dream. The film cut to a different scene: stop-motion clay dinosaurs fighting some cavemen with clubs. The dinosaurs roared, and the cavemen launched spears and stone hammers at the beasts. The effects looked cheesy, but charming. Edda turned the television off, baffled by what she just watched. Making sure not to put too much pressure on her injury, Edda stood up. She slowly hobbled to the kitchen to get a glass of water.

Edda sipped at her drink as she watched a distant storm roll inland. Though she hadn't checked the weather prior, the storm seemed rather sudden. The fog was gone, but in its place was an intense darkness. Swirling dust devils of sand and grass pirouetted near the inlet entrance. Seldom had Edda seen the skies so black and gloomy. The clouds above looked hateful.

Edda cracked the porch door open just a bit. With her head between the doorway, she inhaled the aroma of the air. Storms brought with them pleasant smells Edda very much enjoyed, but there was something else in the air that evening. It was something sweet, prominent, that hit Edda's nostrils the moment she inhaled. It was the smell of oranges, acidic, mixed with sea salt and storm rain. Careless for a moment, Edda put too much pressure on her foot. Pain sang through her toes and through her thighs.

"Fuck," Edda hissed, wincing and leaning back on her heel. Her phone began to ring, which she left sitting on the living room table. Edda limped back to the couch and answered the phone. Her Mom was calling.

"Hey sweetie!" Her mother greeted her.

"Hey, Mom." Edda smiled.

"It's been forever! You never call me anymore!"

"I know it's just..."

"Don't worry about it! I'll call for you..." Edda's mom was a fast talker, a trait Edda adopted at a young age. As a pre-teen, Edda spoke so quickly her sentences blurred together, sometimes rendering her words incomprehensibly garbled. It took Edda a long time to slow down her speech habits and still had to consciously stop herself from rapid-firing off words at lightspeed. As she grew older, Edda found she was less enthusiastic to say anything at all.

"Anyway, I need to tell you about Uncle Ted." Mom said, her voice turning serious-sounding.

"Okay?" Edda raised her brow. She never liked Uncle Ted. He was a bit of a creep and had some shitty opinions that had caused family arguments in the past.

"Well, Ted's dead," Mom said bluntly.

"Oh, that's... horrible." Edda faked it.

"It's okay, hun, you don't have to pretend to be sad." Mom was always honest and upfront, if not lacking in some social graces. "You just need to come to the funeral and put on a face."

"I can do that." Edda agreed. "How'd he die?"

"Pig." Mom blurted out.

"Excuse me?" Edda restrained laughter.

"Yup. His biggest hog fell right on top of him. Crushed him immediately." Mom tried to sound upset, but her strange description of the death and monotone speaking habits lent comedy to the moment.

"Hah." Edda snorted, trying to withhold her laughter.

"Sweetie, he's dead, at least try and have some restraint." A mother scolded her daughter.

"Sorry." Edda apologized half-heartedly.

"It's apparently a more common way to die than you'd think." She continued. "He should have sold that stupid Farm years ago when he had the chance! Dying's a good way to avoid your debts I suppose."

"So, it would seem," Edda replied, rolling her eyes.

Outside, a large boom of thunder cracked. Edda imagined two trains jousting. There was a flicker of light, power went out, then immediately returned. Appliances turned back on, and several beeps echoed throughout Edda's apartment.

"What was that?" Mom asked concernedly.

"Oh, a brownout. There's a big storm going on right now." Edda explained.

"Oh, really? It's gorgeous out here right now. All nice and sunny."

Edda loved her mother, but she had a tendency to talk her ear off for exhaustively long stretches. With some effort, Edda steered the conversation to a close. She had made the mistake of telling her about stepping on glass, which led to a whole rant about how cities should keep their streets cleaner (Edda neglected mentioning she was the one who'd left the glass there). When mom finally did hang up, Edda let out a sigh of relief. At least Mom had provided ample distraction from her throbbing injury.

Afternoon faded into the evening, and 144th Street and Wight found themselves in the middle of an ever-growing storm. Another crackle of thunder burst, shaking the ground, and bright white lightning painted the world for a moment. Outside was marvelous looking, a gorgeous living piece of art made only possible by a sudden storm. Throughout the storm, the wind continued to carry the sweet smell of oranges. The thick fog had mostly receded, yet remained just enough to allow an eeriness to linger in the atmosphere. Lights from homes, streetlamps, and windows pierced ever so softly through the air, creating pockets of hazy coloration in which raindrops pierced. Then the rang stopped as the center of the storm hung over the area.

Standing up from the couch, Edda slowly tottered out to the porch and down the patio stairs, the urge to be in the middle of the storm overtaking her. She was careful of her wound, limping on her heel. Small spats of rain pattered upon Edda's head. The clouds hanging above her formed so perfectly a cylindrical funnel that she could see past the storm and spy the stars in space. Edda gasped at how brilliant the sight was. It felt like she was in the center of the universe, as if around her was a cage made from wind, rain, and lightning. Past the dunes, the waves seemed to point upwards to the sky, the water contributing to the lingering funnel which hung so majestically above her head. Great elation overtook Edda. She felt like a child again, fearful, but driven by wonder and curiosity.

Through all the spectacle, through the beauty and the fog, a sudden, powerful flickering glow called attention to itself. Edda looked towards the flamingo pink house. From the pink home's window, the one which had taunted her all this time, came a flashing light. So powerful were its lumens that they matched the brilliance of nature's lightning. It strobed violently. Wight Street was consumed in a maddening flicker, all of which originated from the second-story window in the flamingo pink house. In the storm, the light felt wrong, amplified, grotesque. Yet it excited Edda. It was as if an invitation.

Not even bothering to close her door and leaving her phone behind, Edda ventured down Wight Street. Just minutes ago, the pressure on her right foot would have sent a great pain through Edda. Now, however, she was striding, oblivious or uncaring of the injury. Edda felt she could step on a thousand shards of glass now and no reaction would come of it. Still, she took care to avoid any more shards.

In front of the pink home, before the cantilevered supports, Edda stared upwards. The simple beachfront house was scowling directly at her, its face formed from windows and rafters and a door frame. It was a mischievous place, one daring Edda to enter, to try something. The estate was hungry, so hungry. The experience roused primal excitement in Edda as every pore in her skin tingled.

The properties on Wight have their addresses listed to the right of the front door. It was the same at the pink home; however, the address was 'scrambling' itself constantly. Each number changed instantaneously every few seconds right before Edda's eyes.

01964...

93593...

10873...

█████...

23512...

The front door swung open slowly, the sound of rusty hinges and creaking wood like the pained cries of a dying child. The open doorframe was a maw. It was a tunnel, pulsating downwards into an invisible abyss.

"This is insane," Edda reasoned with herself, staring into the void that lay in front of her. "This can't be real..."

Edda knew she should turn around, run away, and never think of what she saw again. She knew what the right choice was. She also knew if she didn't go inside, she'd never have another chance. It was her gut, telling her she was standing on the precipice of fate. She could jump off, or she could turn away.

"This is insane," Edda repeated to herself as she stepped into the darkness, veiling herself in blue. The storm eye drifted away.

Back at home, on the living room table, Edda's phone buzzed. She received a text that would go unread:

Hey girl, how's your night? Fran finally replied.

CARETAKER'S MAZE

A little before 7:30 a.m., Ward awoke to the sound of his grandmother calling out, shouting the best her weak lungs would allow.

"Hello!? Ward!? Hello!? Is anyone there?" Darcy paused periodically to regain her breath before shouting again. This wasn't the first time Ward experienced this behavior. Grandma had a terrible fear of being alone and helpless since the fall. Ward couldn't blame her for that, in fact, he sympathized.

Another day. Ward thought to himself, climbing out of bed, shorts hanging from his waist. Ward felt an immense longing to be back outside in the fog-infused darkness of last night. As he passed the front doors, Ward opened the curtains, hoping to see the same mysterious foggy landscape, only to be disappointed, greeted instead with a dull and gray morning.

"What's wrong?" Ward stepped into Darcy's room.

"I really need to go!" Darcy impressed with great urgency. She'd managed to make it through the whole night without ruining the bed. While she'd wet herself a little bit, the diaper contained everything. Ward was genuinely impressed. He couldn't remember a recent day when he didn't have to change his grandmother's sheets.

After getting grandma to the bathroom and through her morning routine, Ward scrambled some eggs and made toast. It was nothing special, but it did require more work than cereal, certainly.

"We have your new appointment at four," Ward reminded Darcy.

She nodded her head, chewing slowly on some buttered toast and eggs.

"I'm gonna call ahead this time to make sure they're open," Ward said, sipping at some orange juice.

"That's a good idea." Darcy nodded.

"Then on Saturday, I'll get groceries." Ward was thinking out loud. Darcy shook her head, not bothering to engage further.

Work was mind-numbing, but positive in a way. Ward needed to zone out, do something repetitive and mindless. It let him temporarily displace his misery into a state of indifference. Days like these, without their manager's interference, were especially tolerable, which was all Ward really hoped for anymore.

Darcy's eleven o'clock game shows were about to come on. She lifted the remote, turning the volume up much louder.

"I'm your host ..." a man from the TV droned on, accompanied by a light jazz band and an audience cheering.

When he was a young teen, Ward found a lot of enjoyment watching game shows and British sitcoms with his grandmother. It was a warm, fond memory. Now, though, as time progressed, the shows felt less dazzling. Perhaps his views on life had grown more cynical. Ward's ever-burgeoning disdain for his grandmother made looking back on memories involving her filter through shit tinted glasses. Yet without being able to find a reason why, Ward still cared for her. It was a strange feeling, to love someone so much and to hate them nearly equally.

Ward received a message, his phone dinging. It was a confirmation text for Darcy's appointment from Kane's office.

"Looks like the appointments on for today."

"Oh, good," Darcy said. "When is it again?"

"Four," Ward answered.

"Could pick something up afterwards," Darcy suggested, passively viewing the television. There was a contestant on a stage with the host. He was holding a giant inflatable hammer while whacking moles with price tags on their heads.

"Okay, sounds good." Another benefit Ward found in being Darcy's caretaker was the free meals. The proposition of takeout was always one of the more especially exciting aspects of Ward's days.

"Could you get me some more water?" Darcy asked.

"Sure." Ward stood up from his laptop, refilling Darcy's cup with ice cold water. The game show Darcy was watching cut to commercial. On the television a quick news promo flashed.

"Tonight, on Newtext News at six," a news reporter, a woman in a yellow dress, spoke on the TV, "Ohio's State Emergency Alert system confuses residents when..."

Ward set Darcy's sippy cup of water on her walker seat. He turned to walk away and didn't even make it a single pace before Darcy whimpered, purposely audible, another one of her favorite cursed catchphrases.

"I wish I could just die. I'm a burden." Her dark message on repeat.

Ward halted in place. Momentarily, he trembled. He wanted to shout, to scream, to assault. He took in a deep breath, one which tempered his resolve slightly. Desperately, Ward tried to hold his tongue. Every time he retaliated, it just ended in tears, hate. He wanted to tell Darcy he loved her and how he hated her for what she was putting him through. Ward wanted so desperately for her to know that there was worth left in a life she now considered only something worthy of being discarded.

Ward made turkey sandwiches for lunch. The shows ended, and the two ate in silence. Once more, Ward prepared to drive Darcy to her doctor's appointment. Exiting the back door into the halls of Grassy Acres, Ward didn't even look in the direction of Paula's apartment. Instead, he took the stairs to his right. While walking through the basement hallway towards the garage, Ward picked up his pace, afraid of encountering whatever made that awful holler he heard last night.

While driving, Ward was nervous; Darcy was going to mention her first son again. The trip was nearly silent, though, save for the radio turned down too low. Some classic rock was playing, the disc jockey obnoxiously spewing commercials and nonsense in between generic oldies.

"I don't like modern music," Darcy said, breaking the silence. "Just noise." She huffed at her oxygen tank.

A high-pitched rock star belted out on the radio some lyrics about his mind not being for rent, not by the government nor by the gods above.

"Most of these songs have been older than me, by a lot," Ward rebutted.

"Really?" Darcy was shocked.

"Yup." Ward smiled as they continued along. The roads were nearly empty. Letterfaux was a small town, but Ward didn't come across a single car on the road today.

Ward parked in front of Dr. Kane's office. The parking lot was nearly abandoned save for a few empty vehicles. The buildings were dark, all of them now. Several curtains were drawn, and no lights appeared to be on inside any of the buildings. Looking through the car windshield into the building's windows distorted the darkness within them even more. Ward's eyes could not adjust well to the interiors. There was depth to them, but most of it was veiled. What little he could see was mundane. Furniture and carpet in low light.

"This doesn't seem right," Darcy observed.

"No, it doesn't," Ward agreed with her for once. He pulled in front of Dr. Kane's office, keeping the engine on and the car doors locked.

"I'm going to call." Ward dialed the office. After wading through menus and waiting a long time, his call got no response, eventually going to voicemail.

"Nothing?" Grandma asked.

"Nothing," Ward confirmed. "I'm gonna try the Mexican place." The restaurant was called El Comida Grande. Ward had been there once. It was alright. Newtext was an extremely white town, so much so that in a census it was determined the population was over ninety percent Caucasian, leaving the other percentages to a small minority of underrepresented ethnicities. Ward didn't speak much Spanish but knew enough to be pretty sure the name wasn't grammatically correct. Looking up the phone number of the restaurant on his phone, Ward dialed the place. Like the doctor's office, there was no reply.

"Weird." Ward felt unnerved; a chill ran down his spine.

"Go try knocking," Darcy suggested.

Ward looked around. It had turned into a sunny day despite the cold. The parking lot was still. A teal sedan was tucked in the corner near the veterinarians, and a Volkswagen Beetle was parked in front of the restaurant. Otherwise, it was empty. No person could be seen around the area. Nothing looked out of the ordinary, yet the scene unnerved Ward, shook him. Everything felt wrong, and his instinct was telling him not to step outside of the car.

"No," Ward replied, hastily backing out of his parking spot.

"What about my appointment?" Darcy asked as Ward zoomed out of the lot.

"I don't know," Ward said. "I want to check something."

Down the road a few miles was another small plaza of shops. There was a liquor store, gun shop, pizza place, and hair salon. Pulling into the outlets, Ward drove through the lot. There were more cars parked here than in the lot by Dr. Kane's, but it was still pretty empty. The liquor store was open. Ward watched as an old lady holding two brown paper bags headed to her car, loading up for the weekend. The pizza place also appeared to be open. The other two stores looked dark.

"Alright," Ward sighed a breath of relief. Seeing other people out in the wild was reassuring. An entire shopping plaza being abandoned midday on a Friday didn't sit right with Ward. Newtext, Letterfaux, and its neighboring towns were rather small, but not small enough to give the impression of a ghost town. It had started feeling like one. Ward's car idled. He looked up into the sky. *Haven't seen a bird in weeks.*

"You picking something up?" Darcy asked, confused on why they had stopped here.

"No..."

"Oh..." Grandma stuttered.

"How about pizza for dinner?" Ward asked suddenly, pulling in front of the restaurant. It was called Rocky's; they specialized in New York style thin-crust pizza.

"Oh, sure," Grandma agreed.

To Ward's relief as he reached for the front door of the pizza place, it swung open to a welcoming business. The two had never ordered pizza from this place before. Darcy preferred just cheese, a simple classic. Ward, however, liked pizzas loaded with toppings. The two split a large pie down the middle. Darcy got her plain cheese pizza, and Ward got his Jackson Pollock of a pizza. This time Ward ordered yellow peppers, jalapeños, mushrooms, onions, bacon, shrimp, and chicken. Some would call it excessive; Ward called it perfection. The toppings were so jam-packed that the slices could not support the weight of the toppings. Returning home, the two had a fantastic, if not early, dinner. Darcy used the meal as an antecedent excuse to start drinking before five.

As he ate, Ward tried to ignore the terrible feeling in his gut. Something about him felt wrong. Something about the outside world felt wrong. Paranoia was exhausting. He really wanted to get high, just a nice buzz to take the edge off.

Time passed quickly for Ward. Hours passed by in what seemed like minutes. He felt like he was on autopilot. His mind was hazy. He had a thought, or perhaps it could be better described as a vision, which floated around in his head. He could not grasp what he was seeing, imagining. It kept nagging at him, making its presence known as a blur in one's peripheral vision, only to be unseen when turning one's head.

"Hello?" Grandma asked, her legs raised in the air trembling from weakness. Ward had halted midway as he was helping her change into pajamas.

Ward snapped back into reality. It was like being hit with all the G-force of a car going from one hundred to zero within a few seconds. Ward was confused. He could have sworn he was sitting at the dinner table eating pizza, and now he was here.

"Sorry. Must be losing it..." Ward excused himself.

"I already have." Darcy let out a rare quip, and Ward forced a laugh.

Once changed, Darcy slowly hobbled toward the bathroom sink to brush her teeth, all the while Ward pulled her oxygen tube along to keep it from getting tangled underneath the walker wheels. Ward felt like he was holding a dog's leash.

With utmost effort, Ward got Darcy into bed. She was panting when she suddenly began grasping Ward's arm tightly. She heaved, sucking in the oxygen as the breathing machine continued to pump and whirl. Minutes passed, her grip ever tightening, before she finally regained herself.

"Okay... thank you," Darcy said, releasing her clutch from around Ward's right arm. She picked up a remote and turned on the TV to do some channel surfing.

"Yeah..." Ward shook. Grandma still had a surprisingly powerful grip considering. "Going to go for my walk." Ward said, his duties temporarily relieved. On his arm, where Darcy had grabbed at him, Ward's skin was agitated and red. Or perhaps he was imagining it. It itched.

"What the fuck," Ward muttered to himself, heading into his bathroom. In the sink, Ward ran water over the rash, which brought relief. He wasn't even sure if Darcy had actually agitated his skin, or if he was turning phobic in regard to his grandma.

Ward wanted to get stoned desperately. The idea of going into the basement alone tonight, however, didn't feel entirely safe. Ward had been smoking in the workout room all winter and never had an issue, save for occasionally having to be quiet if a passerby headed to or from the elevator. Ward considered smoking on the porch tonight. Outside, though, it was nothing but dark, bitter cold, and piercing winds. Ward checked the temperature on his phone. It was twenty-five degrees out, but felt like below twenty with the high winds. It would only get drastically colder in the upcoming week. Even if Ward could endure the cold, which he was not willing to do, the wind would extinguish any flame he lit and blow buds from his bowl.

Armed with logic, telling himself he'd be fine, Ward grabbed his stash bag and keys and headed out into the apartment hallways. Ward didn't want to walk by Paula's room, assuming the door was still ajar. If that door was open three days in a row, Ward would feel obligated to do something. Ward didn't want that burden. So, Ward took the stairwell to the right of his apartment, taking the long way downstairs. The stairs to the basement wrapped around themselves. The railings were teal, and the walkway was hardly lit, save for a dim yellow wall light which desperately needed new bulbs. Ward hastily ran to the strange L-shaped room, imagining some monster emerging from the boiler rooms to chase him down.

Making it inside the gym, Ward turned on the lights and slammed the doors shut, sliding back against them. He felt like a kid running to the bed from the doorway as he turned off his bedroom lights.

The room was the same old, empty, creepy, windowless location it always was. Ward opened his goody bag, filled his bowl, and began to smoke. Ward tried to browse forums on his phone but couldn't get a connection. It happened frequently; he was in the basement after all. So instead, he sat there, puffing on his bowl, blowing dank clouds into the workout room in silence. His pipe, which Ward affectionately had named Phaser, was a slow burn. After grinding the pot, the weed burned at a nice pace in the large, rimmed piece. Minutes and multiple puffs in, Ward was feeling relaxed.

Suddenly, through the hallways of Grassy Acres, a howl, as if the building itself was screeching in agony, boomed through the basement corridors. It was a terrible scream, and with it, powerful gusts of wind kicked up, which bellowed violently beneath cracks in the green double doors. Ward gasped and dropped his lighter, which pattered onto his jeans along with some spilt ash. The noise sounded close. It was similar to the shriek he had heard yesterday.

"Holy shit." Ward restrained a scream, scrunching inwards on himself. For a while, Ward didn't know what to do, hunkering tight. Ward's imagination had him affright, the source of the sound infinite in their possibilities, all horrific.

Ward slowly packed up his paraphernalia, deciding he had to escape the room at some point. He stood up nervously, shaking. His hands reminded him of grandpa's when he was in his later years, when Parkinson's was at its worst. Lingering in front of the double doors, working up the courage to dash to the elevator, Ward could feel an immense pressure upon his eyelids. He didn't want to head to the stairwell, past the maintenance tunnels. Ward imagined some monster lingered in there, like a minotaur stalking a maze. He shook his head, his high now fully replaced with fear and adrenaline.

Ward listened through the crack in the doors as well as he could. No distinguishable sounds could be heard. Some wind howled down the hallway, but it was not the horrific rattle heard minutes ago. Ward listened for movement, expecting to hear someone patrolling the halls, but there were no such footfalls or patters. Ward peeked through the crack in the doors. He couldn't see much, save for dim lit white concrete walls. It looked still, but he could not witness much with such a small sliver of sight. Ward's eyes began to water as he refused to blink. He was transfixed, expecting to see movement at any minute. But stillness prevailed.

No more delaying the inevitable.

Ward slowly pushed the green doors open, which uncharacteristically creaked as if trying to call attention to his egress. Ward, with a combination of stealth and haste, made his way to the elevator, pressing the call button repeatedly. The plastic white circle lit up yellow every time he pressed it. The basement hallways felt darker than usual. The air was heavy, like the mists he watched rolling late last night.

The elevator slowly descended. Ward tapped his toes in anticipation. He felt vulnerable, a sitting duck. He wanted to sprint down the long hallway to the stairwell next to the pipework entrance but was fearful commotion would conjure some imagined monster. Still, the urge to run home compelled Ward. It felt as if the elevator was procrastinating, hesitant to arrive. Ward continued to tap his toes. Wind blew in from the garage; it was cold, sending more shivers Ward's way.

DING!

The elevator arrived, its doors sliding open lethargically. Practically leaping inside, Ward slammed his pointer finger into the first-floor button. The elevator doors squeaked to a close, and Ward allowed himself to breathe again. As the elevator shook, rising to floor one, Ward rubbed his temples, trying his best to suppress an oncoming migraine. The elevator door opened, and Ward stepped out into the familiar foyer, relieved to be out of the basement.

"Never going back down there." Ward swore to himself, fully aware he would have to again at some point to retrieve his car. Walking down the hallway, Ward's relief was replaced with a new tension: he was going to have to pass by Paula's apartment. He prayed the door was closed.

As he walked, Ward found himself looking down at the simple patterns in the carpeted floor, trying to distract himself as he shuffled home. Then, to his left, he saw Mrs. Paula's apartment door. It was fully swung open. Ward stopped to look inside, a macabre fascination overtaking him. He wondered how had nobody but him noticed this? In retrospect, Ward hadn't seen anyone else in the building for days now, maybe even weeks. The same sensation of dread that Ward experienced outside of Dr. Kane's office today reemerged, churning in his belly.

The apartment was shrouded in darkness, save for a small blue light coming from somewhere towards the back of the home. Outlines of furniture, their rims bathed in a subtle blue, gave depth to the inky darkness within. A flash of fear gripped Ward suddenly. He could see someone, standing, motionless, in the back of the house. Their figure was faded, obscured by a blue gloom. It looked like someone, something was looking at him, glaring in his direction. For a moment, a glimmer of white reflected in the dark, and Ward thought he could see teeth, fangs...

Completely gripped by terror, Ward sprinted, his feet stomping on the carpet. Thankfully, home was close by. Reaching his door, Ward grabbed his keys, frantically unlocking it. He made extra sure not to pull that horror movie trope of dropping the keys, lamenting the idea of dying because of terrible dexterity. Once inside, Ward nearly screamed in joy, locking the door behind him. He was thirsty, sweating, huffing. A thrill and tingle ran down from the tip of his skull to the bottom of his pinky toe.

"Hello?" Darcy called out. Ward gave himself a moment to compose himself before replying.

"Hey!" Ward said. "Give me a minute, I need to use the bathroom."

"Okay," Darcy agreed.

Stepping into his restroom, Ward stood in front of the mirror, setting down his smoking supplies. His eyes were blood red, sunken, and his skin pale. Ward splashed some hot water on his face, trying to calm his shaking. Ward flushed the toilet to pretend he used the restroom before heading to check on Grandma.

"What's up?" Ward asked, standing in between the doorframe.

"I think I broke the TV again." Darcy frowned, pointing the remote at the television. "Probably hit the clicker wrong."

Ward headed into the bedroom, facing the television. On the screen was a row of colorful rectangles and squares. A black rectangle with white text sat in the middle of the screen in the foreground. It read: *Off-Air.*

"That's weird..." Ward went to grab the remote from Darcy, hopping over her oxygen tube as he did so. "What channel are you on?"

"I don't know," Darcy groaned.

Ward flipped up a channel, going from thirteen to fourteen. The two were greeted with the same black and white message: Off-Air. He changed to another channel, with the same result. Clicking the remote rapidly, channel after channel, each one was off.

"What the fuck..." Ward trembled. Something was definitely wrong, a subtle apocalypse.

"What is it?" Darcy asked.

"I guess we don't have a signal." Ward rationalized. "Maybe a downed wire or something?" Ward had no idea what he was talking about. He hadn't a clue how the technology worked beyond how to use it and vague concepts of wires plugged into walls.

"Oh..." Darcy said, disappointed. "Well ... I'll go to bed."

"I'm sure it'll be repaired by tomorrow." Ward felt unsure about everything at the moment. Ward refilled Grandma's cup of water at her request and left her to sleep.

Ward double-checked that the front door was locked. He closed the curtains. Being on the first floor, with a direct view of the connecting main road, suddenly felt like a huge vulnerability to Ward. Ward double-checked that the back door was locked as well. He looked through the door's peephole. It provided nothing but a small fisheye view of their neighbor's door. Everything was still and quiet.

Ward pulled out his phone to search for information about the dead air on television. As he opened a browser, the connection stalled. Ward switched to wireless data but still could not make a connection. Heading to the den, Ward checked his laptop, which was also unable to connect to the internet. Whatever was happening, everything was down. Ward's nerves continued to worsen.

Ward killed some time playing a single-player video game. He'd been trying out this indie RPG lately. It wasn't great, but it was charming and strangely addictive. It acted as nothing but a distraction for him, valuable as that may be. A glowing square of entertainment meant to get lost in. No immersion was to be achieved, as Ward's instincts were blaring alarms. Nothing felt right. Still, the game helped pass the time.

Darcy began to snore from her room. When she fell asleep at certain angles, it amplified the sound of her honks. In conjunction with her breathing machine, it was certainly an ambience no comfort could be found in. Ward contemplated just going to bed, but his nerves were so high he knew he'd do nothing but roll around the mattress in discomfort.

As sudden as a flash of lightning, through the walls and halls, through the windows and doorways, through the girders and support beams, a powerful shaking rumbled through Grassy Acres. The intense vibrations only lasted but a moment, but for that brief second, Ward thought the ceiling was going to collapse on top of him, burying him in layers of rubble and people and anguish. Then, just at the height of the shaking's intensity, it stopped. There was a brief calmness... Ward sat motionless, looking around, stunned. Then, a great electrical hum buzzed, just as intense as the previous quaking. With a crackle, the power in the building went out.

Capacitors hummed their last moments before deafened by silence. Everything went dark in the apartment, save for Ward, who was illuminated by his laptop screen, now using reserve power. Several smoke detectors beeped throughout the complex momentarily.

"Ward!" Darcy awoke, panicked. "Ward!" She coughed, struggling to catch her breath after overexerting herself.

"I know, I know!" Ward stood up, powering down his laptop. Now in total dark, Ward pulled out his phone, using its light to guide him as he slowly treaded through the bathroom towards Darcy's room.

"Are you there?" Darcy called out, concerned, once again pushing herself and yelling louder than she should.

"I'm here..." Ward reassured her as he approached her bedside.

"What happened?" Darcy panted.

Ward, using the light, grabbed one of Darcy's portable oxygen puffers from her wardrobe and handed it to her.

"I think we had an earthquake," Ward said. "I didn't think Ohio had earthquakes."

"Oh yeah," Darcy struggled to speak. Sucking down another waft of air, she continued. "Yeah, we get 'em once a while." Darcy coughed and groaned as her withered lungs, like deflated balloons, huffed desperately.

"Hadn't seen one in decades though..." Phlegm clogged Darcy's throat as she wheezed.

"Huh." Ward was flabbergasted. "Don't overexert yourself." A realization popped into Ward's head. Shouldn't there be car alarms coming from outside? He wasn't sure if earthquakes actually caused alarms to go off, but Ward had seen it in movies plenty of times.

"I'm gonna go check outside real quick." He needed to see if there was any devastation or perhaps people congregating outside the building. Maybe someone would know something.

"Okay, be careful," Darcy replied.

Ward crept to the front. Pulling back the blinds, with hesitation, Ward opened the doors and stepped outside into the chilling night. It was a little past 9:00 p.m. at this point. Like yesterday, a great mist had overtaken everything. Ward could hardly see into the parking lot. Shivering, he stepped towards the patio gate. Outside, no alarms were blaring, and everything seemed normal. He couldn't see anyone, nor was there any conversations to be heard. Their patio was undamaged. No cracks in the floor could be seen, and from a general view in the dark, the building itself seemed unphased. If it was an earthquake, it was minor. The dark, as well, could be obscuring some of Ward's perception. In the distant fog, once more, Ward could see indistinguishable movement.

Stepping inside from the cold, while the apartment was warmer, Ward realized he would need to get extra blankets for himself and Darcy if the power was out for much longer.

"Everything seems normal," Ward said as he closed the doors and drew the curtains. His eyes were still slowly adjusting to the darkness.

"Check the lobby," Darcy suggested.

"What?" Ward asked as he stepped back into Grandma's room. "Why?"

"People meet there... The H.O.A. members and such," Darcy explained.

"Oh..." Ward knew what Darcy was saying made sense, a rare occasion these days. Information on what was happening would be useful. Still, dread hung above Ward, a looming shade. Walking the halls in darkness, after what he'd just experienced, seemed like a living nightmare. He tried to think of some reason or excuse not to go but couldn't concoct one.

"I guess I'll go check." Ward grabbed his keys once more. Times like these made him wish the back door didn't auto-lock.

Ward stood before the exit, looking through the spyhole. He saw nothing but darkness. He pressed his ears against the door but heard nothing.

"This again," Ward said, trying to dig up what scraps of courage he hadn't already expended today. "God dammit." Ward cursed to himself. He wished he had a knife, a gun, or pepper spray (bear mace would work too).

"Three," He counted out loud, grabbing the door handle. "Two." His breathing tense, his chest tight. "One!" Ward pulled open the door, leaping out into the hallway, his head looking about the dark halls. Everything was still. Ward was uneasy. He lived in a building where the majority of residents were retirees around the age of sixty or higher. These were people with mundane lives and too much free time on their hands. Surely someone had to be about checking on things. It was late granted, but if any moment called for someone to make adjustments to their sleep schedule, an earthquake was probably that moment.

Using his phone flashlight, Ward headed towards the central lobby of the building, the front entrance. Just a few seconds, and he'd be walking by Mrs. Paula's place. Ward's shoulders were tense, his muscles clenched. With each step, Ward could feel his brain rattle around inside him, all his fears and worries making a wreck of the place. No other doors were open, no people roamed the halls. Ward could hear no sounds in the distance, no people speaking, no concerned residents bustling. The building was quiet, still.

Ward was about level with Paula's door again, which he noticed was still open. He looked away from the room, picking up his pace. Heart racing, Ward barreled forward until he reached the lobby. Everything was empty, quiet. No lights were on, total outage.

"Fuck me," Ward whispered to himself.

Ward was tempted to shout out something, like "Hello?" or "Anyone here?" But he had seen enough horror films to know that wasn't a good idea. Carefully, like he was traversing a minefield, Ward turned around and headed back to the apartment, the tension in his legs like springs ready to launch a pinball.

The walk back home from the lobby through the halls was still equally dreadful. The strange wallpaper, the carpet patterns, the popcorn ceilings, everything took on a different form in the dark. Hallways, mundane and unnoticed, were now turned into frightful tunnels and maddening pathways that twisted about themselves like traversing the intestines of a living creature.

Approaching Paula's once more, the blue light inside her home had once again manifested and was much brighter now, seeping out past the doorframe. Ward looked inside the blue abyss momentarily. It was compelling, magical, frightful. He saw a flash of movement against the glowing blue backdrop. Something was wriggling in the darkness. Ward wanted to run but was curious despite fear. Something akin to a childlike wonder overtook his senses.

The voice of an elderly woman called out from the darkness, her pitch strangely low. The voice sounded like it originated from farther back in the room, tucked into some corner.

"Hello?" A woman called out. "Hello?" The voice repeated itself exactly. "Hello?"

Ward wanted to respond, to greet the woman. In reflex, as if his body was stopping him on its own, he grabbed his own mouth with both of his hands, holding his words in. Ward stepped backwards like he was backing away from a coiled snake. His vision was still affixed on the blue light. It felt special, mesmerizing.

"Hello? Hello?" The voice spoke again. Ward looked towards the blue light, waiting for something to happen. He was shaking in equal parts terror and elation. From within the apartment, sounds of churning flesh, wet meat, and cracking bones echoed. Then, a new voice spoke, that of a little girl.

"Hee-hee... I see you!" The voice was getting closer. "Hee-hee... I see you!" The girl sounded delighted, like she was playing hide and seek with the boogieman. "Hee-hee... I see you!"

Ward, shaking, unable to move, instinctively tried to scream, but he was paralyzed. He pulled against his own muscles, which were tearing and rolling underneath his skin. His veins were popping and blood vessels bursting as he struggled to wrestle control over his own autonomy. With all his might, he tried to push from his throat all his fears. He tried to turn, to move his feet beneath his legs. Still, he was motionless, affixed on the blue glow like moths to a flame.

"Hee-hee... I see you!" The voice repeated once more. Within the dark, gurgling and churning noises bubbled forth. A hefty mass, just a shadow against the bright blue, writhed and squirmed, a mass flailing in the dark. "Hee-hee... I see you!" The voice grew louder as something approached, backlit by the blue.

Ward regained control. He screamed, uncontrollably, as loudly as he could until his throat was sore. He turned from Paula's, sprinting towards his apartment door, his feet pounding against the floor in the dark. He was so close, so close to home. Yet as he ran the hallways beneath him seemed to stretch. It was like his legs had grown shorter, and the walls taller. From behind Ward, something was gaining in speed, headed in sudden pursuit, frantic and eager to hunt. More sounds of breaking bone and churning flesh could be heard; pattering feet and crawling arms thumped and slapped. Again, the voice changed, churning. It sounded like a scared old man, begging, sobbing.

"Stay away from me!" The 'old man' wailed. "Stay away from me!" It repeated.

Ward looked back for but a moment. In the dark, he wasn't sure what he made out, but it wasn't human. Its form was churning, like a slippery mass of living oil. From its body sprouted limbs and tendrils of all sizes, which flailed and kicked and swung in all directions. Wings sprouted from its form, buzzing and clicking like a swarming infestation. The thing's shape seemed to always be changing, sinking in on itself like an ouroboros or a Möbius strip. Ward recognized several faces in the thing, each with gnashing teeth and bulging eyes. They looked in pain, desperate for company to commiserate with.

"Stay away from me!" the pursuer repeated. "Stay away from me!"

Ward reached Darcy's apartment. Trying to unlock the entrance this time, Ward nearly did drop his keys as he haplessly fumbled in terror. Hardly managing to unlock the door, he jumped inside, slamming the barricade behind him. Ward locked the door handle and pulled the chain closed. Just moments after Ward did so, a great thud slammed against the door, rattling the frame and chain. Horrendous sounds came from behind the blockade, sloshing and cracking. It banged against the door again, over and over, frenzied like a carnivore with an insatiable appetite for blood.

"Hello!?" Darcy called out from her room, hearing the commotion. "What's going on?"

Again, the monster crashed against the door, which held firm, the chain rattling on each hit. Then, it ceased the assault for a moment.

"What's happening!?" Darcy called out once more.

The thing's voice shifted anew. The sound of twisting mass, like crunching bones, would haunt Ward the rest of his miserable existence.

"What's happening!?" The thing beyond the door now sounded just like Darcy. "What's happening!? What's happening!?"

"Stop!" Ward screamed, unsure what to do, praying to a God he long stopped believing in as he leaned all his weight against the door in resistance. The building was old. The doors made from quality wood. Still, the frame splintered.

"What's happening!?" The beast pounded on the door, continuing its mimicry.

"Stop it!" Ward wailed. "Stop it!"

"Ward!?" Darcy called out. "Are you okay?"

"What's happening!?"

SLAM!

The monster feverishly clawed at the entrance again, desperate for a way inside. "What's happening!?"

BASH! The door frame splintered slightly.

"What's happening!?"

Ward rushed into Darcy's room, unsure what to do. He didn't know if he could protect himself, let alone Darcy, but he felt obligated to try.

"Ward!" Darcy gasped for air, huffing from her tank. "What's..."

"...happening!" The mimic outside their door continued to repeat.

"I..." Ward didn't know. "There's..." Ward tried his best to articulate the situation but was at a loss. Again, the thing pounded against the door, rattling the frame, repeating its words like it was a demonic parrot.

"Who's banging on the door!?" Darcy heaved in concern.

"I don't..." Nothing about this made sense. Ward wasn't opposed to the idea of the supernatural but was never particularly a believer in ghosts or ghouls. What he was about to say felt insane. "There's a monster..."

BANG!

Again, the creature slammed against the door. Its voice shifted once more, back to the sound of the 'woman' previously in Paula's apartment.

"Hello?" The thing called out as if it was lost. "Hello?"

"A monster?" Ward could feel the skepticism radiating from his grandmother. Grandma was a bit of an idiot, but she wasn't taken for a fool easily.

"I know... I know what it sounds like," Ward rambled. "But there's something... there's something..."

"Hello?" The thing continued to call out. It seemed to have ceased bashing against the door, now only repeating itself. *Knock. Knock. Knock.* It pattered on the door.

"Hello? Hello?" It continued to knock occasionally, as if politeness was a way in.

"That sounds like Paula," Darcy coughed. "Is she okay?" She nervously huffed at her oxygen.

"That ..." Ward stuttered, ready to scream and cry. "That is not Paula!" He shouted, his voice raw and burning. "That thi... thing is not human." Ward felt sick, his head pounding and his legs heavy. Darcy heaved, inhaling more oxygen. If it wasn't dark, Ward would see that Darcy was shaking as much as he was.

"She sounds like she needs help," Darcy said, her voice laden with concern.

"Grandma, please!" Ward shouted. "It—it attacked me! It chased me!"

"Why are you doing this!?" Darcy began to cry. "What's happening!?"

"I'm not doing any..." Ward didn't know how to console her, himself. He didn't know what was real or what to believe. All he knew in the moment was a presentiment instinct that things would get much worse.

From the hallways outside came a familiar sound. There was a screech, the same one he had heard before. It was a howl, unnatural, like a starving wolf gnawing at its own legs for sustenance. Accompanying the wail was the sound of stampeding, like a hundred feet hitting the ground in unison, a million joggers starting a race. The monster, the demon, continued to howl as it 'ran' away, its screams growing ever distant until it could be heard no more.

Darcy was crying, panting. So was Ward.

"Cunt." Ward cursed.

"What is this?" Darcy asked. Ward rarely heard her sound so serious. The last time Ward heard Darcy sound like this was when Grandpa died.

"I don't know," Ward replied bluntly. "We're not safe."

"Evidently," Grandma sobbed. The two lingered in the dark. The silence was haunting. It brought with it a dreadful anticipation.

"I'm going to call the police," Ward exhaled, breaking the silence. That was a sentence Ward never expected himself to say. He wasn't the biggest fan of the police, for a myriad of reasons.

"Good idea."

Ward pulled out his phone. Noticing the battery was low (around forty percent), he put the phone on power saver mode. Ward then dialed 9-1-1. The tone rang, dialing, and dialing, in perpetuity. Ward sat, at first for a few seconds, then a few minutes. Still, the phone just continued to ring with no reply. Nearly an eternity passed in the miserable cold and dark, and Ward sat confused, in disbelief of the situation he found himself in. Ward's perspective on life shifted drastically these last few minutes. He'd never believed in the supernatural, religion, or mythology. Now he wasn't sure. The phone continued to ring, to no response.

"Did it go to voicemail?" Grandma asked.

"I don't think 9-1-1 has a voicemail." Ward almost laughed. Still no answer.

"No one's picking up?" Darcy huffed some oxygen.

"No one." Ward hung up the phone, wanting to save the battery's charge. "Maybe lines are down or something."

"Oh, Jesus," Darcy cried. "Let me die. I don't understand this world anymore." She inhaled oxygen at a rapid rate.

"Try and conserve that," Ward scoffed, ignoring her comments. "We have no idea how long power will be out."

"Oh, God," Grandma cried. "Just let me die." Ward had a morbid thought. If the monster made it inside, perhaps he could use Darcy as a scapegoat, a sacrificial distraction to allow for an escape.

Ward slid the living room recliner against the interior apartment hallway door. He then slid the living room couch in front of the patio doors. The apartment was growing exponentially colder in the winter night. Ward brought Darcy more blankets and put on extra layers of clothing himself. He was exhausted, but fear and adrenaline wouldn't allow rest. He knew it would be a long night, and he would have to be vigilant.

Bringing the recliner out from the den into the living room, Ward leaned back just enough to be comfortable, but not so much so that he couldn't get up swiftly. He spent what felt like hours trying to call almost everyone on his contact list. No matter what, his calls would not go through. The same went for text messages. *Message failed to send*! There was something blocking the connection. Deciding to conserve battery, he stopped.

Ward stared at the front door. It felt like an open wound, a sore waiting to be stabbed at. He sat in the dark, looking at the entrance, contemplating reality. Hours passed, and his eyelids weakened. Ward tried his best to stay awake, vigilant, but fell into a powerful slumber. He slept for a long time.

. . .

"Ward!?" Darcy's panicked voice called out. "Ward!?" She huffed. The power had yet to return, so she continued to suck down on her dwindling supply of artificial air.

Ward emerged from sleep. His eyes were fuzzy, and momentarily he felt paralyzed, the room around him a blurry darkness. Everything was pitch black; no light came from outside.

"Ward!?" Darcy called out again, weaker. Hearing this, Ward snapped to attention, rising from his seat. Flashes of recollection, flashes of yesterday assailed him. It felt like a dream. With his muscles still sore from sleep, he stumbled to his grandma's room, panicked.

"What? What!?" He said, fearful of some new monster's emergence. As he lingered, he could smell it. The room was stale; it reeked of piss and shit.

"Of course," Ward sighed.

At least now that the power was out, Ward didn't need to maneuver Darcy's oxygen hose on her journeys. Sitting on the seat, she relieved herself. Afterwards, Ward helped Darcy clean up and change her diapers. The lack of running water was made apparent by this task.

"It's so dark," Darcy commented as she huffed down on her oxygen, taking long inhalations. It sounded like someone holding down the spray button on a tube of air freshener for an unnecessarily long time.

"We've only got one more refill of that," Ward said, concerned. Darcy moaned and scowled as she relieved herself.

"What time is it?" Darcy asked, rubbing her eyes as she stood up from the toilet. Ward pulled out his phone, checking the time.

"That... can't be right," Ward said softly, concerned. He unlocked his cell, opening the clock application, and still the same time was listed.

"What? Darcy asked.

"Nine-thirty." Ward frowned. "A.M." It was still dark outside, pitch black, like the middle of the night. There was no sun poking past the curtains, no glow around the rims of windows. The apartment was very much a cave, but even with every blind drawn, the home would not be entirely pitch black as it was now.

"That can't be." Darcy scowled, standing up from the toilet, clutching her walker. "Your machine's broken."

"Maybe," Ward said, escorting Darcy to her seat in the living room. "But it does feel like I overslept a bit."

"Me..." Darcy gasped. She struggled to talk and walk, but it didn't stop her. "...too."

Ward decided he needed to plan for the worst. He didn't know what the situation was or how long it would last. Ward found a flashlight, but it had no batteries. He tried to find something to use as a weapon, a hammer or a crowbar. He found a fireplace poker tucked away in the laundry room. It was an old relic of a former past made from a dark black metal, covered in dust. His grandparents' old home did have a fireplace, but why they brought it to an apartment without one, confused Ward. Regardless, it was a heavy metal stick with pointy bits, so he was thankful to have it on hand.

With paper and pen, Ward began to take inventory of all the food they had available. It took a moment for his eyes to adjust as he started writing. Everything in the fridge had an expiration timer on it now that there was no power. Some things had probably already spoiled or were beginning to.

The cheese was still good, the deli meats still passable as well. The milk had begun to sour. The juices were still fine for the moment. In the freezer, the raw meat would be a total loss without the ability to cook it. There were also a lot of frozen meals that would be no-go. Some of them may be technically consumable since they were pre-cooked, but Ward decided to put them off till last.

Ward made a strange breakfast, composed of ingredients that needed to be prioritized in eating first. Cheese, strawberries, lettuce, and some bagels with cream cheese. While they couldn't get water from the fridge, fortunately, Darcy had a little less than a dozen water bottles tucked away at the bottom of the pantry. He poured each of them a small cup of water.

"What is this?" Darcy puffed as Ward plated her breakfast in front of his grandma and sat down to join her.

"We need to be smart about how we're eating," Ward said.

"Why?" Darcy seemed confused.

"Do you not remember last night!?" Ward raised his voice.

"Yes..." Darcy was trepidatious, her voice quiet.

"Well, no power means food will spoil. And I have no idea when we can get more."

"Can't we go to the grocery?" Darcy seemed to be breathing well for the moment.

"I am not going out there." Ward shook his head. "Not until things get normal."

"Why?" Darcy asked once more. The concaves in her face were like deep, bottomless pits in the darkness. The pupils of her eyes could not be seen, but instead, she simply had black orbs which rotated in her skull. Even though the unnatural shadows distorted Darcy's form, Ward could see the confusion and fear in her. He could hear it, too. Yet, Ward was angry. Frustrated with her obliviousness.

"Oh my God ..." Ward tightened his wrist, rolling it. "Because of whatever's... out there." He pointed to the barricaded front door, then the back door behind him, then lifted his hands in frustration.

"What's out there?" Darcy asked.

"How clueless can you be!?" Ward shouted in his head, baffled. "A monster, a demon, I don't know!"

Darcy looked down, away from her grandson. She nibbled on some cheese in silence, fearful anything she said would upset him.

"Listen... I don't know what's happening," Ward admitted. "For all we know, it's the god-damned apocalypse. We need to ration."

"Just like the war..." Darcy huffed more oxygen down. Ward bit his lip. If power didn't restore soon, Darcy wouldn't die from starvation, dehydration, or monsters in the dark. It'd be her chronic disruptive pulmonary disease. Darcy was already getting stir crazy without her shows. In the dark, she couldn't read, so all she could do was sit in silence or talk. She chose the latter, despite how it wore on her lungs.

For Ward, the feeling of being trapped was now amplified. He was living in his grandmother's coffin, and he felt he would die alongside her. It was a dreadful prospect.

"What time is it?" Darcy asked. A new catchphrase was

developing. She kept asking Ward every few minutes or so. Time didn't feel like it was passing in the dark, and the only way to know for certain was by checking Ward's phone or laptop. In this way, Ward was transformed into a clock.

When dinner came, Darcy demanded a glass of wine, which Ward complied with. There wasn't much left. Ward decided to have a drink alongside her. He wasn't a big fan of wine at all, especially pinks, but Ward figured he might as well enjoy a buzz at the end of the world. The two ate some salami sandwiches. They dipped it in cold red sauce, which strangely complemented the wine well in an unconventional way. They also ate some bananas for dessert. It was a strange meal. Despite no shows to watch, Darcy was a woman of routine. After dinner, she sat in her normal chair, quietly humming to herself in the dark between bouts of sickly coughing and oxygen inhalations. Ward kicked his feet, tense.

Ward tried to dial for help once more, tried to call several loved ones and friends. Nobody picked up, his phone just rang and rang, not even going to voicemail. He sent text messages, but none would go through. Every text was like a message in a bottle lost at sea, floating nowhere, never to be received.

After endless dial tones and several unsent messages, Ward gave up on that pursuit again, wishing to conserve battery, for what good it would do. Desperate, Ward walked around to each light switch, praying that flicking one on would do something, cause anything to occur. He looked through closets, cabinets, dressers, and drawers. Ward wasn't sure what he was looking for, just that he was seeking something useful, some McGuffin to fix the situation. No such thing was found. Eventually, exhausted and resigned, Ward gave up on that pursuit as well.

"Fuck it," Ward said. He retrieved his stash bag, filling a bowl with pot. Thankfully, he'd visited the dispensary recently, but marijuana was a limited commodity now, too.

"Smoke it while you got it..." he mumbled. If it was the apocalypse, he might as well get high. Sitting down on a stool at the kitchen counter, Ward unpacked his supplies. It was difficult to pack a bowl in the dark, but Ward managed through a combination of focus and muscle memory. He lit his piece, enjoying each smooth puff.

"What is that smell?" Darcy sniffed, turning toward the kitchen.

"I'm smoking some weed." Ward puffed at his pipe. He felt some satisfaction in this action.

"You can't do that." Darcy inhaled her oxygen, waving her hand in the air.

"If it really is the end of the world. I'm going to enjoy the little things while I still can." Ward puffed a large cloud of smoke into the air. It felt liberating, in a way, to be able to smoke in the apartment. All this time living here, and it was never a privilege he was allowed. Now, feeling trapped in this dark, gloomy place, Ward was allowed one meaningless little token of freedom.

"I always thought it was a liquid," Darcy said suddenly, as she watched her grandson in the dark.

"What?" Ward laughed. "Really?"

"Yeah." Darcy huffed her oxygen. "I thought you drank it."

Ward broke out into hysterics. It was the first time Darcy had made him laugh in a while. For a moment, Ward remembered how much he loved his grandma.

. . .

Another sleepless, uneasy night passed. In the morning, there was still nothing but darkness inside and out. Ward's phone was in the red, so he checked the time sparingly. His laptop had died overnight. That piece of junk had long since lost its ability to hold a charge without remaining plugged in. The entire apartment was beginning to smell like trash, excrement, and rotting fruit. Additionally, they were down to just five water bottles. Darcy was also nearly out of her portable oxygen as well as diapers. Ward wished he could take a shower. Sparingly using bottled water to wash up was not very effective, especially after continually helping Darcy use the restroom. Ward could feel Grandma's stink lingering upon him. Supplies were going to force Ward's hand soon. He would have to commit to a choice, an action, with no pre-informed knowledge on what to prepare for or what to do.

Ward stared at the alert he'd received on his phone a few days ago. *Couldn't say he wasn't warned.*

It was sometime around noon, give or take, lunch had just wrapped up (they had eaten the remaining bread, some peanuts, and the last banana). Peeling back the curtains, Ward looked through the patio door window. Outside, it looked as if it was the dead of night during winter. No light could be seen, natural or artificial, only blackness. Ward realized how accustomed to the dark his eyes had grown.

"What do you think's out there?" Ward spoke out loud. He wasn't expecting a reply. But Darcy did, in fact, provide one, hauntingly so.

"Nothing." Darcy sucked down more fleeting oxygen. "I've seen the sky for ninety years and that's not the sky."

Ward gulped, closing the curtains, leaning his head against the door. He could feel his warm breath radiate from the curtain cloth back onto his face.

"Then ..." Ward headed back to the couch, sitting in the seat closest to his grandma as he spoke. "What is it?"

"I don't know," Darcy sighed. "Bad news bears."

Dinner came around. Ward's culinary creativity was being put to the test. He 'made' spam with onions and some assorted celery, cutting around some decaying bits. Ward hated spam, but it was protein. He set their plates down on the dining room table.

"I'll have some wine," Darcy said confidently.

"We..." Ward felt like he was about to tell a child Santa isn't real. "We finished the wine yesterday."

"Oh, Lord," Darcy muttered disappointedly. "Can we get more?"

"I don't know," Ward sighed. "But we're running out of more important things than just wine..." Ward sighed, sitting down in his seat. "Grandma?" He needed to ask her something.

"Yes?" She huffed in another puff of oxygen. The spray mechanism sounded faint, like not much was left in the canister.

"Do you really think nothing's out there?"

"Oh ..." She thought for a moment, continuing to huff. "There has to be."

"Maybe you're right ..." Ward sighed. Finishing dinner, Ward helped Darcy into her recliner. He lay back on the couch, looking up at the ceiling, lost in thought, listening to Darcy's labored breaths.

"You look just like him," Darcy commented as she grew comfortable in her recliner.

"Uh-huh," Ward mumbled.

"You two are a lot alike."

"How would you know that?" Ward groaned. It felt wrong to talk about this for some reason.

"Jason visited me last night," Darcy said, no wheezing upon her tongue.

Ward halted, frozen. The implications of his grandma's words sank deep into his essence. Had the darkness driven her mad? Or worse...

"Excuse me?" Ward quivered, skin tingling and fear rising. He sat up on the couch, looking towards his grandma.

"While you were sleeping." Darcy huffed from her dwindling supply of air.

"Was this a dream?" Ward asked as calmly as he could.

"I don't know." Darcy smiled. Her teeth the only thing visible in the dark. "But he's waiting for me. His touch was soft."

"Waiting for what?" Ward asked.

"For me to die," she said plainly.

"You're not going to die, Grammy." Ward tried to comfort her.

"Oh, please." Darcy coughed. "I'm not stupid. Everything's gone to shit." It was strange to hear Darcy swear. She saved such words for rare occasions, like using the good plates when guests arrived. She'd always said she didn't like cursing. "You'd be better off leaving me to die."

"Maybe," Ward sighed. "But I'm not going to."

There was a moment of silence, brief, lingering between the conversation.

"I hope everyone else is safe," Darcy lamented.

"I'm sure they are." Ward wasn't sure about anything, but he hoped whatever was happening was contained locally around this accursed apartment building.

"I know they are," Darcy cried.

. . .

Two long, dark, tense days later. Supplies were at their lowest. Ward thought it was around lunch time. His phone had died, and telling the passage of time had grown increasingly difficult.

Ward had sequestered Darcy to her bedroom. She was nearly out of oxygen. Ward had swapped out her tank a day or so ago, and there was not another replacement. Either way, Darcy's condition had worsened, and she used the portable supply almost constantly as if it were her new set of lungs. The apartment was a complete mess. Ward had given up on any hope of sanitation. Shit lined grandma's bed, and Ward's hands smelt of foul excretions. Without diapers and running water, Darcy was left to fester in her own stew. The bathrooms were starting to overflow, and floors were beginning to grow sticky. Ward only used baby wipes now on his hands before prepping food, but even soon that would no longer be an option (both eating food and access to baby wipes).

"Here ya' go." Ward set down Darcy's lunch on her overbed table. She hadn't had to use it since the early days of recovery when moving back into her house. Lunch was abysmal. They had about two, maybe three meals' worth of food left, though calling them meals may be a bit generous. On Darcy's plate were some pretzels, peanut butter, and a few wilted apple slices. Ward had used up the last of the remaining perishables with that, or at least the ones that were still edible, though Ward feared they may have to reevaluate that definition soon. They were also down to the last water bottle. Darcy was given just a small glass of water with her meal.

"Try to drink after you eat," Ward suggested. "Those'll make you thirsty." He pointed at the pretzels.

"What..." Darcy huffed for a long time on her oxygen, looking down at her plate with disdain. "What is this?"

"Lunch..." Ward droned, miserable.

"NO!" Darcy screamed. "I'm tired of pretzels! All you feed me are pretzels!" Her voice was cracking, her lungs strained. She quickly sucked down more oxygen. The tube sounded empty, or like it was close to it.

"Gram... it's all we..." Ward tried to rationalize with her, but was explosively interrupted.

"NO! NO MORE!" Darcy slammed her hand down on the overbed table, sliding it violently and with a surprising amount of force. Her meal and glass of water collapsed to the ground, the plate shattering. Peanut butter smeared across the floor. The glass cup managed not to break, but water splashed everywhere. She began to heave, desperately sucking life from a tube.

"What is wrong with you!?" Ward screamed.

"STOP!" Despite her weak breath, Darcy seemed to wield a fury that allowed her to boast with great volume a powerful declaration. "NO MORE OF THIS!"

"I don't have a choice, I..." Ward tried to cut in, but Darcy screamed like a train whistle.

"WHY ARE YOU DOING THIS!?" Her lungs were like thin water balloons, overinflating and ready to pop. "WHY!? WHY ARE YOU DOING THIS!?"

"I'm not doing..."

"WHY!? I JUST WANT TO DIE!" Darcy raged. Her arms were flailing and her legs kicking. Her portable oxygen inhaler fell from her lap. The metal capsule-shaped canister collided against the wood floor, sending a clanking sound echoing through the house. Darcy was panting and crying, snot running down her shabby clothes.

"Why... why..." Darcy tried to keep screaming, but her anger was snuffed by her gasps. She'd begun gagging and wheezing. Desperately, she tried to reach for the oxygen inhaler on the ground. She looked as if she would topple off the side of the bed, but it seemed she didn't even have the strength to turn herself over. Darcy looked towards Ward, arms outstretched. She looked pitiful, and for a moment, it felt like Ward had night vision.

Ward looked into his grandmother's eyes, and she looked into his. In the dark, in her last moments, Darcy didn't look much like herself. Still... she looked scared, angry, feral. Ward wanted to grab the oxygen and give it to Grandma, but something stopped him. He loved her so much yet resented her so vastly. It felt like both an execution and a generous gift, Darcy finally receiving what she'd been begging for. So, Ward watched as his grandmother flailed on her soiled bed, fighting against death despite her wishes to embrace it. Darcy's face turned red, then purple. She continued to gasp and cough, seemingly trying to scoop air into her mouth. Her eyes bulged and grew bright pink. The sounds his grandmother made were grotesque, indescribable, horrendous fluid filled gargles and desperate, sorrowful screeches. After minutes of Ward's unblinking attention, Darcy died. When she finally stopped flailing, he blinked. When he opened his eyes again, her corpse was still there, motionless in the dark.

"Hehghu..." Ward whimpered, both a laugh and a cry. "Oh god. Oh no, I... What?"

Ward stumbled backwards, turning from Darcy, never to look upon her again. He bunglingly shuffled from her room, eyes facing down at the floor. He stumbled into his bedroom, lying down on his mattress. He wept for a long time.

"I'm..." Ward spoke out loud to himself momentarily. He wasn't sure what he was, but he knew what he wanted. "I need out." His tears had subsided, but not much. But the sobs did not restrain Ward's actions.

Ward launched from his bed. He changed into a new set of clothing, putting on several layers to protect from the cold outdoors. Grabbing his backpack, he filled a few extra changes of clothes. Raiding the pantry for what little was left, he stuffed it into his pack. Whatever was out in the darkness, Ward knew he didn't want to go on foot. It was cold, miserable enough in the apartment.

Fortunately, he could enjoy some heating for the first time in ages via his car, assuming he could reach it. He would have to head through the basement to get to the garage. There was a button to open the garage doors remotely, a clicker. However unfortunately it was in the car in the garage hanging from the driver's sun visor. *Would be useless without power anyway.*

"Weapon," Ward said, remembering the fire poker. He may need a way to defend himself. Ill-prepared, reckless, and terrified, Ward cleared the barricade around the back door. He unlocked it, and the chain rattled as it was unlatched. The locks clicked open with an ominous springing sound. Ward stepped out of his apartment, onto the carpeted floors of Grassy Acres.

CLAY HOUSES

From the darkness, the blue formed itself, the interior of the home, from nothing. Edda watched, mesmerized. It was as if the void was both the clay being molded and the sculptor. Floors unfolded beneath Edda's feet, rolling out like a tatami mat. The walls rose and expanded in an instant. Details, furniture, and all were manifested into being. The interior was gray momentarily. Then in a flash, the house was filled with color and light, texture and vibrance. Edda wasn't sure if she was awake or dreaming; her head was foggy, and eyesight blurry. She smelled sweet things, like fruits dripping with gasoline.

Looking around, the interior of the home appeared rather normal, considering what Edda had just witnessed. It didn't feel lived in, like a house that's not a home. The first floor was a simple layout. Past the front door was a stairway to the left and a hallway to the right. The floor was tiled in mundane, tiny white squares. Above was a popcorn ceiling, which looked yellowed and blackened, as if someone spent a lot of time smoking cigarettes downstairs.

Edda walked down the right-hand hallway. There were closets embedded in the walls, as well as a washer and dryer. The hallway ended at the entrance to a large room. The room was rectangular and spacious, with no apparent purpose. It was windowless and connected only to the hallway leading to the front door. The floor was a disgusting pink shag carpet, which was wet and moldy. The wallpaper was simple, yellow and white striped, but it was peeling and ruined by water damage. The ceiling here was a drop tile. Edda turned around.

Heading up the stairs, Edda noticed several pictures and

paintings mounted on the walls, at least, their frames. Most of the photos and paintings seemed to have been ripped out and torn apart, leaving behind only scraps of torn prints and canvases. There was one piece that remained, however. It was an oil painting, much larger than the rest. It looked old, neglected, baroque.

Edda stared at the painting, entranced. Edda was standing lopsided on the stairs, so she tilted her head slightly to get a better angle. The painting depicted a lady sitting on a stool. She was beautiful, with strands of golden hair flowing in the wind. She seemed to be looking out of the painting, staring back at Edda. Behind the painted woman was a field of wheat, blown out in brilliant white light. On the horizon was a sun which poked out from behind a mountain range, glowing in a way in which its radiance nearly drowned everything else in a golden aura.

One element of the painting, however, seemed opposed to the light, shrouded in its own unnatural darkness. Next to the woman, most startlingly, was a bird cage, equal in size to her. Only black paint was used to depict the cage. So much was used in fact that it created layers upon layers of dark which popped from the canvas, drawing Edda's eyes to its black form, almost inhibiting her from seeing the surrounding beauty. The cage always drew attention to one's eye, even if you simply wished to stare at the brilliance of the sun or the blush of the woman. It was like live pornography performed in the corner framing of a presidential address. One inherently drew more attention than the other.

Continuing upstairs, Edda arrived at the second floor. The story opened to a large kitchen with a center island. The cabinets were gutted, and no appliances were present. The kitchen did have a lovely black granite countertop, however, which was nicely polished and reflected its surroundings almost as well as a mirror could. The kitchen connected to the living room, another bathroom, and the outdoor balcony.

The view through the balcony window was strange. The beach itself looked normal, the dunes familiar, but distant in the ocean were tremendous monoliths, at least a dozen of them, all in varying heights and locations. They towered out of the sea like skyscrapers, spiraling monuments in which the waves of the ocean corkscrewed around, creating vast, raging whirlpools. They looked like whittled bone, carved from giants or gods long since forgotten and decayed.

Edda felt equal parts terror and elation. Her instincts told her she was in danger, to leave and never come back to this place. Her imagination and curiosity, however, excited her. She felt honored, in some bizarre sense, to be given sights that possibly no human had ever witnessed before. All her life, Edda had been reserved, meek. Now, in this moment unexplained, she felt emboldened to charge forward, undaunted by the unknown, defiant to terror. In the abnormal, she was determined to thrive.

Edda headed into the living room. It was, in contrast to the other rooms she'd seen, nicely furnished. There was a large grey leather couch, one that could probably seat around ten people, as well as several ottomans that extended the seating potential. A television was mounted on the wall, and below it was an entertainment center. There was a glass table in the middle of the room, on which nothing sat. Above, a ceiling fan, which had collected layers of dust, lazily spun. While the room was nicely furnished, it felt soulless, empty. There were several windows in the living room. Edda kept an eye out for the window through which she saw the flashing light. None of them seemed right. The interior of the house felt off, much larger inside than she had expected, or perhaps much smaller.

Edda turned the corner of the living room. There were stairs, which led upwards into an unlit corridor. Edda climbed into the darkness. The stairs began to spiral around themselves until it felt like she was ascending in circles. Eventually reaching the top after several minutes of walking, Edda found herself in a long, drab corridor that stretched outwards like a rubber band. At the end of the corridor was a single window, and above it, hanging from the ceiling, was a covered light, which dangled from a loose thread of wire. From that light, a bulb flashed on and off at random intervals.

It really was just a dying light bulb after all.

"Heh," Edda chuckled. *Why not?* Edda made her way down the

dimly lit hallway. The walk was long, and the floor seemed to twist and turn underneath her feet like a rickety rope bridge. The hallway was absent of detail, nearly pitch black. No decorations adorned the walls, nor other passageways. At the end of the hallway, through the window, Edda could see Wight Street, which looked as it always had. Adjusting herself at the correct angle, Edda could barely see her patio. She extended her hand out to the lightbulb, screwing it in place. It no longer flickered.

"Okay," Edda smiled. "Done." A calmness overcame her. She felt relaxed, lulled into a sense of security. Turning around, Edda noticed a doorframe. She stepped inside to find a small room with carpet. The walls were carpet, the ceiling carpet, the floor carpet, all of the same blue color. Besides that, it was empty. It made her feel uneasy, so she did not linger. Heading back, Edda descended the stairs to the second floor. She strode through the living room into the kitchen, admiring the sea view as she did so. Edda headed back down to the first floor, wood creaking under her feet, a sense of enlightenment and accomplishment emboldening her.

Edda's invigoration immediately ceased as she stopped midway down the first set of stairs. Standing in front of the previously described painting, she now looked upon it in horror. The fog from Edda's head receded, and her focus sharpened.

"Holy fuck." Edda startled herself, realizing she wasn't dreaming. The absurd nature of the house, its impossible sights, only now did Edda truly comprehend its implications. It felt as if she was previously moving along as a puppet, and now suddenly her strings were cut. Edda reached towards the painting, feeling its texture on her fingertips. She slid her hands down the canvas slowly, its thick layers of paint an affirmation of her consciousness. Edda looked up at the woman, smiling. The figure looked just like her. Edda touched her hand to her painting doppelganger, expecting it to move or lunge out at her. But the painting remained motionless.

Continuing downstairs, Edda returned to the entranceway. The front door, to her surprise, was wide open. She was expecting to be trapped, for this home to be her new prison. Edda could see out past

Wight Street to her small corner home. The eye of the storm had since passed. Some of the rain was blowing in through the front entrance, causing water to slowly pool near the doormat. Edda could leave, never to return to this strange place. Yet, despite her desire to flee, the outdoors felt like a trap as well. If she exited, she'd be returning to a fake world, a stage-play of her former life.

This is insane, Edda thought to herself on repeat. She turned around, heading back down the first-floor corridor to the large, empty, rectangular room. In the corridor, all the closet doors were open. Inside them were hardly any contents, only stains and dust, and a few empty coat hangers.

Entering the rectangular room, the wet carpet sloshed under Edda's shoes. The soggy room was no longer empty. In the corner, farthest from the entranceway, was a cage, empty, haunting, rusty, familiar. Edda glared at the contraption, its proportions exaggerated, its presence somehow expected. Inside the cage was nothing. Inside the cage were her mistakes. Inside the cage were her desires. Inside the cage were the people she'd lost and forgotten.

"I'm not a prisoner," Edda whispered to herself.

Opening the cage door, Edda crawled inside. Sitting down on the rusted metal plate, Edda crossed her legs, leaned back, and waited for a very long time. First, a day passed, then a week, then a month. She experienced hunger unfathomable. She experienced thirst unquenchable. But she never left the cage. She felt closer to a father she never had the chance to know. She felt his hands warm, clutching her tightly as if she were but a newborn.

Slowly, Edda and the cage sank into the depths of the moldering Farm, embraced by its halls.

"I'm not a prisoner," Edda affirmed.

A WORKING TITLE FIT FOR ANY HOUSEHOLD IN THE NEIGHBORHOOD

It is so strange to me, these squares through which we see.
It is so strange to me, these holes through which we breathe.
It is so strange to me, these dreams through which we scheme.
It is so strange to me, these lives we seldom glean.

CALDERA

He had asked her out on a second date. After what felt like an awkward disaster last dinner, she was thankful for the change of scenery. She felt much more at ease in the park than in an overpriced steakhouse. The two had set up a blanket by the promenade. They were under a nice tree, a weeping willow, which provided the perfect amount of shade. The weather was just below eighty, and the breeze was generous. Sounds of dogs barking and children playing echoed throughout the park. Couples and friends sat on benches, conversing. A few cyclists and skaters rolled by now and then. There was a kid with his mother, flying a kite. It was picturesque.

As spontaneous as a bird's chirping, a loud-pitched ringing sound pierced through Bethany's skull. She held her right ear for a moment. It felt like she was being stabbed and beaten, but just as suddenly as the pain came, it disappeared.

"You alright?" Carl asked. He looked so young.

"I'm fine," Bethany replied. "Tinnitus."

"Oh. That high-pitched thing?" Carl asked, unsure.

"Yeah," Bethany affirmed. "It's going away, only lasts a few seconds."

"You… go to a lot of concerts?" Carl was nervous. Though he was less jittery than he was on their first date, Carl still stuttered and felt like he struggled to say the right things. What he didn't know was that Bethany was also nervous; she just hid it better.

"No," Bethany laughed, looking at the muddy river which slowly chugged downstream. "Why?"

"Ya' know …" Carl waved his hand as he spoke, trying to think of how to articulate himself. "Loud music, screaming people, ringing ears, all that …"

"Oh no," Bethany smiled. "I got it after a concussion. Fell off a horse."

Carl laughed for a second, holding in his chuckle when he realized how rude it seemed.

"I'm sorry, I shouldn't have laughed ..." Carl forced an awkward smile.

"It's okay," Bethany laughed alongside him. "Shit happens."

The environment grew cold. It was no longer a warm day by the creek. The muddy river was still, frozen by a winter's cold, and like it, a kite hung motionless in the sky. Clouds fell backwards into the atmosphere and stars long dead, only known for their glow, reignited.

"You ride horses?" Carl asked. He was wearing an older face now.

"Oh, no ... not anymore. Haven't since I was a kid." Bethany began to shiver. A winter air carried on it a deceptive warmth.

"Honestly, I'd probably bust my ass falling off," Carl laughed, taking a sip of his drink.

"I'm sure you'd do fine." Beth smiled.

Bethany often wished she could replay moments in her life, like a relived scrapbook.

Bethany often wished she could replay moments in her life, like a relived scrapbook.

Bethany often could replay moments in her life, like a relived scrapbook.

Bethany often could replay in her life a relived scrap.

Often, she replayed life, relived.

Often, she replay, relived.

She replay, relived.

She, relived.

Relived.

"You can't die here." Carl's tone of voice changed. His face grew serious, the shadows beneath his eyes like punji pits; they stabbed like the cold air.

"What?" Bethany gasped. "Carl..." She felt sick. "I can't..."

Bethany awoke, her ears ringing and head spinning. Her face was pushed down into the hard soil and grass. Blood trickled from her head, which had a substantial gash in it. Grunting, Bethany tried to lift herself up. As she exerted herself, a tidal wave of pain shot through her right arm. The agony was more terrible than anything she'd experienced in life, even childbirth, all twelve hours of it. Bethany, with her neck cracking as she turned, looked in horror upon her arm. It was broken, shattered, unrecognizable.

Where her wrist used to be was now but a stump. The skin wrapped around Bethany's arm was frayed in many places, torn to strands of bloodied flesh like peeled pieces of string cheese. Bethany screamed, her lungs coughing up blood, pus, and mucus.

Her howl was carried by the night wind, lost in obscurity on the highway. She could hardly hear herself shout in the dead winter night. Somewhat fortunately, Bethany's left arm and legs were mostly functioning. Strenuously, fueled entirely by instinct and adrenaline, Bethany propped herself up, turning around on her back. As she did, her arm flailed and dragged against the ground and underneath her weight.

She screamed again. If one could die of pain this surely would be the threshold. Bethany couldn't see her own breath, perhaps she had. Eventually, Bethany pushed past the blaring pain, trying to orient herself. It was dark. There was a cutting wind, so unbearably cold. She was in a ditch filled with dead grasses and frost-nipped foliage. To the right of the highway was an empty field with a few dead trees scattered around. To the left of her was the road and her car ... It was crumpled. A pulverized deer was embedded into the bumper and hood. Her windshield was shattered outward, like a missile had launched from the interior of the vehicle. Most of the car had folded on itself like a discarded tissue. A little bit of smoke trickled from what once was the hood.

Bethany looked down at her functioning arm and hand. Her clothes were torn, her skin cut, covered in blood and dirt. A few shards of glass and metal embedded themselves into areas of her skin at random. Her palm, shoulder, neck, and chest were all filled with shards of debris. Bethany, shivering, bloodied, and delirious, wanted to lie back down and go to sleep forever. It seemed like the only option to hide from the pain. Just as she was about to accept her death, Bethany remembered.

It filled her with rage, hate, and sorrow, all of which rivaled the physical pain immensely. A maddened determination, something both natural and super, spurred deep within Bethany. She tried to stand. Her first attempt, she essentially flailed. Her second attempt, she nearly found footing, but her left leg gave way, her bones cracking and skin shredding. As she lay in the cold, frost-topped ground, Bethany looked forward, the wreckage of her smoldering car a surreal landmark. A burst of winter wind cut through the night, stabbing at Bethany's exposed skin. She felt Mother Nature's knife penetrate her broken bone and mangled nerves. Bethany raged continually, a roadside banshee.

Eventually, she managed to stand. Newtext's border was about eight miles from Letterfaux. They were slightly further into town, so realistically, it was about nine to eleven miles away. Bethany had covered some distance driving but wasn't sure how much before the accident. She was in no condition to walk an inch, let alone eight miles. Bethany saw no other alternative other than to persevere or die trying. Home was the last chance she had to save Leon; she had to get there no matter what.

Bethany took a step, stumbling forward. Her front right foot could barely support her weight as it connected with the ground. Her left leg dragged behind. With boundless pain, she managed to stay standing then began walking. Beth tried to climb up the small rise from the ditch to the road past the wreckage, one step. Bethany wobbled, the slope tricky in her condition, and the ground slippery. Another step. Still, she stood. Upon the third step, however, Bethany fell forward, crashing face-first into the ground, her chest slamming against rock, and her mangled arm shattering even more upon impact.

Beth landed in a section of grass that was splattered in gore and viscera. Blood and decay from the deer splashed upon her face and body. The smell was repulsive, and combined with the blow of the fall, Bethany found herself vomiting a mixture of bile and her wounds. Panting, drained, she managed to stand on her feet once more. Bethany knew if she fell one more time, she wouldn't stand again. Reaching the top of the hill, Bethany found a large tree branch, which she began to use as a cane. Limping down the dark, cold road, Bethany thought of only one thing: Leon.

. . .

You're listening to 91.5, home of the Boulder! Up next, we have another hour of all your favorite hit country singles...

The voice on the radio, dull and muffled, came through the speakers. Harold Dellinger was driving his Explorer from Newtext back to his home in Letterfaux. He'd met up with some friends to go drinking. He'd suggested going to Chesire's so he could drink closer to home, but the majority of his friend group lived in Newtext. Harry was mostly sober. He'd made sure to drink more water this time than usual at the very least. About three years back, he'd gotten a DUI, so he was trying, slightly, to be more careful. He felt confident to drive, and though the country roads were dark as usual, he had this route memorized and his mind focused.

Harold flipped his turn signal on towards his left, taking the turn gently down Vogele Street. The road was a long stretch of nothing, just cornfields and woods with occasional family homes dotted behind private driveways here and there. Sleepy, but vigilant, finger tapping along to a catchy tune, Harry was taken by complete surprise when his headlights illuminated a brutal wreck ahead of him. Instinctively, he slammed his brakes, rubber burning and tires squelching.

"Wow." Harold gazed slack-jawed, his car idling in the road for a moment. The wreck was impressive. He could have been forgiven for mistaking the car for a crushed soda can, were it not for its size. Momentarily, Harry thought about fleeing the scene, wanting no involvement, but his caring nature beat out such an instinct. Pulling out his cellphone, Harry attempted to call for help but found he had no reception. Hesitantly, he slowly drove up the road, emergency blinkers on, as he inspected the scene.

"Hello?" Harold rolled down his window, the biting winter wind stabbing at his pale face. "Anyone alive?" His shouts were absorbed in the empty road and wilds. The deer, or what was left of it, was merged with the front of the car, creating this grotesque sculpture of fused metal and flesh. It was a roadside gargoyle, a menacing sculpture. Harry was a bit of a car guy, but the wreck made identifying the vehicle impossible. Harry spotted droplets of blood, leading from the wreckage directly parallel to the road ahead. Leaving his car and putting on his emergency blinkers, Harold followed the trail and soon enough found a woman. She was lying face down in the ground, breathing slow. The car blinkers flashed on and off, illuminating the scene in red bursts of light.

"Are you alive?" Harold stuttered. There was a stick next to the woman. He had an urge to poke the potential corpse but felt disgusted with the idea. Her body looked like a battered pincushion, or a voodoo doll ripped to shreds by a hound.

Bethany looked up from the ground, struggling to move. In front of her was a tall, skinny man with a shallow face and bushy beard. He was wearing a red and black checkered flannel jacket, jeans, and boots. He looked terrified, unsure of what to do.

"Call ... nine ..." Bethany tried to plea.

"My ... my phone's got no signal, I ..." Harold was scared. He wished he'd taken a different route home; he wished he'd been oblivious, just driven by the wreckage. "Fuck ..." Harold swore. He felt sick. It felt like somehow this would be pinned on him. He couldn't afford court or jail.

"I'll go get help." Harold declared, turning around.

"Wait!" Bethany gurgled out a shout. "No time."

"We need to get you to the hospital." Harold seemed to know the area well. "There's one down in Central Burk... I can drive there, get someone!"

"NO!" Bethany screeched, spiting into the dirt. "I need to get home!"

"Lady, no fucking way!" Harold insisted. "Fact that you're alive and talking right now is a damned miracle. You're in shock, we need to get you to..."

"NO!" Bethany screamed again, bits of blood, spit, and mucus shooting from her mouth as she did so. "THEY STOLE HIM!" Beth shuddered, her body convulsing and her mind raging. "THEY'LL KILL HIM!"

"Christ, lady, what are ..." Harry was shaken. "Slow down, what happened?"

"My ..." Bethany huffed; her tears mixed with her blood; her inhalations mixed with her shouts. "My son was," Beth's words burned her insides, "kid... nap..." She felt woozy. Staying awake was growing increasingly difficult. Her head nodded up and down, her eyes heavy and body numbed.

Hesitantly, Harold helped Bethany stand up. She was defiant to her crumbling body, defiant to her pain. Trembling and struggling, blood trickled down all parts of her body, some of which ran down Harold's clothes and skin. Bethany's face was painted in both her own and the animal's blood, and similarly, her body was smeared in viscera. Her clothes were torn, and pieces of glass and metal could be seen still wedged into her flesh. Bethany shouted in agony as she flailed into the car, Harold doing his best to prop her up.

Harry had never heard such screams before. It was a struggle, but with a lot of exertion, Bethany was strapped in. Getting into the driver's seat, Harold turned down the radio and took off, tires screeching, the car lurching. Blood covered the passenger seat and floor within minutes. Harry wished he had a towel he could have set down, or a tarp.

"Jesus ..." Harry weaved down a winding road. He was still driving with the goal of reaching the hospital. "They in the accident to?"

"No ..." Bethany grunted, her throat rumbling. "Just a damn deer."

"So why home?" Harry asked. "Dying there won't save your kid."

"They." Bethany held in her screams. She tasted nothing but copper in her mouth. "They'll kill him."

Harry didn't know what to say, how to react. He was afraid he was getting embroiled in something dangerous. "Lady! Is this some kind of mafia shit?"

"Bethany," she muttered in reply.

"Excuse me?" Harold asked.

"My name." Beth grew weary speaking.

"Oh ... pleasure, I guess. Uh ... Harry."

"Harry ..." Bethany whispered. "Please." Bethany's words were desperate, soft, weak. "Please. Home."

Reluctant, fearful of the outcome, Harold continued to drive with blind intent.

"Okay fine." He bemoaned. "Where do you live?"

Fortunately for Bethany, Harold had spent most of his life in the area. With a little guidance, Bethany pointed Harold in the right direction. The most difficult part of the journey for Bethany was the labor of staying conscious and articulating directions. Beth could feel her soul slipping from her body. She felt closer to death than she ever had. The radio was on, not muted but on the lowest volume. Occasionally, strange near near-inaudible sounds came through it.

"Left," Bethany wheezed, speaking as minimally as possible.

"So... crazy ex?" Harry asked as he turned the car, spinning the steering wheel with his right palm while the wheel slid through his loose-gripped left hand.

"No." Bethany's movements felt delayed, her words echoed. Harold was as much of a blur to her as the road.

"Okay ..." Harold sighed, nervous. He wanted to know what he was getting involved with. Obviously, Bethany had gotten into a wreck, and helping someone who was in an accident felt righteous. However, he didn't want to be implicated in some crime or, worse yet, collateral damage to something nasty. The last thing Harold wanted was another record. And a dead woman in his passenger seat certainly would be a hard sell to the local authorities.

"The right after... Then straight a bit." Bethany pointed to their next turn with her functioning hand; her body trembling to lift the weight of her arm even slightly.

"Well then..." Harry felt like an asshole, but his own safety was a prime concern. "Let me put it bluntly. Be as vague as you like, but it seems I'm liable to be driving you to your own death sentence. I don't want that, if avoidable."

"Nobody's die..." Bethany tried to speak, crumbling in pain, she curled in her seat, shivering. Bethany scarcely managed to squeak out two words: "It's fine."

"Fine? Fine doesn't involve an arm looking like that." Harold shook his head slightly, brow drawn and teeth clenched. He couldn't stand looking at Bethany's injury. It made him feel queasiness and dread like never before. Cleaning the interior was going to be a nightmare. Harold found himself thinking guiltily.

"Just please ..." Bethany shuddered, blood trickling from every part of her. She took a long time in between each labored word. Her voice was phlegmy, the kind of voice that belonged to a habitual smoker with lung cancer. "Get me home and I'll do the rest."

"Jesus, you can't even talk, lady! Let alone go play action hero! What are you gonna do when you get there, anyway? Bleed on 'em? How many people we talking, huh!? You said they! Means at least two people who are willing to kill a kid! I mean, Jesus, what am I even doing right now!?" Harold was worked up. He wanted to re-route back towards Mercy Hospital, but the time wasted seemed like it would just lead to Beth dying in his car. Harry wished more than anything that he was home in bed and sound asleep. He didn't feel like a hero or a good person, only a victim making the wrong decisions for another victim.

"I can't ..." Bethany sobbed, her deep breaths painful, each spasm like a knife in the chest. "It has to be me..."

"Okay. You're more stubborn than my ex." Harold, exasperated, complied once more. He wasn't interested in dying tonight. "But when I get reception, I'm calling the cops."

"Mhmmh," Bethany mumbled in agreement.

Bethany, struggling to stay awake, managed to guide Harold

to her home. Harry pulled up to the driveway. From here, with a limited view, behind the foliage and in the dark, the home looked more akin to a fortress; a dungeon for vile and wicked prisoners who would render upon each other hells of a collaborative creation.

"Take this." Harold retrieved a pocketknife switchblade to be precise. "I like this knife. I'm hesitant to part with it, but, well, anyway, this shit's not exactly legal, so don't go telling anyone where you got it."

"I don't need a weapon." Slowly, Bethany pushed open the passenger door. Harold was going to offer to help, but Bethany leapt to the ground, her shaking legs like beams struggling to support a roof covered in snow. She fell to the ground.

Quickly, Harold jumped out of his car and came to Bethany's side.

"Lady, I'm telling you this is a bad idea!" Harold was not the crying man, but such a sight shook his constitution.

"I've no choice." Somehow, Bethany stood on her own. It was like watching someone disobey the laws of gravity.

"Then I'm coming with you." Harold insisted.

"No!" Bethany spat. Though she knew his help would be immense, she didn't want a stranger involved any more than they had to be. All of this had started because of a stranger entering their home all those years ago. Bethany felt some strange obligation to keep this within the family. "I have too, alone."

With a long, long pause. Harold Agreed.

"Okay, go save your kid." He sighed. "But I'm calling the cops."

"1459," Harold repeated the address out loud to himself as he climbed into his truck, trying his phone for reception once more to no avail. "1459." He repeated to himself over and over as he drove home. He had the ominous feeling he would be one of the last people to ever see Bethany alive.

. . .

Bethany stood before the fortress. This place was no longer her home, not without Leon. It could hold anything now, be anything now. All the rules for Bethany changed tonight. No assumption could be asserted with any confidence. All she hoped for was Carl's love, Carl's help, and Leon's safety.

Carl had been drinking. He just finished taking a piss. Stepping back into the living room, he picked up his bottle, which was almost empty. Carl's buzz was excessive. His head was spinning. Demons seemed to be all around him, in his head, in the corners of his home. When Carl was young, his grandfather would tell him stories from the Old Testament. He would warn him of damnation and hellfire. Carl never had much of an opinion on religion. He wasn't sure if he believed in God, and wasn't sure if he wanted to, especially in one that cruel.

From the front of the Parson's house came the sound of a door swinging open. Howling wind poured into the parlor. Heavy, slow footsteps stomped on the floor as the front door slammed shut from intense wind speeds.

"Oh, fuck'n what?" Carl sighed upon hearing the movement.

"Carl?" A soft, pained voice cried out.

"Beth!?" Carl excitedly slurred his words, scurrying to the front door.

Carl ran to the entranceway. What he witnessed was the most horrific thing he'd ever seen in his life, a terror unmatched. His beautiful wife was now mangled, broken. She looked like a walking corpse. Her skin was grey, her lips a pale blue. Her eyes were bulging from the recesses of her sunken brow, pink and burning. Her hair was matted, and it looked like pieces of her scalp were ripped from her head completely. Her clothing was torn, and like her body, nearly entirely soaked in blood. Far beyond anything else, though, was the brutal state of Bethany's right arm. Carl held back sickness in his throat, swallowing the taste of sick.

"It took him." Bethany stared into Carl's eyes, unblinking.

"What ..." Carl tried to speak, heaving. "What ..." His was jumbled.

"Is it still here?" Bethany asked. There was no time for comfort, for assurances. She was dying, and quite possibly her son, too.

"What happened to you!?" He shouted. Carl had never cried so much in a span of twenty-four hours.

"Crashed ... Deer ..." Bethany huffed. She could feel her internals churning. "Took Leon. Is it still here!?" Her screams held a deafness, her mute whimpers a pitiful shout. Each screech, each sound she made, was like sandpaper that scratched at her insides.

"We need to call an ambulance!" Carl felt dizzy. His inebriation amplified with absolute adrenaline.

"No!" Bethany screamed. "Leon!" Bethany stumbled, nearly crashing to the floor. Carl managed to catch her, holding her as gently as one could a bloody ragdoll. Beth nearly blacked out in pain, screeching in agony. Carl helped Bethany hobble to the living room, where she sat on the couch, painting it and the carpet red. Beth lay backwards, unable to hold her eyes open, her body going limp.

"No, no, no!" Carl shouted. "Stay awake!" He snapped his fingers rapidly near Bethany's ears. Pulling his phone out, he dialed for an ambulance. After a few rings, an operator answered the phone, asking for the nature of the emergency.

"I ... uhm, yes, my wife." Carl was sweating, stumbling over his words in a panic. He took a moment to figure out what to say.

"Sir?" The voice of a kind woman on the line spoke. "Are you still there?"

"Yeah, yes." Carl shook his head. "I ..."

"Leon ..." Bethany tried to stand.

"Sir?" The operator asked again.

"Yeah ..." Carl leaned his head against the wall. All he could see was white plaster and the top of his stain-covered shirt. "My wife's been in an accident, she's ... she's dying." He was sobbing. Tonight was just like the night of Hurricane Nester. The storm Mannhouse brought with him all those years back was still managing to crash right through Carl's life.

"Okay, sir, I'm going to need you to stay calm. Can you provide me with your address?"

"Yeah, yeah. It's fourteen fifty-nine, Farmstead Drive. Letterfaux. We're ..." Carl swallowed, his neck and chest tense. He could hear muted but rapid typing on a keyboard over the phone. "We're right on the outskirts of Main Street..." He banged his head softly against the wall repeatedly, leaving a tiny scuff on the drywall.

"Okay, sir, I'm sending help. I'm going to need you to stay on the line. Is your wife awake? How's she doing?"

"She's..." Carl turned to look towards Bethany.

She was gone, no longer seated on the couch. A new trail of viscera, which partially overlapped the old one, led through the kitchen and towards the garage.

"Gone..." Carl gasped.

"Sir?" The operator asked in concern.

Carl dropped his phone. It landed on the carpeted floor, speaker face up. Carl followed the trail, terrified, confused, amazed. How Bethany was managing to move or speak in her state was a miracle. He always knew his wife was tough, but this was absurdly so.

"Sir?" The operator continued to speak, growing more and more concerned. "Sir? Are you there?" Carl followed the droplets, the smears of crimson. He approached the garage door which hung ajar slightly. From within the dim lit garage came a terrible scream, one which made Carl's blood curdle.

Bethany wailed from the garage a holler so impressive it sent a shockwave through the atmosphere, piercing the ozone layer. The house began to shake, the ground violently unstable. Lights flickered on and off, and dust and debris crumbled from the ceiling.

"What the hell," Carl whimpered, wide-eyed. It felt like an earthquake, a big one.

Bethany bellowed louder than any concert, any firework, any noise Carl had ever heard. It made her childbirth seem like a light nap. He covered his ears, stumbling towards the garage as the intensity of the shaking continued. Cabinet doors flung open and closed. Items crashed to the floor, furniture slid, and paintings swung. The rusty red door leading to the garage was slamming open and shut, back and forth wildly.

Carl held his head back, pushing forward with his shoulder. The red door slammed into Carl's side as he made his way into the garage. There, Carl witnessed his wife do something he didn't know a person was capable of. It was so gruesome, so awesome, so insane. Carl winced, but he could not turn away. On Bethany's face, she scowled, her teeth nearly shattering under the pressure of her jaw, her eyes blood red, and her neck muscles pulsating from the brutality of the moment.

Bethany clawed at her broken arm, grasping it with her good hand. With a force that could shatter boulders into pebbles, Bethany tore at her wound. She was uprooting her bad flesh and bone like she was pulling a weed from the ground. Tremendously she raged, ripping and howling, the ground shaking in violence matched only by her. Strands of flesh snapped like steel wires from a bridge. Bone splintered and muscles unraveled like twine. With one more great forceful rage, Bethany ripped from her body her broken, dangling arm. It fell to the ground, and upon impact, all the rumbling and quaking ceased. The house was still, silent.

Carl looked at his wife directly in the eyes, speechless, trembling. She smiled back at him, her eyes burning like volcanoes. From the ground, she picked up her amputated arm, which still spurted blood and marrow and pus. Holding it where the wrist once was, wielding it like a hammer, she spoke clearly, her voice calm and loving.

"It wasn't enough," she snarled.

Bethany raised high her detached arm, blood trickling down from it onto her head like she was showering. With all the force she could muster, she slammed it upon the ground. The ground cracked and tremored. The arm shredded apart with the blow, almost unrecognizable as a limb. Carl whimpered, looking upon his bloodied wife. She was hitting the same section of the floor Carl had destroyed with a hammer all those years ago.

"It wasn't enough!" Bethany grew louder. She slammed her mangled arm into the ground once more. On impact, it ruptured, viscera spraying everywhere, flooding the garage with gore. The arm was now merely bone and dangling pink strands of meat. The garage floor quivered under the power of the blow once more. Rubble seemed to disintegrate into sand.

"Bethany ..." Carl looked up from the floor in awe, speechless.

"IT WASN'T ENOUGH!" Drawing upon strengths gods could seldom muster, Bethany came down with such a force that she ignited in flame like a meteor burning up in the atmosphere. When her bony, ruined arm impacted with the floor, it splintered like dry wood into a hundred pieces. A boom more impressive than a supernova echoed throughout the neighborhood. The floor cratered underneath the Parsons', as if a meteor had just struck the center of their garage. Bethany toppled to the floor. She had reached her limit, physically and mentally. Carl rushed towards his wife, shaking in disbelief, then...

The garage was swallowed in a blue, eerie light. In this bloom, everything seemed to implode in upon itself. All gave way to a deep, dark pit, a chasm bottomless and blue. The Parsons and their home tumbled downward, swallowed whole by the Farm. Into the sinkhole it all fell, raining debris.

POWER WINDOWS: MIASMATIC INFOGRAPHIC MEMORY EXCHANGES

The cage descended into darkness. Looking above, like a reflection on a lake, Edda could see the Flamingo pink house shimmering in a body of black waters. Edda's legs dangled in the abyss, her hands by her sides. Below her, Edda could see nothing. Only the rattling of the chain suspending the cage made any sound in this place. It was a near total deprival of the senses.

Edda held her head in anguish. It spiked with surgical pain, like threads sharper than needles being strung through her brain. Though she tried to scream, she only could gasp soundless cries. Collapsing backwards against the cold metal bars, Edda choked for air, then felt a great reprieve wash over her body.

She incorporated into a vision.

· · ·

"WHAT IS YOUR NAME!?" The hooded man screamed once more.

"Tom ... Tomas," Tom huddled against the cage bars. He was naked, bloodied, beaten, scared. Tomas was shivering, soaking wet on a cold day.

"WRONG!" Master berated. Clutched in his leather gloved hand, Master held a personal taser. Reaching through the cage, he pressed the device against Tom's bare thigh, electrocuting him with a quick volt. Tomas shook, banging his head and limbs against the cage. He convulsed violently as he bit down hard on his bloodied tongue, ripping shreds of flesh from his lip.

"YOUR NAME IS DRULL!" Master screamed, kicking the cage with his steel-toed boot, causing it to rattle. In his other hand, Master clutched a hose. He sprayed down 'Drull' with the hose, aiming for the face as Tom helplessly covered his eyes.

"Again," Master said, relenting with the hose. "WHAT IS YOUR NAME!?"

Tomas shivered, looking away from his captor. Just yesterday, he was home with his family. His wife, his daughter. Tom wasn't sure how he'd gotten in this position. His memory was fuzzy; it felt like he'd been drugged, and the hangover was brutal. The last thing he remembered was talking to his wife. Then, he awoke in the cage. The first thing Tom saw upon awakening was his new self-proclaimed Master towering above him.

"Silence isn't an answer." Master reached out, tasing Tomas once more, who shook violently for a moment before going limp. "DRULL!" Master screamed through his hood. "YOUR NAME IS DRULL!"

Master kicked an empty bottle of beer, and it flung forward from the force, colliding with a wooden support beam and shattering. Glass sprayed everywhere on the hay-covered floor.

"Okay," Master said, looking at the sorry state of his captured prize. He didn't want to kill Drull, not with so much work to be done. "Enough for today."

Tomas slid up from his seat, head pounding, vision scarcely functioning. He'd vomited in his mouth, which had trickled down his chin and neck.

"No dinner ... Not until you say your real name." Master laughed, turning to leave for the day.

"Tomas... Macsen..." Tom spoke in defiance, just audible, a whisper under his breath. Master heard him, nonetheless.

"We'll see how long you can keep that up." Master laughed, shaking his head as he walked towards the exit. "Your name is Drull." Master slammed the barn door closed behind him.

Tomas cleaned the vomit from his face the best he could. He was shivering and huddled up into a ball, trying to warm himself. His body was in agony, his muscles flaring, and his skin bruised. He had cracked some teeth, and his jaw felt like it was an inch farther back in his skull.

"My name ... My name is Tomas Macsen." Tom repeated to himself, over and over, shaking feverishly. "My name is Tomas Macsen. My name is Tomas Macsen." Tom chanted to himself for as long as he physically could. He wept, closing his eyes, picturing the faces of his loved ones, refusing to forget, begging for salvation.

. . .

Edda cleaned the vomit from her face the best she could. She was shivering and huddled up into a ball, trying to warm herself. Her body was in agony, her muscles flaring, and her skin bruised. Her teeth had somehow cracked. Her jaw felt like it was an inch farther back in her skull.

"My name is Edda Macsen."

Edda, shocked, leaped back into her own body, now behind her eyes once more. She flailed, wincing, like awakening in a fright from a nightmare. She felt sick, like she needed to vomit up something that wasn't hers. The cage was rattling, shaking violently from her startled awakening.

What, what was... Edda thought to herself, head cloudy, unsure if she was in a dream. *Where?* Edda looked around. She was in an abyss, which was the only word she could think of. She had no idea how she got here, or why she was in a cage. She had no memory of entering the Flamingo pink house, but ... It felt like she had new memories, vague, fuzzy ones.

Edda checked her pockets, frantically looking for her phone. She had nothing on her but a single quarter and a couple of pennies. Edda kicked her foot in frustration, causing the cage to swing more. Looking down, towards a bottom unseeable, made Edda feel incredibly uneasy. Holding a penny in her hand, Edda dropped it from the cage, listening for any sound. But no indication of a collision was heard.

Edda was trying very hard not to panic, not to scream and cry, and even to her own surprise, she was managing quite well. Grasping her head, Edda leaned against the cage, closing her eyes, thinking of Francesca, of the beach, of Mom and all her friends back home. Hell, Edda even wondered if Carter would notice her absence, the nosy old creep. Again, Edda's eyes widened, and she went limp. She saw more flashes, glimpses through the looking glass, more memories.

. . .

"Hey Chuck!" An old, bearded man wearing a jean vest smiled, interrupting the conversation, waving his hand as he walked by toward the dartboards. Chesire's was rather slow on Thursday nights, though a little more packed when the biweekly dart leagues were in session.

"Who's that?" Mannhouse laughed, a pint of light beer in his hand. Mannhouse grabbed a peanut, cracking it open. He ate it, then tossed the shell to the floor.

"No clue." Chuck laughed. "I'm always too drunk to remember most of y'all's names."

The two laughed. Chuck and Mannhouse didn't interact too often, mostly because Chuck didn't come out to drink as regularly as Mannhouse did. When Chuck did go out, however, he drank and made sure everyone else did, too. Chuck and Mannhouse had known each other through interacting at the local bars near exclusively for the last three or so years. Small town run-ins are like that in certain crowds, especially bars.

"Anyway," Chuck continued the conversation prior. "It ain't about respect, or character. No sir." Chuck shook his head.

"How so?" Mannhouse inquired.

"Ya' want someone to listen to ya? Really listen to ya? Obey? It ain't about respect, no nothing like that," Chuck rambled.

"Whatcha' boys on about?" The bartender, Page, eased herself into the conversation as she walked behind the bar, setting down a tray of dirty glasses and empty bottles.

"Well," Chuck, the boisterous person that they are, raised his voice theatrically. "Mannhouse's kid here's being a disrespectful little cunt." Chuck waved his beer at Mannhouse like he was throwing a fastball.

"Hey!" Mannhouse raised his voice. "Watch your tongue about my son!"

"Ohhh!" Chuck laughed, raising his hands in the air like he was surrendering to the cops. "Apologies, apologies."

"Well," Mannhouse laughed. "No, Chuck's right, he's being a dick."

"What?" Page leaned against the counter, her cleavage purposely on display (got her better tips). "Bad grades or something?"

"No, no," Mannhouse sighed. "He's a good kid, surprisingly good grades considering all he does is smoke pot and ditch class. Just won't listen."

"Sounds like me when I was a kid." The bartender laughed.

"Me too, sorta." Mannhouse shook his head. "And that's the problem."

"Well, you talk to him about it." Page wasn't a parent.

"Yeah." Mannhouse laughed. "Good luck trying to get him to say anything to me." Mannhouse hung his head.

"And that's what I'm saying!" Chuck spoke up again, chugging from his glass so that bubbles of beer stuck to the hairs around his lips. "Okay, so look..." Chuck swiveled on his stool, pressing his left shoulder into the side of the bar. Mannhouse looked him in the eyes, and Page leaned in closer.

"I got ..." Chuck tried to think of a way to phrase his words carefully, pausing for a moment. "I got this dog back home, dullest hound there is, and I'm its Master. I keep em in a kennel when I'm going out. Now, this dog, despite being a dumbass, is a persistent bastard, and was always trying to defy me, trying to get out."

"Ominous," Page, the bartender, laughed.

"So," Chuck continued, "One day I decided I'd had enough. I got me this big stick, one that could give a good wallop. Every time that hound acted out of place, SMACK!" Chuck slammed his hand on his thigh for emphasis. "Eventually, after days of these beatings, that damned mutt quivered every time I'd even look as if I was reaching for my beating stick. So, I tried something. You know what that is?"

"No," Mannhouse replied.

"I left the dog's kennel door wide open, put my mutt inside. Now I

set the stick down in front of the cage. Dog was terrified, backed up as far against the kennel bars as it could be. Then I left. Now, sure enough, when I got home, that dumbass dog was gone. You know why?"

Page and Mannhouse were both looking at Chuck, both engrossed in the story, but with a look of concern in their eyes.

"Because," Chuck explained, "It ain't the stick the dog's afraid of. It's the person wielding it."

"Jesus, man," Mannhouse took a hefty drink and shook his baffled head. "What are you suggesting? I beat my kid like a dog?"

"No, no," Chuck sighed, frustrated.

"You're wild, Chuck," Page laughed, getting up to help a customer.

"What I'm saying is..." Chuck looked Mannhouse right in the eyes. "That stick is what I needed to teach the respect I deserved. Now, I close the door to that hound's kennel each time I leave, sure ... But I don't lock it no more. That dogs to afraid to defy me, and I make sure to keep it that way. It's fearful more than anything now. So, it needs to think I'm close, holding the stick, and it needs to be terrified, of me, of the consequences..."

"Holy hell." Mannhouse's eyes were wide. "Sage advice, I guess..." Mannhouse was always baffled by the people you could meet in bars. "I need another drink. You thirsty?"

"Of course!" Chuck smiled, patting Mannhouse on the back. Mannhouse waved to Page for another round, who was helping some darts player with an order.

"Ya know though..." Mannhouse said. "It ain't respect, not true respect. Just fear."

"Oh." Chuck smiled. "There's no difference at a certain point..."

"Whatever you say, Chuck." Mannhouse smiled. The two drank another round.

. . .

Edda felt like a million selves. She shook at the cage she found herself trapped in, which swayed in the dark abyss like a child's swing set hung from a tall tree's branch. The flailing sensation and rattling of the chain only worsened the oncoming sickness. Again, Edda's eyes dilated, pupils wide and white. Through her visions, she wandered deeper:

"...yes... yes, I understand, but if you just..."

Edda looked up. Looming tall above her like a giant was her mom, Cheryl. She looked young, distressed. Edda found herself floating, as if a disembodied pair of eyeballs watching her mother cry as if it was a television show.

"It's just he hasn't been home in..." She was trying to explain something to someone. Edda couldn't make out who was on the other end of the line, their voice was just a muddled cluster of mumbles. Whoever it was sounded dismissive, or at least the intonation of their muffled speech did.

"Okay..." Mom pinched her nose in frustration. "No, I'm sure he'll be home any minute." More obnoxious sounds came through the phone, almost cartoonish sounding.

"Yes. Okay, thank you..." Cheryl huffed, silent tears running down her face. "Jackass." She slammed the telephone down on the receiver.

Edda tried to hug her mom, but found she was only hugging the bars of a rusted steel cage instead.

PARTISANS RED

Bethany felt warm, safe. All of her pains were gone. Around her, she was blanketed in a blinding blue light, which hugged her tightly like a parent comforting a teary-eyed child. She felt bliss. No worries assailed her mind, no trauma, physical or spiritual, weighed upon her. She felt fantastic, like she was young again.

"You put too much on yourself," Carl said. They were in the car. Carl was driving them somewhere. It was a holiday, Thanksgiving, Christmas, or some other sort of family gathering. Beth couldn't divine which. Around them, the highway moved and churned, as their car sputtered motionless in the air, its wheels like paddles wading through an invisible river.

"No work puts too much on …" Bethany felt light feet-kicking against the walls of flesh within her womb. She gasped in excitement. "He's kicking …" Bethany's body was always shifting. Sometimes, it never felt like it was her own. Carl put a free hand on her belly, keeping his other on the wheel and his eyes on the road.

Carl's mouth peeled backwards, his face opening up like a zipper on a backpack. From the moist dark crevices deep within his throat, a small eyeless face emerged. It spoke, its lips like razor blades and tongue serrated. It said terrible things.

· · ·

Bethany landed face-first upon cold, hard ground. The impact didn't hurt but was shocking. It took her a moment to orient herself. Eventually, out of her daze, Bethany lifted herself up from the ground. She was somewhere familiar but couldn't place it. An unnatural shadow clung to the air, obscuring her vision.

"Hello!?" Bethany called out into the darkness to no reply. Her voice was different somehow, but she did not even recognize it as her own initially. She winced suddenly from a reverse phantom pain, clutching at where her wound hurt the most, only to realize something incredible. No longer was she in her broken state. Her arm had returned to her. Even more horrifying, Bethany was a kid again, at least physically. Mentally, she felt like the same person. She was wearing an old outfit she had as a child. Though she hadn't thought of it in years, the green, homely dress was instantly recognizable.

Bethany stepped forward. The walls around her were cheap white cinderblocks, and the ceiling was drop-panel. To Bethany's horror, the place she recognized where she was, it all came back to her. She was in the halls of Bright Futures, all alone. Everything looked exactly as she had remembered it as a kid.

"No..." Beth whimpered to herself. "No, I don't want this." Yet the halls remained, manifestations of fuzzy agony left unsorted. Her head hurt. Bethany wanted to call out for her father. She wanted to curl up in her old childhood bed and cuddle with her long-lost teddy.

"I'm still a mom." Bethany reminded herself. "No matter how I look." She wasn't going to let herself forget about Leon, even in hell. She was determined to let nothing, be it supernatural or mundane, stop her. On the walls surrounding her were dormitories, each with their doors shut. As she walked, each step she took echoed in the empty halls. She passed by one dorm, then another, then another. All the doors were stretched, elongated on their hinges. Then, progressing a bit more, one of the dorm rooms was slightly ajar. She peeked inside.

Bethany peered past the crack in the door. She could see four kids sitting on the ground, huddled close to each other. Each child had no face, which instead was like a blank glob of clay, formed to an approximation of a head. They jittered. Everything seemed familiar, though Beth didn't know why. She didn't remember a lot about camp, but she told herself she enjoyed it, told herself it was important to her life somehow. Bethany stepped back from the door, her heart pounding.

"Sixteen-Fingered Man..." Bethany whispered to herself, recalling vague parts of that night. It was a dumb story her brother had concocted to scare her as a kid, that's all. She was pretty sure he made it up on the spot. Still, somehow the story seemed real. It was more than just a story.

"What have I done?" Bethany looked down at her legs, so frail and small once more. She felt as if she had condemned her son to the exact same cruelness, she was tossed into all those years back. She was just as careless a fool as her mother had been. Bethany walked down to the end of the hallway, which turned at a ninety-degree angle to the left. She was in the boys' wing. On the other side was the girls, and between those dorms were the counselor's chambers and the shared bathrooms. A gulp slowly slid down Bethany's throat. Her head was spinning, her vision blurry, and her arms trembling. It was hurting to remember. She hadn't in so long.

Bethany's small, muffled footsteps hit the floor as she hesitantly treaded forward. She could only hear her restrained breath and meek footsteps. Beth took great care to make sure she was as quiet as possible, but her shoes squeaked slightly on the polished floor, and the pleather materials creaked. Bethany scratched her left arm, a nervous itch. Her skin felt different, like she was wearing someone else.

It was about twenty paces past the counselor's rooms to the girls' hallway. Bethany felt compelled to head that way. One pace. Four steps. Six. Seven, eight, nine, ten. The boy's counselor's door opened slightly ajar, a quiet creek that might as well have been an explosion. Bethany froze in place, her chest tightened, and her mouth sealed shut. She couldn't remember his name, though she knew it started with an A. Why now? Bethany wondered. Why now was she reliving this?

The counselor's room was pitch black. Bethany could not see past the crack in the door; it was a line of darkness, an implication. Bethany wanted to run, but her borrowed body refused. She stared at the gap between the doorway, an entrance to a separate reality. From the darkness in the back of the room, like dim Christmas lights, two white specs, eyes, and a near-invisible sunken face, focused on Bethany. Through the crack, their eyes met, and upon realizing someone was looking back at her, Bethany gasped. The eyes behind the door did not move, but the creature spoke. The voice sounded like the mourning of mothers, like the death of fathers. Its inflections were of a shallow vassal, a puppet, whose only words were pre-manufactured, spoken off stage by some ventriloquist.

"What are, what are..."

Bethany wanted to run, but she was shaking, her legs trembling, and her eyelids quivering. With her, the whole world shook.

"What are you doing up so late?" It was his voice, the counselor whose name started with A. The eyes in the darkness grew a little closer to the door, his face now visible, though the rest of his form was still shrouded in black. His face was vile, a reminder of everything Bethany hated. She was paralyzed with fear.

"Coming from the boy's wing?" The counselor asked. Beth remained still, like a deer in a field. She just hoped her body would allow her to run soon.

"Lights out is at ten, miss ... What's your name again?" The beast behind the door had a cadence in its voice which no man could reproduce. It was like someone repeating the sounds of the words without knowing the meaning of them.

"Bethany ..." Beth gasped, grabbing her mouth, trying to restrain her voice while speaking anyway. She was willed to reenact her past, unable to change it.

"Bethany ..." The counselor with a name that starts with A said. The door creaked open all the way. Beth tried to turn around and run, but still her body was locked in paralysis. All she could do was look forward in terror. Suddenly, Bethany remembered his name. Adrian.

From the doorway emerged Adrian, the Sixteen-Fingered Man. It was a mangled imitation of life. Its face was a poor snapshot of counselor Adrian's. It was a hazy recollection of the real counselor who'd long forgotten about his crimes against Bethany. While "Adrian's" features were somewhat defined, parts of his face were blurry, missing distinct detail. Its face was stretched over a long phallic neck made from nothing but exposed pink and purple pulsating tendons. The neck was about the length of a yardstick. His legs were like tree trunks, and his chest wide. Bethany could see muscles rolling under his skin like worms burrowing in the dirt. It was wearing loose tennis shorts, though the material they seemed to be made of was that of some blue fleshy leather. A large bulge pulsated from his crotch. Of all the horrific descriptions, though, most deserving of detail was of the monster's fingers.

It had no thumbs. Each finger was abnormally long, reaching down past its knees, nearly dragging to the floor. They were almost as if claws or bladed pendulums. At the end of each finger were sharpened stumps of bloodied bone. Each splintered appendage seemed to move as if independent tentacles. They were chains, lashes, formed of battered meat and broken bone.

"I've missed you." It smiled. With a sudden, violent force, the Sixteen-Fingered Man extended his arms outward, his fingers cracking like whips, flailing like tendrils. Bethany was tripped, as fingers grasped at her legs like tentacles. She was pummeled, falling onto her back as she cracked her head against the floor, jostling her brain.

Bethany screeched, covering her face as fingers scratched and prodded at her tender skin.

"Screaming will only make it worse for you." The horror grimaced towards Bethany, its stretched back face and long smile quivering. The creature began dragging Bethany back into the room, the pitch-black dorm. All she could see of the interior was a mattress, splattered with dried blood. Next to it were some bottles of empty beer, a few shattered into shards of broken glass. She tried to resist the attack, kicking, clawing, and biting at the fingers that restrained her. Just as she was about to be pulled through the doorframe, she spread both her legs outward, her feet pushing against each end of the frame in resistance. She was hardly able to pull herself back, the resistance a mere inconvenience for the beast. The monster's fingers wrapped around her neck and head, choking and throttling her, shaking her violently back and forth. Her neck felt as if it was about to snap. Up her thighs, the monster's fingers tangled, its flesh like acid against Bethany's skin. Losing all strength, Bethany's resistance gave way. She was now fully enveloped by the monster's grasp.

"Stop!" Bethany begged. "STOP! ST..." Multiple fingers entered Beth's mouth, silencing her pleas. They rolled down her throat as she gagged, begging for oxygen. She kicked and screamed, but soon the monster restrained her movement completely, so all she could do was quiver. With her legs spread open wide, the monster began to mount her. From its pants emerged several strands of flesh, which wrapped around each other forming a crooked purple rod. Green liquids dripped from the tip of the foul bladed thing.

"Good," Adrian smiled. "Good."

"BASTARD!" Carl raged. "Leave her alone!" Sprinting down the hallway, Carl leaped, kicking the Sixteen-Fingered Man to the ground, who relinquished his grasp on Bethany. The monster fell backwards into the room, landing upon shards of glass with a loud crack.

Released from the beast's hold, Bethany stood up, coughing and gagging. Bright Futures was suddenly much smaller, or she was much larger. She was back in her old, bloodied adult body, missing arm and all. The pain she felt was immense, somehow amplified by this place. Still, she stood, defiant.

"I'm so glad I found you," Carl cried. "What the hell is..."

From the darkness, the creature howled. Sixteen meaty tendrils harpooned from the dorm room, past the frame. They rocketed towards Carl at speeds rivaling meteors hurtling through space. Multiple fingers pierced through his body like spears. Blades cut through each of his limbs, his chest, and neck.

Carl gurgled, blood trickling from his mouth. His eyes grew pale, lifeless.

"Not him, too!" Bethany screamed, wiping blood from her face.

With great anger, she leaped from the ground toward the monster. Carl began to go limp, impaled by the manifestation. The daggers pulled Carl into the darkness; his head flung backward from the speed. Bethany sprinted towards him, practically running on air, her only arm extended, palm outward. Carl was slammed against the wall, his body smashing into the brickwork with such force dust was kicked up in a cloud of particulates.

"You'll both do fine," The Sixteen-Fingered Man chortled.

"No more!" Bethany screamed, latching onto several of the monster's tendrils. Beth bit down upon one while tearing at the flesh with her hand, her fingernails digging into the beast's rotten rind. Bethany tore from the monster one of his fingers, holding it in her mouth for a moment before spitting it out, upon which it plopped to the floor, flopping like a fish out of water for a moment before growing still in a pool of pus. The Sixteen-Fingered Man screeched an inhuman wail as its grasp on Carl loosened. Carl slid down the concrete wall before slumping motionless to the floor.

"YOU WHORE!" the thing screamed, curling backwards in reflex. It was bleeding. For a moment, it looked fearful, like a wild animal. The Sixteen-Fingered Man formed a fist with his uninjured hand. His appendages looked like a jumble of tree roots or a rubber band ball. Slamming down upon Bethany, she collapsed under the power of the monster's strike. She wheezed, unable to scream, no breath in her lungs. Again and again, the monster slammed down upon Bethany's hips. The force was so great that beneath her, the tile flooring cracked and sank.

"Good." It smiled. Beth was huffing, nearly unable to breathe, her eyes glazed. Above her, the Sixteen-Fingered Man crawled on top, hatefully eager. Adrian's face twisted around itself until the thing's features were nothing more than a fatty spiral. Its long phallic neck pulsated, expanding and compressing.

"There is nothing you can do." The Sixteen-Fingered Man pushed its waist against Bethany, who squirmed violently, desperately trying to crawl out from beneath her assailer. Some of the monster's fingers entered her open wound. She could vividly feel it; they were like worms that burrowed through her body as if she was a plot of soil. Just like all those years ago, something awful pressed hard against her crotch, digging deep into her. Suddenly, the Sixteen-Fingered Man gasped, growing silent. Blood and green pus spurted from its mouth. Bethany could see in its eyes a wild, animalistic fear.

Carl was standing behind the monster. He had stabbed a shard of glass right through the center of its neck, which was spurting milky white fluids. Though he was laboring to even stand, Carl refused to stop fighting as long as he was able.

The monster's words and shrieks were garbled, now wild shouts. It turned to Carl, slamming its fist into his body. He held his arms in front of his face defensively, absorbing the tremendous blow the best he could.

Blinded by rage, all of the monster's focus was upon Carl. Bethany, shaking, panting, lifted herself once more. Rushing behind the Sixteen-Fingered Man, she grasped at one of its tendrils. She tugged on it, pulling the monster away from Carl, causing it to stumble for a moment. Carl also grasped at a finger. The two of them tugged with all their force against the fingers that they clawed. As they did so, the Sixteen-Fingered Man was stretched between the two. It flailed, stabbing and scratching at the defiant two. Tendrils and meaty blades slashed violently, the beast desperately trying to break free. Husband and wife yanked at flesh as it began to tear. It was like a horrid game of tug-of-war. Down the middle, starting at "Adrian's" twisted face, the monster began to split in half, white ooze, green pus, and crimson blood spurting out from the top of its head like a fountain display.

"MORE!" Bethany commanded.

"MORE!" Carl echoed.

The monster was split in half, shredded. Viscera sprayed from its body, which was razed to the ground. The fingers of the thign began spasming and hissing like snakes for a moment before growing still. Then it was but a motionless corpse of an abomination. The stench was horrible, like rotten fruits and semen. It was done.

"Fuck." Carl coughed.

Bethany was exhausted, delirious, in more pain than any one human should possibly be able to endure, let alone remain conscious through. "We have to find Leon."

"Yeah," Carl agreed. He sounded terrible, like he was drowning. "I'm sorry. I never meant for any..."

"None of that," Bethany panted. "We're going to get through this."

"I don't think I can..." Carl huffed as he fell to the ground, breaking the fall on his right shoulder. Bethany saw it as he fell. There was a hole, deep in Carl's chest, adjacent to his heart. The fact that he had managed to lift himself up and fight in the first place was a testament to his conviction.

"Oh shit, oh Christ!" Bethany gasped, rushing to her husband's side. Sitting next to him, Carl leaned against Bethany, enjoying the warmth of her love. Bethany ignored the great physical pains surging through her; it was nothing compared to the idea of losing Carl. Her eyes welled up as she began crying. "You're going to be fine ... We, I can ..." Bethany didn't know what to do, what to say.

"I..." Carl coughed, blood oozing from his stab wounds. "You never stopped inspiring..." Carl grew limp. He died smiling in his wife's lap. Bethany held Carl tight, weeping. Each sob was like a brick, each tear a razor, each of which battered her bruised form. As Bethany mourned, the corpse of the Sixteen-Fingered Man dissolved, puddling into a swamp of bleach.

A bright flash of blue crackled with power. Bethany turned to face it, her face wet with sorrow. The light boomed, shaking the halls for a split second. It formed an orb, which was vibrating violently. Then, with a burst of energy rivaling splitting atoms, it exploded into a trillion geometric patterns. Its color also shifted. The once melancholic blue was now a deep, brooding red, formed from Bethany and Carl's blood. The view through the window was spectacular, like nothing Bethany had ever seen.

"Goodbye." Bethany kissed Carl on the forehead. "I'll see you in heaven soon."

EXTRICATION CASCADE

Ward stepped out into the halls of Grassy Acres, closing the door quietly behind him. He had a backpack of supplies draped over his shoulders, and Darcy's old, rusted fire poker clenched in his trembling hands. Cautiously, he headed to the stairway to the right. Ward crept down the stairwell, making as little noise as possible. His eyes were flashing, dashing, and his head was swiveling; he was ready for something, anything to attack. Yet everything was quiet, still, lingering. Ward refused to drop his guard; there was a monster loosed by some cruel force, and Ward didn't want to confront it if possible.

To escape, all Ward needed was to get to the garage and manually open the tilt-up garage door. He believed there was a crank he could turn to open it, but never had to do it manually before. Perhaps it was just an optimistic misremembering. Ward didn't know what was out beyond the dark and fog, but it had to be better than his current circumstances. The plan sounded simple in concept. Ward expected the worst while hoping for the best.

Ward opened the stairwell doors in the basement, a howl of wind coursing through the dark halls as he did so. It was even colder in the basement than it had been on the first floor. Ward was wearing several layers, but still he found himself shivering.

Cautiously, Ward stepped out into the hallway. To the right of the stairwell was the path that led to the pipe maze. Ahead of him was the hallway that passed the L-shaped room towards the garage. It seemed much longer in scale than usual. He had walked this path several times before, and the layout was clear in his head, but it was always illuminated up until now. His eyes, over the week in the dark, had adjusted well to the blackness, but now he found his sight playing tricks on him. Corners, pipes, walls, all things could be perceived as vile abominations skulking in his peripheral vision.

Dark's playing tricks. Ward shuddered. His gut was telling him he wasn't alone. It felt like he was being watched by prowling eyes. Ward didn't want to risk using a flashlight, despite having one on him. The last thing he wanted to do was draw undue attention to himself. Ward held the fire poker in his hand tightly, ready to lash out at anything malicious.

The garage entrance door squeaked as it was opened, betraying Ward's presence sending an echo through the open space. The sound bounced off the concrete walls, pillars, and vehicles. Ward froze, expecting a shriek or something else horrific, but all was quiet save for the humming winds. Hesitantly, Ward stepped into the garage, making sure the door didn't slam shut.

The garage could hold twenty-three cars in total. Twelve spots were on the west side, and eleven on the east. Ward emerged on the east side. Parking spots were designated to residents numbered one through twenty-three. Additionally, residents had small storage areas designated for them. These were next to their numbered parking spots. Residents kept all sorts of things, usually in chests or on wall-mounted shelves. One resident had a canoe leaning against the wall in their spot. Another resident kept a disassembled drum set in their storage area. It was a good place to keep things that were too difficult or cumbersome to be stored in a small apartment. Darcy's parking spot was number twenty-three, which was tucked away in the corner at the very end of the east side, close to the exit.

Pillars supported the ceiling, which connected above to a repeating pattern of concrete beams. Ward grimaced each time his footsteps sent a slight patter vibrating through the underground chamber. Still, Ward heard nothing abnormal. He felt as if perhaps he was lucky, and the monster was somewhere else. Perhaps it had long left the building or was back in Paula's dingy den.

The garage door was rather tall and wide enough for two vehicles to pass through it simultaneously. The thing was not meant for a human to manually open it. It was motorized, and a chain, much like ones found on bikes, opened and closed the contraption. Ward checked the east side of the door. Nothing. He checked the west. Again nothing. Ward swore there would have been some way to manually open the door. He thought he recalled seeing a crank of some kind but came to the assumption he either misremembered or was overly hopeful. Looking down, Ward checked to see if there was a handle or release latch, but none existed.

Gently setting his makeshift weapon down on the cold concrete ground, Ward crouched, slipping his hands underneath the rubber seal, gripping tight the bottom of the door. He tugged, with all of his might, pulling upwards. At first, it did not budge, but with extreme exertion, the door squealed, moving upwards by an inch. Cold air rushed in beneath the cracks, chilling his exposed fingers. Ward huffed, already red in the face, struggling to pull it up higher, but it would not budge further. Ward groaned, the metal rattling, but still, it would not give. There was something preventing the door from rising any higher.

Shit. Ward restrained a loud curse. Resting for a moment, Ward attempted again. Once more, the metal rattled, colliding with something that stopped it from opening. Even when using his flashlight, Ward wasn't able to identify the mechanism preventing the door from opening. He was no engineer, and the deep dark and long shadows made identifying mechanisms difficult. Ward looked up at the garage motor. It was hanging from a metal mount connected to the ceiling through which the garage chain looped. It seemed plausible that if he could move the chains through the motor manually, the door would open. He just needed a way to reach it.

Creeping around the carport, weapon back in hand, Ward kept expecting to be ambushed at any moment. Regardless of paranoia, everything was still perfectly quiet. Ward was looking for a ladder, something tall enough that would allow him to reach the motor chain. He checked each resident's storage area. He found some interesting things, but nothing useful. Fishing rods. A folded-up electronic keyboard. Several cardboard boxes and bicycles, but nothing substantial to climb on. Occasionally he'd jump at the shape of a pile of boxes or discarded junk, expecting a monster only for his eyes to reveal a mundane every day object. After a quick search, to Ward's dismay, there was no ladder. He contemplated going to the other garage port, but didn't want to risk heading back through the connecting hallway. Resigned to the fact that he had no ladder, Ward came up with a new plan.

Unlocking his car, it flashed, the front and rear lights like flickering candles in the dark, briefly illuminating the space a deep red. Sitting inside, Ward set his weapon on the passenger seat and started the car. It rumbled to life, loudly idling in the empty dark. Ward drove the car directly underneath the garage door motor. Putting the car in park and letting it idle, Ward stepped out, leaving his door open. Ward climbed atop his car. Balancing himself on the roof, his feet clanked on top of the flimsy metal, which was surprisingly slippery.

Ward reached upwards towards the motor, grasping at the chain. Upon his tippy toes, stretching with great strain, he could just reach it. Grabbing tight with his right hand, which became covered in slick black oil, Ward tugged at the chain. Briefly, it moved, and to Ward's amazement, the door rose slightly higher. Slowly, with aching muscles, Ward raised the garage door. It was a strenuous and difficult process. Ward began panting and, despite the cold, began to sweat profusely. His arms cramped, and the back of his legs felt like he was post charley horse. With the door raised about a quarter of the way, escape started to feel possible.

Yanking on the motor chain once more, Ward's balance was lost. From under his feet, he fell backwards. As he did, Ward's ring finger tangled in the chain. It snapped at a horrendous angle, breaking immediately as he fell before being ripped from the chain, which somehow remained on its cassette.

Ward bellowed from the hurt, his screams bouncing through the garage and all corners of the basement. He crumbled on top of his car roof, slamming hard into the metal frame.

"FUUUCK!" Ward raged reactively. He'd never experienced something so physically painful.

In the dark, distant halls, past the workout room and elevator, a shrill, wretched shriek vibrated the walls of the once quiet apartment building turned tomb. Ward immediately stopped screaming; the pain was still visceral, but the terror more overwhelming. The source sounded like it was coming from the tunnels past the stairwell. Frantically, as best he could without worsening his injury, Ward stood back up. He had dented his roof slightly. Panting, once more on his tippy toes, using his uninjured hand, Ward desperately tugged at the chain, each yank raising the door only a slight bit more. The door didn't need to be open all the way, just enough that he could get his car through.

"THRREEEAAAKKKK!" The thing, now growing closer, roared its distant mighty war cry. No terror could this thing comprehend, no emotion did it conceptualize. It was merely a beast, a force of nature, acting upon instinct. It was a predator, charging towards its prey.

SHINK! SHINK!

The chain rattled. Now Ward could hear the thing's many footfalls as it approached. Still, he tugged, the door slowly continuing to rise.

SHINK! SHINK!

It continued to rattle and wail, both the chain and beast. The door was a little under and halfway open. Ward could crawl under the door, but knew he would not last long in the dark and cold on foot. Other monsters lurked outdoors as well; Ward had no doubt.

The garage entrance door flung open, echoing just as it had when Ward had opened it. The feeling of a terrible presence entering the room shook Ward to his core. The monster shouted, now not just guttural noises, but words.

It began to repeat itself once more, chanting: "What'd you say!?" it screamed. "What'd you say!? What'd you say!?"

THUMP! THUMP! SLAM!

The thing sprinted into the garage. Regardless of what height the garage door was, it would have to be enough. Ward leaped from the top of his car, landing hard on his knees. He turned, stumbling into the driver's seat. Locking his car, Ward clutched the wheel as he put the car in drive.

"WHAT'D YOU SAY!?," its screams shook the garage, shook Ward. The hair on his skin had never stood so tall.

Ward slammed his foot on the accelerator, turning towards the garage exit. His car swung hard. The car's back tires lost traction for a moment, causing the car to spin and bounce in place, rubber burning and smoke accumulating for but a moment. Then, furiously, the car hurdled forward like a sprinter at the start of a race.

"WHAT'D YOU SAY!?" the monster shrieked again. Ward could now see it in his backup mirror. It was formless, black, hard to distinguish, wriggling like a hundred black leeches in an endless syrupy ocean.

With the accelerator pressed as hard as he could, Ward slammed his car into the garage door with tremendous force. The metal door peeled backwards, and his windshield shattered into a web. The door ripped from its hinges. Individual metal plates buckled outwards from the construct, and the chain connecting to the garage door shattered, pattering on to the floor. The motor ripped from its trestle, crashing with a bang. The body of the car bent like tin, but still it broke through the barricade. Ward was flung forward, bashing himself against the steering wheel.

Normally, past the garage door was a hill leading to the road. However, there was no surface here. The car, revving and puttering, angled downwards, as if sinking into the ground. But there was no ground, and after teetering momentarily on the lip of the garage entranceway, the car gave way, freefalling. From the garage door, the creature howled, its tendrils lashing out towards the car as if a cat swatting at a toy one last time.

"LEAVE ME ALONE!" it gurgled and shrieked, changing its voice. "LEAVE Me alone ... Lea..." The screaming beast's howls grew distant quickly until all that was heard was the howling wind. The car went into a nosedive. It was not dark outside because of some weather phenomena. No, it seemed beyond the apartments of Grassy Acres, was nothing but a void, an abyss.

Ward screamed. The car spun. Ward was launched from his seat, banging his head onto the ceiling. The car spiraled, and Ward hurled like a ping pong ball. Receipts, change, all loose items in his car began to rise then fall violently. For a moment, Ward felt weightless, like he was floating in zero gravity. The car tumbled, ever growing in its momentum. Ward was launched back and forth again and again like a rag doll. It seemed there would be no end to the chaos when, frantically empowered by the laws of physics, the fire poker Ward had brought slammed (sharp point first) directly into the back of his neck.

THROUGH WHICH BORED GODS WATCH

There was an era before life, where eternity lingered in silence, a gaping void of nothingness. In these timeless echoes, primordial beings slumbered undisturbed, formless and blissful. Then, as chaos and maelstrom erupted over billions of years, machinations most peculiar occurred. Life emerged, it began to evolve, change, adapt, thrive. In this disturbance, the ancients were awakened, given bodies befitting of their temperament. Alongside, humans emerged among the sentient. Man found fit to give the known celestials titles befitting of godhood; thus, the first worshiped were proliferated. Eventually, devotions faded, the daemons were scorned by time, forgotten by the masses, or worse yet, they were twisted and perverted into some conjured abstractions of their essence. The zeitgeist was born, and under its umbrella, the weight of mass consciousness pressed down upon all slaves to the invisible, all slaves to the maddening indulgence of whims.

"Goodbye," Mannhouse said, praying he'd imparted the severity of the burden blue upon Carl. Mannhouse jumped into the portal, which crackled with power. He fell through the broken concrete. Mannhouse tumbled downward for a very long time. Surrounding him was a blazing light, so great Mannhouse had to cover his eyes or risk blindness. Mannhouse had fallen through the portal on other occasions, but he was never prepared for its intensity. The previous summons to the Farm were shrouded, the memories lost. Something about the place disallowed recollection; only brief, confusing images could be retained. They were scenes made of melting wax.

In the web, Mannhouse could feel the strings moving. Vast,

they reached to all corners of manipulation. In their tendrils, they grasped at the living like puppets. In the halls, those arbitrarily deemed worthy witnessed the churnings. Vast, they were constructed, only to be rebuilt, gilded walls of moving metals. They guided the weary to slaughters or shelters. No life could be supported here, in a home without windows, of nothing but walls, a Farm with no cattle. They would come to fill the role, to be taken and made into livestock. Only a few pitiful fools, one out of thousands, were burdened with the title Shepard. It was burned into the heart with a cattle prod lit in the flames of war.

Mannhouse appeared naked, like a gust of wind, in a field of white, gray, and yellow flowers. In his right hand, he clutched a standard deck of playing cards, jokers removed. The blue portal in which he fell disappeared in a burst like silent fireworks. The sky was clear, but in the distance, storm clouds accumulated and thunder rolled. This was the same field from all those years ago. The same field where he made...

The covenant with that thing. It was a being made of stars and suns. It had many names. It had offered a pact, extending its hands outwards to him. He shook it, the claws, so sharp and bony, cruel yet honest, warm, and cold. The deal broker could not take away Mannhouse's cancer, but could delay it. Ten months could be turned into twenty years. Mannhouse had seized the opportunity, wanting nothing more than to live a long life with his family. Once his blood filled the fountain, the bond was enacted, Mannhouse was bound to the entity.

He was turned into a glorified courier, shuttling objects and unwittingly trafficking people from the material world into the extra-spatial machines of the Farm. Often, Mannhouse's benefactor would not call upon him for years. Between those delays, Mannhouse's mental state withered slowly. He became paranoid, depressed. His worst tendencies were amplified. A short temper transformed into violent outbursts. Vices became overwhelming addictions. The very deal Mannhouse took to stay close to his family led to their division. Or perhaps it was Mannhouse's true nature to ruin everything he'd built for himself. It was like a bell, ringing in his head. The day Mannhouse realized this, Mannhouse would have died young from cancer, true, but he would have died with his family by his side, a smile on his face, loved.

In the middle of the grassy field, which blew waves of pollen upon the winds, atop a slight hill, was a poker table. It was made from planks of black ash, with streaks of gold and silver resin glimmering from its cracks. Several lawn chairs surrounded the table, out of place in comparison to the artisan piece. In the middle of the table was a black telephone. Its yellow curly wire extended upwards past the clouds and sight. The phone sat upon an old radio, the kind not seen since the 50s. It was playing an old song, the volume very low, carried on the breeze. The tune was something Mannhouse recognized. His grandmother loved that song, but he could not remember the singer's name, nor the band playing.

Mannhouse walked towards the center of the field, the grass and flowers tickling his bare skin, the breeze rustling his hair.

Mannhouse tossed the playing cards onto the table, which slid on its sleek surface, bumping into the radio before coming to a halt. Mannhouse turned the radio off. He wasn't in a music-listening mood. Walking around the table, previously obscured by the radio and his line of sight, Mannhouse saw a rifle. It was his old gun, the suicide stick, which he'd grown intimate with long before he found and lost his true love. Perhaps happiness would only be found in a warm gun now. Wrapped around the gun's stock was a red ribbon. Next to the rifle was a notepad, yellow paper with black lines, the kind you could tear off from the top easily. On it was a message, scribbled in every language. Mannhouse looked at it, baffled momentarily. It read: *You know what to say. P.S.... Sorry for the clerical error.*

Next to the message was a phone number. Mannhouse wasn't sure what to say, but he dialed the number regardless. One ring, then two. Three rings, then four. Five, then ...

"Hello?" a familiar terrified voice answered.

It all became clear to Mannhouse. He did know what to say, like he'd been rehearsing it his whole life. Time obeyed no laws in the Farm, for no laws could constrain the transcendental, the abstract, nor the shapeless. All math here turned to poetry.

"Carl, shut up and listen to me. You'll all be safe if you do what I say, I promise." He was instructing a man and holding him at gunpoint simultaneously, in different places, in different times. "You got what you need in the garage. Tell him to make his own entrance." Mannhouse hung up the phone, its bells ringing lightly.

"Heeh," Mannhouse laughed hysterically. He chuckled again, boisterous and joyful. It really was a gift he was being given, so the illusion held true. Mannhouse picked up the rifle. He turned off the safety and cocked back the bolt. The gun was loaded, a single bullet.

Sitting down in a field of white and grey flowers, Mannhouse crossed his legs. Placing the butt of the rifle between his thighs, Mannhouse rested his chin on the end of the barrel. Calmly, with a smile on his face, Mannhouse placed his finger on the trigger and squeezed it gently, like a lover's caress.

Unleashed from the end of the rifle was a flash so mighty, accompanied by an impressive boom, which sent the distant thundering clouds a roil, their own chorus exploding in a cacophony of stormy sounds. The bullet, Mannhouse's last mortal friend, ripped straight through his jaw. It shredded apart Mannhouse's left eye and pierced through his skull, drilling through brain matter, the slug screwdriving its way out the other end of his eviscerated head. But no blood, or bone, nor bits of brain splattered forth from his wounds. Instead, flowers, seeds, buds, and vines were sent flying upon the wind, splashing forth from Mannhouse's death wound. They were colorful, varied in shape, size, and type. Purple, pink, green, red, orange, and blue, any and all varieties imagined sputtered forth from Mannhouse's shattered skull. Taken by the winds, these flowers and roots and givers of life planted themselves within all corners of the garden. Once fields, only grey and white, with seldom splatters of yellow, now would grow into a rainbow. The garden took on all life, all flowers, fruits, trees, and bushes. Anything which could grow was given a space to do so in this endless expanse of life and death.

Time and space passed, it fell back into itself, and never started. Bugs feasted and birds profited from their abundance. Around Mannhouse, vines intertangled.

INTERSECTIONS

Mannhouse slowly awoke, rising from a deep slumber. They ripped themselves free from Earth's cradle. Upon arising, Mannhouse noticed something remarkable. They felt no pain of any sort. Vines had wrapped around their body, and flowers and grass had grown through their skin. Their entirety, their flesh, their insides, all now were foliage. They were a garden Golem, in which the concept of Mannhouse resided. They were beautiful, the colors and scents which formed their person breathtaking. The concept of Mannhouse felt as if they were the same person, but somehow, all the tension and pain from life was now null. They were content, despite any lack of control, any lack of understanding. The garden golem Mannhouse thing knew they were just another flower to grow within the Farm. This was a reward, a punishment. They felt free now, trapped within the garden.

The concept of Mannhouse roamed the fields, watching stars form and die within the soil. They spoke with the trees. They talked to the insects, which communicated by crawling through him. They listened to stories contained in the wind. Long after his family died, still the concept of Mannhouse remained, counting the blades of grass. Eventually, they forgot their identity, their ego, and they became something new. They were now The Dealer.

The Dealer looked towards the poker table. A red line, like thread, formed, suspended midair, hissing like a kettle. Beams of red light, marvelous, dripping specs of blood, manifested itself above the fields. The Dealer stood entranced by the spectacle. The light grew larger, coating everything around it in a deep blood-red glow. With a burst of power, an echo exploded outwards, and from the portal a body tumbled to the ground, a lifeless ragdoll. Then, without indication or flair, the light vanished, with it the ominous red.

Calmly, The Dealer approached the body, which lay lifeless in a bed of daisies. It was a lady; she looked dead. Her arm was missing, her body mangled. Her skin was ripped to shreds. The Dealer felt no pity for her; in fact, they felt almost nothing. Humanity now seemed as foreign to them as an atom to an ant.

The Dealer rested his hand upon the dead woman's head. Her entire body began to quiver and shake, then, where her injuries once were, sprouted flowers and vines. Dried blood turned to grass, and embedded shrapnel was forced out from the flesh, in their place, seedlings. Where there was no arm, now a display of flowers formed a limb. Coloration returned to the skin, and the woman from the red window began to breathe again, slow at first, then rapid, then, at a normal rate.

. . .

Slowly, Bethany awoke. Her eyes were heavy at first, and she nearly fell back asleep. She lay upon the softest bed of grass she'd ever known. There was a wonderful smell in the air, that of fruits and flowers and freshly harvested crops. Pulling herself up, Bethany remembered what had happened. She launched upwards, vigilant, and veiled in fleeting terror. She was amazed; however, wherever she was, it was gorgeous. Bethany, despite the disarming scenery, remained steadfast and ready.

"Hello," The Dealer greeted. His words were as if cherub nuzzles.

"OHH!" Bethany turned around quickly, startled. There was a floral arrangement in the shape of a person. Blues, reds, yellows, violets, greens, and pinks. All shades and shapes of flowers complemented the mass of moving grass. It would be beautiful as an arrangement, but it was moving, which sent a great fear through Beth. The thing was standing behind her, waving.

"Holy shit." Bethany stepped backwards, her feet trampling the flowers. "Stay away from me, I'm ... I'm ..."

"I'm sorry, I didn't mean to startle you," the floral person said, stepping forward just a bit while holding their hands up in a show of peace.

"What did you do to me?" Bethany quivered as she looked at her arm. She felt good, at least her body did. Mentally, her head was like scrambled eggs. "What did you do to my Leon!?"

"Nothing," The Dealer said, arms fully raised, halting their movements. Their lips did not flap, but rather rustled when speaking. "You were dying, I did what any good gardener would do. I plucked the rot, that is all."

Bethany looked down at her previously ruined arm (now nothing but yellow and white flowers), then back up to the floral man. She did feel no pain, and she was not actively being attacked. Still, after surviving her husband to that *thing,* Beth was not willing to trust anything or anyone in this strange hell she found herself dwelling.

"I'm The Dealer. You?" For a moment, the concept of Mannhouse almost remembered their given name, their past.

"The Dealer?" Bethany looked them up and down, incredulous yet intrigued. They looked nothing like the drug dealers she'd known in the past. Though they seemed more human somehow than the last strange humanoid they encountered in this place.

"It is a name I was born into," they explained. "So ..." The Dealer waved his hand, expecting an answer. "You are?" Conversation sparked a slight remembrance within them. The Dealer found they quite liked pantomiming indeed.

"Be-Bethany." Beth couldn't believe she was talking to a bouquet.

"It's nice to meet you, Bethany," The Dealer said. "You're the first to arrive."

"Arrive?" Bethany asked, looking about the strange place she was in. She felt at peace and safe but refused to accept complacency. She held it down, replacing it with anger and determination to save her son.

The sound of the noise barrier being broken boomed from out of the clouds, and with it, a car fell to the ground a few paces away from the poker table. It collided nose-first, the bumper and hood collapsing into the engine. The impact was tremendous, shaking the ground, kicking up stones and dust. Then, teetering, the car fell backwards, landing on its wheels with a bounce. Smoke flumed from the engine as the exhaust sputtered. There was a figure inside.

Bethany momentarily ran from The Dealer, thinking the sound was the start of their assault. But The Dealer simply gazed towards the wreckage, and Bethany followed suit when she noticed what was happening. The driver's door opened, and from within it emerged a young man, unscathed by the severity of the collision. He didn't seem to notice Bethany and the flower man. There was a bright red welt on his face.

. . .

"Holy shit, how did I survive that!?" Ward laughed to himself, kicking and jumping with excitement from the adrenaline burning beneath his skin. He pumped his fists momentarily in celebration before looking around at his surroundings. Ward's excitement turned to confusion. Ward locked eyes with Bethany before averting her gaze out of fear.

Been there. Bethany sympathized. Climbing from the roadside of her crashed car felt like a lifetime ago now. She wondered if she had never left home, would Carl be alive? Would Leon be safe?

"Welcome!" The Dealer waved, slowly walking towards the wreckage. "Are you alright?"

"Am ... am I dead?" Ward laughed nervously, frantically looking around. "This like ... heaven?" Ward looked down at his finger, the one he mangled in the chain. It had healed, now replaced with a small bouquet of flowers. He found this somewhat comforting despite the surreal sensation.

"No," The Dealer chuckled, pollen bursting out from their lips. They remembered laughter. It was a strange sensation. "I don't think so." The Dealer stepped forward a little more as they talked. "I haven't seen any golden gates."

"Right," Ward said. He looked at Bethany, who glared back at him. The Dealer stepped closer to Ward once more, curious and wishing to touch them, to fix any remaining wounds.

"Hey! Hey! Stay back now, don't get any... any ideas." Ward had dealt with enough monsters for a lifetime. He retreated from the flower man, stepping behind his ruined car.

"It's okay..." Bethany gave her approval. "They're not dangerous, I think..."

"You think!?" Ward huffed, ducking behind the crumpled metal frame of his totaled car. "And who says I trust you, lady!?"

"Excuse me." The Dealer turned to Bethany. "I have a name." Indignance ... that was a fun feeling as well. They were quick to remember, to relearn.

"Right. The Dealer." Bethany rolled her eyes.

"Can someone PLEASE!" Ward shouted from behind the heap. "PLEASE just tell me what the hell is happening!?"

"I'm just as lost," Bethany said.

"Oh, and don't think I'm not on to you!" Ward pointed at Bethany. "You're with him, aren't you!? Your weird ass flower arm! Don't think I don't see it!"

"Yeah, I really didn't get a say in this ..." Bethany sighed.

"I just met her." The Dealer espoused. "Though I have been waiting."

"Creepy ..." Bethany commented.

"What!? What!? You gonna turn me into a fucking wreath!?" Ward spat, hyperventilating. He grit his teeth.

"You know it's a wonder I'm not freaking out as much as you are, frankly," Bethany commented, looking towards the young man. "You're the one with your normal body intact!"

"Come on!" The Dealer shouted. Anger... that one felt all too familiar. "Can we just do introductions?" He raised his right hand, announcing himself. "I'm The Dealer."

"Oh my god, I'm Bethany," Beth said, looking down at her arm. "This is pretty new to me too..."

Ward hesitated to reply, looking back at The Dealer and Bethany. They sounded genuine, and he wanted them to be.

"I'm..." Ward thought of Darcy, alone, dead, rotting at home. "My name's Ward..."

"Nice to meet you," Bethany said, forcing a smile.

The breeze picked up, and the three enjoyed its company. The grass and flowers danced, and distant trees waved. The sky was blue and the clouds puffy and wonderful. In the distance, a small, never-ending storm rumbled on the horizon.

"So," Ward hesitated to keep speaking, slowly approaching the two. He was tense, ready to run for his life at any moment, fully expecting to walk into some trap. "Anyone know what the hell is happening?"

"I've had the answers growing within me. Soon it will be harvest." The Dealer said. "When our last participant arrives, I'll explain all I know."

"You..." Bethany stuttered. "You keep saying that... participant!? What are we playing a game or something here!?"

"Precisely. I'll explain when our last participant arrives..." The uncanny animated hedge maze man was beginning to remember everything it was to feel human, save old memories. Perhaps that aspect of themselves never retreated but simply refused to blossom until the time was right.

"Fuck this!" Ward shouted. "I'm getting out of here! There's gotta be some exit in this damned... atrium."

"You can go if you like," The Dealer attempted persuasion. Human conversation was so different than that between the birds or chittering soil dwellers. It was pleasant, this returning oral and mental sensation. "But I wouldn't leave the gardens of the Farm if I were you. It's not safe out there alone... but I think you already know that."

"Why," Ward stuttered, motionless, lost in thought. "You mean..." Ward could still hear the monster's screams, the sounds it made as it banged upon the apartment door.

"The Farm?" Bethany asked.

"Well..." The Dealer sighed. Again, they almost remembered their true name. They were coming into themselves, their old personality. "Don't really know why, but this place just kinda' named itself, I guess. I don't know, it always sounded right in my head. The Farm!" The Dealer waved his arms in the air like he was forming a rainbow. "Does kind of sound stupid, actually. Never really said it out loud before..."

"Uh-huh." Bethany raised her eyebrow. Everything seemed too... amiable, compared to the trials that brought her here.

"So," Ward whispered to himself, head turned away from Bethany and The Dealer. He raised his voice, fear deep in his soul. "You saw the monster, too?"

"Kid," The Dealer said. Though they could not recognize their own voice, it still sounded as if their own. "This place is nothing but monsters..."

"This game of yours doesn't sound any less monstrous." Ward frowned.

From the sky, the booming sound of rattling metal echoed momentarily, synchronized with distant thunder. It was like the noise made by raindrops, but without the water. Then, parting through the clouds was a metal thing, dangling from a chain. There was someone inside it.

"And here is our last participant..." The Dealer pointed towards the sky.

"Whoa..." Ward looked upwards.

The three watched as a cage lowered from on high, stabbing through the mists and clouds. It grew closer and closer until it eventually reached the ground. The cage was about the same distance away from the table that Ward's car was, but on the opposite side. The chain was miles of metal, taut and strong, unwavering even in the high-altitude winds, spanning upwards endlessly, much like the yellow phone cable.

"That's an entrance," Ward said, as the cage made contact with the grove floor.

"You fell out of the sky in a car," Bethany laughed, a genuine laugh.

The cage door swung open slowly on its own accord, the metal hinges squeaking an appalling cry. Emerging from inside was a woman. She looked as though she'd been crying for hours, her eyes bloodshot and wide, lips quivering and red. She wrapped her hand around the cage door frame, using it to leverage her body, and she crawled out from behind the cruel, rusted bars. The gentle flowers beneath her feet were much more of an appealing sensation than the cold, brutal metal of the cage. As her tears fell they turned to tulips.

"Welcome," The Dealer said, waving his hand, beckoning to the woman in the cage. "We've been expecting you."

"Again... not ominous at all..." Bethany sighed, tapping her foot nervously on the soft grass.

There was a long pause. The woman who'd crawled from the cage said nothing. Everyone was waiting, watching. Then, the person spoke.

"Hello?" Edda said, looking at the three strange persons in front of her. "Am I dead?"

"Why does everyone keep asking that?" The Dealer put his hands on his hips inquisitively.

"Might have something to do with..." Bethany pointed at her arm and gestured to the surrounding environment with said limb.

"I'm still not convinced I'm alive," Ward laughed nervously.

"Well, I've never met a dead man who can talk," The Dealer replied.

"And I've never talked to a plant person." Ward snapped back.

"Uhh, I'm not really sure how I got here," Edda whimpered. "Are you Fran's friends? Did I blackout? Sometimes when she..."

"No," The Dealer said. "Where not Fran's friends. I am The Dealer." The flower golem extended his leafy green arm out for a handshake, which was declined.

"I'm Bethany," Bethany waved cautiously towards the woman from the cage. The Dealer and Bethany looked at Ward, waiting for him to introduce himself.

"Alright!" Ward shook his head in disbelief. "Fucking sharing circles in Heaven ... Name's Ward."

"Uhhh... I'm, Edda..." Edda was hesitant to say her name but saw no reason not to. Bethany looked somewhat familiar but Edda could not pinpoint it.

"Can someone tell me what's going on? Are you like, a puppet or something?" Edda looked The Dealer up and down.

"I can explain what I know." The Dealer hopped up from the grass onto the table. Their leap was high; their body felt light. As they landed, a large amount of dust and pollen kicked up. "Each of you were invited here to play a game. You've been sponsored by one of many potential benefactors."

"I think I'm in the wrong place," Edda interrupted, raising her hand slightly. "If you could just show me how to leave ..." Edda struggled to retain which memories were her own, and which were visions she had suffered. For a moment she wasn't sure if she was looking through her eyes or her father's. She looked around, for the first time truly grasping the nature of her surroundings. The field she was in was endless, the sky impossibly shaped. The plant person, at first assumed a trick or costume, now became apparently real. Edda could see bones exposed, being moved by vines that tugged at it.

"If you ended up in the Farm, Ma'am," The Dealer said, meeting Edda's panicked gaze with deep, pupil-less, flowery eyes. "That is no accident. It's either fate or a misjudgment on your part. Either way, the results are the same."

"What's this game you keep mentioning?" Bethany asked.

"Yeah." Ward nodded.

The Dealer reached down, picking up the pack of cards he'd set upon the table so long ago. He wiped some dust from the pack of cards, its cardboard container nearly crumbling, but the cards inside were still in good condition. The table was immaculate, as if it maintained itself. So, too, were the lawn chairs.

"We're going to play a simple game of poker. Texas Hold 'Em," The Dealer announced.

"Poker?" Ward laughed. "All of that? For a fucking card game?"

"How is this going to help me find my son!?" Bethany screamed at the top of her lungs. "I don't have time to waste on tricks!"

Edda stood near the cage, unsure what to do, what to say.

"Listen," The Dealer said. "You don't have to play, but it's the only merciful option you have." The Dealer turned to Bethany. "And you don't have to play for yourself."

Bethany gulped, a lump in her throat that she could not swallow. She was never very good at cards.

"Why can't Leon play?" Bethany asked.

"I don't know..." The Dealer shook his head, still standing atop the table, box of cards clutched in hand. "I'm only telling you what my seeds tell me. Otherwise, I know nothing."

"No thanks." Edda waved at the plant person dismissively.

"Excuse me?" The Dealer was surprised.

"I'm not going to be held prisoner by some sort of flower boy." Edda pointed towards the horizon, towards the storm. "Besides, today seems like a good day to go for a walk, and I need to think things over." Edda began heading away from the table towards a large tree on the horizon.

"I wouldn't leave..." The Dealer reached out. "It's dangerous beyond the garden..."

"It's..." Edda turned to the Dealer, a powerful, determined expression on her face. "It's going to be okay."

. . .

Edda ignored The Dealer's continual warning, walking at a casual pace, never looking back. She kicked her shoes off, then her socks. The feeling of flowers and grass beneath her toes was almost as wonderful as the sensation of wet sand back home. Edda walked farther and farther till she was out of sight, extending the boundaries of the Farm, never to be seen or heard from again. She saw many wonderful things and never retreated from any threats. It was the greatest walk she'd ever taken, and the daydreams were like nothing else.

. . .

"Well, she made her decision." The Dealer was disappointed, or rather felt the disappointment of some nameless anger.

"Can this game really save my son?" Bethany asked, putting her flower hand upon The Dealer's leafy shoulder.

"If you can bankrupt the house." The Dealer smiled.

"And if I lose?" Bethany asked.

"I don't know." The Dealer confessed. "But at this point, what else do you have to lose?"

"I'll play," Ward said. "If winning can make my life normal again."

"Why not?" Bethany sighed in agreement. "Beats walking aimlessly..."

"Fantastic." The Dealer smiled. Bethany and Ward took a seat at the table while The Dealer began to shuffle the deck of cards.

"Does everyone know how poker is played?" The Dealer lived up to their name. They made shuffling cards look like acrobatics. His fingers fluttered and bounced the cards, making them appear as if flowing rivers.

"Nope," Ward replied. Suddenly, he did. "I mean... yes." He'd never played before in his life, but suddenly felt a modicum of experience under his belt and a deep comprehension of the mechanics of the game.

"Yes..." Bethany nodded her head, also never having played.

"Once more, fantastic."

"The house will fill in for the empty seats." From the grasses and the dirt and flowers formed simulacrums of people, living shrubs and entangled roots, much like The Dealer, though all distinct enough in shape and expression, their own person. Six manifested in total, making for a total of eight players with Bethany and Ward, nine including The Dealer.

The Dealer sufficiently shuffled the deck, then set the cards down in front of them. They plucked from their body several small yellow flowers, dozens of them.

"Here." The Dealer handed to each of the players twelve flowers in total. "These will be your chips."

"Okay..." Ward grasped at the flowers, sneezing a bit. "This is great for my allergies..." The flowers did in time form more and more a resemblance to chips until no other distinction could be made.

"Each chip is worth ten points. There is no limit to your bets; however, you must bet at least a single chip at the start of each round," The Dealer explained. "When you run out of chips, you're ejected from the table and lose the game."

"And how much does the house start with?" Bethany asked, staring The Dealer down, determined to win.

"Oh, simple," The Dealer explained. "When you can no longer pluck a flower from my body, the house is bankrupt. If anyone manages to bankrupt me, you all win. Simple enough?"

"Simple enough," Ward agreed, counting the flowers on his opponent. There were hundreds, and more seemed to sprout from within them.

"Fine with me," Bethany said. "I've survived worse odds."

"Very well." The Dealer smiled rows of daisies.

Bethany and Ward took a seat around the table, the simulacrums joining them.

"Shall we play a hand?" The Dealer began to distribute the cards rapidly, house first. The hands were dealt, and the contestants left to play, beneath the sun, among the flowers, in the fields of the Farm; thunder could be heard rolling in the distance. Unknown to all who sat at the card table, several primordial gods watched the game play out. It was a nice way to pass the eternities. Unknown to these old beings, they too were being watched by other, greater old gods. And they, too, were being watched. On it went, endlessly, all around a game of poker, this spiral of anomalies. Through the window, bored gods watch.

BLUE SUNSET

Carter walked up the sidewalk on 144th heading towards Wight Street. The sun was setting. It was a strange color, a mix of blues and greens. It was a marvelous spectacle to behold. He made a point of passing by Edda's apartment, hoping to see his cherished neighbor; instead, Carter saw something rather distressing. Edda's porch door was left open. It looked like rain from yesterday's storm had pooled a little bit inside.

"Hello?" Carter climbed up the patio stairs to get a better look. "Edda, are you alright!?" But Carter got no response.

. . .

"Want anything specific?" Peter called from the kitchen.

"If you're making it, I'm not too picky," Greg said. He was in the living room, lounging on the couch in his pajamas. Peter had offered to make breakfast, and Greg never refused a free meal. The television was playing in the background, news, weather, nothing interesting. Greg scrolled on his phone, killing time.

"How about pancakes?" Peter asked. "Simple, got that premade batter."

"Fine by me." Greg was reading some article about black holes. He didn't understand much of what he was reading, even with it broken down into layperson's terminology.

"... going live with Jenny Kennedy of Channel Nine with exclusive coverage of breaking news in your region," some reporter spoke on the TV, *"Tell me, Jenny, what's going on?"*

"Whoa." Greg looked up at the television.

"Dave, I'm standing a few blocks away from what I can only describe as a humungous sinkhole..." Jenny spoke, standing as close to a police line as she could get. Behind her, though hard to see, was a large pit; it looked deep. There was a crowd of people accumulating at the scene.

"Yo' Peter, come check this out!" Greg shouted, sitting up from the couch, focusing his attention on the TV.

"...just outside of fourteen fifty-nine Farmstead Drive. Multiple neighbors reported violent shaking and a large explosion around four ..." Jenny continued to report.

"Holy shit, that's down the street," Peter said. "I didn't feel anything last night, did you?"

"No..." Greg shook his head.

"...the reported explosion at Newtext Motel seems to be unrelated, but Police aren't counting anything out as of yet. Meanwhile, rescue efforts are underway as..."

"I've driven by that neighborhood a hundred times, never paid it any mind," Greg said.

"I didn't think a hole could be that deep..." Peter gaped dumbfounded.

In the background, behind the reporter, several people started running towards the hole. Shouts of amazement, elation, fear, and hysteria could be heard as people seemingly began to riot. A few men started fighting, clawing at each other. People started jumping into the pit. They began to throw themselves into the maw.

"Wait, Dave... I think something's happened! We're going to try and get a closer look." Jenny tried her best to stay on frame as she and the cameraman scuttled to a new position. They managed to find an angle mostly unobscured. The cameraman zoomed in on the pit, the focus blurry for a second.

From all around its borders, emerging from homes and tree lines, hundreds of people were rushing towards the pit. They seemed to be coming out of nowhere, as if they had traveled for days to get here. They threw themselves into the hole, laughing and screaming as they tumbled down into the darkness. Several people trampled over each other, as if the only thing that mattered to them in life was getting into that pit. Several people smashed into the sides of the shaft walls, mangling and ruining themselves as they were swallowed by the depths. Like an endless stampede, herds of people continued to rush towards the abyssal deep.

"Dave, I can't believe what I'm witnessing, it appears to be..." Jenny ranted on as the crowd became more violent. Suddenly, her voice changed. *"I need..."* the reporter said, turning away from the camera. *"I have to jump."*

She sounded crazed, frantic. Suddenly, like the others, she began sprinting, climbing, and clawing over mounds of accumulating people toward the mysterious pit. The camera dropped to the ground, landing in the grass. It pointed upwards to the sky. The happenstance composition of the frame allowed one just to see the swarm of people around the rim of the pit. Within minutes, there were thousands of people, like a mob tsunami, all leaping to their deaths. Greg and Peter held each other tightly, unsure of what else to do but embrace each other and keep watching.

Emerging from the darkness, floating like a balloon, was a boy, hardly a teenager. He was rising from the darkness while others threw themselves into it. The child was hovering almost motionless midair, arms by his side, head pointed towards the heavens. Around him was a powerful blue aura, which sent sparks from his skin.

"Well, you don't see that every day," Cactus said out loud. Peter and Greg simultaneously turned to look at their talking plant in shock; their world views shattering moment by moment.

"Oh, yes, hello," Cactus greeted the two. "I guess we've never spoken..."

www.ingramcontent.com/pod-product-compliance
Lightning Source LLC
LaVergne TN
LVHW010603100826
845148LV00014B/2829
9781628064759